Seven Stones

Julia Lee

Life,

My aunt has told me so
much about you and your work. I
am honored that you want to
read my novel. Thank you, and
happy reading! :)

Julia Lee

201 West Laurel Street
Brainerd, MN 56401

218.851.4843

www.riverplacepress.com

First Edition

ISBN: 978-0-9903563-2-5

To Katie, I couldn't have done this without you, buddy.

And to Shane, I wouldn't be able to do anything without you.

Acknowledgements

This book is my baby. Like raising a baby, it takes more than one person to help it grow and mature. I am truly lucky to have so many wonderful family members and friends who helped me turn my story idea into a novel. If I tried to write everyone's name down who has helped me, the list would be about as long as the novel itself.

Thank you especially to Chip and Jean for making my dream a reality, and putting up with all my constant stream of emails. Thank you to my fabulous editor, Angela, for taking my rough manuscript and polishing it into a novel. Special thanks to Laura Reddish of the Native Languages of the Americas organization for helping me with the Anishinaabe language and names. In addition, thank you to the great people of the Mille Lacs Indian Museum, especially Travis Zimmerman and Bradley Sam, for allowing me to use their research materials and answering my questions. Thanks to my beta readers, especially my mom and dad, Shane, my aunt Eileen, Kathy Blake, Crystal Johnson, and Katie Futrell, for meticulously reading my work and giving me feedback.

Thank you to all the people who read my manuscript drafts, offered criticism, asked me how my writing was going, let me ramble on about story ideas, liked my Facebook updates, and above all gave me an unending supply of support, encouragement, and love. I appreciate it more than I can say.

"We did not weave the web of life.
We are merely a strand in it. Whatever
we do to the web, we do to ourselves."
Chief Seattle

"Every action of our lives touches on some chord that will vibrate in eternity."
Sean O'Casey

1

It was only a dream. Already the details were blurred, images falling through the cracks of her memory like grains of sand.

Go back to sleep.

Keilann glanced at the neon clock next to the dark form of her suitcase and groaned into her pillow. Four hours—she had to say goodbye to her life in less than four hours. She rolled onto her back and stared at the ceiling, struggling to connect the frayed ends of her dream. Someone had called out to her, and she was almost certain there'd been a fire. Or had it been a crash?

A police siren wailed past her open window, the flashing lights threw harsh shadows against her walls. Her *old* walls. Tomorrow, they would be someone else's. A nameless, faceless someone who would paint over the green Keilann and her mother had picked out together with God knows what horrible color. She stared at the blank spot on the wall where her old dreamcatcher used to hang. It used to comfort her when she woke from nightmares as a child. What Keilann wouldn't give to have it with her now.

Keilann kicked off the blankets and sighed. It was too hot to sleep. Her bare skin stuck to the air mattress and beaded with sweat. Next to her, Fiona slept untroubled by the heat or the move tomorrow. Her little sister's chest rose and fell evenly, her splayed black hair glinting with gold in the glow of the street lights outside.

You have to sleep. Go back to sleep.

Tomorrow. It was hard to believe that Keilann would no longer live in Chicago— that she'd no longer even live in the United States. Even though she had packed up and shipped out most of her belongings weeks ago, it still didn't feel real.

Squeezing her eyes shut, Keilann tried to will herself to sleep. It was no use. She rubbed the heaviness from her eyes and heaved herself up, closing the door noiselessly behind her.

At first, Keilann thought she imagined the light. Curious, she abandoned her original plan for a glass of water and followed the bright glow to the living room. Keilann had always loved the cozy brick-lined walls and big bay window. It was strange how big and sad the apartment looked without her mother's dreamcatchers on the walls or the fat purple couch squatting in the middle of the room. Keilann peered into the empty room. There, standing alone in the glare of the city streaming through the window was the stout silhouette of a woman. Her warm, cinnamon skin seemed to glimmer in the amber light, a thick woven shawl huddled around her shoulders despite the stifling heat. Even in the semi-darkness, Keilann could pick out the intricate floral beadwork, the bright, jewel-like colors shouting across the black fabric. Keilann's mother had brought the shawl with her from the Rez. She wore it when she needed comfort, and wrapped it around her shoulders like a hug.

Keilann hung in the doorway.

"Hey," she whispered.

Her mom jumped, rapping her knuckles against the window pane. It was strange, but Keilann almost thought she looked guilty, as if caught doing something inappropriate or wrong.

Her mother made a show of rubbing her reddened knuckles.

"You scared me," she laughed. "Everything okay?"

Keilann shrugged and shuffled into the room. Leaning against the cool window pane, she soaked in the familiar view—old brick buildings and stately maples lining the narrow street below.

"Mom, are you scared?"

"A little," she admitted. She looked at Keilann over the rims of her glasses perched on the end of her nose. At forty-five, her mother's face was still smooth and youthful, but tonight Keilann could see the lines beginning to creep around her eyes and mouth when she smiled. "But I'm also excited. You saw Dad's pictures. Scotland is gorgeous." Her mother wrapped her arm around Keilann's shoulders and gave her a squeeze. "It'll be an adventure."

Keilann gave her a limp smile. "Yeah."

Her mom looked out the window.

"I know this is hard on you, changing schools and making new friends—"

The word 'friend' was razor sharp. Keilann tried not to think of the friends she was leaving behind, or the year of plans they were making without her. They promised to Skype, promised to call, but it wouldn't be the same. Senior year should have been the best: trips to Navy Pier, Broadway shows at the Cadillac Palace Theatre, the traditional class cruise on Lake Michigan. All that was gone now.

"—but after a while, I think you'll love Aberdeen as much as you love Chicago. Maybe more."

Keilann pressed her forehead to the cool glass. "Why did he have to take the job? I thought Dad was happy at the U."

"He was happy, *Akiiwin*," her mom said, using Keilann's Ojibwe name to emphasize her point. "We both were happy teaching there, but this is his dream job. Head of the English Literature Department at one of the most prestigious universities in Britain—

how many people do you think get that chance?"

"But I thought you wanted to move back to Minnesota after we finished school."

Keilann's mother picked at a loose thread in her shawl. "I did."

"So what happened? Are you an apple now?"

A car alarm blared in the distance. Keilann's mouth tightened; she hadn't realized she was so angry. It was one of the worst insults she could've hurled at her mother. Namid used to tell her daughters stories about life on the Rez, a place Keilann had only visited on short trips during summer vacation. She told how people there called her an "apple" because she left to get an education: red on the outside, but white on the inside. Not really Ojibwe anymore.

She expected her mom to snap. Instead, her mother sighed again, her shoulders slumping wearily.

"Sometimes you have to make sacrifices for the ones you love." There was a tremble in her usually strong voice. "Sometimes you have to give up more than you ever thought you could and hope that it's all worth it in the end."

She pressed her hand to her mouth, her shoulders shuddering. With a horrified jolt, Keilann realized that her mother was *crying*. Keilann didn't know what to do, where to look; she could feel her face growing warm.

"Mom, I'm sorry. I didn't mean it," she said. "I'm just tired and crabby. Forget it, please."

Her mother waved away her apology. "It's fine," she said, dabbing her eyes on her shawl. "It's not you—"

"I didn't mean it."

"I know, *Akiiwin*. I know you didn't mean it." She smiled, her eyes red and puffy. "Look at us. We should get to bed, huh? Big day tomorrow."

"Yeah," Keilann's stomach sunk. Tomorrow. "Night, Mom."

"Good night."

Keilann shuffled back to her room, but her mother turned back to stare out the window as if saying good-bye. She crept past her parents' door where her father's snores drowned out the light scuffle of her feet. No wonder her mom couldn't sleep.

Keilann rolled onto the mattress and closed her eyes, but her mind refused to be quiet. She'd have to begin in a new high school, walk into the cafeteria on the first day of school with not a friendly face in sight. Keilann had never been quick at making friends like Fiona. Would she have to eat her lunch in the bathroom stall? Her stomach flip-flopped.

Sure, she had dreamt of traveling before, but more along the lines of a road trip to the East Coast or maybe somewhere exotic like Hawaii. But never, not once, had she ever dreamed of going to *Scotland*. What the hell was in Scotland, anyway? She'd seen *Braveheart* a few years ago—to her, Scotland meant a bunch of white guys in ugly skirts with weird accents and bad hair.

What more was there to know?

Keilann yawned. Her eyelids were getting heavy. Far off, the steady swish of traffic on the Interstate lulled her to sleep.

She was riding in a car with William Wallace; he was a terrible driver. The car kept bumping and swerving all over the road. She was going to say something to him, but the car disappeared.

She was running. The high rise of downtown Chicago disappeared as she drew nearer like a mirage. She was running through a forest alone. Trees rushed past her on all sides, dark and silent.

Where was she?

She craned her neck from side to side, recognizing nothing. A spasm of fear shot through her. Where was the Braveheart guy? How could he have left her like this? She could smell smoke; a billowing black cloud rose above the trees and closed in around her. There was a noise like a tea kettle whistling, and it kept getting louder and louder. Keilann pressed her hands to her ears, but the scream roared in her head. Only it wasn't a tea kettle anymore, it was a person. Someone was screaming.

Keilann held her breath as a face began to emerge from the smoke—wide forehead, high cheekbones, dark eyes smoldering, burning. Keilann could feel the heat of the fire from his eyes on her face. Without warning, the trees burst into ferocious, hungry flames, consuming the shadow man instantly. He reached for her, blackened flesh peeling from bone as the flames licked up and down his arms. He opened his mouth. Keilann was sure he was going to speak to her.

His scream ripped through the flames. She stood, frozen, helpless as she watched him fall to his knees, one arm still reaching to her—

The sharp crack to her head woke Keilann instantly, wood meeting bone with a dull thud. Pain throbbed in her temples, her heart beating somewhere behind her eyes. She'd fallen off the air mattress.

"Keilann?" A voice whispered from the darkness.

She turned, a flutter of surprise turning to joy as she recognized the dark face of her little sister not a foot away. A wave of gratitude rushed through Keilann. For once, she was glad that Fiona had insisted on sleeping in Keilann's room the night before the move.

Fiona was staring at Keilann intently; her smooth forehead was crinkled, her eyes wide. "Are you okay?"

Keilann propped herself up, her limbs still tense and cramping. She touched two fingers to her forehead; an egg was already beginning to swell. Perfect.

"Yeah. Just a bad dream," she muttered.

Fiona kept staring.

"What were you dreaming about?"

Keilann rolled away from Fiona and stared at the blank wall. How could she explain the dream to Fiona when she didn't even know what it was about? All she knew was that it was terrifying.

"I don't remember," she lied.

Keilann lay in the dark a long time before she finally could close her eyes. When she woke up the morning of the move, all she remembered was her stiff neck, the lump on her head, and the vague sense of a terrible dream.

2

Keilann's fingers fidgeted with the starched pleats in her required uniform skirt. She was desperate to loosen the thick knot of her necktie—she wished it wasn't so tight.

A necktie. Last year she had worn a new pair of jeans and an orange paisley tunic she'd bought at Navy Pier, her thick black hair tumbling down her back the way she liked it. This year, she was dressed like a corporate executive.

"I look like an idiot." Keilann stared into the bathroom mirror, aghast at her own reflection. Next to her, Fiona tucked a stray hair into her glossy French braids.

"Well, good," she said, flashing her sister a devilish grin. "You won't be fooling anyone, then." Keilann pulled at the plaid skirt, fanning out the perfectly measured and pressed pleats.

"They actually *wear* this stuff here?" She picked up a brush and began attacking the knots in her hair. "Maybe it's all part of a stupid joke, like an initiation or whatever."

But it wasn't. Keilann had double-checked the letter she and Fiona had received, the strict policy stamped on official school letterhead. Right under the pompous school crest and pretentious Latin motto, *Ex Scientia Lux*, glared the ominous words: **SCHOOL DRESS CODE.**

There will be NO EXCEPTION to the following mandatory uniform. While at Mary Arden Academy, students will be outwardly representing the caliber of their education with their dedication to personal appearances. Full parental cooperation is expected and appreciated.

- WHITE collared shirt (off-white, cream, ivory, etc. are NOT ACCEPTABLE)
- Mary Arden Academy school tie (yellow, black, and red plaid ONLY)
- Tartan skirt/black trousers: girls may wear trousers during cold weather months
  NOTE: knee-length, WHITE socks MUST be worn with skirts at ALL TIMES

Keilann stared at the list. Where were their parents sending them?

She glanced sidelong at Fiona who was straightening her necktie for the third time.

"I can understand the humiliating tartan skirts, but *neckties*?" Keilann's reflection pouted. "I look like Dad."

Fiona giggled. "You look like an angry bee." She flipped her collar and smoothed its crisp edges.

Keilann scowled and thrust at her hair with new vigor. The humidity and constant rain had teased it into a rebellious, knotty nest. As she struggled to beat her hair into "a high standard of appearance" that would "represent the caliber of her education," it was hard not to hate Fiona. Floating into the bathroom a half-hour after Keilann had begun her desperate Academy makeover, she breezed past in a uniform that looked fresh and intellectual without effort. Her snow-white shirt was immaculate and tucked without a wrinkle, the thick, tight kilt rested lightly on her trim hips.

Despite her numerous attempts, Keilann could not keep her shirt from bunching in the back, the unruly wrinkles shouting disgrace from across her midriff. The heavy wool skirt did its best to press and squeeze Keilann to conform to its standards, the uncompromising waistline digging into her stomach painfully. To her despair, a thick roll of flesh overflowed the thrifty allowances of precisely calculated tartan, ignoring the size Mary Arden thought she ought to be. Keilann's heart dropped. She looked like she was wearing a spare tire.

Checking her reflection for the last time, Fiona flipped her braids across her shoulders, her lustrous jet-black hair and mahogany skin contrasting against the stark white collar. She flashed her older sister a confident smirk and flounced down the stairs where their parents were already eating breakfast.

In the end, Keilann gave up and simply pulled her barely tamed frizz into a chunky ponytail. She faced her reflection, taking a long, steadying breath.

"Well, this is as good as it gets."

By the time Keilann finally made it down to the kitchen, Fiona and her mother were already half-way through their breakfast. She sat down at the avocado green Formica table her dad had salvaged from an old Chicago diner before Keilann had been born. At least something was familiar this morning. Keilann glowered at the cold stone walls of the "quaint" cottage her parents had stuffed them into. Just like the rest of the country, their new house was damp, cold, and grey. Deciding they'd had enough of the city—and without bothering to ask Keilann her opinion—her parents had chosen a drafty old house tucked away in the countryside. Surrounded by glum trees and dark hills, Keilann had felt cut-off from civilization since the move. At least going to school was an excuse to get out of the house Keilann could *swear* didn't like her any more than she liked it.

Keilann sat down in her chair as carefully as she could, trying not to make the wrinkles in her uniform any worse. Her mom had cooked, which meant the toast was stone cold and the eggs were limp and rubbery. Just as well; her stomach fluttered with nerves. A mouthful of eggs and a few nibbles of toast were all Keilann could manage.

"Ready for your big day?"

Fiona speared a mouthful of eggs onto her fork. "Did I tell you I just *love* these uniforms, Mom?" She grinned at Keilann.

Keilann stirred her eggs with her fork and glared. *Brat,* she mouthed.

"Good, they were expensive enough," their mom said. She arched an eyebrow. "You feeling alright, Kei?"

"What? Oh, yeah, I'm fine," Keilann lied. "I just couldn't sleep again last night. I keep having this dream—"

Her mother looked up from her coffee and yelped.

"Oh, god—Reid! Get down here and grab your breakfast!" She jumped up from the table and began clearing away dishes in a frenzy. She was in such a hurry she didn't even notice that Keilann had hardly touched her food. Usually, this would warrant a speech on waste and privilege, but today her mother just scraped it into the trash bin without a second glance. "We have to leave in ten minutes if we're going to make the meeting!" She dumped the dishes into the sink.

"What were you saying, Keilann?" she asked over the rush of water as the dish tub filled.

It had been this way for weeks. Her parents had always been busy, but now that her father was a department head, Keilann had hardly seen him. After her mom had found out she got the associate art professor position, they'd both been running mad trying to learn schedules, classrooms, and plan lessons. In that time, Keilann's dreams kept getting worse. The screams and fire had intensified so much that Keilann woke up in a cold sweat nearly every night. Whenever she tried to talk with her parents about it, there never seemed to be enough time.

I'm adjusting to the move. She nibbled a soggy corner of cold toast. *They'll go away after I get used to Scotland.*

Getting used to Scotland. It's all Keilann had been trying to do for the past three weeks. Days of unpacking and reorganizing their lives, getting to know new train schedules, and what her dad called "discovering the town." Owing to the fact that the nearby "town" only consisted of a rusty antique shop, a tiny grocery store, and a weathered pub, their whole exploit took about two seconds. Her parents called it charming and relaxing. Keilann and Fiona called it boring. She didn't like the thought of living in this cold, dreary place, but it was better than the nightmares. That's what she kept telling herself, anyway.

It hadn't all been bad, though. Determined to show their children that Scotland wasn't completely awful, the Douglas' had devoted the first week almost wholly to sightseeing. Keilann was surprised to find that within driving distance were royal castles, complete with turrets and gardens that looked like fairy tales come to life. Even she had to admit the ornate ballrooms and looming towers were pretty cool.

Best of all, there had been a few trips to Aberdeen to see the college and go shopping. Castles and ghost stories were one thing, but as soon as Keilann's feet hit the pavement of the big city, she finally felt at home. The streets of Aberdeen were crowded with people, smells, and the congestion of too many buses and cars. She loved it. Walking between the high rises and shops, lost in the bustle of life, Keilann could've been in any city. Despite the constant threat of rain and gloom that seemed to hover over Scotland, at least there was Aberdeen to keep her sane.

After her mother was offered an associate professorship because of an emergency vacancy, the sightseeing trips had to be put off for a while. There was work to be done, and the first day of school loomed ever closer. Now that it was here, Keilann wasn't sure if any of them were ready for it.

"Any breakfast left for a starving man?" Keilann's father bustled into the kitchen, shrugging his favorite tweed jacket. He winked at Keilann. "Anything edible?" He said only loud enough for her to hear.

Keilann smiled. "Barely," she whispered back.

Her father nodded. "Coffee it is, then."

Fiona giggled into her orange juice.

"There's toast and eggs on the table, Reid," Keilann's mother said from the sink. She glanced at the clock. "But we really have to get going."

"Relax, we've got eight whole minutes." Nevertheless, he poured his coffee into a travel mug. He turned to the girls. "How do I look? Smart and important?"

Keilann's father was as tall and lanky as her mother was short and stout, with carrot-colored hair and a neatly trimmed beard. Aside from the tweed jacket, he'd put on a hunter green shirt and a matching green-and-gold plaid tie. Keilann looked down at her uniform and frowned. She didn't think the fact that she and her dad were wearing practically the same thing for the first day of school was a good thing. He at least made the tie look respectable.

Fiona gulped down the rest of her orange juice in one swig. "You look good, Dad."

He held up a hand. "Before I forget—" He spun around and reached into the fridge. "Lunches for both of you. And don't worry, *I* packed them," he said with a wink.

"I heard that," their mother said, snapping a towel at her husband. She dried the rest of the dishes and scurried over to the girls, her heels clicking against the wood floors.

"Good luck today." She gave Fiona a swift kiss on the forehead. "I know this isn't how you imagined spending your senior year," her mom said, putting her hand on Keilann's shoulder. "But I know you'll make the most of it."

Keilann tried to smile back.

"Don't worry!" Their dad called after the girls as they crunched down the long gravel driveway to wait for the bus. "Today will be a great adventure! You'll see!"

An hour later Keilann sat in the main office of Mary Arden Academy, feeling as far away from adventurous as possible. The eggs and toast she'd choked down danced in her stomach. Everywhere she looked she saw spotless, polished floors and buffed wood paneling. It was like no other school she had ever been in—even the trash bins looked clean enough to eat out of. Her old school in Chicago had been a blend of colors and languages that Keilann had just fit into like a square on a patchwork quilt. So far at Mary Arden, she'd seen two kids who weren't white.

Keilann tugged at her kilted skirt. Waiting in the office was worse than going to the doctor. Keilann sniffed at the air scented with mild disinfectant; now that she thought about it, the main office actually *smelled* like a doctor's waiting room.

Tap, tap, tip, tap.

Seated on an identical chair next to her sister, Fiona began absently drumming the tiled floor with the toe of her stylish black flat. Keilann studied her from the corner of her eye. Perhaps Fiona wasn't as composed as she pretended.

From somewhere in the back offices, a latch clicked shut and a wizened receptionist shuffled into view. The woman was extremely bony with a sharp, gaunt face and chin-length, graying blonde hair cut at a severe angle. She puffed toward them, hunched under a thick bundle of color-coded files. Keilann marveled that she could hold them at all; they had to weigh at least as much as the old skeleton. She tottered over to the lacquered main desk, organizing the files into neat piles behind a yellow Formica placard that read "MÓRAG FREER, ATTENDANCE" in fat block letters. In the midst of such smart surroundings, the aged name card seemed drab and outdated. Much like its owner.

Both girls sprang from their seats at once, practically splitting the seams of their identical uniforms with nervous energy. Keilann sucked in a deep breath and made one last vain attempt to hide the stubborn bulge of her belly.

Here we go.

She stood at attention next to her sister, her hands clasped behind her back, and waited. And waited. A distant tone echoed and the glaringly white halls erupted in a din of chattering voices, slamming lockers, and scuffling shoes. Apparently well desensitized to the routine clamor, Mórag's eyes never left the mound of files she inspected with intense concentration. Keilann watched those eyes, absurdly distorted by thick cat eye glasses, sweep across the facts and figures, stopping to scratch a note or frowning as she bent to correct an error. The long, single tone blared again, a stern warning to any stragglers. Though the thought of going to her first hour class didn't hold any particular enjoyment for Keilann, missing it entirely didn't seem like a good idea either. Fiona threw her a meaningful glance, chewing her bottom lip. It was one of Fiona's only nervous habits.

She is worried. The realization gave Keilann a surge of comfort and just enough courage. She stepped toward the desk and cleared her throat loudly.

Reluctantly, Mórag's eyes left the pages and snapped to the sisters' anxious faces. A polite, appropriate greeting was on the tip of Keilann's tongue when the woman cut her off with a sharp sigh.

"Not again," she mumbled, her wiry shoulders slumping by a fraction. A weary, age-spotted hand passed over her eyes.

Keilann stared back at the woman in dumb shock, her feet glued to the floor, a bitter taste filling her mouth like blood. Even the receptionist didn't think she was good enough? Was it that obvious?

Mórag picked up a phone and punched the numbers as if each had personally wronged her. Was she calling someone to take Keilann away? Where would she go? What would her parents say if she got kicked out after less than an hour at the best academy in Scotland?

"James? Mórag. Can you please send down one of the Spanish teachers?" She paused, listening for a reply.

Keilann blinked. *A Spanish teacher?*

She sighed, clearly relieved this time.

"Thank you. I don't understand what they think I can do without an interpreter for these people." She clicked her pen and shifted the phone to her other ear, her voice dropping to a hoarse whisper.

"Why do they keep wasting our time with these foreign exchange students? Cannae speak a lick of proper English," she huffed in a thick Scottish burr. "And we get dumped with them every semester."

Keilann's mouth hung open.

She was talking about *them*! This horrible woman was talking about her and Fiona like they were filthy, discarded rags. Her shock boiled and hardened into anger, coating her nerves with steel.

"I don't know what they expect me to do," Mórag repeated. She plastered a wide, forced smile on her face and nodded at the girls.

"Excuse me," Keilann growled.

Mórag's smile wavered; she finally noticed the sparks shooting from Keilann's fuming eyes. It was her turn to be too shocked for words. She let out a terrified squeak, the phone clattering from her hand. It would have been a comical sight if Keilann hadn't been ready to tear her useless head from her scrawny neck.

"I don't mean to be rude or anything, but we don't need an interpreter," Keilann spat. "If you would have bothered to ask us, we would've told you we're American."

Keilann could feel Fiona bristle beside her.

"That means we understand everything you've been saying about us."

The woman at least had the decency to look mortified. A flush of pink crept up her frail neck, tinting the spidery lines of her face with an ugly rouge.

"I...I...my mistake," she stammered an apology. "I didn't...I...well, you do look a bit exotic...." Mórag faltered, her color rising. "I only meant—"

In the end, she was only all too happy to process them as quickly as possible. Keilann hovered over the desk in tightlipped fury, meeting Mórag's standard registration inquiries with surly, curt responses only when absolutely necessary. Of all the things they'd brought with them from America, this was one that she had naïvely hoped to leave behind.

By the time Mórag shoved the bright orange hall passes at them, Keilann was exhausted. She felt like they had been at Mary Arden an entire day, and was more than ready to turn her back on the whole horrible country.

"Welcome to Mary Arden Academy, ladies. I'm sure you will each share an illustrious academic career while within our walls," Mórag said, not meeting Keilann's eyes. Clutching their new files to her chest protectively, she retreated from the desk and darted out of sight behind a file cabinet.

Fiona's anger reared as soon as the main office's heavy double-doors clicked behind them. "Exotic? That stupid, racist piece of—Ow!"

Keilann jabbed her sister in the ribs and smiled politely. The teacher walking by raised an eye brow, but said nothing. Keilann waited until the click of his penny loafers faded into the adjacent hall. She spun on the still blazing Fiona.

"Watch it," she hissed. "You make a big deal out of it, and it is only going to get worse. For both of us."

Fiona blinked. "Are you serious?! That woman should get fired for the way she treated us! Why should we just take that crap?"

Keilann shook her head. "Just forget about it, okay? Don't let it bother you. People are dumb; they make assumptions." She sighed. "It's not as if stuff like this has never happened before."

Fiona opened her mouth to argue, but Keilann could see the anger dissolve out of her. She stared at her shoes.

"Well..." but she couldn't find any words.

"Well."

Fiona bit her lip. "What's your first hour class?"

Keilann consulted the color-coded map and class schedule Mórag had given her. "English. Down this wing, I guess. Yours?"

"History." There was a pause as Fiona decoded her own map. "First floor."

"Ah."

So that was it. Comforted by her sister's familiar presence during the last few weeks of summer, Keilann had forgotten how little she would actually see Fiona during the school day. They had to go their separate ways. After such a dubious start, Keilann had a difficult time looking forward to what lay ahead. Or believing her time at Mary Arden would amount to anything close to describing an "illustrious career."

Fiona smiled weakly. "Good luck." She gulped.

"You, too."

Fiona turned toward the stairs and paused. She looked back at her sister, a broad grin spreading over her face. "Just try not to be such a loser, okay?" Another glittering flash of teeth, and Fiona disappeared down the stairs.

3

Keilann remained a moment longer, breathing in the seconds that trickled by. Every audible tick of yet another incessant clock was a steady reminder that her time was not her own. The sweaty pass in her hand was quickly expiring—it was now or never. Heels clacking against the cold tile, Keilann hesitantly wound her way down the hall labeled LANGUAGE ARTS in blue on her map.

1041...1043...1045...

Keilann ticked off the numbers as she passed classroom after classroom of identical students. Here and there she caught snippets of a teacher's lecture, emphatically gesturing to make a point or lulling their class to sleep with dull slides crammed with dates and definitions. What impressed upon Keilann most was the hushed, almost reverent, quiet that lay upon the students like a thick blanket.

In her old schools, there had been too much noise. Because Keilann was often silent, teachers had either seen her as a sullen underachiever or not seen her at all. The latter suited her best. If she could stay off of a teacher's radar, then she could sneak by without causing waves. Her grades had never been perfect, but she made sure that they were never a reason for someone to take notice of her either. At Mary Arden, however, Keilann could already sense that her carefully balanced strategy was not going to be an option here.

1047...1049...1051...The classrooms marched on.

As Keilann paced down the muted hall, the only sounds that reached her ears were the droning voices of lecturers and the regimented whisper of pens furiously scribbling notes.

Hypnotized by the blur of white walls, white floors, and white faces, she almost walked straight past her destination.

1057.

Keilann halted just outside the open doorway. She double-checked her schedule and glanced back up at the room number. This was it. Lingering at the door, she took advantage of the fact that no one seemed to have noticed her uninvited interruption.

Color blared from the walls. Every inch of the classroom was swathed in pictures. Bright, colorful Van Gogh prints were taped lopsided along with modern art and scraps of poetry. Plastered in rows were large, black-and-white pictures of long-dead white men with strange beards, along with a few more contemporary ones of women and minorities—famous authors, no doubt. Keilann didn't recognize any of them.

"Can I help ye?"

With a jolt, Keilann realized that every student in the room had taken a break from copying notes to stare at her. How long had she been standing there? The woman approaching her was only an inch or so taller than Keilann and very plump. Her round frame was draped in a breezy, wine-colored dress that tapered down to high-heeled leather boots, her long, mousy hair pulled back in a loose bun.

"Um,—"

Sniggers rippled through the classroom. Keilann flushed. She could hear Fiona's voice in her head: *just try not to be such a loser, okay?*

She took a deep breath.

"Uh, yes. I'm looking for Ms.," she glanced at the schedule. "Ms. Spark's English class?"

The woman gave Keilann a warm smile.

"Then ye've come to the right place. Ye must be me new student from the States?"

Keilann nodded as Ms. Spark ushered her into the classroom. She could feel the eyes of her peers sizing her up as she concentrated on not tripping. Ms. Spark took the pass from Keilann without glancing at it and lumbered over to a large desk so littered with papers it would've made Mórag Freer faint.

"Now let's see. Douglas, is it?"

She scanned a clipboard crowded with class rosters, her eyes halting half-way down the list. At once, Keilann knew she had reached the legal name her parents had registered her under: *Douglas, Akiiwin*. An all-too-familiar frown tugged at the corners of her teacher's mouth, as if she thought Keilann's first name must be a practical joke.

"Akai-? Akee-?" Ms. Spark clumsily sputtered the Ojibwe syllables, looking to Keilann for help.

"Uh-kee-win," Keilann said clearly, raising her head defiantly against the smirks spreading across smug faces.

"It's Ojibwe. Native American," she clarified, when Ms. Spark's brow puckered at the unfamiliar words.

Keilann heard a loud snort. She turned her head in time to see a blonde boy with broad shoulders and too much gel in his hair raise his right hand toward her.

"*How,*" he said in deep, mocking tones.

The class erupted in howls of laughter, and the docile façade of Mary Arden Academy was swiftly cast away. Underneath the posh manners and etiquette were the same merciless, bloodthirsty cannibals that seemed to rule every high school social hierarchy. They pounced upon any sign of weakness or abnormality, and Keilann was a deer in headlights. The boy's smirking face blurred as hot, mutinous tears threatened to spill from her eyes.

Don't cry in front of them. Don't let them see that they can get to you.

Try as she might, Keilann wasn't certain how long she could choke back the onslaught of rage and humiliation that welled inside of her. Luckily, it took only a matter of seconds for Ms. Spark to snap back from her initial shock.

"Enough!" she barked. Her voice cracked through the air like a whip.

The laughter died instantly, replaced by a thunderous silence. The smirk fell from the boy's clean-cut features as Ms. Spark's glare honed in on the cause of such a disruption. Her bulk seemed to puff up with anger like a bullfrog, her gentle face distorted with wrath. Even Keilann shrank away from her.

"Connor McBride!" she seethed through gritted teeth. "Once again, I have ye to thank as a source of ignorance and infantile behavior in my classroom."

The air suddenly seemed much heavier; the students tried to look anywhere but at Ms. Spark and her prey.

"It would be a shame, would it not, if the football team had to play its first match of the season without its star keeper because he had gotten his foul-mouthed hide thrown in detention?"

The boy's eye's bulged, his face turning a violent shade of purple that almost matched Ms. Spark's dress. "But—no—you can't!" the boy stammered. "Ms. Spark, I was only joking!"

She did not yell. Her voice was a deathly calm that was much, much worse.

"I think ye will find that *I* am *not*, Mr. McBride."

In a flash, Connor's face rearranged itself from an outraged snarl to respectful and contrite. "I deeply apologize, Ms. Spark. The comment was thoughtless and immature."

"It is not I you have offended. Apologize at once to Ms. Douglas, and report to my office for detention next Friday."

"But, Ms. Spark, the match!"

"Now, McBride!" she thundered.

The blistering anger and revulsion written in his features was much more difficult to conceal as he turned his scowl to Keilann.

Deep purple blotches darkened Connor McBride's flawless complexion. "Sorry," he muttered, glaring at his desk.

"Very well, McBride. I expect no more outbursts from you for the remainder of this semester, is that understood? Excellent. Well, my dear," she added in a much warmer tone, turning to Keilann once again. "I apologize for such a rude interruption. Would you mind telling me your name again?"

"I usually just go by my middle name," Keilann said in a rush. She had no desire to endure such mocking a second time. "Keilann."

Ms. Spark glanced at her over the top of her clipboard, but made no comment as she scribbled in Keilann's name. Keilann's hand trembled as she accepted the course syllabus and required reading list from Ms. Spark and was finally allowed to take a seat.

"Just ignore Mr. McBride. It's what I try to do most of the time," Ms. Spark added, dryly, breaking the lingering tension.

Keilann fled to a desk in the corner of the room, far away from the poisonous glare of Connor McBride. What had she done to deserve such blind hatred?

"Now, although I believe we've had quite enough excitement for one day, I propose that we return to something of a much more exhilarating nature."

Ms. Spark's voice was light, but unmistakably commanding. Keilann forced herself to look straight ahead, feigning rapt attention so she wouldn't have to bare the tangible loathing of Connor or the disapproving scowls of his friends. As Ms. Spark addressed the class, she felt the weight of those leering stares begin to shift.

"In a few short weeks, we will be delving into much more enthralling and rewarding work." Her voice grew louder, more passionate. "You will experience first-hand the dazzling word play and spectacular genius of arguably the greatest writer in human history: William Shakespeare."

The students, who had seemed to be holding their breath during Ms. Spark's theatrical introduction, now let it loose in one loud, unanimous groan.

"As thrilled as I know you must be to read Shakespeare," she continued over the din. "You will be equally tickled to be studying one of his most famous—or perhaps, infamous—works, *Macbeth*, known in the theatre simply as 'The Scottish Play.' Anyone know why?"

A wisp of a girl with short, spiky hair in the front row waved her hand insistently. "Chrisselle?"

"Everyone in theatre knows that 'The Scottish Play' is cursed," she said, breathlessly. "Terrible things happen. People have died performin' it. If you sae the name, ye'll bring the curse on yer show."

Keilann's eyebrows shot up. *Curse?*

Ms. Spark was nodding as Chrisselle spoke, passing out thick stacks of books to each row.

"Exactly: a show so evil, it is said to be cursed and actors fear performin' the work. But why? That is what we are going to discover. What is the attraction—or revulsion, as some of you may feel—of Shakespeare's only Scottish-based play? It deals with a fair bit of witchcraft, betrayal, greed, and murder. In the end, it will be for you to decide."

The boy a row ahead of Keilann turned and flopped a shabby book onto her desk. A disturbing couple adorned the disintegrating cover. The man's hands were dripping with blood, a stricken gasp frozen on his face. Behind him, a haughty woman with deep red lips sneered over his shoulder, a bloody dagger clutched in one hand, a crown in the other. The image would have been startling if a previous student hadn't penciled in thick eyebrows and a curling beard over her wicked grin.

"Laird and Lady Macbeth." Ms. Spark scrawled their names on the whiteboard, connecting them with a thick line. There was a flurry of rustling papers and pens as students rushed to take notes.

"Two of the most infamous characters in all of literature—and based on actual historical Scottish rulers, however loosely. Laird Macbeth is a loyal nobleman coming home from war when he encounters three witches who hail him as king. Macbeth is tempted by the power and glory of the crown, but he doesn't really plan on doing anything—until he decides to write home to his wife to tell her all about the witches' prophecy.

"Now," Ms. Spark drew a large circle around Lady Macbeth's name. "Here is our true villainess of the play. As soon as she reads what the witches have said, she decides to act. The witches' words are more than just a prophecy to her—they are an excuse to commit cold-blooded murder. It is Lady Macbeth who comes up with the plan to slaughter the kindly old King Duncan in his sleep."

She wrote his name above Macbeth's, two lines sprouting roots underneath it.

"She plans to blame it on his two sons, who are only children at the time. With Duncan's sons out of the way, the crown would pass to the next in line: Macbeth." Ms. Spark grinned. "Pretty evil, eh? Macbeth resists at first, but his wife ends up using her, ah, feminine charms to convince him to drug Duncan's guards, sneak into the old man's room, and stab him to death."

Ms. Spark turned away from the whiteboard and brushed her hands together. "Seems like a pretty solid plan, yes? Seems like that old hag had thought of everything to make sure her husband would become king. A flawless plot, but old Rabbie Burns knew something that Lady M didn't.

"Robert Burns," Ms. Spark clarified as Keilann's brow knotted in confusion at the strange name. "The most celebrated Scottish poet of all time. Some call him the 'Scottish Shakespeare.' He wrote a poem nearly three-hundred-years after *Macbeth* was written that emphasizes one of the plays main themes: ye cannae plan for everything."

This time, Ms. Spark passed around a thin sheaf of bright blue paper. On it was one of the strangest poems Keilann had ever seen. On the right side of the paper was an illegible jumble of words that Ms. Spark explained as "Scots," the language in which Burns had written all of his poems. Thankfully, Ms. Spark had also included a translation into English on the left, though it hardly helped Keilann make sense of anything. The whole poem was about a man who ran over a mouse's nest with a plough, and how unfair it was that the mouse went through all of that hard work for nothing. Keilann couldn't see how that related to anything Ms. Spark had said about *Macbeth*, until she read the final stanzas to the class in Scots. Keilann followed along with the English translation:

> *But Mouse, ye are not alone,*
> *In proving foresight may be vain:*
> *The best laid schemes of mice and men*
> *Go oft awry,*
> *And leaves us nothing but grief and pain,*
> *For promised joy!*
>
> *Still you are blest, compared with me!*
> *The present only touches ye:*
> *But oh! I backward cast my eye,*
> *On prospects dreary!*
> *And forward, though I cannot see,*
> *I guess and fear!*

"'*The best laid schemes of mice and men go oft awry,*'" Sparks repeated. "Can anyone tell me what that means? Beathan?"

The ginger-haired boy in front of Keilann started at his name, but responded without missing a beat. "I think it means that no matter how guid of a plan ye make, it can always go wrong."

"Absolutely! '*Leaving us nothing but pain for promised joy.*' Laird and Lady Macbeth think that getting the crown will make them happy. They think that their plan is foolproof. The one thing they do not account for, however, is the human conscience.

"'*But oh! I backward cast my eye,*'" she quoted again. "We will find that many elements are working against Laird and Lady M, but the biggest enemies they have is guilt. '*And forward, though I cannae see, I guess and fear.*' What does that sound like?"

"Sounds like they would be paranoid," a burly, spotty-faced boy from across the room offered. "If they were able to kill Duncan for the crown, who's to stop someone from doing the same thing to them?"

"Excellent!" Ms. Spark whooped. "I want ye to keep all of these things in mind as ye complete yer first assignment."

Keilann stifled another groan, though a few of her classmates weren't able to contain their discontent.

"Before we begin reading about Macbeth's plans going awry, I want ye to think about yer own best laid schemes. Ye are to write a two-page essay on the theme we just explored: why plans go wrong, and what becomes of us lowly mortals in the aftermath.

Write a narrative of a personal experience of what ye thought was a perfect plan, and not only how it went wrong, but also how either guilt or fear changed how you handled the situation."

The low, steely tone Keilann had heard from the office now blared through the classroom.

"Two pages due by the beginning of class on Thursday!" Ms. Spark shouted over scraping chairs and chatter bubbling from the hall.

Keilann pushed back her chair, taking extra time to pack her bag until Connor McBride was well out of sight.

Plans going wrong, Keilann thought glumly. *Where do I begin?*

By the time the final bell tolled, Keilann had a mounting pain throbbing behind both eyes. Her head was jam-packed with facts, and her book bag crammed with homework. The feeble groan of her locker as she clapped it shut for the final time was an exhausted sigh of relief. Home was the only thing on Keilann's mind as she lugged her book bag over her shoulder.

She never saw it coming.

Wiggling through the mass exodus of shouting, kissing, laughing bodies, she was eager to reach the main entrance where Fiona would be waiting and leave this day behind her. Keeping her eyes fixed on her feet, Keilann slammed into the broad chest of a boy muscling himself through the crowd. Her ears rang with the raucous laughter that filled the hall as she bounced off of the brick wall of a boy, spilling onto the tiled floor with her books and papers sprawled around her.

Dazed, she scurried to stuff her things back into her bag.

"I'm so—" the apology stuck in her throat. Keilann was staring up at the smug sneer of Connor McBride.

Oh, no.

"Well, look what we have here, lads!" the snub-nosed boy shouted to a posse of lean, athletic boys. "It's Pocahontas!"

A few of the boys whooped, bellowing and beating their open mouths with their palms. Keilann's face burned, scalding the tears that had been trying to free themselves from her eyelids since that morning. She scrambled to her feet and tried to step around Connor. He cut off her escape, planting his long legs directly in her path.

"Where d'ye think yer going?" he jeered. "Don't ye want to stick around for the powwow?"

He leaned toward her, a wave of chokingly sweet cologne making her gag. The back of her heel struck a locker door with a hollow thud.

She was trapped.

"I had a spotless record," he hissed, jabbing a manicured finger in her face. "Never had a detention, never missed a game—*never*!" The minty tinge in his breath couldn't cover the reek of cigarette smoke. "Yer gonna pay for what you did to me."

His threat stunned Keilann into action.

"What *I* did?!" she sputtered. She slapped his meaty, tobacco-stained finger out of her face. "What did I do to *you*?! I didn't ask you to be a racist creep!"

Where was a passing teacher when she needed one? Keilann leaned as far away from Connor as she could, her back pressed against the cold metal lockers. The boy's face twisted into a snarl. He opened his mouth, but it was Fiona's voice Keilann heard.

"Keilann?! Hey! What's going on?" She flew down the stairs, the group of boys parting to get a better look at her.

"Get away from her!" Fiona shouted.

It was enough. Connor's head swiveled and Keilann darted behind him to where Fiona's head was bobbing between the thick shoulders of most of the boys' soccer team.

"Keilann, who was that guy—ow! You're hurting me!" Fiona cried, bewildered.

Keilann latched onto her forearm with vice-like strength, dragging her little sister away from Mary Arden Academy as fast as she could. Fiona's long, slender legs stumbled to adjust to Keilann's short, quick strides. Though she had almost sprinted from the double-doors, she was not fast enough to out run the final insult Connor McBride hurled over the grounds.

"I'll see you tomorrow, *Pocahontas*!" he shouted through cupped hands.

Once they were on the bus, Fiona tried to ask what had happened. All Keilann could hear was the chorus of spiteful laughter echoing in her ears long after the boys and their perfect school had disappeared in the diesel exhaust behind them.

The bus belched and heaved along the narrow country lanes, but still Keilann wouldn't say a word. Finally, the bumping and rocking came to a halt outside of the winding gravel drive and nodding flower beds that lead to the house—Keilann still refused to think of it as *her* house. The girls jumped from the steps as soon as the bus came from a halt. For once, it was Fiona who had difficulty keeping up.

"Just tell me what happened!"

Keilann had reached the stoop, the dark row of windows glaring down on her intrusion. She slid her school bag from her shoulder and kept walking.

"Keilann!" There was fear in Fiona's voice this time.

Keilann's steps picked up into a full run.

"Keilann! Keilann!" Her sister's voice tapered away.

She didn't know where she was going.

I just need to get away.

The pounding in Keilann's head was much louder than the pine-softened thuds of her footfalls. Louder than Fiona's fading cries.

I just need to run.

Chest heaving, Keilann ran, the chill breeze washing over her face like a cool stream. She drank in the relief and freedom of the fresh air, pausing only for a few steadying breaths. She cocked her head and listened, but heard no more footsteps or calls. Fiona wasn't chasing her. Good. Keilann had to get away from that house, that school, her new life, if only for a few minutes. Taking a deep breath of crisp air, she set out again at a brisk walk, the sodden green turf squishing under her sneakers.

Her parents had relocated them to a rural Scottish town with an unpronounceable Gaelic name. Far different from the sleek, manicured cosmopolitan landscape she had always known, this was a world of forest and stone carved only by wind and rain. When she first glimpsed the hills, Keilann had thought they had a wild kind of beauty to them. But that had been before she knew she was going to be stuck with nothing but hills and sheep for company. Strictly a city girl by nature, Keilann hadn't had much of a desire to explore the woods surrounding her house.

Until now.

The trees became denser and the gentle slope of the land began to even out. The light came only in splotchy patches filtered into an emerald gloom through the canopy above. The temperature dropped suddenly in the cool air beneath the trees. Keilann crossed her arms tightly, drawing her sweater close.

Truly alone for the first time in weeks, Keilann's mind looped back to her old life, marveling at the moments that had led her to this secluded wood in Scotland.

Scotland. I live in Scotland. This is my home now.

She was hardly aware of the trees passing around her. Winding through trunks absent-mindedly, her thoughts were shattered by a sudden, stinging pain in her foot.

"Gaaaah!"

Keilann's ankle twisted under the rock. Propelled by her own momentum, she fell forward, scraping her shin along the stone as she fell. She landed painfully on a bed of sticky pine needles, dirt flying into her open mouth.

"Son of a—!" Keilann spit out grit and curses, wiping her mouth on her muddy sleeve.

She rolled over, her throbbing shin shooting needles of pain down her leg, a small pool of blood blooming on her knee. She peeled back her sweaty knee-high sock and dabbed off as much blood as she could with the rough acrylic threads of her sweater.

White hot pain pulsed from a series of ragged, indented slashes that were already bruising into deep purple.

Wincing, Keilann applied pressure with her sleeve and waited until the gash was only trickling a faint ruby streak into her sock to try to stand. Shaky and bruised but otherwise unharmed, Keilann limped over to her attacker. The boulder was the size of a large cat, overgrown by long grass and crowned with rough points smeared with red from Keilann's fall.

She turned about her, all of her attention now focused on finding any other booby-traps hidden on the forest floor. At first, she could only see wild grasses and generations of pine needles carpeting the otherwise innocent-looking ground. As Keilann picked her way through the trees, she began to feel like she was navigating a mine field. Dozens of stone heads peeked above tufts of grass and heather, their craggy faces upturned and eager for another misstep. Turning about, she found several fat, saw-like boulders clustering behind her, nestling against a grove of tree trunks.

"I hate nature," Keilann said. She twisted around. "Just how many of these things—?" She raised her eyes and froze, her sentence ending in a gasp.

Keilann had been too engrossed in her careful dance around the stone minefield to notice where it had been taking her. She was standing on the edge of a small tree-ringed clearing, face-to-face with a massive hump of greyish-black rock nearly a head taller than her father.

The stone's surface was covered in lichen and moss, its grizzled face deeply pitted from hundreds of years of rain and wind. Despite its size, the stone reminded Keilann of an old man; slightly leaning on a fallen tree for support, its once sharp features withered into trivial lumps. She placed her hand on the coarse surface gingerly, as if afraid to hurt it with too much pressure.

This must have been here for hundreds, maybe thousands, of years. She gaped up at the stone's full height, shielding her eyes from the sun with her free hand. *How did it get here?*

Keilann was sure that this rock was not a natural feature of the landscape. The other, smaller stones were squat and sand-colored, thrown hodge-podge throughout the trees as if they were forgotten toys. The dark slab under her fingers had been shaped and hewn by human hands. There were still traces of carved knots and spirals, though the craftsmanship had long been blunted by the elements. Keilann's head spun as she tried to imagine how many hands had touched this very spot and how many more were yet to come long after any trace of her life had crumbled to dust. The thought made her shiver, though her pulse beat defiantly against the lifeless stone.

What *was* this thing?

Keilann's fingers lingered across a deep fissure that splintered like a lightning bolt, a singular imperfection in the otherwise unbroken rectangular stone. It must have taken months to chisel and shape the rock and drag it to this one spot. Hours of sweat and devotion, all for what?

Keilann sighed and let her hand fall from the stone.

She had bigger problems to worry about than a big ugly rock. Keilann tore her gaze from the stone, glancing up at the sky to where the sun was crowded out of view by thickening clumps of dark, rain-heavy clouds. A fat drop of water plunked onto her forehead.

Time to go.

Keilann turned, reluctant to weave her way back through the sharp stones, when something out of the corner of her eye made her double-take. Wide-eyed, she peered through the leaves, hardly believing what she saw. A second pillar stood about twenty feet behind the first, blocked from view until she had stepped back. As soon as she noticed the second pillar, another stone nearly twice the height of the other two appeared almost diagonal to the second, leaning against the gnarled trunk of an ageless oak tree not ten feet away from her. A thrill of excitement shot through Keilann's stomach. Her head spun as her eyes darted from stone to stone, seeing the full circle for the first time.

Seven identical stone monoliths stared at each other in a perfect ring. Some of the pillars had been chipped or broken; another had been smashed in two by a tree trunk. Keilann crept along the perimeter of the stone circle, careful not to make a sound, as if her footsteps could wake the slumbering stone giants. From the instant she noticed the presence of the stone circle, the atmosphere seemed to change. The air was breathless, as if the trees held back the wind in anticipation.

Then without thinking, without really knowing what her feet were doing until it was too late, Keilann walked into the circle. She vaguely recalled television specials about people supposedly becoming sick or overpowered by mysterious forces at places like Stonehenge, but she had never believed any of that psychic crap.

Why should I be afraid of some old rocks?

She paused in the very heart of the circle, waiting for something to happen. Keilann closed her eyes and felt....

Nothing.

She was standing in the middle of the woods, just as she had been on the other side of the stones. Disappointment mingled with relief. No mystical force was going to show itself today. Keilann's face burned as she imagined how foolish she must look, thankful that no one was around to see her. Her eyes flitted to her old watch.

I should go back. They're probably looking for me.

She leaned forward slightly, listening for the echoing sound of her father's voice or Fiona's light footfalls snapping twigs or crashing over boulders. With a start, Keilann realized that she not only couldn't hear any sounds of her family, she couldn't hear any sounds at all.

The forest was quiet—absolutely silent. She listened for the chirp of a bird or the rustle of leaves, but the forest was suddenly still as if everything had stopped moving at once. She could hear no sounds or sense any movement except the wild beating of her heart.

For the first time since she could remember, Keilann wished she wasn't alone.

When she thought about it later, Keilann wasn't quite sure why she turned around. There was no sound, no breaking twig or rustling leaves. No, had there been a sound—any sound—then she could explain what had happened next. A sound would have made it easier to believe.

It had been a feeling. A cold breath on the air as if someone had opened the door of a long unoccupied room. The stone circle suddenly seemed to crackle with the energy of a thunderhead just before lightning strikes, every hair on Keilann's neck standing at rapt attention. Her nerves were so electrified she had to clench her jaw to keep her teeth from chattering.

There it was again: the quiet presence, the feeling of invisible eyes watching her. The cool draft tickled her skin, sending shivers down her spine, warning her of danger. Keilann wheeled on the spot, ready to face whatever beast or imaginary predator had stalked her from the shadows of her nightmares—and nearly crashed into a complete stranger.

Keilann was too shocked to scream, her mouth silently gaping as she staggered backward. Her shoulder hit the rough stone, jarring her senses enough to focus them on the impossible stranger that had materialized out of thin air.

It was a young girl, probably her own age, if not a little older. She had messy red hair that tumbled to her shoulders and piercing grey eyes that stared at Keilann with the same wide-eyed disbelief. She crouched in the center of the circle like a hunted animal; her muscles taught and ready to pounce. She wore a long, plain dress that hugged the curves of her slim figure, her lips parted in surprise. The girl might have been beautiful had she not been streaked and spattered with mud. Clots of mud were tangled into her wild hair, trailed down her face, and embedded into her clothing. Her arms were the worst. Streaked with mud to the elbow, her outstretched hands were black under the nails.

The two girls stared in mutual shock and confusion, each seemingly dumbfounded at the other's existence. Keilann wanted to speak, but her mind went blank.

Say something.

She couldn't remember how to form words. It was just too impossible. How could this solid girl be standing where Keilann had been not five seconds before?

The girl straightened from her feral crouch. Her sudden movement made Keilann jump. Drawn at her full height, she looked nearly as tall as Fiona. She was cold and regal, her severe eyes narrowed. Keilann squirmed under her gaze, feeling as though the girl were a lioness calculating whether such a pathetic meal was worth the effort. The girl's mouth began to open and close rhythmically, absurdly reminding Keilann of a gasping fish.

It was a few moments before Keilann realized the girl was speaking—or trying to, at least.

Though her lips moved, Keilann had to strain her ears to hear any sound at all. It was almost like watching an old movie, unable to decipher the meaning until the sound had time to catch-up with the picture. By the time her voice had finally reached Keilann's ears, it had become garbled, distorted somehow in the two feet of space between them. Keilann couldn't help but think of the game she and Fiona would play as girls, revealing secrets to each other underwater if the other could decode the message.

The girl paused, frowning. When Keilann didn't respond, her eyes narrowed further until they were nothing more than cold slits. As the girl seemed to gauge her next move, something clicked in Keilann's brain.

"I can't—how did you—where—?" There were too many questions. Keilann decided to try the simplest one first.

"Who are you?"

Before Keilann could finish speaking, the girl lunged forward.

"Hey!" Keilann stumbled away from the stone. The girl reached for Keilann's arm, her muddy fingertips brushing the blood-stained fabric of her sweater. "Wait! Stop!"

The girl was a breath from Keilann, her face contorted in savage anger. Keilann had nearly reached the edge of the stone circle, desperate to run, but her feet tangled over each other. She landed hard, the impact making her wounded leg blaze with new pain. Keilann threw her arms out and closed her eyes, preparing for the blow. But it never came. She remained motionless, her eyes squeezed shut, but nothing happened—no cries, no footsteps, nothing. Slowly, she opened her eyes and looked about her.

The girl was gone.

Keilann lay in the open glade for a few moments, hardly daring to breathe. Gingerly, she sat up and looked about her. She had fallen just outside of the stone circle which was...*empty?*

Her mind spun. The nerves in her legs howling in pain.

Was she hiding?

Keilann's eyes darted left and right between the trees, searching for a flutter of cloth or the flash of skin.

Why would she run away?

Bewildered and shaken, Keilann felt more vulnerable than ever. Five agonizing minutes trickled by without any signs of the girl. She stood slowly, every muscle in her body shaking. Stunned, scared, and more confused than she had ever been in her life, Keilann peered behind the pillars of the circle. Her legs shook with adrenaline, her shin throbbed with a shooting pain that traveled all the way down her foot.

What the hell just happened? That's impossible! She couldn't have—

Behind her, a twig snapped, but Keilann was ready for it. She knew the girl couldn't have disappeared that quickly.

"It's about damn time!" an angry voice shouted from between the trees.

Keilann wanted to drop to her knees and cry in relief as she turned in time to see Fiona thrust out her hip and cross her arms irritably.

"Mom and I have been looking everywhere for you! Didn't you hear us calling for like, the past hour?" Fiona snapped.

Keilann stared, licking her dry lips. "Did you see her?"

Fiona huffed and tossed her head, brushing aside a stray lock of hair.

"See who? Mom? Yeah, and she's pissed as hell that you just ran off like that. You are in serious—"

"You didn't see her? But—I saw—she was right here." The trees seemed to close in on Keilann like a cage. The girl must still be hiding in there somewhere, watching them.

"What are you talking about? Hello? Earth to Keilann?"

Keilann said nothing, her eyes searching the trees behind Fiona. Fiona dropped her arms, her annoyance turning into concern. She stepped toward her sister who still seemed oblivious to her presence.

"Keilann, what is wrong with you? You're acting really weird."

Keilann jumped at Fiona's soft touch on her arm.

"Are you bleeding?"

"It's nothing," Keilann mumbled. She shrugged off Fiona's hand. "I...tripped."

"Yeah, right, or you could try telling me what actually happened, starting with school," the edge had returned to Fiona's voice. She planted herself in front of Keilann, making it clear that she was not moving until she got some answers.

"No, really, I tripped over a rock," Keilann pointed to the edge of the grassy glade. Her face darkened. "But that's not important, Fiona. Someone was here. I saw her. This girl snuck up on me when I was walking and then she just....She's gone."

Fiona's brow puckered. "Wait, someone was here? As in our backyard?"

Keilann grabbed Fiona's shoulders, meeting her startled gaze. "Are you sure you didn't see anyone?"

"Ow! I'm sure!" Fiona wrenched herself free, rubbing her arm tenderly. "Is that what you're freakin' out about? Someone playing a dumb prank on you?"

Keilann could feel her ears reddening. "I don't think it was a prank, Fiona."

"Some bored local probably saw us drive up and decided to freak out the new Yank neighbor, and you're going to let that scare you? It was probably somebody's idea of a joke," Fiona shrugged, willing to dismiss the event without a further thought.

"Besides," she added, "You can always tell Mom and Dad if it really bothers you."

Ashamed of her fear, Keilann's face boiled into a lobster-red. When Fiona put it like that...She began to follow her sister back to the house.

Could it really have been a joke? Her cold glare, the anger blazing from her eyes—did she do it all just to scare Keilann? Again, Keilann imagined the girl hiding behind a clump of pines, this time rolling with laughter at the stupid American who was so easily tricked.

By the time they cleared the trees, the house looming over her once more, Keilann was nearly convinced that Fiona was right. There was only one nagging doubt at the edge of her mind: Fiona said that she had been calling her name for over an hour. Keilann should've heard her, but from the moment she had set foot inside the stone circle, she hadn't heard anything. Nothing. Even the strange girl's voice had been impossible to hear from two feet away. No matter how talented of a prankster that girl may have been, she could never have caused such a distortion. But what could?

"So, what did you think?" Fiona asked, jerking her head back toward the trees. She paused at the front door, her hand resting on the knob. Keilann followed her gaze, watching as the red sunset turned the leaves of the wood into golden tongues of fire. "Find anything cool back there?"

"Nothing," Keilann turned her back to the forest. "Just a bunch of rocks."

5

For a while, the nightmares diminished. Keilann was so fixated on the strange girl in the woods that thoughts of the burning man were pushed aside and briefly forgotten. The image of him reaching for her smoldered in the back of her mind while she wrestled with the memory of the red-haired girl lunging for her arm.

She would never admit it to Fiona, but Keilann was still not entirely swayed by her sister's prankster theory. The girl had seemed too terrifying, her anger too intense for a simple joke—or had that been the point? Even though Keilann had not dared to venture beyond the sight of the house again, the girl followed Keilann into her dreams. They were not chillingly real or crisp like the dreadful death-rattle of the burning man. Often, Keilann would wake to only hazily remember a blurred image or a muffled voice in the dark. It was almost as if she were looking at the girl's reflection in a stream—the more she tried to focus on the details, the harder it was to see what lay beneath the current. Once or twice Keilann had been wrenched awake by the creak of a floorboard. Was it a footstep on the stair? In the dead of night, she was wildly convinced that the girl had found a way into the house, that she was watching her from the dark corners, waiting for Keilann to be alone.

One rainy afternoon while Fiona was unpacking boxes in her bedroom, Keilann finally decided to voice her fears aloud to her sister.

"It just makes me nervous, I guess. The fact that I don't know who she is or what she wants. I haven't seen her since that day in the woods." She paused. "Isn't that weird in a small town like this?"

"Don't be stupid, Keilann."

Fiona didn't even look up from hanging a poster of her favorite band on her bedroom wall. Keilann had been reluctant to talk to Fiona—she knew how paranoid she sounded—but the latest incident had pushed her over the edge. Though Fiona dismissed it with a disdainful snort, Keilann was sure she hadn't imagined it: someone had been calling her name last night.

"Old houses make a lot of weird noises, don't they?" She paused to rip off another square of tape and stamp it on the poster with her thumb. "I mean, c'mon, who would actually want to come out here just to bother you? Just listen to me, okay? Let. It. Go."

With no legitimate argument as to why someone would actually want to stalk her—

and unwilling to share any more details about what had really happened in the circle—Keilann let the subject drop.

What if Fiona was right? If the stone circle had been nothing more than a prank, the girl would have certainly told her friends by now. Friends like Connor McBride. Wouldn't he just love to use the red-haired girl to torment her?

It was not long after she heard her name whispered in the dark that she began to dream of the burning man again. While Keilann occupied her days unpacking and adjusting the pieces of her old life into her new Scottish one, her nights were once again spent never running quite fast enough to escape hungry flames and the blood-curdling scream of a dying man.

This time, however, Keilann wasn't alone.

Sometimes, Keilann chased someone else through the fire: the red-haired girl. In each dream, Keilann was frantic, desperate to catch up to her though she couldn't say why. Every night when she'd finally close her eyes, the girl was always there. It was becoming too much. Keilann let herself become obsessed with the mystery of the girl in the circle. She tried to focus on building a new life, but during the endless hours of unpacking, her mind wandered back to the secret mystery hiding just beyond the tree line.

Two weeks after she had stumbled upon the stone circle, Keilann's nightmare worsened yet again.

The dream began in the usual way—a sprint through the cemetery of ghoulish trees, the all-too-familiar sting of smoke behind her eyes, the fire greedily consuming the gap between itself and her heels. Keilann pitched through the grey curtain of smoke as fast as her ragged lungs could push her. She could hear the river up ahead, the promise of cool water willing her body forward. Her feet sunk into mud, the current dragging at the hem of her dress—when the world around her suddenly shifted. The forest and flames melted into a wide, lush meadow. Instead of water rushing around her hammering legs, gentle waves of grass kissed her skin. A strong wind whipped a curling auburn lock into her eyes.

Red? Keilann's groggy subconscious struggled to remember. *I have red hair*?

The soft fields rose and fell with the breeze, making the earth breathe and sigh. She squinted into the rolling sea of green. Keilann had been looking for someone, but she couldn't remember who. The sun beat down on the heavy wool of her dress, needles of sweat prickling beneath her arms. Keilann's small hands scratched and pulled at the itchy material. She stamped her foot impatiently. She was beginning to tire of this game, she was hungry and her shoes were pinching her feet. But was it Keilann's imagination, or was the grass getting taller? It now reached her shoulders, her eyes barely peeking above the soft blades.

"Mama?"

A flash of red floated on the horizon like a cloud.

There! Her mother had appeared like a mirage in front of her, her back turned away from her small daughter.

"Mama! I'm here!" Keilann cried out.

She broke into a run, her dress dragging behind her, catching on briars. It seemed to grow yards of fabric as she ran, billowing behind her like a sail. Though she pumped her legs with all her might, the dress pulled her back again and again. Her muscles burned, but she ran on until she could feel ropes of sweat pouring down her back. Why did it have to be so hot? Dark clouds began to pile overhead, blotting out the sun, but the heat only seemed to intensify. Without warning, the thunderheads burst with the force of a torrential gale, turning the long grass into wriggling snakes. Keilann began to panic as the storm's twisting black funnel descended on the valley. She *had* to get her mother to safety.

"Look at me! Turn around! We have to get inside, please!" Keilann shouted into the wind.

But her tiny voice was lost in the screaming frenzy of the tempest. Again and again, she called out, but her mother didn't even seem to know that she was there. The wind wailed in Keilann's ears, and something else—a deep, resonant boom of thunder exploded into a strange name that she somehow knew was supposed to be her own.

"Mama!"

Keilann grasped her mother's wrist, almost shaking with relief. In an instant, however, her relief turned to horror. She recoiled, cradling her hand in pain. Her mother's skin was *boiling*.

She stared, frozen, as her mother finally turned to face her. Instead of her mother's warm, friendly smile, a thin crack of a grimace rested just below the hollow black gaze of the burning man. His blackened skin hung in dead strips of charred flesh. A gnarled hand reached for her; Keilann opened her mouth to scream, but no sound came. She wrenched herself free of his grasp, the corpse toppling onto her. She was falling, falling, falling.

"No!"

A sharp spasm of white hot pain shot through Keilann's limbs. Clawing frantically at the dark creature of her nightmares, she had wound her sheets into a jumbled mass and crashed to the floor below, landing hard on her left shoulder. For one wild moment, enclosed in the smothering cocoon, she thought she was still trapped underneath the dead man, tearing madly at the linen around her head and legs.

Her arm thrashed out and collided with her wall.

All at once, the world turned straight again. She was on her floor. She had had a nightmare. It was her own bed sheets that held her captive, not the man's disfigured limbs. Despite the relief that washed over her as she recognized her own room, a stabbing pit of fear in her stomach refused to unclench itself. The wind moaned through the trees outside her window, creating sinister shadows on her wall, crouching, slumping, and falling, over and over again as the image of the man replayed in her mind. She shut her eyes against the visions, still shivering at the thought of his touch. Keilann was too afraid to move, as if the hidden monsters of her nightmare hovered overhead, watching for her movement in the semi-darkness. The sheets were sour and damp with sweat, but she clung to them.

Keilann could barely see the bed in front of her face, yet her eyes flitted from wall to wall, too frightened to move.

It was a dream, she thought, *just a dream.*

She stood up into a stiff crouch, shuffling toward her bed with both arms groping blindly for the light switch. After a few moments of nothing but black, the lamp suddenly flicked on, revealing her bedroom in a harsh light. The walls were dark, almost as black as the night and looked as sinister as the knotted trees twisting in and out of her dreams. She examined them carefully, as if whatever had lurked within her nightmares hid in the shadows cast by the small pool of light. Her shoulders sagged. Keilann passed a weary hand over her face and rubbed the sleep from her eyes. She glanced at the clock on the wall, her brain taking a few beats longer than usual to decipher the hands and numbers. Even when her head finally digested the information, Keilann still couldn't make sense of it.

4:45? In the morning? She blinked at the clock face.

Cold radiated from the floorboards, creeping up her ankles, pricking and needling her flesh until her toes were numb. Keilann stood in the middle of her room, icy fingers of dank air chilling her to the bone. The stone walls held little sympathy for her. They stared back as impassive and frigid as the morning air.

"Another beautiful Scottish morning," Keilann said, using her voice to fill the silent void of her room.

She groaned and stretched, her head buzzing. It would be useless to try and go back to sleep now. Keilann was just beginning to make out the details of her room. The half-unpacked boxes dotted her floor like landmines, their contents strewn over the smart new furniture. Though her bed had finally arrived last week, her room was no more familiar—or comforting—than the first day she had arrived. She shivered again, not certain whether it was from the early morning chill or the haunting scream that still echoed in her ears.

Staggering around her room, she stubbed her toe on a nearby box and cut the morning air with curses. Every morning there were fewer boxes left to steer through, yet every morning she always managed to find the biggest one with her toes. The pain jolted the slippery details of the nightmare from her attention. There was a sweeping meadow, an eerie wind, and a strange woman. Was she supposed to be her mother? The pieces fell through her memory like grains of sand. By the time Keilann had shuffled into the hall, the entire nightmare had faded into a few fuzzy images.

She padded down the steps, feeling her way around the edges of the unlit living room, her back pressed firmly against the wall. A dim glow ahead told her she was going the right way; soon her feet connected with rough stone. Keilann sighed, the tension in her shoulders releasing as she passed through the archway. Why did she always feel the safest, the most welcome in the tiny kitchen? Someone had left the window shutters open—a soft, grey light illuminated the sparse, utilitarian room with a ghostly glow. Early morning mists still gathered in deep pools throughout the valley, swirling past the windows and painting them with fog.

A dull, muffled growl rumbled from her stomach in the stillness.

"Breakfast time," Keilann announced to the empty room. Her voice filled the creeping silence, fighting back any of the nightmares that lurked just out of sight. She turned to the miniature gas oven, rifling through cupboards and drawers to find the stowed matches. Lifting the tea kettle from the burner, she paused, frowning, and set it back in its place. The matches abandoned on the counter, Keilann gingerly touched the back of her hand to the worn copper kettle. It was hot. Only then did she notice the thin, snake-like vapors trailing from the spout—someone had made a cup of tea not five minutes ago. Something like courage thrilled up her spine; just the thought of another person sharing the darkness made the shadows of the night weak, almost pathetic.

Keilann glanced around the kitchen, poking her head back into the living room. The new leather couch and plush arm chairs her parents bought after the move were deserted.

"Hello?" Her voice bounced around the blank walls and scattered boxes, but met no sister or parent before returning to her. An unbearable silence slithered back into the room.

"Hello? Anyone there?" She inched forward. Faltering steps took her past the yawning fireplace, the dark staircase, and the gleaming locked door of her parents' office. The further she wandered away from the kitchen's safe haven, the faster her resolve crumbled. Keilann was already turning back when a golden glint sparkled in the peripheral shadows, catching her eye. At the other end of the house, one of the large, paneled French doors stood slightly ajar, its golden latch glinting mischievously in the strengthening light. The sight of the open door dropped a hard lump of panic in Keilann's stomach.

Did someone break in to rob us? Did the red-haired girl break in? Her mind raced with panic for a few seconds, but then she remembered the tea kettle.

Wait. Think about it. The sane, cool voice of logic interrupted the jumble of hysterical fears. *If someone was breaking into your house, would they really stop to make themselves a cup of tea before ransacking it?*

The rationale was a calming salve to her inflamed imagination. *That must mean if no one was breaking in, then someone must've been breaking out.* Keilann rushed to the windows.

And there, huddled in the dew-soaked grass, was the shrouded form of her mother, her small fingers curled around a mug of tea. She hovered at the edge of the tree line, her back turned to Keilann, bundled in a heavy shawl the color of the evening sky. Mist coiled around her, threatening to envelope and dissolve Keilann's substantial, practical mother. Set against the sleeping pines, her mother looked like she had sprung from the earth overnight. She was solid and sure, rooted in the traditions and beliefs of the past, much like her eldest daughter. Like her daughter, those roots had been shaken from their native soil and violently transplanted. Could either of them survive such a shock?

Keilann watched her mother in the half-light. Her shoulders were bent and tensed. Though she did not seem afraid, there was something in her body language that Keilann could not quite read. Dread welled up and washed images over Keilann's mind—a woman standing with her back to her daughter, the darkness covering the sun, the scream of a dead man. Déjà-vu stabbed Keilann so hard that it knocked her out of her door.

"Mom?" Her voice felt rusty, though the cry that echoed in her ears was all too familiar. Her mother did not turn. Blood pounded in Keilann's ears; her feet were drenched in dew as they flew over the turf.

"Mom!"

"Keilann! What's wrong?" Shocked, Namid's head snapped toward the sound of her daughter's voice. Thick hair flew over her shoulders in dark ripples dipped in silver, tea sloshing down her shawl. "What are you doing out here? Don't you know what time it is?" Though still clearly taken aback, her mother's maternal, authoritative edge had recovered. She bent down and touched a cool, reassuring hand to Keilann's shoulder.

"I couldn't sleep," Keilann said. She pointed backwards to where she had left the door wide open. "I saw the door and—" she raised her head to meet her mother's gaze. "Are you okay, Mom?"

There was no masking it. Her mother's wide-eyed stare was blood-shot and puffy.

"Have you been crying?" *Again?*

In Keilann eighteen years, she couldn't remember ever seeing her mother cry until the night before they left Chicago. Now she was crying again. Her mom drew back her hand and stiffened as if Keilann had slapped her.

"Of course not!" She turned to hide her face, hastily dabbing at her eyes with her shawl. "It must be my allergies. You know they always irritate my eyes."

When her mother turned back, her cheeks were scrubbed dry. She flashed her daughter a smile that was a bit too big to chase the sadness from her swollen, red-rimmed eyes.

"Couldn't sleep," her mom said. "I thought some fresh air would do me some good. I should've remembered what pollen can do to me." She shrugged. "I didn't mean to scare you. I forgot about the door. I didn't think anyone else would be up for..." Her mom checked her watch and started at the early hour. "Why are you up, Keilann?"

"I couldn't sleep either. I had a nightmare and couldn't get back to bed," Keilann stammered out the truth. She was too bewildered by her mother's odd behavior to think up anything better.

"Another nightmare?" Her mother's voice was gentle. Her eyes softened. She regarded her daughter quietly. "How many is that, Keilann?"

"I don't know. Not many. It's no big deal, Mom."

"Still, Keilann, I'm not certain that this is normal."

She knew that her nightmares were anything but normal, but hearing her mother say that out loud made Keilann feel like a freak.

"Are you sure you're okay, Mom? You look upset." Keilann fumbled blindly to switch subjects. "Is anything wrong?"

"Look at this shawl!" Her mother cut in mid-sentence, her tone shrill. She made a huge show over the now tea-stained wool. Large, dark splotches flourished across most of the fabric.

"How clumsy of me!" She shook her head, a plastic smile on her lips. "I might be able to save it if I soak it right away."

"Mom—"

"Come, Keilann. I don't want this to be ruined." Her voice was thick. Without waiting for Keilann to speak, she began to walk back to the open doors.

"Come inside," she called over her shoulder.

Dumbstruck, Keilann stared after her mother. Never, in all of her life had she seen her act like that. She couldn't decide which was worse: the fact her mother was lying, or the fact that Keilann had never noticed it before. She followed the soft imprints of her mother's footsteps in the grass. Inside, she could hear her mother already running the tap, attacking the blemish in her otherwise flawless shawl.

Wearied by more than the early hour, she crawled back beneath her covers. As she drifted into sleep, her mother's quiet step worked its way up the stair and into the bedroom down the hall. Bed springs squeaked as her mother lowered herself onto the bed next to her father. Would she tell him about her restless night? Keilann pulled the covers over her head, her last thought of her mother. Was she, too, haunted by a secret and just as desperate to hide it?

Hours later, Keilann was wrenched from sleep by the same sharp fear, the same wicked storm and strange wind. This time, she was ready. Before the details slipped into oblivion, before her mind had a chance to separate from subconscious, Keilann dove for the box that served as her makeshift nightstand. Grasping the pen and paper she had prepared, she scrawled a word on a yellow sticky note and slapped it on her wall. She fell back on her pillows, exhausted from her effort, but heart thudding with a swell of pride. She did not know what it meant. If she was truthful, it probably meant nothing, but in a way the letters staring down at her were symbols of triumph. They were a beginning, a gateway to unraveling the strange labyrinth of her nightmares. Yes, the burning man would come for her again, but she had captured his voice. Of all of the terrors Keilann had endured, she had finally heard the mournful name on the wind and snatched it out of the dream. It had fluttered on the wind, was caught and wrestled into the real world, and trapped beneath ink.

Gleaming faintly against the neon paper was a single word that Keilann was almost sure was a name: *Grewock*.

6

Keilann's feet had hammered down the woodland path, beating the pathetic stubs of grass into the hard-packed earth with every footfall. Blinded by anger and pain, the stone circle was the only place where she could be alone—at least, that's what she was thinking when she had sprinted away from the house again. Another day of insults, another day of *Pocahontas* trailing her down the halls. She couldn't stand another day like this one. Keilann thought she had found a way to avoid Connor, hoped that he had forgotten or grown bored with tormenting her. She'd been wrong. This time, he tripped her as she ran up the stairs to catch her bus, sending her and the contents of her backpack sprawling on the floor.

"Stay out of my way, Pocahontas." He kicked a book out of her reach and laughed. Tears stung her eyes, her knee smarting from the fall.

Ignore him. Ignore him.

That's the advice almost everyone had given her. Twig-like Chrisselle from Spark's English class approached Keilann the second day of school, full of apologies and insults for Connor McBride. That alone was more than a good enough reason to become friends in Keilann's eyes. Chrisselle immediately invited Keilann to join her circle of theatre friends at lunch, and they all gave her the same advice: ignore Connor. He was a notorious bully, and Keilann was not his first or only victim.

Ignore him. He's not worth listening to.

Easy to believe when sitting comfortably at a lunch table surrounded by friends, but impossible to remember when alone on the bus with a bruised knee. Keilann couldn't keep his ugly words out of her head.

Keilann hadn't stopped to consider what she'd actually do when she got to the circle, or how being there would scour the bitter taste of Connor McBride's foul words from her mouth. She only saw his smirk, heard his harsh bark of a laugh, felt his clammy breath against her cheek. The monster of his memory had been enough to propel her forward without worrying about consequences or reason.

When the top of the tallest stone burst into view, a small, quivering fear inside of her whispered a warning. The mad churning of her legs slowed to a walk as she picked her way around the infantry of barbed, ankle-high rocks.

What are you doing here, Keilann? A small voice pressed. *What do you want?*

Keilann brushed it aside, flicking it from her thoughts with a stray branch in her path. Old fears bubbled to the surface—the red-haired girl hid behind every tree, each massive stone. Keilann ignored her, her eyes resting resolutely on her goal.

I've taken enough crap from one bully today, a stronger voice snarled against the cowering fear. *If she wants to mess with me, I'll be ready for her.*

"Pocahontas!" rang in Keilann's ear. Her hands clenched into fists.

Just let her try.

Keilann inhaled a gulp of air as if jumping into a pool of water, and crossed into the circle.

Something was different today. Hollow. It was a sensation that reached up from the soles of her shoes to the pit of Keilann's stomach. She knew, without realizing or caring how she knew, that the girl was not here. The air was flat and dry. No electrifying current raised the hairs on her neck. Though the woods were hushed, it was a natural quiet that enveloped the sleeping trees and gently nudged leaves.

Keilann was alone.

The tears she locked behind her eyes all day flowed unchecked down her cheeks and trailed into her hair. Keilann would never let her parents see how much she hated her new home, but here in the stone circle she finally let herself cry. She curled her body against a stone and sobbed into her hands. A burst dam of emotions flooded her and all of the homesick, longing, fear, anger, and loss rushed out at once.

Keilann felt broken. It was as if someone had cracked her protective shell like an egg and there was nothing she could do to stop herself from oozing through the cracks. Sobs shuddered through her body, her face drenched with salty tears and thick bubbles of snot. She mopped her face with the starched sleeve of her Mary Arden uniform, smearing disgusting streaks and blotches into the white fabric.

She looked at the once primped shirt smeared with mud, glop, and sweat.

It's totally ruined, she thought. *Mom's going to kill me.*

An odd feeling crept up her throat, quirking the corners of her lips into a grin until it spilled out into mad laughter.

Take that, Mary Arden, she wanted to scream. Though Connor may see her as nothing but a stain on a white shirt, he didn't realize how powerful a stain can be. A stain can cling and fight until it changes the very fabric of the weave, becoming inseparable and unchangeable. A stain can endure.

Keilann giggled, clutching a stitch in her ribs. She would have cried again if she had any more tears to shed. Her stomach ached from sobbing and laughing, her legs burned from running, but she couldn't stop herself from giggling.

Finally, Keilann collapsed on the ground, gasping for air. She was lightheaded and giddy, her temples throbbing. Lying sprawled on her back in the feathery grass, Keilann stared at a steely patch of sky caught in the spiky, sheltering arms of the trees.

"What do I do now?" Keilann asked, searching the clouds for an answer.

She never expected to actually receive one.

"Funny, tha's jess what I was thinkin.'"

Keilann jerked at the sound, yelping at the sight of a nervous boy leaning against the nearest stone pillar. He had a lean, almost scrawny build that was half lost in the bulk of a thick black sweater. His eyes were an icy shade of slate grey, thrown wide in surprise. He held his hands up in front of him, plaintively, as if he had startled a wounded animal.

"Sorry! I'm sorry! I was trying not to scare you." He sighed, raking his hand through his hair in frustration. "I knew I was going to scare you," he said under his breath.

Keilann was on her feet, backing away from the unwelcome stranger.

"Who are you? What do you think you're doing here?" Had he been watching her this whole time? The image of the red-haired girl flashed across her mind. Were they friends? Did she tell him about Keilann, of the hilarious joke she had played on the stupid new girl? Now he had come to see for himself, and what a show he had gotten. The thought of him witnessing her hysterical breakdown made her face blaze with shame.

"How long have you been watching me?" she whispered, horrorstruck.

The boy shifted uncomfortably.

"I wasn't watching you. At least, I didn't mean to. You seemed upset." He stopped abruptly, quickly shifting courses. "My name is Beathan MacAlpin. I live jess over there." The boy pointed through the trees in the opposite direction of Keilann's house. "I've been rovin' through these woods since I was a bairn. The people who lived on the other side did nae mind."

The boy paused. He kicked at a loose stone, grinding the toe of his trainer in the dirt. "I did nae know it was your house now."

Keilann's brow furrowed. The more the boy spoke, the more familiar he seemed. She looked at him closely. His name sounded like "Bee-an" to her clumsy American ears, the rough Scottish burr cantering syllables faster than she could keep up. She thought she had heard that name somewhere before.

Keilann gasped.

"*Bee-an!* But you're—!" She stared as Beathan shook the ginger fringe of hair out of his eyes.

"Spark's English class. I sit in the row ahead of ye." He sighed dramatically and placed a hand on his heart.

"And here I was beginning to think ye did nae remember me." He winked at her, grinning broadly.

Keilann's face darkened.

So, he had been privileged to her humiliation that morning as well? Now she could see the Mary Arden logo on his black sweater. Why hadn't she noticed before? She was suddenly very aware of how she must look. Her face was smudged with snot and dirt, any hair not stuck to her face was hopelessly tangled. Beathan's cool, tidy presence brought Connor's taunts fresh into her mind. What gave him the right to stand there and stare at her like some sort of savage?

"That doesn't give you the right to sneak up on me!" Her nostrils flared. "What kind of name is *Bee-an* anyway?"

The boy shrugged, a curious smile on his lips. "The same kind of name as *Uh-kee-win*, I suppose."

Beathan might as well have punched Keilann in the stomach. Her mouth fell open, but she clenched her jaw shut almost at once, her mild irritation quickly changing to a white-hot fury.

"How dare you," she spat.

The ferocity of her tone wiped the smile from Beathan's face. She stomped toward him and it was the boy's turn to back away, his back against a slab of stone.

"Now, listen," he pleaded.

"No, you listen!" Keilann shouted. "I didn't ask to move here, and I don't want to go to your stupid school. So if you've come to continue what your friend Connor started this morning, you're gonna be sorely disappointed. If you are not out of my sight in five minutes, I'm calling the police."

Ben crossed is arms. "Connor McBride is an oily bastard who doesn't know his arse from a hole in the ground. And he is not my friend."

Keilann's attack screeched to a halt.

"I—what?" she blinked. "He's not?"

"Not," Beathan said, curtly. "Ye would've known that, if ye'd bother to listen to something other than the sound of yer own righteous indignation."

Keilann opened her mouth for a quick retort, but her words came out in a stuttering jumble.

"You seemed—when you said—I just thought—"

Beathan glared.

"Yeah? Well, you thought wrong," he said. "I was only tryin' to point out the irony of you insulting my name. Funny what happens when people start assuming things, isn't it?"

Keilann flushed to the roots of her hair with shame. He was right.

An awkward silence filled the circle. Why couldn't he have just left her alone? She stared at the pleats in her kilt, careful not to meet his frosty gaze. What could she say?

"Sorry," she muttered, throwing the apology between them like a peace offering.

When Beathan said nothing, Keilann thought he might have left as noiselessly as he had come. But when she raised her eyes he was still there, standing just inside the circle. His face had softened and he was considering her with what looked almost like concern.

"No harm done," he shrugged. "I cannae blame ye. It's not like ye've had a very warm welcome." He took a few steps toward her and held out his hand. "Let me change that. Can we start over?"

Keilann hesitated.

Could she really trust him? There was only one way to find out. She met him in the middle of the circle and took his hand into her own. It was warm, if not a bit calloused. He had a strong grip, shaking her hand heartily in his bony fingers.

"There now," he gave her another lopsided grin. "I'm Beathan MacAlpin."

Keilann found herself smiling despite herself. His gap-toothed grin was innocent and sincere, like a small child's. "Keilann Douglas."

"So, what brings you to our illustrious land, stranger?" To Keilann's horror, he plopped himself down, crossing his legs in the short, soft grass.

She paused again, unsure of what to do. In the past, she had been only too happy to ignore and be ignored by the opposite sex. How did Fiona talk to boys? Keilann remembered a lot of fluttering eyelashes and hair-tossing, but quickly ruled out both tactics. Beathan noticed her hesitance, his eyebrows arching until they disappeared in the shaggy fringe of hair that fell onto his forehead.

"I don' bite, ye know." He bared his teeth, exposing a wide cleft between his front teeth. "See? No fangs."

Keilann smiled weakly and finally sat down, carefully placing at least a foot between her and this new boy. She tucked her legs behind her, conscious of how little her uniform kilt managed to hide.

"So-oo," Beathan pried, spreading his arms wide. "What brings a fair lass like ye to a place like this?"

Keilann sighed. "My dad. He was offered a job at the university in Aberdeen. He accepted, so we left Chicago and here we are." She shrugged, trying to sound more nonchalant than she felt.

Beathan wagged his head enthusiastically.

"Chicago? Wicked! A bit more exciting than this place, I'll wager." He grimaced and gestured to the trees whose traffic was limited to the hustle and bustle of squirrels and birds.

Keilann smirked, imagining the wooded paths replaced with ten-lane freeways, the birdsong with the steady beeps of horns and curses of city drivers.

"A bit," she agreed.

"Hmmm...quite a change for ye then." He sat back and cocked his head to the side. "How are ye likin' it so far?"

Are you kidding? Keilann swallowed her sarcasm.

"It's really beautiful and, uh, different." Looking up, she stopped mid-sentence. Beathan's face was bulging with the laughter he was struggling to hold back.

"Sorry!" he burst out, his laughter rolling out of his chest. He wiped his eyes with his sleeve. "Ye were trying to be so diplomatic. Ye could've just said it's all been shite."

She blinked at him, shocked by his bluntness.

"How could it not be?" he continued, easily. "Ye've had to deal with Mudbrains McBride. But please don' let him ruin yer opinion of Scotland. Not everyone is as thick-headed as him. In fact, most people are pretty damn decent."

Keilann shot him a skeptical look.

"Yeah, well, 'decent' seems to be in short supply around here," she said, ripping up short tufts of grass as she spoke. Not daring to meet Beathan's eyes, Keilann found herself recounting the scene with Mórag in the attendance office. She hadn't meant to bring it up. It wasn't like she relished being embarrassed.

Why am I telling him all of this? she wondered as the details spilled from her mouth. *What if he thinks I'm making it up?*

When she got to where Mórag had told her she and Fiona looked "exotic," Beathan interrupted with a loud snort.

"That dried-up old haggis," he snorted. "Don' ye worry about her, Keilann. The most 'exotic' thing she's seen in the last fifty years is an electric typewriter."

As Beathan continued on with a string of insults, Keilann felt a steady, warm glow spreading from her stomach. For some reason, hearing Beathan insult Connor and Mórag's ignorance eased the sting of their words. It filled the aching hole her home had left. For a few minutes, she let herself bask in the wholeness of his company. After Beathan ran out of abuses to hurl, an awkward silence fell between them again. From the struggle on his face, Keilann could tell that there was something else he wanted to say. Though she was curious, she didn't pester him. Already in unknown territory, Keilann didn't want to push her luck.

Beathan bit his lip, reminding Keilann of Fiona's nervous habit.

"Keilann?" He paused. "Why don't you use yer first name?"

Keilann shrugged. She had been expecting much worse. In third grade, a boy had asked her if she wore feathers at home and lived in a teepee.

"Dunno, it's just...easier, that's all."

Beathan frowned.

"Easier?"

"Easier than trying to explain how to pronounce it every time, than dealing with jerks like Connor. It's just easier blending in that way."

Beathan's frown deepened. "Well, why should ye have to blend in? There's nothing wrong with being different."

"Yeah, that's easy for you to say." Keilann felt her face getting hotter, her voice rising. "You fit in. You're the same. You have the right skin, name, and pedigree—that's really all that matters. Everyone always tries to say how individual they are, but individuality is a load of crap. In the end, it comes down to whether you can look and act the way everyone else wants you to." The steam ran out of her vehement words. She was suddenly aware of how loudly her voice was ringing off the trees.

Keilann sighed. "You just get tired of doors slamming in your face."

Beathan was quiet. Keilann could feel the pulse thudding in her head, the rush of blood in her cheeks. She hadn't meant to get so worked up. *What's wrong with me?*

Beathan shrugged. "I'm not the same. And I don' think ye should have to be, either."

"Right," Keilann snorted. Her eyes ran down his lean build and freckled, pale complexion. "And how exactly are you different? You seem pretty much the same as everyone else around here."

Beathan crossed his arms. "Ye cannae think of any differences, Keilann?" He cocked his head to the side. "Or are you the one thinking like our dear friend Connor now?"

"If you're so different then why did you come here?" she blurted, more harshly than intended.

The boy gave another dismissive shrug.

"I told ye, I've been coming to this place since I was little—"

"No," Keilann cut him off sharply. "When you must've heard me—" she flushed. "When you knew I was here?"

Now it was Beathan's turn to look uncomfortable.

"Ye sounded upset, and I jess thought—"

"And you just thought you'd come here and get a good laugh, right?"

Beathan blinked. "Sorry?"

"Your friend must've told you all about me by now. Did she promise you a good show from the stupid American?" Keilann's voice was rising to a shout.

Beathan's brows knitted together.

"Who told me what? What are you blithering on about?"

"Don't try to tell me you don't know about her. The red-haired girl? If you've been coming here since you were little, you two must be great pals."

"Girl? What girl? Yer the only girl I've ever seen here."

"Stop! Just stop!" Keilann shrieked. "You come here acting all nice and genuine, but I know what's really going on."

Beathan jumped up, confusion and anger etched in his scowl.

"Yer insane! I don't know what girl ye are talking about! I only came over here because I heard ye cryin' and I felt sorry for ye. End of story."

Keilann's temper flared, her pride bristling at his words.

"Yeah? Well, I don't need your pity."

"Great. Why don' I jess take it with me then?"

"Fine!"

"Fine," he said in a strange, cold voice.

He dusted off his pants without meeting her eyes, turned, and stormed out of the circle.

The peace of the woods, the comfort of Beathan's friendship shattered around her. Keilann felt hollow again and it was all her fault. He had reached the edge of the stones. At the last moment, Beathan stopped, placing a hand on a broken stone that only reached his shoulders. He inhaled sharply, but did not turn around.

"I only came here because I thought ye could use a friend. My mistake."

His words knocked Keilann back into her senses. There was no mistaking the hurt and bitterness in Beathan's voice. Maybe he was telling the truth. Maybe he didn't know the red-haired girl at all. What had she done?

He thinks I'm a lunatic. I am *a lunatic.*

Keilann could have gone after him, could have made him listen to her apology, but her limbs were oddly frozen. She stayed in the circle like an idiot, hating herself for losing the one person who had shown her any kindness.

The next few weeks were a steady blur of alarm clocks, homework, and the constant, dreary tones marking the beginning and end to every day. Keilann had little time to think about going back to the stone circle, let alone unraveling the mystery of the red-haired girl.

Despite being at Mary Arden Academy for nearly a month, Keilann had never managed to find a trace of the girl. Normally, this would have been at the forefront of her concerns, balancing precariously on obsession. Keilann was so swamped with homework that she buried the girl in the back of her mind under calculus equations and the dates of the English Renaissance. For now, the red-haired girl remained a quiet murmur right before she fell asleep, a nagging tug of doubt, nothing more. Her dreams, too, finally began to fade. There were still nights when Keilann woke in sweat-drenched sheets, shivering from the screams, but soon the nightmares grew dim and vague; a blurred face or whisper was all she could remember most mornings. Some nights she did not dream at all.

Keilann should have felt relieved by this, but in truth she had barely noticed the absence of her nightmares. The bright neon note faded into a sickly yellow, fluttered from the wall unnoticed and collected dust beneath the bed, its secret forgotten. She had bigger problems to deal with during her waking hours.

Connor McBride had kept his word. He was careful to ignore her in Spark's class, but once out of the sight of teachers, his taunts and insults grew worse. Rarely without several members of the football team, they would dance and whoop whenever they caught her off-guard. Connor would trip Keilann, smash her books from her hands— he even spat on her. She tried to disregard him as much as possible, shielding Fiona from the worst of it when she could not. Chrisselle and her friends, who were used to Connor's bullying, told her to keep her head down. Her only hope was that he would eventually grow bored and torment some other hapless target.

The plan did not seem to be working. Keilann scrubbed off another racial slur from the face of her locker. The sticky red paint ran watery streaks down the dented metal as she blotted the foul words away with paper towel. For a fleeting moment, Keilann entertained the possibility of reporting Connor and his lackeys. She smirked at the thought of the look on Connor McBride's stupid face as scenarios of vendettas flashed through her mind's eye. She imagined the school permanently suspending him from the football team, or having his precious record tarnished with the black mark of expulsion. The smile instantly faded into a scowl as Keilann remembered the last time she had received a teacher's help. She may have been subject to Connor's revulsion and disgust regardless, but Keilann was only the victim of his hate-fueled revenge because of the punishment he blamed her for. What would he do to her if she gave Connor the excuse of reporting him to the headmistress?

Keilann gritted her teeth.

She had never felt more alone. Throughout the long weeks since their first meeting, Keilann couldn't bring herself to talk to Beathan again. So many times she had lagged behind after class with the intention of apologizing, but she would barely catch the flurry of his bag disappearing out the door before she could think of what to say. After several failed attempts, Keilann decided to try and confront him in the lunch line, where there would be little chance to run off. She waded through the multitude of ravenous teenagers until she spotted a gingery mop of untidy hair half-way up the line.

"Beathan!" she called, forcing her way through a bulky pair of rugby players.

He turned his head, laughter from a recent joke still on his face.

"Beathan!" Keilann waved, vigorously. She would have felt like an idiot in any other situation, but right now she didn't care how she looked.

Beathan's eyes locked onto the source of his name, the smile vanishing into a thin, grim line. His head swiveled as he searched for an escape or a way to hide, but Keilann worked her way out of the crowd before he could take a step.

"Beathan," she panted. "I've been looking all over for you."

"I'm not hungry," he mumbled to his friend. Not meeting Keilann's eyes, he backed out of line and jogged into the throng.

The sting of bitter, disappointed tears threatened to overwhelm her sturdy defenses. Keilann stood rooted to the spot until she noticed Beathan's friend, a scholarly-looking boy with a long, dark ponytail, giving her an odd look. Darting from the cafeteria, Keilann arrived at her next class twenty minutes early. Her stomach rumbled a demand for food, but she couldn't go back. She slumped down in the deserted math corridor, leaning her head against the locked door of her classroom.

Why do I care? It's not like we're even friends or anything. I shouldn't care what he thinks of me.

But she did. Chrisselle and her friends were nice, but Keilann just wasn't cut out for theatre. She didn't get excited about musical lyrics or monologues, and she was not about to audition for the school plays. She liked eating lunch with them, but wished she had someone she could really talk to. Though she willed herself not to, Keilann couldn't help thinking about when she had met Beathan in the stone circle. How easy it was to talk to him—before she ruined everything. Though she pretended to work on homework, all

Keilann could see was Beathan's face, his mouth set in a grim frown at the sight of her.

That night, Keilann's nightmare changed.

She was running through the woods again, but this time the figure she chased was Beathan. His shaggy hair bounced just outside of her reach, but he wouldn't turn around no matter how many times she called his name. As the trees and rocks flew by, she realized that he was leading her back to the stone circle. The stones suddenly broke away from the trees, colossal monsters twice the size of their real-life counterparts. Beathan ran into the stone circle and stopped dead in the middle.

"Beathan!"

Keilann's voice sounded distant, echoing around the exaggerated stones. She raced to his side, grabbing his shoulder. Determined to make him listen, she spun him around and flinched away in horror. Beathan's face was twisted into a sinister grin, his features eerily distorted. When he spoke, it was with Connor's voice.

"Don't touch me!" The nightmarish Beathan tore his shoulder from her grasp. "Pocahontas!"

Keilann staggered into a stone, tangling her arms and legs in a vicious, thorny vine. She watched as Beathan's figure blurred into Connor McBride. He strode toward her, shouting insults until his face began to blur. Wild, auburn hair sprouted from his head. His eyes turned a dark, steely grey. Keilann opened her mouth to scream as the red-haired girl lunged.

Keilann's blaring alarm clock hurtled her back into reality. Hands shaking, she swiftly clicked it off and huddled under her blankets. She hadn't had such a vivid dream for weeks, but the return of her old demons was not the reason she lay shivering despite layers of thick quilts. The image of Beathan's face twisted with hatred seared through her every time she closed her eyes.

Hours later, the cold tone rang a merciless warning through the halls of Mary Arden Academy. Keilann skidded into her seat just as the final bell tolled, skirting around Connor McBride as she flung herself into her desk.

Breathlessly, she dug for *Macbeth* and her collection of notes scratched on the complex characters and plot. Throughout the long weeks, *Macbeth* continued to plod on through betrayals, murder, conspiracy, and lots of bloody fights. It was difficult to remember who was slaying whom on any given day. Despite the archaic language, Keilann found herself enjoying the play more than anticipated. Ms. Spark was an excellent reader, and with the help of the always dramatic Chrisselle, the story was even interesting at times. Keilann found herself drawn to Lady Macbeth most of all, who proved as fascinating a villainess as Ms. Spark had promised.

They were just getting to the part where Lady M goes mad with guilt. Night walking and hallucinating, she unwittingly confesses to the murders of not only the king, but also Macbeth's best friend and several women and children. As Ms. Spark read the "Out, out damned spot!" monologue to the class in her deep, booming voice, Keilann couldn't help but think that Lady Macbeth got what she deserved.

Ms. Spark finished the monologue and closed her book shut with a snap.

"So much for Lady Macbeth. That's the last time we hear from her alive. The calculating strategist has lost her mind, her once passionate relationship with her husband dissolving as he becomes ever more steeped in blood. The murders he has committed since assassinating Duncan are too much for Lady Macbeth to cope with. Macbeth insists that they were necessary to keep his crown safe. Any thoughts?"

Ms. Spark's sharp gaze swept the groggy faces of her students.

"Keilann," she called out.

Keilann jumped at the sound of her name, nearly dropping her pen.

"Why would Macbeth, who was once so reluctant to commit one murder, be so willing to do it again and again?"

Tongue-tied, Keilann tried to digest what Ms. Spark was asking. She had always kept her head down in class, knowing that any eye-contact with a teacher meant danger. Keilann's strategy had helped her slip by—until now. Ms. Spark had picked up on Keilann's reluctance to participate, her fear of being humiliated stopping her from voicing her opinions. Spark had been lenient for the first few weeks, but was apparently unwilling to give any student a free pass from thinking.

From the other corner of the room, Keilann could hear Connor whisper something to a chorus of muffled sniggers. She stared at the back of Beathan's head. To her relief, his shoulders did not shake with repressed laughter.

"I think that murdering Duncan corrupted Macbeth," Keilann ventured, cautiously. "You know, he was afraid of someone doing, like, the same thing to him and so the more he killed people, the easier it became."

Ms. Spark was already at the front of the room writing *corruption* in a large scrawl on the board.

"Thank you, Keilann. Ye've introduced one of the main themes of *Macbeth*: the corrupting nature of absolute power. This theme, among many others, will be the focus of yer final projects."

A sporadic wave of synchronized groans was instantly squelched by the dangerous gleam in Ms. Spark's eye.

"Since you are all so thrilled by the prospect of celebrating yer new Shakespearean knowledge, I'll just double the length of the essay, shall I?"

Keilann swallowed the groan rising in her own throat, the classroom fearfully quiet.

Ms. Spark smiled.

"Hmmm...I thought so. Now, before ye get too eager, allow me to explain yer assignment. As we finish up the last act o' the play, I want ye to choose a character that interests ye the most. If none interest ye, I will pick one for ye." Ms. Spark paused from passing out rubrics, laying an icy glare on several more troublesome students. Keilann smiled inwardly when her gaze lingered on Connor McBride.

"The essay will track the changes yer character has undergone in the play, describing how he or she was affected by each of the main themes and whether the character was corrupted by each."

"Now," Ms. Spark continued. "This essay is just the basic work ye will be required to fulfill. If any of ye wish to take a more creative path, or have another angle you wish to explore, please feel free to come and speak to me about it. If I decide that yer new idea fulfills the requirements for time, effort, and analysis that the essay does, you will be permitted to choose yer own option instead. Any questions?"

Yeah, why do we have to do this? Keilann didn't dare say the mutinous thought out loud. Ms. Spark was usually her favorite teacher. Her class was far more motivating and thought provoking than the other mind-numbing lectures that were often as monotone and lifeless as the steely bell that broke up the day. Lately, however, it seemed that all of Keilann's teachers were consorting to give their students lengthy midterm assignments. Ms. Spark's essay was only the latest on an ominous pile that made Keilann's hand cramp just thinking about it.

The sharp tone of the bell jolted Keilann out of her thoughts. She peeled herself from the chair and stuffed the shabby books into her bag as cruelly as she could, nearly ripping the seams as she took her frustration out on her battered textbooks.

Without thinking, Keilann let out a loud, exasperated huff.

The raw frustration in her voice made Beathan turn, still half-bent over his own books. He met Keilann's eyes for the first time in weeks, a lopsided grin playing on his lips.

She froze.

Seconds trickled away as the rest of the class fled around them. Beathan opened his mouth as if to say something, faltered, and tried again. He stood there with his mouth hanging open for a few seconds as Keilann watched his face break out in vivid red blotches.

He dropped his eyes.

"Excuse me." He shouldered his way past her and escaped through the door before Keilann had recovered her wits.

She walked to her next class in a daze. Beathan had looked at her—what's more, he had smiled at her. He was even about to speak to her before...before what? What had stopped him? Keilann had almost given up on making things right with her almost-friend, but that one stolen moment gave her hope. The memory of his smile gave her courage. She would do talk to him today, after school.

Keilann practically floated the rest of the way to Biology, her feet barely touching the ground.

The passing hours were unbearably slow. By the time the final tone sounded her freedom, Keilann was jumping out of her skin with nerves. Not wanting to miss her chance, she didn't bother to stop at her locker. Keilann sprinted up the main stairs, her feet landing on every other step as she raced toward the main entrance. Thin trails of students leaked out of the school. Most were still gathering books and gossip near their lockers before the weekend. Keilann sidled along the entrance and took a post near the grassy lawn, warily stepping around a large, murky puddle from the latest bout of rain. She inspected each face that passed her as a healthy stream of students ebbed away from the building. After a few unsuccessful minutes, she checked her watch.

Where is he?

"Keilann!"

Fiona had broken away from a small cluster of girls. She grinned and waved.

"Hey," she said breathlessly, running to Keilann's side. "A few of my friends are going out for some food after the soccer match tonight. Wanna come?"

Keilann only half-listened to her little sister's giddy chatter. Of course Fiona would be going out again tonight. While she had merely managed to attach herself to a group at lunch, Fiona had acquired a large circle of friends within the first few weeks of school. Fiona was on the phone almost every night, making plans and sharing whispered gossip. Keilann spent her nights with a book.

Keilann's eyes flicked from face to face, but only a few looked familiar and none were Beathan.

"I can't tonight, Fiona—thanks," Keilann added, trying to keep the edge from her voice.

Fiona stepped directly in front of her sister and cut-off her view of the main doors. Keilann tried to sidestep her, but Fiona would not budge.

She crossed her arms. "What's up with you?"

Keilann could just barely see above Fiona's bony shoulder. "I'm just looking for someone, okay?"

Fiona's face brightened at once. "You mean that boy you met? The one that lives behind us?"

Keilann had told Fiona the barest of details about meeting Beathan in the woods. After she had run off without explanation, it was the least she could do. The only other alternative involved Fiona reporting Keilann's odd behavior to their parents.

"Um, yeah."

"Oooooh!" Fiona squealed. She flashed her older sister a thumbs up. "Good luck! Tell me all about it later!" she added, grinning wickedly.

Fiona wriggled her eyebrows knowingly and strutted off in the direction of her friends. Keilann sighed, watching her depart. Sometimes, it was very advantageous to have such a distractible sibling.

Keilann, on the other hand, stayed focused on the task at hand. She turned away from Fiona, determined not to fail at this self-appointed quest.

One minute, she was watching the last remnants of students burst from the heavy oak doors into the weak sunlight, her agitation at its peak. Fiona's diversion had only taken a few seconds, but those precious moments could have been Keilann's only chance.

The next thing she knew, Keilann felt like she had been slammed by the force of a semi-truck. Her head snapped back as her body hurtled forward from the powerful thrust. She was shoved off of her feet, her arms flailing as she landed face-first in the mud puddle with a sickening crunch. Keilann tasted the metal tinge of blood as she coughed mud from her nose and mouth. For a few horrible seconds, she was blind. Her eyes burned with muck and water. She scrubbed her face with mud-drenched hands, blinking frantically.

She lifted her throbbing head and her stomach dropped. Sneering down at her was the gloating face of Connor McBride.

Keilann had never been in a fight in her life.

Sure, she had had arguments with Fiona, but those generally ended in one of the girls refusing to talk to the other. Usually, when Keilann had to deal with the occasional bully at her old school, she used the same strategy she employed in the classroom: become invisible. If no one ever noticed her, then she couldn't possibly upset anyone. The closest she had ever come to hitting someone was when she had been seven-years-old. Fiona had stolen her favorite blanket, so Keilann pulled her little sister's hair until she finally let go and went sobbing to their mother. Hardly a compatible experience to what she now faced.

Keilann lay soaking in three inches of mud. Her face and wrist exploded in white hot pain. Her mind reeled. Blood dripped from her crushed nose into her open mouth, mixing with the mud she had swallowed. Her stomach lurched as she tried not to gag.

She had no idea what would come next. Connor circled the muddy hollow lazily, his glittering eyes fixed on Keilann. He reminded her of a well-fed cat toying with an injured mouse. Keilann shivered in her sodden jumper.

Am I supposed to punch him? Even in her head, the thought sounded ludicrous.

Connor stopped pacing and planted himself directly in front of his prey.

"Miss me?" he sneered down his nose. His black shoes shone inches from her face, not a single speck or scuff besmirching the buffed leather.

The shoes stepped back a fraction as Connor took in Keilann's appearance.

"I thought that mud would go nicely with your skin," he said, nodding slowly. "Would you look at that? Perfect match!"

While Connor gloated, Keilann scanned the school yard in vain. Fiona and her band of friends had cleared out. Her throat tightened. It was Friday afternoon. Teachers and students alike had bolted at the final bell. Even Connor's usual entourage of brawny footballers were nowhere to be seen. A few stragglers lounged under trees or waited for rides on the stone steps, but they were all either too afraid of Connor or didn't care enough about Keilann to stop him. A few looked on with polite interest, hoping for a good fight. The frightened ones stuffed headphones in their ears, pretending they couldn't see what was happening twenty feet away.

"Now that I have yer attention," Connor's eyes gleamed. "I thought ye'd like to know that I willna be using tha' childish nickname 'Pocahontas' anymore."

A cold sneer stretched across his lips. "It really doesn't suit you."

Keilann's stomach cramped from another mouthful of mud and blood. Her legs were fine, but she couldn't remember how to stand. She was crippled by the thought of what Connor might do if she tried to get up. The mud might have well been quicksand. Though her mind whirred with desperate escape plans, her body had simply forgotten how to move. Keilann was frozen.

"I've come up with a much better name for ye: Eating Bull! I really believe it fits yer looks much better."

Even with the promise of another slimy mouthful of muck, Keilann couldn't stop herself from gasping. Connor cocked his head to the side, grinning at her reaction.

"Oh, I hoped ye'd like it." He clapped his hands together in mock excitement. "I put so much thought into it."

"That must've hurt."

Connor jumped at the voice directly behind him. He turned toward the sound and into a well-aimed blow. The punch thumped against his jaw with a dull thud.

Connor teetered on the edge of the concrete, his arms wind-milling like an old cartoon before he pitched headfirst into the mud. Keilann had just enough time to realize what was happening and rolled out of the way. Her wrist screamed in pain. Connor's face was frozen in dumb shock, but she knew it would only be a matter of seconds before he regained his wits. Keilann crawled out of the puddle. The muck sucked at her trembling legs as she tried to stand. Her head swam as she staggered to her feet, her muscles like pudding. Without warning, her knees buckled. Keilann would have collapsed if a strong, wiry grip had not clamped tightly around her shoulders.

"Whoa! Steady on!"

She knew the voice had sounded familiar, but Keilann hadn't dared to meet his eyes until now. His face, though lined by a pained grimace, was not warped by hatred or disgust. Keilann's heart contracted at the sight of his lopsided grin. Then it sunk in: Beathan had just punched Connor McBride in the face. For her.

Beathan held Keilann at an arm's length, his nose wrinkling at the generous coat of mud that spattered her from head to foot. "Ye look like a pig's breakfast."

Despite the icy mud that trickled down her back, Keilann was suddenly very warm. She returned a weak smile. She wanted to thank him, ask him a million questions, and apologize all at once. Keilann opened her mouth, unsure of what to say first. She needn't have worried. Connor was over his initial shock.

"You filth loving bastard!" Connor choked out, apoplectic with rage. He staggered to his feet, the force of Beathan's punch making him swoon like a drunkard.

Beathan cocked an eyebrow, taking in McBride's mud stained uniform.

"Filth loving?" Beathan asked, coolly. "Ye really aren't in a position to call anyone filthy now, are ye?"

"How dare ye!" Connor splashed toward his adversary. "I'll smash yer ugly mug in! Then maybe ye'll look more like yer girlfriend."

Beathan's cold expression never changed, but Keilann felt the grip on her shoulders tighten.

"I thought swine like you would love a bit o' muck," Beathan said, as if Connor had never spoken. "Maybe that's why yer Da' drives piss drunk into so many ditches. It reminds him of home."

Connor froze mid-stride. His face darkened to a dangerous shade of purple. "Don't ye ever talk about my father that way!" Connor roared.

"Then I suggest ye never talk about my friend that way or yer gonna have more than mud to worry about, I promise ye that," Beathan growled.

Connor's chest heaved. He stood ankle-deep in the mud, flexing his meaty fists. His eyes narrowed. "I'll kill ye," Connor hissed.

Beathan's eyes flashed. "I seriously doubt that even yer that stupid." He let go of Keilann and spread his arms wide. "But yer welcome to try."

Keilann darted glances between the boys, waiting for someone to make the first move. Beathan might have a leg up in the wits department, but there was no question in her mind who would win a physical fight. Connor's toned bulk was barely concealed by the fitted uniform shirt. Beathan's jumper hung from his frame in loose folds. Connor stood on the edge of the puddle. He cracked his knuckles menacingly and glared at Beathan with tangible hatred.

For all of the withering glares Connor threw at Beathan, he had yet to throw a punch. He wavered in mid-attack, as if he didn't dare cross some invisible line between him and a scrawny boy half his size. What was he waiting for?

Connor drew his leg back and swung it forward like a pendulum. The kick was well short of hitting Keilann or Beathan. Instead, his foot skimmed the puddle and sprayed both of them with a fresh splattering of muck. A clod of mud slapped Beathan in the face. He staggered back and cursed.

"Yer daddy's name cannae protect ye forever, MacAlpin!" Connor roared. He turned on his heel, sloshing more water onto Keilann's second ruined uniform and kicked deep rivets in the sodden grounds as he stormed toward the soccer pitch.

Beathan spit black grit and gravel at his back. "Neither can yours, McBride!" Beathan shouted after him.

Connor halted in his tracks. Keilann could see the tips of his ears burning with scarlet fury. Her heart constricted. It looked as though he was going to turn around and charge Beathan after all. For a fraction of a second he hesitated. Connor's shoulders twitched in a half turn.

Oh god, here it comes.

Beathan wouldn't stand a chance on his own. What would she do if Connor came after them? Would she, could she, fight him? The adrenaline thundered through her veins and screamed in her head. Her thoughts swirled in panic.

She had almost decided to grab Beathan and run when Connor seemed to change his mind. He squared his shoulders and continued on without another word. Stunned beyond words, Keilann watched him stomp from view. Her knees quivered, relief and shock overwhelming her.

Keilann turned to Beathan, wide-eyed. "What was that all about?"

A war of emotions raged inside of Keilann, and her head was pounding from the fall. She had just been saved from the first fight of her life, but still wasn't sure how it had happened. Keilann was terrified of what Connor was capable of, but couldn't deny that her heart had flipped over when Beathan had called her his friend.

Beathan wiped his mouth and spit another mouthful of mud in the grass.

"It's a long story," he frowned. He looked Keilann up and down. "What say we get ye cleaned up first, yeah?"

Following his gaze, she finally looked at herself. Keilann's black jumper was splattered beyond recognition. Thick clumps of mud and slimy clods of grass clung to her hair. Her nails were black with dirt. Staring at her mud-caked arms, Keilann couldn't stop herself from thinking that she must look exactly like the red-haired girl, plastered with muck.

"Beathan, I'm so sorry!" she blurted. "I must've seemed insane, and all you were trying to do was be nice to me when no one else was. I was such an idiot! That girl, she snuck up on me in the circle and I thought that you and her...."

"Keilann! Keilann!" Beathan threw his hands up to stem the frenzied flow of words. "It's all right! Ye have nothing to apologize for."

"I was such an idiot," Keilann mumbled.

She didn't dare look at Beathan, the memory of their last meeting burning her face with shame. Any second now, he would remember how crazy she really was.

She heard him heave a much heavier sigh this time. He scratched his head as if searching for the right words.

Keilann imagined the phrases running through his mind: *"I'm glad I could help you out, but I really only said you were my friend so Connor would leave you alone."* Or, perhaps the less tactful: *"Yer insane. Don't talk to me. Ever."* She heard his sharp inhale and closed her eyes, waiting for the blow that would be so much worse than any punch Connor McBride could wallop her with.

"It's me who has to do the apologizing, Keilann."

Keilann's head shot up. *What?*

She finally met Beathan's eyes. He squirmed under her gaze.

"I'm the one who acted like a prize idiot," he said. He raked a hand through his hair, ruffling the shaggy mane into disarray. "Ye were right. I should have left ye alone. I knew ye were upset when I saw ye in the circle. I knew ye must've come there to be by yerself, but I thought I could make ye feel better. Instead, I only made ye feel worse."

Keilann's mouth hung open, astounded by the words ringing in her ears. Beathan was apologizing to her?

"After I lost my temper," Beathan continued, "I cooled down and realized how stupid I'd been. Of course ye'd be angry with me. It must've seemed like I was sneaking up on ye. Me, someone ye didn't know, when ye were all alone in the middle of the woods."

He shook his head. "No wonder ye freaked out." He picked at a clod of dirt on his jumper. "I cannae say that I blame ye. I wanted to apologize, but I was too embarrassed to talk to ye. I ran away from ye in the lunch room 'cause I was afraid ye were going to tell me off in front of everyone. Not that I didnae deserve it," he added.

Keilann's head spun. She couldn't believe what she was hearing.

"I promised myself that I would find you after school today and finally do this, so here I go. Sorry I was a manky git." Beathan held out his hand.

Keilann absently reached out a hand to meet his, her head swimming.

"You were going to meet me after school today to apologize?" she asked. Her fingers squeezed Beathan's.

A spasm of pain disfigured his features into a grimace.

"Ow!" His hand shot out of her grasp as if Keilann had given him an electric shock.

"Sorry," he mumbled, apologetically. "I've never punched anyone before."

Beathan stretched his reddened knuckles, wincing.

"It really hurts. I guess Connor has a thicker skull than even I had figured." He threw Keilann a sheepish grin.

Keilann leaned over his hand. The knuckles were swollen and bleeding, crisscrossed with angry cuts that bloomed fat purple bruises. "Those look terrible."

"Yeah? Well, ye should've seen the other guy," he said with a weak smile.

Keilann tried to smile, but her bottom lip had begun to swell painfully. She reached for her face, shuddering when her fingers touched dried blood over her nose and mouth. Now that her fear and shock had ebbed, the pain was coming back full force. Her whole face was hot and sore, and her wrist stung when she made a fist. Beathan's eyes watched her.

"You okay?"

Keilann gently touched what used to be her nose before it had collided with the ground. It didn't feel broken. Then again, she wasn't really sure what a broken nose would feel like. Her whole body felt like one big bruise. Keilann opened and closed her injured hand. The pain sent needles down her fingers, but it wasn't unbearable.

She nodded. "I think so."

Beathan reached out a hand as if to touch her face. He checked himself at the last second. His hand hovered in the air before he let it drop.

"Come on," he said, quietly. "Let's get ye cleaned up inside. Ye look awful."

Keilann sloshed back toward the double doors. Mary Arden Academy had never looked so welcoming. Now that the show was over, most of the spectators had either wandered away or were furiously texting exaggerated blow-by-blow accounts to their friends.

Keilann winced. The story would spread over the entire school by Monday morning. For now, however, the hallways were empty. The only sound was the wet squelch of her shoes stamping muddy footprints on the pristine marble floors.

Beathan led her down to the main stairs, stopping at his locker to grab his spare gym clothes. He tossed an oversized t-shirt, baggy shorts, and a ratty towel at Keilann.

"These'll do much better than that sopping mess o' rags. Plus, they're dry. And clean," he added. Keilann held the dubious clothing at arm's length, giving the air a tentative sniff before trusting that Beathan was telling the truth.

Half sprinting, half slipping to the nearest girl's locker room, Keilann checked underneath the stalls for feet and scrambled to deadlock the door behind her. Her teeth chattered as she began to peel off mud-drenched pieces of her uniform, all stained and streaked the same gritty brown. The chill of the water soaked through more than just her clothes. It seemed to sink through her skin and settle in her bones. The sodden clothes landed on the floor one by one with heavy, sticky plops, but Keilann couldn't strip off the cold that seemed to have burrowed inside of her.

Cranking the shower as hot as it would go, she watched muddy rivulets pour off of her fingertips and toes. The worst was her face. She carefully splashed hot water on her nose and mouth, gingerly rubbing the dried blood from her skin. The shower floor swirled reddish-brown as she scoured away Connor's insults and ignorance. She rinsed her hair the best she could, clogging the drain with grass and clods of mud.

Finally warm and clean, Keilann toweled off and pulled on Beathan's t-shirt. Designed for the narrow hips of a pencil-thin boy, it hugged her generous curves. But it was warm. The simple cotton was dry and held a whisper of lavender detergent, and of Beathan. Keilann wiggled into the elastic gym shorts and combed the tangles from hair with her fingers.

When she was finally satisfied, Keilann looked at herself in the mirror. She tilted her head left and right. Her nose was puffy and red, her lower lip fat and tattooed with a serrated cut from where her teeth had bit down as she fell.

What will Mom and Dad think? Keilann gulped, staring at her distorted reflection. *What will I tell them?*

Keilann spent the last month pretending she had assimilated into Scottish life as easily as Fiona. She was often times so consumed with school work that her parents hadn't harassed her much about friends or a social life. As of yet, Keilann had never mentioned any trouble at her new school. If Connor was content at throwing snide remarks at her, then she was content to ignore him. But this—Keilann prodded the tender skin of her inflamed lip—this was different. How much longer would this go on?

What would Connor do next time?

A rapid, staccato tap on the locker room door jolted Keilann from her trance.

"Keilann? Everythin' okay?"

"Fine!" she called over her shoulder.

She gave her hair one last squeeze until only clear water dripped from the ends. Bundling up her soaked uniform, Keilann darted a final glance at her reflection, her mind still divided on how to handle the onslaught of questions that awaited her at home.

She unbolted the door to find Beathan leaning against the row of lockers across the hall in his shirtsleeves, a clean jumper bundled in his arms.

"Alrigh'?"

She nodded.

"Much better. Thanks."

"Here. Catch." Beathan threw the sweater between them. Keilann's numbed fingers fumbled to snatch it. "It'll be warmer."

Keilann pulled it over her head greedily. The air was even colder out in the hallway. The thick cable-knit wool clung to her hair and neck, but blunted the chill that had crept back into her bones. Much too big for Beathan, the sweater fit Keilann better than his other clothes. She looked at him in his flimsy white shirt. He reminded her of an understuffed scarecrow.

"Won't you be cold?"

"Nah, I'll be fine until I get home. Ye looked like a drowned cat," Beathan laughed.

Keilann raised her eyebrows. "Gee, thanks."

Beathan slung something off of his right shoulder. With a start, Keilann realized he had been carrying her bag.

He must've gone back to get it when I was changing.

He handed her the book bag and fell into step beside her.

"I'll wait with ye—jess in case," his voice dropped to a murmur as they pushed open the double doors. The courtyard was almost deserted by then, but Keilann still felt safer with Beathan walking next to her.

Stealing glances over her shoulder the whole way, Keilann sunk onto the cold metal bench, grateful for Connor's absence. She would never make the mistake of letting him catch her off her guard again.

"Yer daddy's name cannae protect ye forever, McAlpin!"

"Neither can yours, McBride."

The strange finale of the fight resurfaced in Keilann's mind, though it made no more sense than before.

"Beathan." Keilann paused.

Beathan wasn't looking at her. His eyes flitted around the school yard, wandering over the faces of the remaining stragglers.

"Yeah?" he asked absently.

She bit down on her lip before a sharp stab of pain reminded her that it now resembled a fat purple caterpillar. Keilann floundered for words, unsure how far she was allowed to pry.

"Did something happen between you and Connor? I mean, no offense, but he could have flattened you back there and he just walked away," Keilann stammered out as she saw the muscles in Beathan's jaw bulge. "I just was wondering why. Do you know?"

Beathan did not answer. He was still looking away from her, but she had the feeling that he wasn't seeing the empty school yard anymore. The noise of the street filled the silence: car horns hollered belligerent warnings, snatches of songs blared from radios, tires whisked past on the pitted concrete.

"Connor and I...it's a long story," he sighed, passing a weary hand over his eyes. His voice was tighter than usual, slow and strained as if he brooded over every word.

Keilann hazarded a glance. Beathan stared straight ahead with his arms crossed over his slight chest, his brows knit together.

"We used to be friends." Beathan turned to face Keilann, smiling at the disbelief on her face. "A long time ago. We used to play football together even when we were still in Primary school. Believe it or no', he wasn't always such a prat. Back then, he was my best mate."

Keilann shot him a skeptical look, her eyebrow cocked as high as it could go.

Beathan laughed. "It's true! He was always kind of pig-headed, but game for a laugh, ye know? Nothin' serious. Until a few years ago." Beathan sighed and leaned back against the bench. "It started wit' his Da'. His drinkin' was always steady, but it got worse when he got sacked from his job. Big company bloke, yeah? His work was his life, and without it..." Beathan ran a hand through his hair.

"Look, I didn't have any proof at first, but I knew that his Da' had a wicked temper when he was on a binge. Connor and his mum got the worst of it. Would come to school with bruises that he'd say he got from football, but I knew better.

"Ye know the thing he said about my Da'?" Beathan asked, turning to Keilann. She nodded.

"Me Da' is a police sergeant. They started getting' all kinds of calls from the McBride place. Mostly his mum would call them in, but a few times it was Connor."

Beathan shook his head.

"Well, it started changing him. His family has always been pretty well-off, really old name and proud of it. They didnae want anyone knowing about what was happenin'. Tried to hush it up as bes' they could. His mum never pressed charges, afraid of word leakin' out. Connor could lie to everyone else, but I knew where my Da' was called off to every other week.

"We stayed friends for a bit, as long as I pretended I didnae notice anything. But, like I said, he started changin'. Teasin' became bullyin' and he was cruel like he had never been before. I tried to ignore it for a while. Made excuses for 'im."

Beathan shrugged.

"I was hopin' he would snap out of it, get it out of his system, but it jess got worse. Then, one day, I ran out of excuses."

Beathan stopped, his lips pursed as if he wasn't sure if he wanted to finish the story.

"The football team has a zero tolerance policy on drugs and alcohol," he said. "There was a bloke that Connor didnae like on the team—was afraid he would take his starting spot. Before practice one day, I went down to the lockers early and found him diggin' through someone's bag. He sort of froze when he saw me. Started yelling about not sneakin' up on him. Then I saw it. He was messing with this kid's water bottle. Spikin' it with somethin' so he wouldn't be able to play. Connor was tryin' to get the guy kicked off the team.

"I saw what he was holdin' and what he was tryin' to hide behind his back. I put two an' two together. I went ballistic. I started screamin' at him, sayin' that he was a loser, jess like his father who had to beat up his mum to feel important."

Keilann gasped. "What did he do?"

"Broke my nose, o' course," Beathan said with a bitter laugh. "He woulda done worse than that, but I told 'im that he could hit me all he liked. It wouldn't keep me from tellin' everyone the truth about his family."

"And he just left you alone?" Keilann asked, taken aback.

Beathan shrugged again. "Sure. One word from me and generations of his family's reputation would be brought to its knees. Needless to say, we haven't exactly seen eye-to-eye since that day, but at least he hasn't tried anything like that again. As long as he toes the line, I keep my mouth shut."

Keilann let the weight of his story sink in. As much as she despised Connor

McBride, there was the smallest nudge of something like pity taking root inside of her. She tried to imagine living in fear of her own father. Waiting in terror for him to come home. Listening to the screams of her mother, knowing she was helpless, alone.

Keilann shuddered. What wouldn't that do to a person? "Wow."

Beathan nodded. "Yeah. I wasn't really sure if I should tell you all o' that, but I think ye have a right to know."

A rasping engine rumbled over the whizzing hum of traffic. Keilann looked up to see the bus wheezing around the corner. She stood awkwardly, shouldering her pack in Beathan's borrowed clothes.

"I'd better go." She shuffled toward the curb.

Beathan shot up from the bench.

"Keilann!"

She turned.

"Would ye want to...do ye want to meet me after the match tonigh'?"

He didn't need to say where. Her heart thundered in her chest, knocking against her ribcage.

He wants to see me?

"Yeah," she said, breathlessly. Her face felt warm again. "Sure."

Beathan's face broke into another gap-toothed grin. He gave her a short wave and began strolling back toward the school. The bus screeched as it pulled alongside the curb, choking out black plumes of exhaust.

"Hey."

He turned back, the smile still on his face.

"Thanks. For everything, Bee-an."

The doors of the bus squealed open behind her. Beathan was chuckling to himself, shaking his head.

"Keilann, why don't ye jess call me 'Ben' like everyone else?" he asked with a wicked smile. "After all, it would be a lot easier that way. Wouldn't ye agree?"

9

"I'm home!" Keilann announced to the dark, empty house. She slammed the door behind her, latching the bolt more out of habit than necessity.

To her great surprise, the muffled voice of her father answered from down the hall. "In here, Keilann!" he called from the study.

She dumped her bag on the living room couch and knocked twice before opening the door.

"Come on in!"

The heavy door moaned as it swung inward, revealing another white-washed room with dark, polished floors carpeted in plush throw rugs. The walls were covered almost to the last inch with shelves stuffed and sagging with books. High up sat stately, leather-bound tomes that Keilann had never been allowed to touch. Well-loved paperbacks were shoved willy-nilly into every crack and crevice, along with rigid hard-covered encyclopedias, dictionaries, histories, and dozens of novels. Keilann's father sat behind an old whale of an aluminum desk, one that had been abandoned by the university in Chicago before Keilann had been born. It was dented and scratched, but her father refused to get a new one. In the opposite corner, her mother's desk—a wooden roll-top relic from her family—sat empty.

Keilann's father was buried in a formidable stack of papers, several books lying on their spines around him.

"How was your..."

Keilann jumped at the sound of shattering china. She had been running a hand over the familiar shelves, not noticing that her father had looked up from his work. His teacup had slipped from his hand, its contents splashed across the floor in a steaming puddle.

Her dad didn't seem to notice. He was out of his chair and halfway across the room, his shoes crunching on the shattered cup.

"Keilann! Your face!"

He cupped her chin in his hand gently as if he were afraid that she, too, would break. Her dad looked down at her bruises over his reading glasses. They perched on the edge of his nose, forgotten like the ruined cup.

"Oh." Keilann's stomach dropped into her shoes. "Yeah."

In the post-euphoria of making things right with Beathan—Ben—Keilann had forgotten about the fight. Her nose was throbbing and swollen, but at least she wasn't bleeding anymore. Her dad stared at her wide-eyed. Keilann gulped, her mind spinning. She had never decided what she was going to tell her parents.

"What happened?" He turned back to his desk. "I'm calling your mother. Her afternoon class might be finished by now."

"Dad, no!"

The panic in her voice shocked her father. He froze with the receiver in his hand, his fingers poised over the speed dial button for his wife's office phone.

Keilann took a deep breath. If she was going to tell the truth, it was now or never. But could she? After everything Ben had told her?

What would Fiona do?

She smiled.

"It's no big deal. I was playing, um, rugby," she stammered out the lie as quickly as she could think it. "With a few people after school. Just for fun."

Keilann's mind raced to remember all of the rugby terms she had learned in gym class.

"We were in a scrum and, you know how graceful I am. I tripped over my own feet and got a face full of dirt."

She held up the muddy bundle of clothes, shrugging her shoulders dismissively.

"One of my friends gave me a spare change of clothes. It's no big deal, really Dad. It looks a lot worse than it is."

Keilann kept her tone light and impassive, but her father's eyes bore into her own, watching her face intently.

His brow furrowed. "You were playing rugby? For fun? You? But you don't even like sports."

She tossed her head, in what she hoped resembled Fiona's frivolous attitude. The pain in her face spiked. Not a good idea.

"I know, but I thought I would try something new. I mean, that's why we moved here, right?" Keilann pulled a face. "I should've known better. Don't worry, Dad, I'll be sticking to books from now on."

She flashed him a sheepish smile and the worry melted off of his face. She could have laughed with relief. She'd done it.

"I should say so," he said. He placed the phone back in its cradle and gave her shoulder a quick squeeze. "You gave me quite a start."

"I'm sorry, Dad. Here, let me help you clean up."

It took the better part of an hour to gather up the broken shards of porcelain, wipe up the tea-spattered study, and brew a fresh cup for each of them. Keilann was careful to stay and chat with her father about school and homework long enough for him to forget about his fears. After promising she would put an ice pack on her nose, Keilann shut the door of his study just as the afternoon light faded into evening. Racing up to her room, Keilann grabbed her nicest pair of jeans and shrugged into a flattering green camisole and gold-beaded sweater. Just because they were comfortable, she told herself as she spritzed the air around her shoulders with a fruity body spray.

Grabbing a light coat, she shouted to her father that she was going for a walk.

"Your mom and Fiona should be home in about an hour!" Her father called as she reached the door. "Make sure you're home by then!"

She finally closed the door behind her. She kept her steps slow and even until she was well out of sight. Once the tree tops had closed around her, Keilann picked up her pace, her heart lighter than it had been in weeks.

Yes, she had just lied to her father, but what else could she have done? If she had told him the truth about Connor, he would have asked too many questions. He certainly would have called her mother, and quite possibly the headmistress.

And would all of that stop Connor or add fuel to his hatred?

For all of her parents' good intentions, their interference would only cause problems. Besides, had she told the truth, there was no way Keilann would have been able to meet her friend in the circle. Friend. She liked the sound of that word. And friends keep secrets for each other, right? So there was no point in feeling guilty about the tiny lie she had told. It would all sort itself out in the end. In another year, Keilann would be off to attend a university back in the States. She would never have to worry about Connor McBride again.

By the time the stone circle had come into view, Keilann had convinced herself that she had done the right thing. She sped up her pace, peering between the stones for a glimpse of Ben.

The circle was empty.

Keilann checked her watch. It was still a bit early. She jogged into the circle. As soon as her feet crossed the ring of stones, Keilann was hit by a brick wall.

The air was thick and humid, almost unbreathable, like a sticky summer night before a tornado hits. She gasped for air and clutched at her chest. The little hairs on the back of her neck and arms stood on end, electrified by an unseen storm. Her head began to swim from the sudden climate change. She stumbled. Her stomach lurched.

What the hell?

Keilann tried to steady herself on a stone. A sense crept up her spine, catching her breath. Without looking up, Keilann knew she wasn't alone in the circle. She could feel someone next to her.

And it wasn't Ben.

10

Keilann's nightmare had returned. All of her old fears came rushing back in one breath, stealing the air from her lungs. Dread filled her legs like sandbags. All she could do was stare in horror at the form huddled at her feet.

The red-haired girl was curled over her knees, hunched into a ball at the center of the circle.

How could Keilann have missed her? Her mind worked furiously. The stone circle had been empty just a moment ago. She was sure of it. But there she was, again. The red-haired girl was so close that Keilann could reach out and touch her. How was that possible? She couldn't have snuck up on her this time. The girl was right in front of her. There was no way the girl could've made it past her in that time without Keilann noticing. It didn't add up.

The girl didn't look like she was interested in Keilann at all. She didn't even seem to know Keilann was there. The red-haired girl looked very much like Keilann had the last time she had run to the stone circle. Curled around herself protectively, the girl's thin shoulders convulsed with heavy sobs. She wore the same kind of simple dress as last time, but it was torn and prickled with burrs. Her feet, just visible beneath the stained hem, were bare and lacerated with tiny cuts. It was as if she had crashed through the woods in a blind panic, with no time for shoes or paths. Keilann held her breath as the girl let out a low moan like a wounded animal, tore at her hair, and rocked back and forth on her heels. Keilann didn't know what to do. The girl was obviously in pain. However she had gotten there, it was clear that scaring Keilann was not her objective.

Keilann hesitated. Should she say something? *But I don't even know this girl. It's none of my business. If I leave now, maybe she won't notice me.*

Keilann began unbending her knees, her whole body tense and rigid with concentration. Her breath was slow and shallow. Her ears strained for the crack of twig or dry rustle of leaf that would give her away. She was almost standing...just a bit more. As soon as she was upright, Keilann would sprint away as fast as her legs could carry her. She knew that she was a pretty pathetic athlete, but with the state the girl was in and the element of surprise on her side, she might just get enough of a lead.

The red-haired girl let out a wail that shot through Keilann's heart. She stopped dead. The seconds trickled by.

Go, go! What are you waiting for? A voice in her head urged. But another, quieter whisper tugged at her conscience.

How could you just leave her?

Before she knew what she was doing, Keilann reached out a hand and laid it gently on the girl's shoulder.

You idiot! The voice in her head screamed, and Keilann had to agree that touching an aggressive stranger had not been the best plan she could have come up with. As soon as her fingers made contact with the rough linen on the girl's shoulder, she had choked on her sobs, her entire body rigid. Her head snapped up, and Keilann saw her face for the first time. Tears dripped from her chin, her face flushed from crying. Her heart-breaking grief was visible for only a moment, instantly replaced by the fierce, hardened mask that haunted so many of Keilann's dreams. Her grey eyes, though swimming in sorrow, blazed with a burning hatred that scorched anything they fell upon. When they locked upon Keilann, she expected the girl to lunge at her. What she didn't expect was for the girl to scream in her face.

"Ahhh!"

The girl fell backwards, recoiling from Keilann as if she had brandished a knife. She backed away, scampering on her hands and knees, pressing herself against one of the stones on the far side of the circle. The girl stared at Keilann in wide-eyed horror. Her chest heaved rapidly.

Keilann was frozen in a half-crouch with her arm still outstretched where the girl had been not five seconds earlier.

Is that why she tried to attack me the last time? She's afraid of me?

The revelation made her head spin. What was so frightening about Keilann? She looked down at the frilly beaded sweater peeking out of her dark wool jacket—definitely not an outfit that would strike fear into the hearts of total strangers.

Her brow furrowed in concentration.

Does she think that I want revenge for her prank? That made some sort of sense at least.

Minutes of silence passed. Neither of the girls moved or spoke, the red-haired girl's ragged breath the only sound. Keilann was uncomfortably aware that the girl was watching her. After a few more minutes of stunned silence, it became clear that she was not going to rush at the girl like a madwoman. The red-haired girl's breath slowed, becoming deep and even. Still, she didn't speak, her eyes fixed on Keilann. Both of them waited for the other to do something. Keilann's thighs began to quake from being crouched for so long.

Okay, maybe this is all just a misunderstanding. Stifling a groan, Keilann straightened. The girl flinched as though struck, and tried to scoot closer to the stone.

Oh, boy. Say something. "Um."

The girl jumped at the sound of her voice, her sharp eyes darting left and right for an escape route.

"Sorry!" Keilann held her hands up, apologetically. "I didn't mean to scare you." She let out a bubble of nervous laughter. "It's funny. My friend, he just did the same thing to me the other day."

The girl's eyes widened even farther as she spoke, her fingers grasping at the stone so tightly the knuckles had turned white.

"So, I—I know how you feel. I really didn't mean to scare you. I think we got off to a bad start. See, you really scared me the last time I was here and, well, let's start over, okay?"

Keilann took a step toward the girl, her hand held out in front of her. The girl yelped and dissolved into terrified sobs, burying her face in her hands. Bewildered, Keilann stared at her proffered hand. What was with this girl? The last time they had met, she had seemed so wild, so fearless. Keilann watched the girl of her nightmares disintegrate into terrified whimpers. She certainly didn't seem very likely to try lashing out now, much less stalk Keilann in her sleep.

I've been freaking myself out this whole time for nothing. This girl is just as scared of me as I am of her.

Frustration churned waves in Keilann's stomach. She had to find a way to make this girl see how stupid this all was. Something terrible must have happened to her, something that Keilann could help her with, perhaps. She just had to find the right way to get her to understand.

A thought struck Keilann like a lightning bolt. The thunder that followed was a voice from a long forgotten dream. A deep, resonant boom that exploded into a graceless word she had been certain was a name.

"Grewock?" she pronounced each syllable slowly, trying to imitate the jangled sounds of her dream.

As soon as the word began forming in her mouth, Keilann already regretted saying it.

Why the hell would this girl know what you are talking about? You don't even know that it's a real name!

She was fully prepared for the awkward silence, humiliation welling in her belly. But it never came. As soon as the word was out of her mouth, the girl stopped crying. She gasped, her hands dropping from her face to hang uselessly at her sides. The girl gawked at Keilann, her mouth slack.

Sensing her chance, Keilann raced into action before the girl had recovered from her shock.

"Look!" she shouted a bit too loudly. "Look."

Keilann backed away slowly and planted herself, cross-legged, in the grassy center of the circle. She sat down and raised her hands, palms up to show that she didn't have anything.

"I'm not going to hurt you."

The girl watched Keilann closely as she spoke, eyeing her warily as if uncertain whether this was some sort of trick or not. Then, very slowly as if she were afraid to make any sudden movements, she peeled herself away from the stone, embracing her knees tightly. Keilann was stunned by the dramatic change in the girl's attitude.

Could it really be her name?

She sat back on her hands, dazed. What did this all mean?

A quiet, almost lyrical murmur began to fill the air. With a start, Keilann realized the girl was speaking to her. The sound of her voice—though choked and tight with emotion—was light and clear. There was none of the unnatural distortion this time, and yet... Keilann's brow furrowed as she fought to understand her accent. It seemed thicker, heavier than any other she had heard before. If Keilann hadn't known any better, she would've sworn that the girl wasn't speaking English at all.

Though they were in the middle of the forest, the girl's voice seemed to echo off of the stones as if they were occupying a vast, empty room. Combined with her heavy Scottish burr, it gave her voice an eerie, ethereal quality that was almost impossible to understand. Maybe it was just the stones themselves, or the sound resonating off of the trees. She tried to remember if Ben had sounded strange.

Keilann's head suddenly felt fuzzy. She couldn't think clearly. She blinked slowly, trying to clear her mind. There was something really important she was forgetting. Something to do with Ben. Why couldn't she remember?

Keilann shook her head, trying to focus. The girl had inched closer to her. She was now just a few feet away, a puzzled expression on her face. She looked even worse up close, pale with dark circles under her eyes. Tracing her high cheekbones were several jagged slashes that looked as if they had been carved by branches whipping against her face.

"What happened to you?" Keilann asked thickly. "Are you all right?"

The girl's brows dipped together, as if intensely concentrating on Keilann's every word.

Does my voice sound weird to her as well?

"Do you need help?" Odd, that she couldn't hear an echo when she spoke.

At last, the light of recognition dawned on the girl's face. Tears welled in her eyes and she screwed her features together, her chin quivering.

"Mathair," she choked out in her thick accent. *"Mathair."*

Keilann's brain worked to place the word. *Mother.*

"Mother?" Keilann stammered out. "Did something happen to your mother?"

The girl's face drained to an ashen grey. She closed her eyes, tears spilling from beneath the lids. She seemed close to collapsing.

Instinctively, Keilann's arm darted out to soothe her. This time, grabbing the girl's bare hand had definitely been a bad idea. A jolt of pure electricity danced down the nerves of her arms to the ends of her hair as if Keilann had shoved her finger into a light socket. She was frozen, unable to move, the shock tearing her raw nerves to shreds. Just as she thought she couldn't stand the pain a second longer, there was a blinding flash of light and then total, complete darkness.

Keilann was falling.

No, not falling. Running. Lights winked into existence, dancing along a narrow tunnel. They sputtered like candles, growing brighter as she ran until she could feel the heat of the flames on her cheeks. The tunnel took shape. Damp stone walls closed in around her, the dim light pooling into a long, narrow corridor framed by dozens of fat, dripping candles.

A massive wooden door, intricately carved and festooned with large iron nails, guarded the end of the hallway. Keilann skidded to a halt, pausing for breath in the semi-darkness. Sweat trickled down her forehead, her hair plastered to her sticky neck. Her hand hovered over the worn wrought handle. Keilann felt like she had to open the door, though the very thought terrified her.

Tears stung at her eyes, her hands shaking against her will. She had to go in, even though something awful waited on the other side. Keilann closed her eyes.

Go in, something whispered. Go on.

She steeled her nerves with a long, shuddering breath and pushed the door open.

A pungent wave of acrid smoke billowed from the room, hitting her in the face and making her cough. Keilann squinted through the gloom.

The room was shuttered and hushed, the only light glowing from smoldering embers in the hearth. She could just make out a few dim forms throwing bundles of sweet herbs onto the fire—healing herbs. Her Gram burned sage when someone was sick. Keilann recognized the sharp, earthy smell. Keilann inhaled again and choked on the thick smoke, resisting the urge to cover her nose with her sleeve.

The air was stifling, the smoke and heat sticking to Keilann's lungs like a grimy film. Burned bundles of sage were not enough to conceal the sour stench of sweat and old blood emitting from the bed in the center of the room. Though every nerve in her body screamed for her to get away, Keilann felt her legs walk forward. She had never been more aware of her body before—the blood pounded in her ears, her head buzzed from lack of air—but she also felt strangely disconnected. It was as if she were watching her body move from somewhere else. How else could this be happening?

Her eyes were glued to the motionless figure on the bed, bundled in heavy blankets despite the sultry heat of the fire. Keilann noticed her hair first, her vibrant red hair set like a flame against the cold marble of her skin. It fanned out around her like a saint's halo, un-

naturally bright against the pallor of death, the woman's face whiter than the linen sheets around her. The once regal features of the woman's beauty had been ravaged by illness. Her face was a skull with sallow skin stretched over it. Her hollow breath rasped in and out of white, cracked lips. Keilann stood at the edge of the bed, transfixed and horrified. A spasm of pain convulsed through the woman's body. She clutched her distended belly and groaned.

Forgetting her horror and fear, Keilann fell to her knees and took the woman's cold, clammy hand into her own.

"Mother," she whispered. She brought the lifeless fingers to her lips, kissing them softly. "It's me. I'm here."

The woman's eyes fluttered, but never opened. Though her mind blazed with fever, her body froze, her fingers and lips a dull bluish color

"You can't die!" Keilann cried. "You can't leave me!"

But she was already almost gone. More than anything, Keilann wanted her to smooth her hair and tell her that everything would be all right.

Her tears ran unchecked down her face. Keilann hovered over the woman as if she could prevent her death by keeping watch over her shrunken body. She was prepared to sit for hours, but a small cough near the fire made her turn. Though he stood outside of the fire's glow, she recognized the square, unyielding set of his shoulders instantly. Her body went rigid, her hand tightening around the woman's protectively. Something in the silhouette was evil.

A man stood at the edge of the room, half-shadowed in a corner, his mouth set into a grim line. His eyes glinted red in the flickering glow, the only part of him Keilann could distinguish from the darkness. The hand clutching the woman's began to tremble under his gaze. Keilann looked at the man, and a cold, hard word floated into her head: Father.

He looked at his dying wife as he would a horse with a lame leg, something useless that should be dispatched quickly and without emotion. In his eyes, Keilann saw the truth: she was past the age of child-bearing, and so had outgrown any marketable value. Not having borne her husband any living male heirs, her death was nothing more than the end of a bad transaction. And the beginning of new, more lucrative ones.

Keilann met his cold eyes. In that moment, Keilann finally realized that her father saw her as the same: a commodity for sale to the highest bidder. She would be weighed, measured, and haggled over for the best price. In the end, she would probably die in childbirth or live with the shame of producing a worthless girl. She may even suffer the same fate: dying alone, married to a man who feels nothing but ambition and values nothing but power. It would be her fate, and she was powerless to stop it.

Her skin suddenly felt like it was crawling with ants. She couldn't stand this man of stone, the smoke from the fire, or the cries of the dying woman. Keilann had to get away, had to escape even though she knew it wouldn't be forever. Without a word, she bolted from the room and didn't look back. Not when she heard her father calling her name, when the sharp stones bit into her feet, or her lungs begged her to stop. She ran far away from her dying mother, away from her heartless father, into the only place she would ever feel safe again.

Keilann's head lolled from side-to-side. She could barely see the path in front of her, but she couldn't stop her head from rolling. Her shoulders kept hitting branches, knocking her back and forth.

"Keilann..."

Her father was calling her name again. But that wasn't her name, the name he used before. What was her name?

"Keilann..."

Why wouldn't he stop following her? Why wouldn't he leave her alone? Not paying attention to the path ahead of her, Keilann's shoulder rammed into a huge tree limb, the knock sending her spiraling to the ground.

Her eyes shot open as she threw her hands out in front of her to catch her fall.

"Ow, watch it!" Ben cried, rubbing the side of his face where Keilann's flailing hand had slapped him. "Christ, Keilann, ye sleep like the dead! I must've been shaking ye for a whole minute before ye even noticed."

Dirt, Keilann's sluggish mind acknowledged, *there's dirt under my head.*

The world was tilted on its side. Keilann picked up her head. She was lying on the ground. She must've fallen when she hit that tree branch. She remembered running, trying to get away from her father.

Wait. Her father? His gentle, earnest smile and kind blue eyes clashed with the cold, black image in her mind. That didn't make sense. Why couldn't she remember? Keilann look around for clues, her eyes traveling to the seven stones encircling her. She had been heading for this place because her mother...something had been very wrong. Keilann's brain strained to put the broken images together.

"Sorry I'm late," Ben said with an apologetic grin. "Match went a bit long."

Keilann blinked at him.

Match?

She looked up at the fading sun, the sky deepening to a velvety navy blue. There was something she had to remember, something important. Her brain finally found the missing piece and slammed it into the empty hole in her memory. The day rushed back to her in a flash.

Keilann sprang to her feet. "Where is she, Ben? Where did she go?!" she shrieked.

Ben jumped back, alarmed by Keilann's sudden panic. "Where did who go? Who are you talkin' about?"

The girl had disappeared again. *But why? Did something happen to her?* "You didn't see her at all?"

Ben was giving Keilann a very concerned look.

"I dinnae know what yer talkin' about," he said, shaking his head. "Ye must've fallen asleep waitin' for me. There was no one else around."

"But why would she just leave?"

Ben was looking at Keilann as if she announced she would take on Connor single-handedly.

"Keilann, are ye listenin' to me?" he asked. "Ye really think that ye would jess fall asleep talkin' to someone? Ye were dreamin'."

Keilann closed her eyes, trying to concentrate.

She had been dreaming, but had the whole thing been a dream? The last thing her waking mind could remember was the girl telling her that her mother had died. Wait, had she told her that?

Her head swam.

The girl was crying. Keilann was trying to comfort her and then...nothing.

Ben's voice broke her focus. The memories slipped through her fingers like water.

"Keilann? Are ye okay?" he asked quietly, as if afraid he would frighten her. "Ye look—Keilann!"

She opened her eyes, but it was more than just her head that was swimming. The whole world swirled around her in patches of bright color. Keilann felt light and dizzy, then the ground slanted up to meet her.

Ben caught her arm.

"Keilann! Keilann!" he yelled.

She closed her eyes, willing herself not to throw-up on his shoes.

"I'm fine!" she gasped. Her stomach gave a queasy lurch. "I just need to sit down."

Ben helped her to the ground.

"Put yer head between yer knees and breathe slowly. Tha's it. Easy now."

After a few deep lungfuls of cool air, the bile rising in her throat subsided. When she was certain she could open her mouth without puking, she recounted the red-haired girl's return. Something told her to leave out the part about her mysterious appearance, telling him that she had simply stumbled upon her while waiting for him to show up.

"And then what?" he asked, watching her very carefully.

Keilann didn't like the look he was giving her. "What do you mean?"

"Well, ye say that ye were talkin' to this girl and then ye woke up with me standin' over ye. So, what, ye just decided to take a nap? And she just left you, passed out in the middle of nowhere?" he asked. He couldn't hide the trace of sarcasm in his voice.

Keilann's anger flared. "What are you saying? That I'm lying?" she bristled.

Ben's voice softened. "No, Keilann. I don' think yer lyin'."

"Then believe me when I tell you that girl was in serious trouble. She came to me for help." Keilann hadn't realized this before she had said it. But as soon as the words tumbled out of her mouth, she knew they were true.

"How do ye know tha'? Did she say so?" he asked gently.

"She...I..." Keilann's voice trailed away.

I was there.

The thought popped into her mind before she could stop it.

I saw it.

But how could that be? Keilann's head spun as logic and instinct warred within her. A wave of dizziness clutched her stomach. She dug her hands into the ground to keep from vomiting.

"Keilann, listen to me." Ben shuffled forward a few inches, looking directly into Keilann's eyes. "I know yer confused and sick, and I think I know why."

Keilann stared back, dazed. He knew?

The grip on her shoulder tightened.

"I don' want ye to panic, but I think ye have a concussion."

"A concussion?" Keilann echoed. What was he saying?

"It explains everything," Ben continued quickly, as if quoting a textbook. "Your memory lapses, falling asleep without warning, the strange dreams. Ye must've had a much harder hit than we thought."

Keilann considered what he was telling her. It would explain a lot. From somewhere far away, Ben's words filtered through her ears.

"I've seen it before plenty of times in matches. Someone gets slammed and they go mental. Don' know who they are or what day it is."

Ben fell quiet.

"Thing is, Keilann, concussions can be right dangerous. Yer brain wants te repair itself, so it does the best thing it knows: makes ye fall asleep. Most times though, if the concussion's bad enough, ye never wake up. If I hadn't come in time...." Ben shuddered.

Keilann heard his words, but found herself unable to comprehend them. It was all a dream? All of it? Unbidden, a single image swam before her eyes: a gaunt face as pale as death, surrounded by a wreath of flaming hair. The sweet decay of the death bed filled her nostrils as if she were lying in it.

Ben grabbed her shoulders, shaking her gently. "Keilann? Keilann, can ye hear me?!"

She couldn't hold it back any longer.

Keilann pushed Ben away and staggered to her feet. She careened over to the brush at the edge of the circle, doubled-over, and heaved. Ben rushed to her side, holding her shoulders as she emptied her stomach. If she hadn't been so sick, she would've been mortified. She retched until only the bitter sting of bile was left in her throat. Grabbing at a handful of leaves, Keilann hastily wiped the vomit from her mouth. She slumped against Ben, exhausted.

"What's happening to me, Ben?" she moaned.

"Christ, it's worse than I thought," Ben said, fighting to keep the panic from his voice. "C'mon, we've got to get ye home. Ye'll be all right, Keilann, ye'll be all right."

Ben began leading her away from the stone circle, and she let him without a fight. There wasn't enough left in her to protest. He tried to keep her talking as much as possible, asking for directions to her house, what her favorite food was, how to spell her first name, anything to keep her mind from slipping into a coma. She answered as best she could, struggling to connect thought and meaning, but her head cleared the farther they walked. Before they had rounded the last bend in the path, Keilann was almost back to normal, her head thudding with the promise of a nasty migraine.

She threw a glance over her shoulder as Ben chatted away, catching one last glimpse of the stone circle before it disappeared from sight. Keilann had dreamt it all. The thought should have relieved her. A concussion made perfect sense. There was nothing bizarre or sinister about it.

Instead, Keilann only felt a sharp pang in her stomach. Not from sickness, but a deep sadness like loneliness stabbed at her. The red-haired girl had been a dream. She turned her back to the circle, shivering slightly in the cool shadow of the trees. The last of the sun's rays had long retreated from the valley, leaving the dark cloak of twilight to cover their approach. Keilann could just make out the black silhouette of the house up ahead, lights blazing like eyes through all windows but one. Her stomach cramped, and she suddenly felt like throwing up all over again.

What the hell was Keilann going to tell her parents this time?

Keilann's eyes shot open.

For one dizzying moment, she couldn't remember where she was. Unfamiliar shadows looming from the darkness around her. She wanted to sit up, but something in the back of her head sent a warning to stay motionless. She had been dreaming again. A woman's face swam into view, pale and skeletal and a man in shadow, his eyes burning. The hairs on Keilann's neck tingled as she thought of it. Those eyes could be lurking in the darkness right now, waiting for her to give herself away. A floorboard near her head cried out. Keilann's heart hammered in her ears. Her breath caught in her throat.

There was a furtive whisper in the dark, so close she could feel her hair stir.

"Keilann? You okay?"

She jumped at the sound of her name. Her hand knocked sharply against a corner of the coffee table.

The coffee table?

The drowsy shutter was lifted from her eyes, and the world slid back into focus. The unfamiliar shadows filled in and became her living room, the leather of the couch under her hands, the lingering smoke of the cold fireplace hanging in the air. Someone had draped a blanket on her while she had slept, and her mother's brightly beaded shawl was wrapped around her feet. A slim shadow stumbled to the end of the couch. Keilann felt a slight pressure on her feet as the cushions groaned underneath the weight of another occupant. A wave of new smells wafted toward Keilann: fried oil, fresh air, and a potent, flowery perfume that masked neither.

Keilann relaxed back into her pillow, rubbing the slumber from her eyes.

"Fionawhatimeizit?" she slurred, her tongue still half-asleep.

"Just after midnight." Fiona's voice was gruff.

Midnight. Keilann had been asleep for over an hour. She hadn't realized how tired she had been until her parents had finally relented and let her sleep.

Keilann grimaced.

It had been a nightmare talking her way out of that one, until Ben had mentioned the word concussion. Suddenly, her parents no longer cared why Keilann had been in the woods or how Ben had happened to find her. They threw a volley of questions and once or twice mentioned "emergency room" before Keilann put her foot down. She was sore from the fall in the circle, bruised from the almost-fight with Connor, and more exhausted than she ever remembered being in her life, but she absolutely refused to go to the hospital. Besides her fatigue, Keilann felt normal.

So instead of doctors prodding her with needles, Keilann had to suffer through being interrogated and cross-examined until she felt dizzy. Her parents made her recite their address, both the new one in Scotland as well as their old Chicago one, her birthdate, and the days of the week. Worse, they insisted that she stay awake for hours of observation. Keilann was forced to sit on the couch and pretend to watch television as her parents watched her. Finally, her father felt confident that she was out of danger. After checking her eyes for a final time, he had insisted that she sleep on the couch, lit a bumbling, smoky fire to keep her warm, and left with a promise to check on her periodically. At least Ben hadn't been a witness to her humiliation. He had retreated to call his own parents as soon as they arrived, and only had time to flash Keilann a quick smile before ducking out the door.

"Mom asked me to see if you were okay before I went to bed. She told me that you had a concussion?"

Keilann nodded before realizing that Fiona wouldn't be able to see her.

"I guess," she said, trying to sound nonchalant. She quickly changed the subject. "How was the game?"

There was a shrug in Fiona's voice.

"It was all right. We lost by two goals, but it was still a good game."

"And you're just getting home now?" Keilann asked. She could just see the glint of a smile in the gloom.

"Yeah, a couple of us went out for chips afterwards."

Keilann arched an eyebrow.

"Chips? Since when have you ever said chips, Fiona?"

Fiona didn't respond. Even without being able to see her face, Keilann knew Fiona was biting her lip. She was biting something back, something she desperately wanted to share.

Keilann gasped.

"Were you with a boy?" When her sister didn't answer, Keilann knew she had guessed right. "C'mon, Fiona, what aren't you telling me?"

"I should be asking you the same thing." The bitterness in her sister's voice made Keilann start.

"What d'you mean?"

"Oh c'mon, Keilann, rugby? Really? You might be able to get Mom and Dad to buy that, but I saw you, remember? I know you weren't playing rugby, so don't bother trying to lie to me."

Seconds ticked by. She knew Fiona was waiting for an answer. Could she trust her sister with the truth?

"Are you protecting someone?" Fiona hesitated. "Did that boy do this to you?"

It took Keilann's sleep-deprived mind a few moments to realize that Fiona thought Ben had hit her.

"What? No. It's just...," she could hear Connor McBride's insults ringing in her ears. What if he grew bored with Keilann and began attacking her little sister for fun? Keilann closed her eyes.

Wouldn't it be better to protect Fiona? The less her sister knew, the better. Fiona couldn't help Keilann. She would only get hurt if she tried to get in Connor's way.

"It's nothing, Fiona."

"Nothing?" she said. "Nothing? You never talk to me anymore. You lie to Mom and Dad all the time, and from what I heard, you're getting into fights after school. I wouldn't call that nothing."

A sick swoop of dread turned Keilann's stomach upside down. "You heard what happened?"

Fiona snorted. "Of course I did. Everyone knows. You think you can keep it a secret when you go around punching people in front of the school? Jesus, Keilann, you're lucky a teacher didn't see!"

Keilann's eyes bulged. "Me punch someone? Listen, Fiona, whatever you heard is a lie. I've never punched anyone in my entire life!"

"Oh, yeah, and I'm supposed to believe you because you've been so truthful about everything else, right? Bite me."

"Fiona!" Keilann hissed. Her eyes darted to the foot of the stairs. Fiona was being way too loud.

"I know you're hiding something. I know that something else is going on that you're not telling me. You've been acting weird ever since we moved here. Is that what's bothering you?"

Fiona paused. Her voice cracked with emotion. When she spoke again, her words were so quiet Keilann had to lean forward to hear them.

"We never used to keep secrets from each other, Kei. Ever since the move I don't even feel like you're my sister anymore."

Fiona was close to tears. The couch shook as she heaved great, shuddering breaths to calm herself.

Keilann was stunned.

She had no idea how much she had hurt Fiona these last few weeks. Fiona had new friends calling her every day, and old ones Skyping from Chicago. Convinced that she was alone in her struggle to fit into her new life, Keilann had never imagined that Fiona had noticed the new distance between them. Her sister was always so even-keeled, so flexible and adaptable. Keilann had just assumed that Fiona was too absorbed in her social life to care about her loner older sister.

Keilann had been wrong. Worse than that, she had been thoughtless. Could she really tell Fiona everything? It was a tempting thought. Keilann wasn't worried about whether her sister would believe it all or not—she wasn't even sure if she did. At least Fiona would listen. The great weight that had settled on her chest seemed to lift a little at the thought. She could tell Fiona.

A light in the hallway flickered to life.

"Fiona! Keilann! What are you still doing up?"

Fiona straightened as if zapped by an electrical current. She swiped at her cheeks with a sleeve and turned to her father with a dry, innocent face.

"Mom told me to check on Keilann before I went to bed."

Their father's silhouette stood in the doorway, motioning to Fiona with a wave of his hand.

"All right, come on then. Keilann is still alive enough to wake me up with your chattering. She needs her sleep and so do you. Bed."

Fiona stood, her warm, comforting weight leaving the couch like a sigh. Keilann threw her sister a meaningful glance.

Later, it said.

Fiona gave the tiniest of nods, and followed her father up the stairs.

12

Sunlight filtered through dozens of lead-paned windows. The warm, shimmering glow beckoned to Keilann, inviting her to bask in the promise of late summer glory, but she knew better. Her cheeks were still raw from the bite of the cold day and her hair a tangled mess from the blustery autumn winds. Despite the damp chill outside, beads of sweat pricked her underarms. In the stagnant heat of the library, the weight of her coat was unbearable. Keilann shook it from her shoulders and readjusted the strap of her book bag.

It had been Ben's idea to meet here. They had tapped out Arden's Shakespeare section, thanks to Ms. Spark's requirement of at least five non-digital sources for their lengthy projects. Keilann had never been to the local public library before. Chicago libraries had been enormous modern structures of glass and steel or regal Gothic masonry, with sections of books that took up entire floors, constantly full of harried students cramming for exams. Hopeful for a Scottish version of her favorite Chicago libraries, Keilann had almost missed the squat, square building set far back from the main stream of traffic.

She hadn't been very optimistic about finding much inside. The dingy stones and dirty windows were not promising. Inside the library was bright and clean, organized and cheerful. The bright orange carpet was worn but well cared for, and the smell of dust and aging ink covered everything. Large, ornamental fixtures hung above Keilann's head, remnants of gas lights, she guessed. A hushed silence hung over everything, but it was different from the one that filled Mary Arden's sterile hallways. Here, things were allowed to be old and shabby because they were also well-loved and comfortable. Keilann inhaled the smell of books and felt the tension of the day slack, the pulsing knot behind her eyes loosen. No one here cared if her shirt wasn't tucked in or her hair was cut the wrong way.

Keilann had wandered her way through Juvenile, Fiction, and most of the Biographies before she found what she had come for. Tucked into a small table near the History section, a ginger-fringed head was hunched over a notebook, long fingers clenched around a pen that scribbled notes at a feverish pace. Keilann took a few steps toward him, suddenly very aware of how tangled and messy her hair had become. She smoothed it with her hands, cursing herself for not keeping a brush in her bag like Fiona. Placing her heavy bag onto an open corner of the packed table, she slid into the seat opposite Ben.

"Hey," he said without looking up.

He hastily finished a note, flourishing his pen with a triumphant dash. Ben smiled over the mound of books that surrounded him like a fortress and brandished a ratty notebook.

"Here are the notes ye missed from this mornin'."

Keilann's windpipe constricted as she took the notebook from Ben. She cleared her throat, forcing her voice to work despite the anxiety that squeezed her vocal cords like iron bands.

"How was class?" she asked offhandedly, trying to sound nonchalant.

The question sounded innocent enough, but Ben knew what Keilann was really asking him. Her parents had insisted that she take the day off school and go straight to the doctor Monday morning. Despite the mounds of homework awaiting her, it had been a relief to be away from school. She dreaded seeing Connor again, hearing the whispers flying behind her as she walked through the hallway. Fiona had said that everyone knew about the fight. Based on the details she'd given Keilann over the weekend, there were at least three different versions, each one more ridiculous than the last.

For someone who likes to be invisible, you're doing a great job of getting noticed by all the wrong people. A cold lump of lead dropped into her stomach when she thought of returning to school. People would've noticed she had missed today. That would probably only make them talk more.

Ben shrugged off the question, saying nothing.

He was just as embroiled in this whole debacle as she was, and he had been left alone to bear the brunt of the aftermath.

"What'd the doctor say?" Ben asked, pointedly changing the subject.

Keilann unzipped her bag and began building her own Great Wall of books.

"She said I was fine. That there was no trace of damage from the concussion, so it must've been pretty minor. She also recommended being more careful when I play rugby in the future," Keilann smirked.

Ben raised his eyebrows.

Keilann's hand found the ragged edge of *Macbeth* at the bottom of her bag. A small prescription bottle of sleeping pills rattled as she yanked the book free.

She froze, nearly dropping *Macbeth* back into her bag. The sound seemed to echo through the muted library corridors like maracas. Keilann held her breath, but Ben never looked up from his notes.

She decided not to tell him about the doctor asking her if she was getting enough sleep and whether she was bothered by nightmares. With one swift glance, Keilann had known her mother told the doctor about the nights she had woken up crying, or worse. When Keilann had hesitated, the kindly, middle-aged doctor took one look at the dark purple shadows under her eyes and scrawled out a prescription for a mild sleep aid.

"It is quite common for students to get wrapped up in A-levels and homework," she said matter-of-factly, giving Keilann what was supposed to be a reassuring smile. "But if you don't get your rest, your brain won't be able to work properly."

She was almost too nice. Her precise English accent sounded harsh and cold compared to the warm, rough burr of Scotland that had filled Keilann's ears for months. Keilann tried to listen to what she was saying, but could only focus on how out-of-place her words were.

What is she doing in Scotland?

Keilann caught herself, realizing that the doctor was probably thinking the same thing about her odd American patient.

"I've only ordered enough for two weeks. Take one about an hour before you go to bed and you shouldn't have any nightmares. Hopefully, by the time you run out of pills, you won't need them anymore. If, however, you are still having trouble sleeping, we'll schedule another appointment and see what we can do."

The doctor pressed the prescription into her hand and waved Keilann from her office. It wasn't until Keilann was shoving the bright orange bottle to the bottom of her bag that she had realized no one bothered to ask whether she had wanted it or not.

Keilann hastily stuffed the bottle back into her pencil case, burrowing the case deep under wads of crumpled paper and forgotten assignments. She hadn't considered whether she'd actually use any of the pills but there they were, clamoring for her attention, rattling whenever she bumped her bag with her arm. Sleep was still hours away, she told herself. Right now Keilann had to focus on more important things. Things like research for her essay, which had not been going well.

Ms. Spark had readily agreed that Lady Macbeth was an excellent subject for her project, and there was a plethora of material to choose from. But that was the problem. Anything Keilann wanted to say about Lady Macbeth's corrupt ambition or twisted morals had already been said about a hundred times. There was no point trying to make an original or arguable assertion about the doomed character. Her book bag was laden with sources declaring the character as a demon, a tragic heroine, a feminist, a strumpet, and everything in between.

Keilann needed a new angle, something to set her assertions apart so she wasn't simply repeating what someone else had already said. That was when she decided to include something that none of her sources had mentioned: an account of the real Lady Macbeth. The diabolical character of Shakespeare's imagination fascinated Keilann. Surely the real person must be equally interesting. Why else would Shakespeare bother to write about her in such detail?

For all of the academic articles written about the fictional character, Keilann had come up with next to nothing about the actual historical person. She scoured the Internet and had come up with a depressingly short list in her notebook. After hours of research, the only thing Keilann could actually say she knew for certain was that there had been a real queen consort of a real King Macbeth.

Not that there was any scarcity of information about Macbeth. Keilann was surprised to find volumes devoted to uncovering the true nature of the infamous Scottish king. Depending on what books she read, Macbeth (or Macbethad or Mac Beatha) was a just and noble ruler. Historians had tracked down his birth, early life, reign, and eventual murder. Macbeth's biographies were choked with drama, political intrigue, and death. Keilann could easily see why Shakespeare had chosen such a controversial monarch to write about.

You can't make this stuff up, she thought, jotting down a few more notes.

But who was this woman, his queen? All of Keilann's books were disappointingly sparse on Lady Macbeth's life details. She was born, she married, she had a son, she married again, and she died, the date unknown. Unfortunately, much of history seemed to only remember husbands, kings, and the number of sons a woman bore him. Lady Macbeth remained dutifully in the shadows. The pages were silent and the authors moved on. Keilann, however, could not.

The life of this unknown woman fascinated her. A queen remembered only as the grasping, heartless murderess that plotted to kill for the crown of Scotland. What would she think of her legacy? Keilann leafed through a book on Scottish monarchs, scanning the short biography of King Macbethad. It didn't even mention his wife.

Keilann sighed. This was getting her nowhere. She threw the fat, useless book on the table in frustration.

"It's useless, it's all useless! This is supposed to be a chronicle of Scotland's rulers, and I haven't been able to find anything about Lady Macbeth in here!"

Ben's eyes flicked from his notes, arching an eyebrow at her outburst.

"What'd you expect, exactly? Women didn't rule back then, men did. They made the decisions and fought the battles that historians wanted to record. Women were little better than property."

Keilann stared at Ben as if she had never really seen him before, her mouth half-open in shock.

He placed a quick hand on hers.

"I'm not sayin' it was right, or that I agree with it," he said. "The people who record history are usually the ones who have the power. We Scots know that better than most." Ben snapped his current book shut and stuffed it into his backpack. "The English wrote the majority of our history. The other half of the story gets left out, lost forever."

Keilann nodded. "I know how you feel. American history isn't exactly what I would call unbiased," she said. "History books gloss over how white settlers wiped out entire tribes just so they could steal all of our land."

"Ignorance and greed," he said with a shrug. "We like to think we know better now, but back then..." Ben gestured with his free hand, his voice trailing away.

Keilann's eyes fell on his other hand, the one that was still lingering on her own. He met her gaze for a fraction of a second, the hand darting back to his side so fast that he knocked over a hefty stack of books.

Ben made a show out of picking them up, hiding his reddened cheeks under the table. When he straightened again, his face was back to its normal freckly complexion.

"So," Ben said, clearing his throat a bit too loudly. "What have ye found so far?"

Keilann took his cue, covering their awkwardness with her frustration.

"Not much, I can't pronounce any of this stuff. These names are impossible."

Ben chuckled. "*Ye* should talk."

"And you. How did you end-up with a name like 'Beathan' anyway?" Keilann asked lightly, relieved to have something else to concentrate on besides the feeling of Ben's skin on her hand.

Ben gave her another casual shrug, stretching his arms stiffly over his head. His elbows cracked from being in the same position for far too long.

"Same as most, I guess. It's an old family name, goes back generations. What about yours, *Akiiwin*? Named after a grandmother or something?"

Keilann squirmed at the sound of her first name. No, even for *Anishinaabe* names hers was a bit different.

"Not exactly," she said.

Ben pushed the notebook aside, his full attention on Keilann, head cocked lightly to one side. He leaned back in the old wooden chair, the dilapidated legs managing a feeble creak.

"So, how did ye get it then? What does it mean?"

Keilann smoothed a crumpled corner of paper in her notebook, aware that Ben's eyes were on her, waiting. She bit her lip, her fingers still fidgeting with the wrinkled page. She rarely talked about the origin of her first name, preferring to pretend that it didn't exist. It wasn't that she was ashamed, as her mother assumed, of her Ojibwe ancestry—quite the opposite, actually. She wasn't embarrassed of her father's Scottish roots either, but Keilann was extremely proud of the long, dark hair and honey-brown skin her mother had given her, no matter what Connor McBride might say about it. No, it wasn't a matter of shame. Keilann was just always wary of telling the story of her naming ceremony to an outsider. An outsider like Ben.

"Uh, well, it's just kind of a weird story, really."

Ben's eyebrows shot up, disappearing beneath shaggy ginger fringe.

"I told ye about Connor and me," he pointed out. "You owe me."

"I don't know if you'd understand."

Ben crossed his arms. "Try me."

Keilann hesitated, watching the shifting afternoon light dance long shadows across the white-washed walls. The black waves of her hair soaked in the heady warmth, making her feel like she could sink into the floor and doze for hours.

"Before I was born, my mother had already had three miscarriages," Keilann began, pausing when she saw Ben's eyes widen. She knew this story by heart, having demanded her mother tell it to her every night when she was little until she could recite it word for word. The story had made Keilann feel special, magical even. Sitting under Ben's keen gaze, however, she felt stupid and childish.

"My parents had almost given up on having kids, so when my mom found out that she was pregnant again she was terrified that the baby would die like the others. They did everything they could to keep the baby safe. They even took a sabbatical from teaching so my mother could go home and be with her family on the Rez."

Ben's brows furrowed at the unfamiliar word.

"Reservation," she clarified. "The Bear Lake Indian Reservation in Minnesota. It's where my mom grew up. She hadn't been back for a couple of years. When she heard the news of her pregnancy it was the only place she wanted to be."

Keilann paused. When she had been five-years-old she had held her breath at this point. Her mother would have reached her favorite part of the story.

"Dreams are very important in our culture," she explained, tentatively. "Not long after my mom and dad moved in with my grandparents, my grandma had a very interesting one. Gram always calls it a vision. She told my mother she didn't have to worry. This time, the baby would live. When my mother asked her how she knew, all Gram would say is that she dreamed it would be so. She still won't tell anyone the details. The only other thing grandma would say was that my parents had to name the child after life so she would have the strength to live and be healthy.

"'She?' my mom asked, 'you know it's a girl?'

My grandma nodded.

My mom couldn't believe it. She asked how Gram knew, but Gram only shook her head. 'Name her *Akiiwin*,' was all my grandmother would say. 'Name her 'Life.'"

Keilann echoed her mother's words, her face flushing with a sudden heat. She stared at the notebook in her hands, unable to meet Ben's probing eyes. Without realizing it, her fingers had absently shredded the edges of the paper into scraggly ribbons. Keilann rolled the strips between her thumb and forefinger, waiting for Ben to speak.

Had he not been paying attention? She hazarded a glance away from the desk. Ben was frowning at her, a strange expression on his face somewhere between mistrust and disbelief.

"I know it sounds weird," Keilann gushed. "But it isn't all that unheard of, and it's not like I believe it or anything. Grandparents and elders have a big say in the naming of a child, and they believe that dreams can—"

"Yer name means 'life'? That's what *Akiiwin* means?"

Keilann blinked.

"Uh, yeah," she said, taken aback. "So what?"

"What's it like on the reservation—the Rez?" Ben changed the subject abruptly. "Have ye ever been there?"

"Well, yeah," Keilann frowned. "We would go for a few weeks every summer. But why—"

Ben rushed over her question, cutting her off.

"Do you miss it?"

"I miss my grandparents," Keilann said slowly, a puzzled frown turning down the corners of her mouth. Ben was acting strange. Did her story bother him that much? "My dad's parents died before I was born. They're the only ones I have."

"Do ye miss the reservation?"

Keilann hesitated. "It's very beautiful up there. I miss the trees and the lakes, but...."

Ben cocked his head to the side. "But what?"

"But my mom left when she graduated from high school. She went to live in the Twin Cities."

Ben frowned. "Twin Cities? Is that in Chicago?"

"The Twin Cities are in Minnesota where my mom grew up. St. Paul is the capital, and Minneapolis is on the opposite side of the Mississippi river, but they kind of grew into one huge metro area over the years," Keilann said. "My mom went there to go to school and that's where she met my dad."

"So?"

"So some people resented my mom for assimilating. They thought she was selling out, in a way. We went to visit the Rez for a few weeks every summer, but we were never really part of the tribe. Not that my grandparents agreed with any of that," Keilann went on. "They were proud of my mom and love my dad. But I know it bothers them that my mom never insisted we were brought up learning all of the traditions. When my dad got the job offer here, my grandma wanted Fiona and me to come and live on the Rez with the rest of our family. My mom said that it was up to us, and I almost said yes."

"Why didn't ye?"

"Well, I told you. We aren't part of the tribe and people treat us that way. Not badly—nothing like what Connor does or says. Everyone was always very friendly and polite, but always a little distant, just a bit cautious. In the end, that's the reason I decided not to go. I didn't want to be reminded that I was an outsider every day, that I did things differently. That I was different." Keilann touched her face where the bruises were beginning to fade. "Kind of ironic, huh?"

Ben snorted. "That's stupid."

Keilann stared at him.

"I don' see why any of that should matter, especially to yer own family."

"You're the exception, Ben. To most people, it does matter to some degree."

"And you? Does it matter to ye, Keilann?" he asked. "Ye sure seem to fixate on it a lot."

"No," she said, firmly. "No, it doesn't matter to me, but you've got to understand. It's about more than skin color. It's about culture and identity. If you're an outsider...."

Ben bristled. "Like me, ye mean?" he asked, hotly.

"No! No, I meant like me."

Ben shook his head in disgust. "Ye know what I think? I think ye make yerself an outsider on purpose."

Keilann's jaw dropped. "What? You think I want Connor to bully me?"

"Of course not, but yer always separating people into who belongs and who doesn't. Who fits in and who shouldn't, the right color and the wrong one. It's only because ye care about that crap that it matters."

"Oh, so you think if I just didn't care that Connor was pushing me in the mud, it wouldn't matter?"

"Yes," he said, bluntly. "Ye let him get to ye because ye think he's right."

"That's a terrible thing to say." Keilann trembled with anger. "How can you say that? How can you think it?"

"Because it's true! It's like yer name. Ye don' use it because it's easier to go by unnoticed that way. Ye stay on the edges, away from everyone because it's easier than getting to know people. People don' fit into yer neat little boxes if ye know who they really are."

Keilann snorted.

"Wow, I really must be some horrible person. A racist bigot like Connor McBride who deserves what she gets."

Ben's expression softened. "No, I think yer scared."

"Of what? Since you seem to know everything about me, tell me what I'm so afraid of."

"Yer afraid of finding out that yer worth a damn."

Keilann was aware of several heads turning in their direction, but the words caught in her throat. She sat, stunned out of words. Whatever she had been expecting, it wasn't this.

"It's so frustrating to watch ye go about, convinced that no one will accept ye and that yer not good enough anyway, so what does it matter if ye don't succeed?"

"So sorry it's been frustrating for you. I must really be some sick creep to enjoy doing this to myself."

Ben leaned forward, his eyes fixed on her face.

"That's not what I'm sayin'—listen to me, please." Keilann had made a move to get up, but Ben had caught her arm. Not hard, but firm enough to keep her from leaving.

She jerked her forearm from his grasp. It was odd how badly Keilann wanted to get away from him, when just a few minutes ago she would have done anything to touch his skin again.

"Why? Why should I sit here and take this crap from you? I thought we were supposed to be friends," she hissed, glancing furtively at the glowering faces behind them.

"We are friends, and that's why I'm sayin' it. I think ye hide yer name because yer afraid of what it would mean if ye actually tried being yerself. It's one thing if people don' like the mask ye wear, it's another if they don' like who ye really are. Yer afraid to take a chance because yer terrified of failing."

Keilann was seized with a staggering urge to run. Run far away from the library, from Ben's dark eyes, from his words that pounded through her brain. Her muscles twitched, but her feet were glued to the threadbare orange carpet.

To her horror, her eyes were welling with tears. "Why are you saying this?"

"Because I don' want ye to do this to yerself anymore. Yer funny, and smart, and nice and...yer beautiful," he said, not looking at Keilann. His face flushed tomato red to the roots of his ginger hair. "Yer a good person. I don' want ye to feel like ye have to hide anymore. Yer too good for hiding."

Keilann stared at Ben in shocked silence, her stomach twisting into knots, all tears forgotten. Her head was spinning with the emotions he had just thrown at her. In the span of a few minutes, Ben had stripped away the protective walls she had been building since middle school. She should've felt raw and vulnerable. But Ben looked more exposed than she felt, his face glowing red. Instead, Keilann was...what was the word for it? Relieved. And confused.

Did he really just call me beautiful? Me?

Ben still wasn't looking at Keilann, his face a dark shade of red rarely seen on a human. "So...so that's all I have te say about that," he told his hands. "Jess think about it, okay?"

Keilann nodded mutely. She knew she should say something, but her mind was stubbornly blank.

"So," Ben said after a few seconds of silence. He raised his eyes and offered her a weak smile. "Ye think we should actually get some studyin' done today?"

Keilann realized that she was still hovering next to the table. Her feet, once tethered to the carpet, now seemed to glide a few inches above it as she floated back to her chair. She picked up her pen and stared at the pages, but her eyes traveled over the words without understanding. Silence stretched between them as they both pretended to take notes.

Gruoch ingen Boite was the daughter of Boite mac Cináeda son of Cináed III.

He's right, I do hide. But isn't it better that way?

She is most famous for being the wife and queen of Mac Beatha mac Findlaích (Macbeth).

Why am I always worried about what other people think? Ben's right. It doesn't matter. I shouldn't be so afraid.

The dates of her life....

I've never been on a date before. Am I beautiful?

Her heart skipped in her chest.

Does he really think so?

Keilann cast about for something—anything—to talk about. Her eyes fell again onto one of the unpronounceable names on the open page in front of her. That's how this all started—names.

She cleared her throat nervously. Ben's head shot up.

"Hey, do you think you could help me?" she asked, willing her voice to stop shaking. "It's just these names again. I keep getting stuck on them."

Ben's face broke into a wide, lopsided grin.

"Let's have it then, Yank," he said, feigning impatience and rolling his eyes to make her smile.

"This first one..." Keilann scooted the book closer to Ben and pointed out the name. "Gruotchinjenboat. How the heck do I say that?"

Ben sniggered.

"Well, *ingen* just means 'daughter of,' kind of like *mac* means 'son of' in the Gaelic. So *ingen Boite* means 'daughter of Boite.' Does that make sense?"

Keilann nodded.

"So really her name is just the first word. You don't pronounce o-c-h like 'otch,'" he mimicked a nasally American accent. "—it's always 'ohhck' like in *loch*."

Keilann sounded out the name in her head, and the smile fell from her face. Ben's voice was drowned out by a deep, howling wind roaring through her memory. It couldn't be. That would mean that...

"Lady Macbeth's name was 'Grew-ohck,'" Ben finished. He saw the look on Keilann's face, her expression wiping away his boyish grin. "Are you okay?"

13

Keilann needed air. Now. The snug warmth of the library, so comfortable just a few moments ago, was suffocating her.

Her eyes were fixed to the page, held fast by that name, that impossible name. Each syllable pounded against Keilann's brain like a tidal wave, drowning out all other thoughts but one: she had to get away from that book. The book held the red-haired girl's name just as Keilann had snatched it from a dream and trapped it under ink. Ben had uttered the name like a spell, unknowingly releasing the nightmarish red-haired girl from Keilann's imagination in her full ferocity. Reason and logic, which should have calmed her, were beaten senseless by shock. Keilann's only option was to run. She didn't have to go far, but she had to go now.

Keilann stood up so fast that her chair was thrown out from under her, landing on the carpet with a muffled clatter. Heads turned, but Keilann didn't care. She didn't even stop to pick it up.

"I don't feel so good," she gasped to Ben. She turned and fled before he had a chance to say another word. If Ben called out after her, Keilann never heard him. The quiet colors and tranquil light of the library melted together into garish streaks as she ran what seemed like triple the length of the room she had just been sitting in.

Her hands collided into the cold metal bar of the door at full force and it yielded without protest. Keilann burst through the main entrance and collapsed on the rough stone steps, scraping her hands on the concrete. She gulped crisp autumn air, its sharp chill cooling the giddy spinning in her head. She forced long breaths of it through her nose, and the more regular her breathing became, the easier it was to stop the light-headed reeling of her thoughts.

After a few minutes, Keilann realized that it was raining. Not the storm of her imagination, but a creeping, misty drizzle that dripped from the barren trees and trailed muddy fingers down buildings. Keilann shivered, but the rain was a relief from the clammy sweat that broke out over her like a fever. Water droplets gathered like a film of ice on her skin, giving her a protective barrier of reality between herself and the name in the book. *Gruoch.*

Keilann closed her eyes and leaned back against the chipped, rusted railing, and let the rain fall freely on her face. The relentless drumming of the name dissolved into the beat of raindrops on slick pavement. Traffic rustled by, kicking up the spicy scent of wet earth, decaying leaves, and exhaust. She opened her eyes. The stately stone houses stared back, their sharp, calculated angles blurred a little around the edges by the fine drizzle. The trim, neat fences and prim flowerbeds were so ordered and purposeful. So unlike the wild, organic tumble of stones Keilann saw whenever she closed her eyes. When she was in the shadow of the stone circle, she could convince herself that there was a mysterious connection between the red-haired girl and her nightmares or the name that seemed to reach out of a dream to haunt her.

But here....

Here the name was just a coincidence, and she chided herself for overreacting. Why let a silly name bother her so much? Even if the red-haired girl shared the same name as a long-dead murderess, so what? What did that prove, except that names can be passed on for generations just as Ben's had been? Keilann took a deep breath of brisk air mingled with the distant, salty aroma of frying potatoes.

That doctor was right, I'm cracking under pressure. The bottle of clattering pills shook in her memory like a rattlesnake's warning. *What if I just took one tonight?*

The door swung open behind her. Slumped against the iron railing just seconds before, she bolted stock straight at the sound of the creaking hinges. She turned in time to see a pair of scuffed black trainers hesitate for a moment before stepping down to sit next to her.

Ben placed a hand on her back just below her shoulders, as if to comfort her.

"Are you okay?" His voice was gentle and soothing. It cemented Keilann into reality, banishing the dark eyes of the red-haired girl from her mind.

Why is he always so warm?

The heat of his palm only made Keilann realize how cold she was. She had allowed herself to become soaked in the sobering rain. She shivered under his touch, and couldn't help remembering another time when Ben had put his arm around her—when she had emptied her stomach in front of him. Keilann's face burned with a surge of heat intense enough to evaporate the rain on her skin.

"I think so," she said. "I just haven't eaten much today because of the doctor appointment. I started feeling—" Keilann met his eyes, desperately hoping that he wasn't struck with the same humiliating memory. "I'm much better now. I just needed some air."

Keilann didn't like the look Ben was giving her. His grim frown made her feel like he expected her to pass out any second.

"Stop looking at me like I'm diseased. I'm fine!" she laughed. "Honest."

Ben finally countered with a limp shadow of his usual toothy grin. He lifted a piece of paper, neatly folded in quarters, and offered it to her.

"I copied Americanized versions o' the rest o' the names ye were havin' trouble with," he said, his grin turning into a playful smirk. "Here. So ye won' have te call me every time ye come across something in the Gaelic."

Keilann snatched the paper, trying not to shudder as she thought about what must undoubtedly be written there. She hastily stuffed it into her pocket without looking at it. Keilann had had enough of names today.

"Thanks," she said brightly, hoping that the hysteria bubbling in her gut had not seeped into her voice.

Apparently, it hadn't. Ben sighed and stood up, stretching his arms over his head.

"No worries," he grimaced as he pulled his elbow across his chest. Shaking out his lanky arms, he offered his hand to Keilann and hoisted her to her feet. "Now, what do ye say about gettin' back to tryin' to pass our English class?"

Something else was beginning to bubble in Keilann's stomach. She opened her mouth to answer, but instead of words, a long, hollow growl emanated from somewhere behind her belly button.

Ben blinked at her for a moment. Keilann tried to apologize, but it seemed that once her stomach had begun demanding food, it refused to stop until it was appeased. Strange squeals and grumbles—along with Ben's deep chuckle—drowned out her attempts.

"I know ye said ye haven't eaten much, but starvin' yerself for homework is jess wrong. C'mon, let's go grab our stuff."

Keilann's furrowed her brows, her stomach emitting a pathetically hollow gurgle.

"Why?" she asked, completely nonplussed. "Where are we going?"

Ben shook his head. "Te get ye some food. Ye can' keep workin' on an empty stomach."

"I can't." Keilann's face fell. "I'm sorry, but I didn't bring my wallet. I didn't think—"

Ben waved away her protests. "Don' worry, don' worry. I'll cover ye."

Keilann gasped. "No! That's not what I meant!" she said, horrified. "I don't want you to pay for me."

"I know ye didn', but I'm going te anyway." Ben shrugged. "I could definitely go for some chips. Besides, I consider it my civic duty to help a fellow starving academic."

Keilann was shaking her head.

"Ben, no. I couldn't."

Ben sighed heavily.

"Keilann," he put both hands on her shoulders and looked directly into her eyes. "Would ye stop arguing and jess let me take ye out for dinner already?"

She stared at him, all objections forgotten—all form of speech forgotten, in fact. Her heart beat a rapid tattoo against her ribcage.

Did he just say what I think he said?

Ben saw the bewildered expression on her face and grinned, his eyes dancing with laughter.

"C'mon," he said. He swung open the library door and ushered Keilann inside. "I know a place down the way. We can get a bite and finish up here afterward."

As they gathered up large stacks of dusty books and scraps of notes, Ben whispered descriptions of the little hole-in-the-wall pub just a few minutes' walk downtown. Keilann half-listened, wading through the jumble of unfamiliar dishes and slang to vaguely determine that he was telling her the food was outstanding. Ben's voice filled her head, but she couldn't focus on anything that he was saying. All Keilann could hear was his exasperated sigh: *"Would ye stop arguing and jess let me take ye out for dinner already?"*

Once again, Ben was holding the door open for her. She stepped through the threshold. The rain had dried up, and the day seemed much brighter than before. Taking a deep breath of fresh air, she fell into step next to her friend. Ben chattered away cheerfully beside her, switching between asking her questions about American football and lamenting the homework that awaited them on the other side of dinner. Keilann forgot everything else. Connor McBride, facing the school tomorrow, sleeping pills, Gruoch—somehow none of it mattered, nothing could touch her. Giggling madly at Ben's impersonation of Connor McBride flailing in the mud puddle, she felt a warm, tingling contentment radiating through her like she had just guzzled a mug of hot chocolate. She caught sight of a rustic half-timber pub ahead with a sign of a scrawny wolf chugging a tankard of ale above the door. As they approached, Keilann could see the name engraved underneath the picture: *The Famished Wolf.*

The pub was bustling with diners packed in among its dark exposed beams and cheery blue tartan carpet. Keilann slid into a wood-paneled corner booth with Ben, determined to let nothing ruin her first truly good night since arriving in Scotland.

Well, almost nothing. The menu was filled with completely foreign—and totally unappetizing—names like *Cullen Skink, Black Pudding,* and *Bangers and Mash.*

This is supposed to be food? Keilann thought, incredulously. *What the hell is it?*

She could feel Ben's eyes on her as she tried to decode what, if anything, was edible.

"Need help?" he asked. To his credit he kept his face straight, but Keilann saw the gleam in his eyes.

She held her head high. No way was she going to admit that she was absolutely clueless. Her eyes quickly scanned the list—there: *Black Pudding.* That sounded safe. Keilann at least knew what pudding was. The brightly colored boxes of instant powdered dessert mix had always sat in the cupboards of her family's Chicago apartment. But what kind of country would serve that as a main course?

Keilann lifted her chin and pointed confidently at her choice.

"No, thanks," she said, primly. "I think I'll just get black pudding."

Ben's eyes popped open, his brows shooting up past his fringe.

"You like black pudding?"

Keilann squared her shoulders. How bad could it be?

"Of course," she sniffed, pretending to be offended. "I'm not the ignorant American you think I am."

Ben pursed his lips, his cheeks taut. Keilann's stomach dropped. That's not how this was supposed to go. She hadn't meant to actually upset him.

"Ben, I didn't mean that."

Keilann stopped abruptly. Before she could get the rest of her apology out, she noticed Ben's shoulders were shaking. She snapped her mouth shut, her face flushing.

He's laughing at me.

Ben fought to hide his wide-spread grin behind his hand. "All righ', Keilann," he conceded after a few breaths. His voice wobbled with barely suppressed laughter. "We'll have black pudding."

She nodded, in what she hoped was a dignified way, hoping that Ben couldn't see how nervous she was. Keilann had never felt more out of her element. She was saved temporarily by the arrival of a friendly waitress with a purple pixie cut and thickly applied eyeliner. The woman took their orders and, glancing between the two, threw them a knowing smile glinting with braces.

"One check?"

Ben nodded and she swept off toward the kitchens.

"Thanks for feeding me." Keilann gave herself a mental slap in the forehead even as she said it. *Feeding me? I sound like a five-year-old!*

If Ben thought her choice of words odd, he didn't show it. But his eyes were still laughing as he spoke.

"Yer welcome. Anytime," he replied, his lips twitching.

Keilann had no idea what she was supposed to say now. The fact that Ben was taking her out to dinner—paying for her dinner—suddenly made her extremely uncomfortable. She should say something clever, something intelligent. Something to make him think that being in a restaurant with a member of the opposite sex wasn't making Keilann's heart throb painfully in her throat. Instead, she nearly knocked over her glass of water and took a deliberately long, slow sip. Why did this pub have to be so hot?

Eventually, Keilann had to either put her glass back down or be in danger of chugging the entire pint of water in one go. She set it gingerly back in its place on the linen table cloth and began pretending that the packed, smoky room was the most interesting thing she had ever seen. She stared in awe at the reproduction art on the walls, was fascinated by the shabby tartan carpeting, and carefully counted the soot-stained bricks in the fireplace. Anything to avoid looking at Ben.

Why? She could usually talk to him with such ease. Why should tonight be any different?

Because he's taking you out to dinner, that annoying, tiny voice crept back into her thoughts.

So? She argued silently. He's just being nice. *I was hungry and had no money.* The small voice wouldn't let up.

No one else has ever taken you out to dinner before. No boy has ever done that for you, it corrected.

So I should be afraid to talk to him because he's a boy? That seemed ridiculous even for her. *Ben is my friend. There's no reason I shouldn't be able to talk to him.*

Keilann cleared her throat awkwardly. Determined to prove herself wrong, she turned back to Ben.

"So, you never told me. How did it really go today?"

Keilann wasn't sure if that was the right question to ask, but it was the only one she could think of. At least it was something to talk about.

Ben hesitated. Judging by the look on his face, he had been expecting her to bring up the subject of school again.

"It was...," he paused, choosing his words carefully. "Uneventful. For the most part."

For the most part? Keilann didn't like the sound of that.

"Was Connor—did he—?"

"Beat the piss out o' me?" Ben finished for her with a roguish grin. "No. He was surprisingly well-behaved, mostly jess ignored me. I wouldn't count on it lasting, though," he added, growing more serious. Ben leaned closer to Keilann, his shoulder brushing hers gently. "He won't try anything again in front of me but I don' trust 'im. Jess be careful. He doesn't like being humiliated."

"Neither do I," Keilann countered, hotly. The cold icicles of fear in her stomach were instantly melted by a white hot surge of indignation. "I'm not scared of him."

"I am," Ben said quietly. "Especially since...."

Keilann arched an eyebrow. "Especially since what?"

Ben exhaled sharply. "Look, I didnae want to tell ye but I s'pose ye'll find out tomorrow anyway, and it's better if yer prepared."

The ice had reformed in Keilann's abdomen, chilling her as if she had jumped into a frozen lake.

"Ye see, there are several very colorful versions of what happened on Friday."

Keilann snorted. "Yeah, Fiona told me. Apparently one of her friends believes that I punched Connor."

Ben shifted nervously on the patent leather seat. "It's not just her one friend."

She froze.

"The version of you punching Connor is actually pretty tame," he grimaced. "There's another one going 'round. People are sayin'...."

Ben paused, and Keilann noticed that he wasn't looking at her.

"People are saying what, Ben?" she coaxed. She didn't know if she really wanted to hear the answer, but not knowing what she would face tomorrow was even worse.

Ben took a deep breath, all of his words streaming out in a rush.

"That ye've been Connor's girl this whole time, and he started the fight because he found out that ye and I were—" Ben faltered, his face turned scarlet. "That you were cheating on him with another bloke. With me."

A heavy, stunned silence followed his words as Keilann's numbed mind tried to make sense of what he was telling her.

"They think me and Connor?" she whispered, revulsion leaving a bitter sting in her mouth.

Ben gave a weak nod.

"And me and—and you?"

Keilann felt an enormous pressure welling in her chest. She couldn't hold it back any longer. Ignoring the fact that they were in a crowded pub, Keilann doubled-over and howled with laughter. She could barely breathe, imagining being the girlfriend of Connor McBride. No, it was better than that. Apparently she was the cause of a jealous love triangle. It was too absurd to consider. Ben looked as if he were somewhere between relieved and alarmed by her reaction. One glance at his expression and Keilann burst into a fresh bout of giggles.

"Oh, come on! This is too good! Connor and I holding hands and skipping down the hall?" Even Ben had to crack a grin at that.

"And me and you!" she gasped, wiping the tears from her eyes. "Who would be stupid enough to believe any of that?"

She looked to Ben, expecting him to agree. He still wore the same grin but it was forced, somehow deflated, as if her words had punctured him.

He gave a short, feeble chuckle. "Yeah. Stupid."

Keilann's insides twisted as if a joke she had told had gone completely flat. She had a terrible feeling that she was doing everything wrong. Was it her imagination, or was Ben acting a bit strange tonight?

Is he that freaked out by those ridiculous rumors? Or is it the thought of us? She hadn't meant to make him feel uncomfortable.

As if sensing the tension, the waitress reappeared laden with dinner plates. She smiled and put a plate of three chunky, blackened hockey pucks surrounded by tomatoes, beans, and sausage in front of Keilann.

"Black pudding for the both of ye. If there's anything else ye need, jess holler."

Keilann stared at her plate.

This is black pudding? What is this stuff?

She poked tentatively at the hockey puck, wondering if anything could be less like pudding. It looked like a black mess of congealed, burned oatmeal, as if the chef had left it on the stove overnight. Keilann turned to make a snide remark to Ben, but he was too busy eating. He looked quite pleased, cutting the discs into bite-sized pieces before popping them into his mouth one-by-one.

Maybe this is what it's supposed to look like.

Keilann brandished her knife and fork as if preparing for battle and copied Ben, taking her time cutting each disc into tiny bits.

Just close your eyes and eat. It can't be too bad.

She lifted the smallest piece to her mouth and jabbed the fork in before she had second thoughts. Chewing slowly, she tested the flavors. Salty, definitely a good crunch, and a taste she couldn't quite place that reminded her of bacon.

Keilann couldn't believe her luck. It was delicious. She fell onto the other discs immediately, the taste of food reminding her how hungry she was. Keilann devoured her entire plate, spearing the last piece of black pudding on her fork and savoring the hearty crunch.

Leaning back in the booth, she was full and sleepy. Keilann grinned at Ben, proud to have come out of her Scottish culinary experience unscathed.

"Thanks for dinner, Ben." she sighed. "That was excellent. You'll have to let me pay you back for this."

Ben shrugged and leaned back.

"Don' worry about it."

"No, really," Keilann insisted. "I want to pay you back."

He reached for the glass in front of him, considering her over the rim.

"Alrigh', ye want te pay me back? Ye can take me out to dinner next time."

Keilann's heart hammered in her ears. *Next time?*

"Sure," she said. "That would be perfect."

Ben smiled lazily.

"Although I have to say, I'm surprised at ye. Ye really do know something about Scottish food. And yer braver than I thought too," he added.

Keilann's stomach lurched. "Brave? Why am I brave?"

Ben shook his head. "I jess never thought ye'd actually be willing to eat blood sausage."

14

A steaming heap of potatoes splattered across Keilann's already brimming bowl. "Eat up!" her father said brightly. "There's plenty more where that came from!" She closed her eyes, fighting back a wave of nausea.

Black pudding, she heard Ben's voice ringing in her head. *There's pork, oatmeal, lard, and dried sow's blood. Ye mix everythin' together and fry it until the blood sorta congeals and blackens.*

"It's so nice to finally be able to eat a meal together in our new home," Her dad continued. Keilann opened her eyes, carefully avoiding the steaming tureens of food on the table. Fiona sat directly across from her, stirring her rubbery vegetables listlessly, staring into a vat of gravy. It was Monday, a night that neither of her parents had to teach. Between the doctor's appointment and Ben—her stomach danced and she forced herself to think of anything but those little black hockey pucks—Keilann had completely forgotten about plans for a family dinner tonight. An excellent cook, her father had been almost painfully excited about cooking real Scottish food.

If only he knew, Keilann moaned inwardly. She had managed not to throw-up during the walk back to the library with Ben, and was even able to pretend to study for another hour after that. When she had come home to a full Scottish meal waiting for her on the table, it was all she could do to keep her stomach from revolting. Seated on her right, Keilann could hear her dad slurping and chewing spoonfuls of meaty stew.

"Keilann, you have to try this," he grinned, holding out a bowl. Chunks of sinewy venison and pulpy carrots swilled together in a greasy broth. The gamey smell of browned meat overwhelmed her, filling her nose and mouth. She tried to pass her grimace off as a smile.

"I'll work on what I've got first, Dad." She winced, not daring to chance a look at her plate. "It's really great of you to make all of this."

Her father waved away the complement with his spoon, tiny droplets of broth spraying the air.

"It's nothing," he tried to shrug off, but swelling a bit at the complement. "I love cooking—gives me a chance to relax at the end of the day, unwind. Especially after what I heard today." Her father plunked the spoon in his stew bowl and laced his fingers together, giving his wife a wearied look.

Keilann saw the look that passed between her parents. She didn't like it. "What? What happened?"

Her mother sighed. "Program cuts."

Keilann pushed the bowl of stew away, untouched. "Are they really bad?"

Her mom tried to give Keilann one of her brave smiles. "Maybe."

The bottom of her stomach dropped like she was falling from the top of a steep hill. "Are you going to lose your job?" Keilann turned to her dad. "They can't do that, can they?"

"I was the last person hired in the department," Her mother said. "I'm only an associate professor."

"But that's not fair!"

Her mom smiled again, but it didn't make it to her eyes.

"It hasn't happened yet."

"And it won't happen," Her father said. "You're a great teacher." He pointed his spoon for emphasis.

Her mother shook her head. "Great teachers get cut all the time."

It wasn't long before her parents were deeply immersed in university politics. Using the distraction, Keilann covered her untouched food with her napkin and pushed the bowl away from her. She leaned away from the table, taking deep breaths of air to settle her stomach.

At least they're talking about something.

For the past few weeks, her mom had seemed so distant, so disconnected from everything around her. Even if this was bad news, at least they were facing it together like they always had.

Her attention drifted from her parents. Keilann turned to her sister. She tried to catch Fiona's eye, but her little sister was still staring mournfully into her potatoes, her fork trailing patterns absently.

Keilann frowned.

Fiona had seemed quiet ever since she had rushed through the door to find her family already seated for dinner. She had just assumed that Fiona had had a long day. Homework was beginning to pile up at an alarming rate that neither of them had ever encountered at their previous schools. But as Keilann watched her, she knew that there must be something much more serious weighing on her sister's mind. Fiona gulped as though she was fighting back tears, spasms of pain flitting across her face. Whatever it was, Keilann highly doubted they could discuss it in front of their parents.

"Keilann?"

The sound of her dad's voice wrenched her from her thoughts.

"W-what?"

"I asked how it went today," he repeated, his brows contracting slightly. "Do you still have a concussion?"

For a moment she must have looked like it. Her brain clicked into place.

"The doctor? Yes. I mean, no, I don't have a concussion," she stammered. "She said that I was fine, and that I should just be more careful in the future."

Keilann was talking to her father, but her eyes were pleading with her mother.

Don't say anything about the pills. Please.

She didn't know why she was treating the prescription with such urgent secrecy. It should have been quite simple to say that she had gotten some sleeping pills to get rid of her nightmares, but admitting that seemed like a confession of madness.

Her mother said nothing.

Keilann's father breathed a heavy sigh of relief. "Those bruises are healing up alright as well. Just please don't play sports anymore?" he teased.

Keilann turned back to her father and gave him a small, sheepish grin.

"Promise," she said, her face smarting with guilt.

"So," her dad continued, shoveling in a few mouthfuls of stew. "How's school going you two?" he asked thickly.

Fiona, who usually talked enough for both girls, was uncharacteristically silent. She continued to stare vacantly at her potatoes, stirring her now cold dinner into a mushy slop. It was Keilann's turn to come to the rescue.

"Um," she stalled, groping her mind. "I've been working on that English project with Ben."

It worked. Her dad turned from scrutinizing Fiona.

"Oh? Ben again, huh?" he asked. "How did that go?"

Without warning, Keilann flushed to the roots of her hair. "Fine. It was fine."

"That Ben seems like a really nice boy," her dad said. He nudged her with his elbow.

Keilann stared at her stew. "He's fine."

Keilann didn't like the smile he was giving her. "You guys have been spending a lot of time together lately."

"In the library!"

And once at dinner.

Her mom came to the rescue.

"This is your *Macbeth* project, right?"

Keilann nodded, grateful for an excuse to turn away from her father.

Keilann's mom put down her fork and leaned back in her chair. "You know, I have a colleague at the university who teaches Shakespeare." She pursed her lips thoughtfully. "I bet she'd love to talk to you. She could probably give you as much information on

Macbeth as any textbook. Maybe more."

Keilann couldn't believe she hadn't thought of that before. Of course there would be Shakespeare professors at the university.

"Are you serious, Mom? That would be amazing. I've found next to nothing."

Her mother smiled. This time it reached her eyes and lit up her youthful face.

"No problem. The only obstacle will be time. I'll have to call and ask her if she has any night classes this week. If she can meet with you, she'll probably want to get some materials ready. What's the subject of your project, again?"

Keilann fought to keep her voice even. She looked directly at her mother.

"Lady Macbeth." It was amazing the effect one name had on her. She grasped her hands under the table so her mother wouldn't see them shake.

"D'you guys mind if I go to my room? I have some homework to finish before I get to bed," Fiona said.

The table stopped. It was the first time Fiona had spoken all night. She had finally raised her face. It was pale and drawn, her eyes rimed with red. Keilann was shocked by the dramatic change in her sister's usually carelessly pretty looks. Was she sick?

Let's find out. Keilann's chair groaned, scraping the tile floor as she stood.

"Yeah, I do, too." Fiona finally looked at Keilann. She threw her a dark, fleeting glance. A warning to stay away.

So she is trying to hide something, Keilann thought. *She's gonna have to try a lot harder than that.*

Keilann gathered up her dishes, hastily dumping her untouched meal into the scrap bin while her parents were still distracted.

"Are you sure that you're feeling well, Fiona? You haven't eaten a thing," her mother fussed.

Edging to the sink, Keilann rinsed the last of the evidence down the drain. She took her time washing her dishes, waiting until she heard Fiona's footfalls pad across the living room, and disappear up the stairs. Keilann patted her hands on a tea towel and followed her sister, keeping her steps relaxed and even.

"Thanks for dinner, Dad!" she called over her shoulder.

She rounded the corner and sprinted up the dark stairs. By the time she reached the landing, Fiona's usually open door was shut tightly in her face. Keilann leaned against the frame, rapping quietly with her knuckles.

"Fiona?" she murmured into the door jam. "Fiona, it's me. Open up."

Nothing stirred behind the door, not even a muffled "go away!" that usually followed Keilann's pleas to enter.

"Fiona, stop it. I know something's wrong. Just let me in."

Keilann waited in silence, straining her ears for some sign that Fiona had heard her. The mundane sounds of scraping dishes and scuffling chairs drifted from the kitchen, but her sister neither moved nor spoke. Her fingers twitched with irritation. How dare Fiona accuse her of not confiding her secrets? What right did she have to make Keilann feel guilty and then go and hide away in her room?

"Okay, Fiona, you don't want to talk to me?" Keilann smoldered. "Fine. Just remember that I'll return the favor."

She turned on her heel and stormed down the hall, no longer concerned about stealth or secrecy. Keilann threw her door open, sending it crashing into several unpacked boxes that her father had been haranguing about for weeks.

"You really should take care of those, you know."

Fiona was sitting on her unmade bed, hugging her knees to her chest, her bare feet burrowed under Keilann's comforter.

For a few moments, neither of them spoke. Heat crept up Keilann's neck, flushing her face. Fiona had been in here the entire time, listening to her temper tantrum.

"Fiona—"

Fiona cut her off, uninterested in apologies or explanations.

"We need to talk," she said brusquely. Though her eyes were still slightly puffy, there was nothing weepy about Fiona now. Her voice was sharp and clear, her face set in a determined frown.

Keilann was taken aback by her spiky tone and almost accusatory glare. She felt like she had been called into the principal's office, and began racking her brain for a punishable offense.

"That's what I've been trying to do," Keilann said slowly, buying time.

Fiona gestured to Keilann's desk chair. "Sit down."

Put-off by being told to sit on her own furniture, Keilann remained in the door way.

"I'm not a little kid, Fiona. This is my room." She crossed her arms and threw her hip out defiantly.

"Are you seeing anyone?"

Keilann blinked. "What?"

"Are. You. Seeing. Anyone."

The black pudding in her stomach turned to lead and sunk into her feet. How could Fiona know that she went out for dinner with Ben?

"Why? What's this got to do with anything?" Keilann asked carefully.

Fiona bit her lip, looking as if she were holding back tears again. "There were rumors going around school today about you and..." Her voice trembled.

Keilann rolled her eyes.

"Is that what this is about? I told you before. Whatever you heard, it's all lies."

Fiona looked at her hopefully. "So, you haven't been seeing anyone behind my back?"

"No."

"You promise?"

"I promise," Keilann shouted, exasperated by Fiona's strange behavior. She knew she would have to deal with this sort of grilling tomorrow, but from her own sister? "What's it to you, anyway?"

Fiona suddenly brightened and released her legs, stretching them past the edge of the bed. She smiled at Keilann and patted the empty nest of crumpled blankets next to her.

"Just wanted to be sure," Fiona shrugged as Keilann dragged herself to the spare bit of mattress. "Anyway, the bigger question is where you were tonight," she whispered, leaning toward her like a conspirator.

Keilann paused, pretending to readjust the comforter. "At the library."

Fiona rolled her eyes. "Yeah, yeah," she waved away Keilann's words. "I mean after that."

Keilann hesitated a second too long this time.

"Ha! I knew it! You weren't studying, you were going out with Ben."

"We weren't 'going out.' We just got hungry." Keilann's face burned.

Fiona pursed her lips.

"Puh-lease! I'm not thick."

"Believe it or not, it is possible to just be friends with a boy," Keilann sniffed coldly. *Not that I've ever even done that before.*

Fiona smirked.

"Oh, really? And did this friend ask you to go to dinner, or did you ask him?"

Her question made Keilann's heart contract, her stomach writhing as if she'd eaten snakes instead of black pudding.

"What does it matter?" she mumbled to her shoes.

Fiona delicately arched an eyebrow, giving her older sister a hard, appraising look. "It matters."

Keilann scowled, her irritation with Fiona's condescending tone just enough to drown out the sick flutter of hope it had inspired.

"He did."

"And did he pay?"

"Well, yes."

Fiona's eyebrows shot up.

"But only because I forgot my wallet!"

Fiona was already shaking her head, deaf to Keilann's defense and protests. "Is he making you pay him back?"

"Not exactly."

Fiona shot her a skeptical look.

"He wants me to pay for his dinner next time—next time we're studying."

It was a flimsy cover, and sounded pathetic to even Keilann's ears. Fiona certainly wasn't taking the bait. She was giving her older sister a genial smile, shaking her head again.

"Keilann, how can you be so dense?" she sighed. "He was asking you out again."

Her heart stopped, and she momentarily forgot how to breathe. Ben? No. *No.*

"We're just...He's my..."

"Friend." Fiona scoffed, drawing out the word in heavy, mocking tones. "So you say," she shrugged, a slow smile spreading across her face. "But you won't be for long. One way or another."

She slipped from the bed and sashayed out of the room without another word. Keilann was too flustered and confused to try to call after to stop her. She stayed in the same rigid position until a dull ache in her knees forced her to move. Springing from the bed, she paced the empty floor between the desk and bed, hardly aware of what she was doing.

Was it possible? Snippets of the day rushed back to her: the warm touch of Ben's hand, his crinkly, lopsided smile, the hearty ring of his laughter, concern for her flickering behind his dark eyes.

Stop it. Keilann shook her head. Don't do this to yourself.

Keilann stopped pacing and ran a weary hand over her eyes. She had been the victim of agonizing, unrequited crushes before, and recognized the warning signs in herself. But suppose Ben really did like her. Was that really what she wanted?

Fiona's sly whisper echoed in her ear. *You won't be friends for long. One way or another.*

A sharp jolt surged through her body, sticking her feet to the hardwood floor. Keilann closed her eyes. She waited until the hammering in her heart had worn itself out, until it fell into a steady rhythm once more. She counted her heartbeats, using the distraction to tame her wild imagination before it erupted into full-fledged fantasies.

Get a grip. When she saw Ben tomorrow, she had to act normally, had to be in control of her emotions.

Oh no. *Tomorrow.*

Keilann's stomach cramped painfully, stinging pangs of dread radiating to the tips of her fingers. She sunk back onto her bed, the cold plaster wall butting against her shoulders. Keilann had been purposely avoiding the bleak reality of facing Mary Arden Academy again. To be in the same class as Connor McBride, with all those horrible rumors.

She closed her eyes, but couldn't stop the images that sprang to her mind: hallways of identical, nameless classmates pointing at her as she passed with whispers igniting behind her like hissing flames. Keilann shuddered at the thought of unwanted attention following her with a spotlight. What had happened to her fail-proof plan to scrape by under the radar?

Without warning, Ms. Spark's clear, cheery voice rang in her ears. *The best laid schemes of mice and men oft go awry.*

Her eyes shot open. Rolling onto her belly, Keilann pressed her face against the wall, peering into the dark crevice between it and her bed. Without thinking, she stuffed her arm down, groping blindly in the crack until her fingers stuck to a gluey adhesive strip. Keilann drew her hand out and the post-it note fluttered and freed itself, coming to rest on the soft denim of her lap. The bright neon had faded under a fine layer of dust, but the name was an unmistakable scrawl, seared on the paper like a brand. *Grewock.*

Gruoch.

Keilann sat on the bed for a long time, staring at her own handwriting. From some far corner of her mind, a deep voice growled two syllables over and over. She could almost feel the heat of the burning man's eyes on her back. Her hand jerked as if to crumple the harmless note and throw it in her empty trash bin. But she couldn't.

Instead, Keilann went to her backpack, dug for the pencil case, and carefully shook out two round powder-blue pills into her palm. Without a second thought, she popped them into her mouth.

Keilann slumped exhausted into the seat of the commuter train, weary but alive. It was an unseasonably warm day: bright, balmy, and amazingly dry, the sun peeking out between occasional gaps in the fat, cotton ball clouds. Tilting her face toward the window, she felt an invisible weight lift from her as the train zoomed farther and farther from Mary Arden Academy. The worst was over. At least, that's what Ben had said, and Keilann fervently hoped he was right.

She couldn't see how it could get any worse.

Over the past five days, every time Keilann had entered a talkative classroom it would instantly go silent, revving back to life like a stalled engine as soon as she darted to a seat in the very corner of the last row. In the hallways between periods, people didn't even bother to lower their voices as she walked by.

"Is that her?" a shrill voiced girl with buckteeth had screeched on Wednesday morning, openly pointing at Keilann as she was rummaging through her locker. "But she's not even pretty!"

Outraged, Keilann had kicked the door shut. Cursing at her throbbing toe, she had hobbled all the way to Biology before she realized she had forgotten to grab her lab workbook. Unimpressed by Keilann's story, her teacher had refused to let her go back for her supplies, giving her a zero for the day and demanding that she stay after school to make up the lab.

Keilann pressed her hot cheeks to the cool window pane, watching as the sloping plum hills of heather and dark thickets of pine trees slipped by as if caught in a swift river current. She closed her eyes, letting the steady tempo of the rail lull her. What was still making her stomach bubble and her face flush had been something more than just a random insult, extra homework, or even Connor McBride. It had been something completely different, completely unexpected, and completely unwanted.

Well, almost completely.

"How can you stand it?" she had asked Ben through gritted teeth at lunch earlier that day. She had just finished telling him about the rude bucktoothed girl when a giggling cluster of younger students had turned in their seats to jeer at the table where Ben and Keilann sat alone.

Ben shrugged and took a hearty bite of his sandwich.

"Jess ignore 'em," he said through a mouthful of lettuce, ham, and cheese. "They'll get bored and move on to the next victim soon enough."

"I can't ignore them. They're everywhere!"

Ben chewed slowly, his Adams apple bobbing up and down as he swallowed.

"Well, we could give 'em somethin' to really talk about," he said, wiping his mouth with a napkin.

Keilann was about to say, "like what?" but her question was cut off by Ben's lips pressing hard against her own. He swiveled so quickly, she hadn't even had time to close her mouth. His warm, scruffy face squashed her mouth into a flat, astonished oval against her teeth. He smelled like mustard and oranges.

Ben pulled away and gave the table an exaggerated wink. The girls shrieked and flapped, buzzing the news around the room like a vicious swarm of hornets.

"That'll do it. Problem solved," he said.

He grinned and took another bite of sandwich.

Keilann's brain was paralyzed. She stared at him, her lips open. She never had time to close her mouth.

"Ben—what did—why—you just kissed me!" Keilann stammered, her voice and temper rising. She tried to ignore the fact that her lips were still tingling from the kiss that prickled all the way down to her toes.

Ben shrugged, that stupid, smug grin still stuck to his face.

"Well, it distracted 'em, dinnit?"

He nodded at the packed lunchroom.

Everyone was looking at her. Keilann's nostrils flared. She could have snorted steam like a cartoon bull.

"You did—just for a joke—never even asked." She choked on her anger, a tidal wave of words building in her throat.

Ben's eyebrow arched on the word "joke." He cocked his head to the side, looking at Keilann as if weighing his words very carefully.

"Who said it was a joke?" His voice was quiet, barely audible above the din of students packing up lunches and shouting across tables.

She stared at him, hardly daring to breathe. The mischievous, swaggering version of Ben was gone now that he had no audience to pander to. Or did he?

Keilann's eyes narrowed.

"Keilann, please don' look at me like tha'," Ben begged. "If I knew ye'd be this mad, I wouldn't a done it. I jess...I thought that mebbe...."

His eyes were still wide, pleading. She wanted to tell him that it was fine, laugh it off as a clever stunt, but her tongue was stuck to the roof of her mouth.

"Keilann?"

The noise of the lunchroom faded and was gone. Keilann's heart was pounding so hard, she could hear little else. Another, almost painful, twinge shot through her veins, but it wasn't anger anymore.

"I have to go to my locker. I'll see ya later, Ben."

She bolted from the room, ducking her head against the sea of pale, jeering faces so they wouldn't see the tears stinging in her eyes.

"Keilann!"

She kept walking, her eyes fixed down the hallway. His patent leather shoes squealed on the tile as he closed the gap between them in a matter of seconds.

"Wait up!" Ben panted alongside her. She had reached her locker but still didn't turn, dialing the combination at a deliberate snail's pace.

"Why do I always end up chasin' ye, eh?" he tried to make his voice sound light, but he was still gasping for air.

Keilann wished she could retort with something terribly witty or scathing—something like, *what kind of soccer player can't run down a hall without getting winded?* But her mind was stubbornly blank.

"I didn't ask you to follow me." Not too original, but each word was as sharp and cold as an icicle.

"True, but that still leaves the question of why yer always runnin' away from me."

Keilann turned on her heel, almost crashing into Ben.

"Well maybe if you didn't humiliate me in front of the whole school just to get back at Connor, I wouldn't think you were such an ass," she hissed in his face.

Ben stepped toward her, his long nose almost touching hers.

"Is that why ye think I kissed ye?"

He was far too close.

Keilann turned away from him and slammed her locker door shut with an echoing bang. The already dented metal emitted a high-pitched, disgruntled squeak, rattling angrily into place.

"Why else would you do something so damned stupid?" she growled, snapping the padlock back onto the handle.

"I could think of a few reasons," he murmured, so close now that his breath was warm on her ear and stirred her hair.

Keilann couldn't stand it another second.

She whirled around, and into the second kiss of her entire life. It happened too quickly to really think about what she was doing or who had even started it. She had spun so fast that her nose collided with his, but so did her lips and that was all that mattered. Keilann was weightless, timeless, a floaty kind of light filling every inch of her as if it had just been waiting to be switched on. This kiss was much, much different than the first: soft, slow, and deep. The math book slipped out of her fingers. It must've clattered to the ground, but she never heard it.

Somewhere far away, a dull tone blasted through an almost empty hallway. Ben gently pulled away from her, and the world came rushing back.

She landed into her body heavily. Her stomach dropped somewhere near her ankles, but her head was light and giddy as if she had held her breath for too long. Shuffling feet and jumbled shouting surged past them, but Keilann's feet were stuck to the floor. Ben bent over and snatched her book before it was lost in the stampede of harried students, calmly placing it in Keilann's numbed hands.

They stood for a few moments, the river of students ebbing and flowing around them like they were rocks in a stream. Keilann couldn't speak or move, couldn't believe what had just happened. She grasped tightly to her math book, resisting the urge to reach out and feel Ben's stubble under her fingers to make sure he was real. She could sense a hurricane of confused emotions brewing inside, but was too shocked to feel the full force of it. Yet.

As if in slow motion, Ben's hand stretched forward, brushing the soft tuft of hair at the end of Keilann's thick plait.

"I'll see ye later, then."

Then he was gone. Keilann stared after him, the herd of students around her thinning until she was alone again.

Did that really just happen?

The bell blared a stern warning, and her brain finally kicked into action. She raced to the math wing and sprinted through the door at the very last second. Her pen trailed along the pages of her notebook for the rest of the day, diligently copying notes in each class. Her teachers droned on about difficult equations, strategic military battles, and the formal variations of conjugating French verbs. But Keilann never heard a single word. It had happened.

Ben had kissed her, actually kissed her. Her, Keilann Douglas. The chubby, awkward girl who had never talked to a boy before, much less kissed one. So what did it mean? She hadn't had a chance to talk to Ben after school. At the final bell, she rushed off to Biology to get credit for the lab she had missed. Keilann had just finished up as the late bus was about to pull out, barely waving it down before it left without her. Would he call her? Should they ignore the kiss, keep on being friends as if nothing had happened? Or—her face bloomed with heat—would he kiss her again?

The train lurched suddenly to the left, sharply bouncing Keilann's forehead on the grubby window. She began muttering a vibrant curse under her breath before remembering her mother was sitting next to her. Rubbing the spot gingerly, she darted a glance across the aisle. Thankfully, Her mom was still engrossed in her lecture notes, scratching out a sentence and making revisions with a quick swoop of her pen. Keilann returned her gaze to the window, watching peak after peak of the distant mountain range crawl along the rushing landscape.

Keilann closed her eyes again, the rapid thumping of her heart making her dizzy. She took a deep breath, exhaling slowly.

What if Ben hadn't meant anything by it? Keilann wasn't naïve. Ben probably kissed many other girls before her. Maybe he had only done it to be nice or because he had upset her. Wherever Ben was right now, she could safely bet that he wasn't fixating on such an insignificant kiss the way she was. By the time she saw him again—her heart contracted painfully at the idea—the whole thing would have blown over with the remainder of the rumors. At least they could go back to just being mates, safe and simple.

Or.

Keilann gulped, a cold sweat prickling across her skin. Or Ben had meant something—a lot—with that kiss. He had meant that he liked her, that he wanted to possibly date her. This thought terrified Keilann more than anything else she had been forced to endure at Mary Arden. She had no idea what that word date implied, no idea how to proceed or what would be expected of her. If—and it was a big if—Ben really did like her enough to be more than just friends, what then? This was Fiona's battlefield, not hers. In the past, Keilann had snubbed plastering on thick layers of goopy make-up and twiddling with the latest hair styles. She had always considered such things a waste of time in the extreme. Now, she fervently wished she had paid more attention to how it was done. If that's what Ben is after, Keilann thought gloomily, she was more or less doomed to fail.

But, a hopeful voice whispered, *if he wanted any of that, he wouldn't have kissed you.*

"Strange, isn't it? It just doesn't seem real."

Keilann's eyes popped open, staring at her mother's smiling face in disbelief. How could she know what Keilann had been thinking?

Her mother nodded toward the window. The sparse farmhouses of only minutes ago were quickly thickening into larger clumps of more and more modern buildings as they neared Aberdeen.

"After all this time, I still can't believe that this is home."

Though her mother's eyes were staring vacantly at the craggy countryside, she was somewhere far away from Scotland. Lately, Keilann had been catching her mother staring out the windows that overlooked the woods, her pencil hovering over a piece of paper, a deep, unspoken sadness lining her usually youthful face. In the shadow of those stolen moments, every year of her mother's life was written on her so painfully that it frightened Keilann to look at her.

"Mom, why did...?"

Keilann's mom started as if she'd forgotten her daughter was there. She tore her eyes from the window, the heavy, purple circles underneath them nearly as dark as the ones Keilann sported.

Keilann cleared her throat. "Do you ever miss the Rez?"

It was a question that neither of them had been expecting. Her mom stiffened, blinking at Keilann as if she hadn't heard her correctly. Besides reminiscing about Gram's fry bread or camping trips in the north woods, she never really talked about her years growing up on the reservation. Keilann herself was taken aback by the words that just seemed to tumble out of her mouth.

Her mother hesitated. "Keilann, I don't think this is the time..." She stopped short. Her shoulders sagged an inch, as if weighed by a heavy burden. Her mother sighed. "I suppose I do. Yes."

Keilann leaned forward.

"Then why didn't you stay?" She had been waiting to ask her mother this question for a long, long time. Her mom had always avoided the subject, talking instead of her college years and the day she had met Keilann's father.

For a few minutes the only sounds in the car were the metallic click of the tracks, pierced now and again by a shrill blare of the train whistle. Someone a few rows ahead coughed.

"You've seen life on the Rez, *Akiwiin*," Her mom began slowly, emphasizing Keilann's first name. "In many, many ways, it's much better than when I was growing up. But its two biggest problems will always be there, feeding off of one another like parasites: poverty and alcohol. Poor families who couldn't pay to keep the heat on in the dead of winter could still always afford a cheap bottle of whiskey. It's everywhere, people self-medicating life at the bottom of a bottle. My parents never touched so much as a beer in all of their lives, and made sure that I didn't. But there were so many who weren't as lucky."

Her voice wavered and broke off. She had never spoken of her childhood like this before. Most of the time, Keilann's mother had told her children stories about things like dancing in her first jingle dress or harvesting wild rice in the traditional way. Keilann and her sister had only ever seen the parts of the Rez their mother had wanted them to see. This was a completely different world.

When her mom spoke again, her voice was just loud enough to hear over the clacking wheels.

"Back then, most white people didn't understand what cultural differences were.

We weren't welcome in their society, and they weren't welcome in ours. Some stores refused to let us in, yelling at our backs that all Indians were thieves—as if we were the ones who stole everything from them and not the other way around."

A bitter taste stung the back of Keilann's mouth and an ugly feeling sank in her stomach. For the first time in her life, she was disgusted that her father was white.

"Most of my friends either dropped out or got pregnant or married, or all three. I wanted more, so I left."

"Was it hard?"

"Yes, it was." She was quiet for a moment. "Still is."

The train clattered on, winding through the bright sunshine. The warm shaft of yellow light shifted and Keilann was enveloped by a cold, thin shadow.

"I didn't know."

Her mom smiled. It was so kind and sad that it cracked Keilann's heart. She had never loved her mother so much as she did that moment.

"It's not the sort of thing people want to hear, but you're old enough now to understand that the ugly things are usually the ones you need to know the most. Her mother's eyes flicked to the window. "We're nearly there."

Keilann hadn't even noticed that the train had slowed to a sluggish crawl. While they were talking, suburbs had given way to stately granite and glass buildings that rose in endless succession as far as she could see. Her mother packed her teaching materials meticulously, filling in every niche of her bag with careful precision. Keilann watched her mother, feeling like she was seeing her for the very first time. She had always taken her mom's calm, indomitable personality for granted. What else did Keilann not know about her mother?

Her mom bent down and as if she could sense what Keilann was feeling, squeezed her shoulder and helped her to her feet.

"Come on," she said. "We've got a bit of a walk, and you can tell me all about what you and Ben have been up to."

Keilann bit the inside of her cheek and switched the subject, marveling at the city around her. It wasn't hard to believe. The train stop was in the very heart of the old town, surrounding mother and daughter with architectural gems wherever they looked. The warm sun bathed Aberdeen in a drowsy light, reflecting off of the granite masonry and making the city shine like silver.

Though the buildings were ancient by American standards, the thick congestion of noise and traffic was wholly modern. People rushed by in colorful blurs of cars, buses, and trains or were lost in the crowded sidewalks. One-by-one, the worries she had been carrying with her from Mary Arden slipped lightly from her shoulders. What did it matter that Ben had kissed her? Who would care if Connor despised her? She was back where she belonged.

They turned a sudden corner and were faced by a wide expanse of lush green lawn dotted with stunted urban trees and crisscrossed with paved footpaths: the university's main campus. Setting across the lawn after her mother, Keilann stared at the imposing halls and harassed-looking students coming and going in every direction. Here and there a few students lounged under trees, their eyes flicking across textbook pages at inhuman speed.

Keilann's mother guided her through the web of buildings, pointing out ones of historical significance and where the best cafeteria was located. They seemed to walk for at least ten minutes before her mother began moving toward a cluster of towering, glass-covered buildings at the far end of campus. Keilann passed under a heavy Gothic archway, slipped past four pairs of double-doors, and was transported into the academic world. The chaotic mingling of city noises and smells was snuffed, and Keilann had the distinct impression that she had just entered a dimly-lit cave. The air felt about ten degrees cooler. Her skin prickled at the sudden change in temperature. It took several seconds for her eyes to adjust. She could just make out a lobby of heavy, dark-paneled wood and several low-lying couches before her mom whisked her toward a large stairwell tucked off to one side.

Once out of the gloom of the lower levels the walls changed to floor-to-ceiling windows, offering a breath-taking view of the campus. On and on they climbed, and Keilann began to wonder why her mother hadn't bothered to take the elevator. Though she was not averse to taking on the streets of Aberdeen by foot, climbing up six flights of stairs was another matter. By the time they reached the floor labeled "Faculty Offices," sweat was beading under Keilann's arms, her breath coming in short, labored puffs.

Keilann's mom flashed a smile and her faculty I.D. badge at the bored student intern behind the reception desk and strolled down a long, twisting corridor of identical doors. They were tall and narrow, each with its own room number and name placard stamped on the front in white block letters. Most had been personalized with posters, flyers advertising various student clubs, or class schedules taped underneath.

Finally, her mother stopped and rummaged for her keys before a door whose only decoration was a smart new name placard that read "NAMID DOUGLAS, ASSOCIATE PROFESSOR." With a discontented squeal, the door swung open.

Despite the unseasonably balmy weather outside, a blast of cold air leapt out to chill Keilann. The office, like the door, was almost completely bare. Rows and rows of built-in bookshelves stared at her like empty eye-sockets, their only occupants a sad pile of six or seven flimsy pamphlets. A large metal desk seemed to hover uncertainly on the glaring white tile floor, its polished surface broken only by the cold presence of a sleek laptop the university assigned to each of its staff members. Gone were her mother's customary stacks of papers and array of student sculptures and paintings she had collected over years of teaching. The only evidence that someone was using the room were several musty cardboard boxes that sat on the floor in the far corner, a light coat of dust covering her mother's name scrawled in black permanent marker. On the windowsill, a single potted plant was dying, its papery leaves brown and curled. Stuck in the cracked dirt was a thin plastic trident bearing a garishly pink card where "WELCOME!" was printed in fading purple ink. Keilann's skin crawled as if she had walked into a room where someone had recently died.

Keilann's mom was busy digging through the top drawer of the desk, sliding a clipped bundle of papers into her briefcase.

"You can put your backpack over there," she instructed, gesturing to the corner already occupied with boxes. As if there wouldn't be room anywhere else.

Her mother swept a dark loop of hair from her eyes and glanced at her watch.

"We'd better get going before I'm late." Keilann scooped up a pen and notebook from her book bag, grateful for an excuse to leave. Her mom followed close behind, locking the door with a click behind her.

"Here," she said, handing a spare key to Keilann. "After you're done talking to Jana, you can go back to my office and work on your project until my class wraps up. I should be done around eight-thirty."

"Perfect," Keilann said. She took the key and shoved it in the pocket of her school jumper. The very thought of sitting in that empty office alone sent a cold shiver down her spine. Keilann rubbed the goosebumps from her arms, glancing around as her mom shuffled through her bag for a final cursory check.

Keilann's gaze washed listlessly past bland department meeting memos and study session flyers until they were drawn to an anomaly at the far end of the hall. A single door was resting slightly ajar, a soft rosy glow spilling out into the hall through the narrow crack. But it was the door itself that drew Keilann's attention. It was covered in—what was that? She took a few steps forward, squinting at the miniscule print of dozens of newspaper clippings.

Comic strips, Keilann realized with a start. She took another step forward, trying to get a better look at the menagerie of gaudy cartoons. *What kind of professor has comic strips pasted to their door?*

Keilann walked up to the door, scanning cartoons of men in ruffled collars and bejeweled tights holding skulls. William Shakespeare. Each and every comic strip had a punch line about or parody of one of Shakespeare's famous plays. Right above eyelevel, encased in a frame of bawdy Shakespearian jokes, was a small rectangular placard with the name "SHUJANA IMAN" engraved in bold block letters.

"Oh, good. It looks like Jana's all ready for us."

Keilann's mom skirted around her daughter and tapped out a light greeting on the narrow glass window—one of the only other places free of comic strips.

"Come in!" called a light, singsong-y voice.

Her mom pushed the door open, the beam of rosy light growing to envelop Keilann in its blush. The harsh fluorescent lights were mercifully shut off and the blinds on the windows drawn low, the soft ambient glow emanated instead from three decorative lamps strategically placed on the surrounding shelves. A young woman leaned far back in her desk chair, feet propped up on her desk, immersed in perusing a fat stack of papers in her hand. She was swathed in a flowing, black dress that cuffed tightly at her slender wrists, the long hem draped around the shins of her fitted leather boots. Her dark, heavy brows were currently rutted together in intense concentration, making it look like a fat, bushy caterpillar had come to rest just above her eyes. It was difficult to say what her hair looked like. All of it was neatly tucked away under a winding hijab that framed her face in gauzy black fabric embroidered with gold flowers.

She glanced up from her papers and pushed them aside at once, her solemn face breaking into a beautiful smile. Keilann couldn't help but stare. Her teeth were so straight and even that Fiona's were dim in comparison, the stainless white exaggerated by the deep olive tones of her skin.

"Right on time! I swear, if I had to read another one of those essays, I would've cracked." She sighed, rolling her eyes to the ceiling. "Undergrads. What do they teach them these days?"

She spoke in a high, clear voice with a very pronounced English accent that momentarily caught Keilann off-guard. Her accent wasn't as clipped or severe as the doctor's had been, however, her voice was so warm and welcoming that it melted any frost.

Keilann's mom gave her a sympathetic nod. "I know. I've got a whole class of freshman who think Donatello and Rafael are crime fighting turtles."

Jana shook her head, clicking her tongue disgustedly. "Disgraceful."

She spotted Keilann and jumped to her feet, another perfect smile blooming over her refined features. "Ah! And this must be your daughter!"

Small and very petite, Jana had a delicate look to her that was emphasized by the yards of fabric billowing with her movements. She only stood an inch or so taller than Keilann, but her eyes sparked with a vivacious tenacity that seemed to fill the entire cluttered room.

"It is wonderful to meet you at last," she continued cordially. "Your mother has told me so many good things about you and your sister. It delights me to help in your discovery of one of the Bard's greatest works."

Jana gave Keilann's free hand a hearty squeeze. She was very warm.

"Thank you so much for taking the time to see me, Professor Iman."

From behind her, Keilann could hear her mother shift impatiently in the doorway.

"Well, I've got to be off. I still need to set a few things up before class begins," she said, her eyes flicking back to her watch.

She turned to Keilann. "After you're done asking questions, you can work on my laptop. I've written the password down here." Her mom handed her a small slip of paper. Keilann took it without a glance and shoved it in the same pocket as the key. "Thanks again for doing this, Jana. I'll see you both in a bit."

With a final wave, Keilann's mom ducked out of sight, the rapid *click-click-click* of her heels fading out of earshot. There was a small, awkward pause. Keilann had never been the one to start conversations, and was slightly intimidated by the elegant, intellectual woman before her.

Sensing her uncertainty, Jana flashed Keilann a friendly grin, beckoning her inside.

"Come in, come in! Make yourself comfortable. I'll just move these." She gestured to a squashy orange armchair occupied by a small stack of *Othello* manuscripts. Jana plopped them onto the radiator and motioned for Keilann to sit down.

"Coffee?"

Keilann had only tried coffee once—and hated it—but it felt rude to refuse.

"Yes, please."

She tiptoed around obstacles of books and papers and sank into a tired-looking armchair in the far corner. As Jana puttered around with mugs and coffee grounds, Keilann tried to take in her surroundings. It was completely opposite of her mother's office in every way. Books stuffed every shelf, tumbling over each other and spilling onto her cluttered desk. Framed pictures of an attractive dark-skinned, smiling woman—also wearing a hijab in several photos—and two small boys took up any extra space. Several smaller pictures of the same woman acted as paperweights, lying atop mounds of essays or jutting from a spare bit of shelf that was obviously cleared as a spot of honor. Jana was behind the desk, wrestling with a battered percolator dangerously balanced on a stack of old coffee-stained art textbooks. The mess would've shocked Fiona. Keilann found it refreshing and inviting after her mother's office.

She leaned back in the cushions, relaxing for the first time that day. Maybe Jana would let her stay here to work.

The sound of Jana's voice refocused Keilann's attention.

"Do you take your coffee black?"

What other way was there?

"Umm...."

With a sweep of her arm, Jana cleared a section of the desk and placed a steaming mug before her. Keilann laced her stiff fingers—still chilled from her mother's icebox of an office—around the hot mug, taking a tentative first sip. Bitter, burnt coffee filled her mouth, coating her tongue with an acrid taste that lingered long after she had swallowed.

Jana filled her own mug and settled behind her desk, smiling broadly at Keilann.

"So, your mother tells me that you are attending Mary Arden Academy. How do you like it?"

The taste of the coffee was nothing compared to the thought of going back to school on Monday. Keilann gulped a hasty swig from her mug.

"Mmmmm," she grunted indistinctly, her mouth brimming with the disgusting liquid. She swallowed, forcing herself not to gag. "Mind if I take notes?" She opened her notebook, the spiral crackling as she flipped to an empty page.

"Not at all, not at all!" Jana exclaimed, waving her hand airily. "How else are you going to remember everything? Now. As I understand, you are doing a project on Lady Macbeth. Is that correct?"

Keilann was midway through a gulp of coffee when the hot liquid burnt her tongue.

"Yes." She coughed, sputtering coffee into her hand. "Sorry."

Jana flourished a wad of napkins from under a jumble of papers. Keilann cleared her throat, and forced herself to smile.

"Yes."

"Excellent. I did my dissertation for my master's on the very same character. Fascinating woman, isn't she?"

Keilann nodded stiffly.

You have no idea.

"Would you mind giving me a rough outline of what your project focus is? It'll help me organize my thoughts. Lady Macbeth is an incredibly complex character. I wrote about her as the blueprint of the modern woman for two-hundred pages, and I could've kept going," she chuckled, shaking her head. "Let's see if we can narrow it down a bit, shall we?"

Keilann launched into a rehearsed summary of how she wanted to incorporate the fictitious character and historical figure into one person, finding just where the truth ended and Shakespeare's imagination began.

Jana listened, steepling her fingers and touching them to her pursed lips.

"Ambitious," she nodded approvingly. "But I can see where you've run into trouble. Just how much have you been able to find on the historical Lady Macbeth?"

"Not much," Keilann admitted. "But I did find a name."

Jana nodded again.

"I ran into the exact problem while researching my thesis. Luckily for you, there are a few more sources on Gruoch than there used to be." Keilann flinched, her pencil jerking a dark streak across the empty page. It had only been the second time she had heard the name spoken aloud. She wasn't prepared to have it thrown in so casually.

Keep it together. Stop being so stupid. She covered her reaction by pretending to reach for her mug. Jana didn't seem to notice.

"Even luckier," she grinned, continuing without missing a beat, "is that you are meeting with someone who has read all of those sources. I was thinking of beginning with the basics: family, background, big life events. Then we can narrow down to specific details, and start discussing possible character interpretations."

Keilann leaned forward, her pencil poised at the ready. "That sounds perfect. I really can't thank you enough for how much you're helping me."

Once again, Jana waved away her thanks.

"It's my pleasure." She leaned back in her chair and propped her feet on her desk, exactly as Keilann had first seen her. "So let's see: the basics. Lady Macbeth was born *Gruoch ingen Boite*, the daughter of a Scottish prince. She was the granddaughter of King Kenneth III. From what we can piece together, it appears that she was her father's only living child.

"Of course," Jana snorted, "she could've very well had an army of sisters, but no one cared about girls. The only births worthy of recording were of sons. As there is no conclusive evidence of Boite producing a male heir, we have to speculate that Gruoch was the last direct descendant of Kenneth III. She couldn't inherit the throne herself, of course," Jana leaned forward, gesturing with her index finger. "But her husband could through her royal blood. So, even though Gruoch was born a useless girl, she still would have been a very marketable marriage pawn."

Keilann scribbled the words *only child, husband inherits throne*, and *pawn*. She looked up from her notes. "Have you ever found any information about Gruoch's mother?"

Jana shook her head, smiling sadly. "Nothing, but that's really not surprising. Gruoch's mother was neither a queen consort, nor did she bear her husband any living sons. There weren't any other reasons a court scribe would bother wasting ink on the life of a woman. Poor thing probably died in childbirth."

Without thinking, a dim memory stirred Keilann to speak. "She was sick."

Jana paused, the faraway look in her eyes replaced by a quizzical frown. Keilann cursed inwardly.

Why the hell did I say that?

"I mean," Keilann stammered. "She could've been sick. There were a lot of diseases and almost no real medicine back then, right?"

"It's entirely possible," Jana considered. Keilann squirmed under the look she was giving her from beneath those heavy, serious brows. "You're right about disease. She may've even been victim to the plague. But all of this is speculation," she shrugged, smiling again. "We'll never know for certain."

"Right. Sorry." Keilann mumbled, her face burning.

"Never apologize for having an opinion, dear," Jana chuckled. "I'm glad to see that you've done a bit of investigative researching of your own."

Keilann forced a limp smile, fighting to block the image of an unnaturally pale face wreathed in a burning halo of red. If only that were true, that she had seen it in a book instead of in her nightmares.

"That's about it as far as her family is concerned. Nothing of significance—historical significance, anyway—happens in Gruoch's life until her marriage to her cousin, Gille Coemgáin, sometime before 1032. Gille was a *Mormaer*, the Gaelic name for a lord," Jana clarified. "With power on both sides of the family, it was quite an advantageous match. A few months after the wedding, Gruoch was pregnant. All was going well until her husband was murdered."

Keilann's head jerked up from the note she was writing about *Mormaers*, her mouth open in surprise. She had never heard that part before. When Jana had said the name of Lady Macbeth's first husband, Keilann had simply assumed he died and she had remarried.

Jana laughed at the shock on her face.

"It's not that surprising. Some speculate that he was killed because of his close proximity to the throne. That is so commonplace in history, it's barely worth mentioning. No," Jana leaned forward, her eyes glinting in the soft light. "What is far more interesting is who murdered him and how.

"You see, no one was ever officially accused. There are no records of anyone claiming credit for the deed. Oh, there've been plenty of theories, but scholars generally narrow it down to two people. One of them—the more likely candidate—is Macbeth himself."

Keilann blinked, the meaning behind Jana's words slowly sinking in. "But that means…"

"That Gruoch's second husband was probably the murderer of her first? Exactly." Jana finished with a wicked grin.

Keilann shuddered. Maybe the cold-hearted villainess of Shakespeare's play wasn't so fictional after all. "How could she?"

Jana was shaking her head again.

"I don't think she had much choice in the matter. Back in those days, a woman was virtually powerless over her own fate, a widow even more so. And a pregnant widow… let's just say that it may have been her only option. Besides, it was Gruoch's own father who orchestrated the match."

"But why would he force his daughter to marry the man who murdered his own son-in-law?"

"Same reason he forced her to marry Gille. For power," Jana shrugged. "Macbeth was also of royal blood, a descendant from Kenneth III's brother. Uniting the two branches of the family tree meant having a stronger legitimate claim to the throne."

"What happened to Gru—to Lady Macbeth's baby?" Keilann asked, not sure if she really wanted to know the answer.

"Now that's where this gets interesting," Jana said, rubbing her hands together excitedly. "Macbeth raised the baby as his own son. He even made the boy heir to the throne."

"Why?"

"No one really knows. Some say that raising the baby as his own proves Macbeth was innocent of Gille's murder, that he married Gruoch because she was the widow of an ally and a kinsman. But I say—" Jana grinned wolfishly. "—I say that Macbeth married the widow of a conquered enemy. There's just too much motive for him to have kept his hands clean. You see, when Macbeth was still a child, his father had been viciously slaughtered by one of his own nephews. Can you hazard a guess at who that nephew could've been?"

"You don't mean this guy," Keilann struggled to pronounce the Gaelic. "Gill-ee Coom-gan?"

Jana nodded.

"So Lady Macbeth ended up marrying two murderers?" Her head spun at the thought. How could she ever have felt safe?

"Looks like it. I think that when Macbeth got old enough, he hunted down his cousin and didn't just kill him, he got revenge. It was the manner in which Gille was killed that gives it away, really. The man wasn't just stabbed in the back or killed in the heat of battle. No, whoever murdered him planned it so he suffered as much as possible before he died.

"Macbeth summoned an army and rode to his cousin's lands, surrounding him and a measly force of only fifty men. Instead of swiftly dispatching the lot, Macbeth ordered his army to capture them and corral his cousin and his men into a small tower. He locked them in, barred the door, and placed his men around the perimeter so none could escape. Then, he lit the tower on fire."

The office disappeared.

Keilann could feel the heat of the fire from his eyes, blackened flesh peeling from bone, the charred slit of a mouth opening to scream. A scream that haunted her nights, the cry she had fought so hard to forget.

"Macbeth sat on his horse just outside the tower, watching more than fifty men die in agony, listening to the sound of his revenge: the sound of Coemgáin burning alive."

The door clicked shut behind her, and Keilann was alone.

She stood in the middle of her mother's empty office, her hand shaking as she wiped the clammy sweat from her brow. The notebook hung limply from her left hand, filled with a scrawl of names and dates that she didn't remember writing. Keilann vaguely recalled Jana droning casually on about character interpretation. Her body had gone into automatic pilot. Her hand took notes, her mouth smiled. She even heard her own voice thanking Jana for her time.

"Are you sure you wouldn't want to stay in here and work?" Jana had offered kindly. "I've got plenty of coffee, and that armchair is all yours."

Jana was really saying that she knew her mom's office, with its one disintegrating swivel chair, was little better than an unused store room. She was offering an excuse to stay, just as Keilann had been hoping.

"Thank you, but I...."

I need to get out of here. I need to be alone.

The warm, welcoming color of the office was suddenly too loud, the soft ambient light blindingly harsh and bright. The air in her lungs felt stale and heavy. She needed to think, needed to breathe.

"I'd like to check out the library, see if I can pick up any of the sources you referenced," she lied quickly, holding up the brief list Jana had dictated to her.

Jana beamed and grasped her hand heartily. The warm touch of human skin made Keilann imagine the charred smell of flesh, skin peeling from bone in thin burnt strips. She had swallowed her vomit and stretched her lips back from her teeth, hoping it would pass as a smile.

Once Keilann was finally alone in her mother's office, a sickening wave of nausea washed over her. She swayed on the spot, her head feeling hot and feverish. She flung the notebook aside and pressed the cold palms of her hands to her eyes. The spiral landed with a pathetic, hollow *thwap* on the tile and all was silent.

Keilann listened to the ragged sound of her breath, trying to ignore the nausea, her mind spinning out of control. First, the howled name from a dream had broken the bonds of reason and become a real person—two people, if the last encounter with the red-haired girl hadn't been just another nightmare. Keilann could handle a name. She could explain that the harmless coincidence, though highly unlikely and intriguing, was nothing more than a coincidence. It could simply be a popular or ancient family name like Ben's, one she could've heard anywhere.

But this was different. How could she explain him? Keilann couldn't count the number of times she had seen him die, haunted by the scream that would never leave her dreams, the scream of a man burning alive. The scream of Gille Coemgáin.

No! That's impossible!

His murder took place hundreds of years ago. It had nothing to do with her. A flash of coppery hair streaked across her mind. The red-haired girl, Gruoch, scowled at her from the darkness.

It's not possible.

Why—how—were pieces of this woman's past haunting Keilann in the present? Something wasn't right and however she tried to pretend otherwise, things just weren't adding up. There were too many coincidences. The burning man, Gruoch, the vivid dreams of a dying woman, the girl in the stone circle—what did they mean?

Keilann dropped her hands and stared at the floor. She was suddenly exhausted, panic and energy ebbing from her body like blood from an open wound. She surveyed the bleak room for a place to sit, to rest for just a moment.

The chair tucked behind her mother's desk sat at an unbalanced, lopsided angle, as if it had simply given up. She stumbled to the windows, clutching at a dusty hanging cord. With fumbling fingers, Keilann yanked the shutters closed, the last ray of light snuffed as the slender shades snapped into place. The room plunged into a thick darkness. Keilann felt her way across the empty space to the desk and sank into the bony chair with a groan.

She lay with her flushed cheek pressed to the cold metal desk, eyes wide and staring. Keilann was grateful for the dark and chill of the barren office. Here, the searing heat and eerie light of the burning man's fire could not touch her. She was safe.

The racing of her mind began to slow, the cool water of reason dousing the flames of her imagination. Even before she had decided upon taking action, Keilann knew what she had to do. It would be the only way to stop the nightmares, the terrifying coincidences, the feeling of being watched. No matter how she looked at it, there was only one option to truly take back her life and end this nonsense once and for all. Though the thought made her skin prickle, she forced back the feeling of dread and clenched her jaw.

Keilann had to talk to Gruoch.

17

Keilann's mind slammed back into place, waking her with a sharp, nauseating lurch. Her heart raced. She lay awake with her eyes closed, groggily sinking into consciousness. A jangle of sounds clanged and echoed. Lights flickered like flames in the distance, yet they were all around her, close enough to burn.

Keilann kept her eyes closed, trying to keep the details of her dream from slithering through her fingers. The harder she tried to trap them, the quicker they slipped away. She gave up and yawned. Keilann nestled deeper into the downy warmth of her sun-drenched comforter. Stretching lazily, she grinned and rolled over. It was Saturday. No alarms, no gossip, no school, no Connor.

No Ben.

Her heart contracted and she buried her face into her pillow at the thought of his name. The kiss...is that what she was worried about? A prick of anxiety rippled through her to the ends of her fingertips. Why? What was she forgetting? Her eyes shot open, the fear and panic of last night rushed back to her in a dizzying wave.

The bed was suddenly itchy and hot. Keilann threw off the coverlet and sat-up too quickly. Blood rushed from her head, making it swim painfully. Keilann swung her legs over the edge of the bed and pushed off on wobbly legs. Clutching the door knob for support, she staggered out into the hallway.

"Gah! Son of a—!"

Keilann hopped in place, holding her throbbing toe where it had struck the corner of a breakfast tray, sending it sliding down the hall, scattering puddles of milky tea and sticky globs of jam in its wake.

"What the hell?"

She yelled out a string of curses that echoed blankly through the empty corridor. Keilann paused mid-hop and held her breath. She cocked her head, expecting to hear footsteps or a shouted warning to watch her language. But Keilann stood alone in her doorway, listening to the sounds of an empty house. Letting go of her foot, she bent down to examine the ruined breakfast; the tea was stone cold, the toast limp and soggy.

This must've been here for hours. Her eyes widened. How late had she slept in? After what she discovered yesterday, Keilann had decided to take one extra sleeping pill last night. A dull throb ached behind her eyes and her throat was dry and scratchy. *I'm never doing that again.*

Mopping up what she could with a bathroom towel, Keilann scooped up the tray and hobbled down to the kitchen in search of an actual breakfast. The vacant house echoed with her awkward steps as if the sound was amplified to make up for the lack of inhabitants. Setting the tray down next to the sink, Keilann scanned the kitchen table and there, just as she had suspected, was a note written in her mother's sloping handwriting. She snatched a glass from the cabinet and filled it with cool water from the tap. Keilann threw it back, gulping and slurping as if she had been running a marathon. Quickly draining the first glass with a satisfied gasp, she refilled it and shuffled over to the large table, the paper fluttering slightly as she reached for it.

Gone into town to do some Christmas shopping.

She started, blinking at the words. Christmas shopping? But it was only...she began ticking off the days on her fingers. Five weeks. She still had five weeks. With the unseasonably warm weather still greening the countryside, Keilann had forgotten about the approaching season. She glanced out the front windows: wilting grass patched here and there with brown as far as the eye could see. Christmas in Chicago had always been filled with dazzling lights, sharp winds, and driving snowstorms. Keilann looked at the sky hopefully, but the fat black clouds looming on the horizon promised nothing but more rain. She sighed and turned away from the window.

Dad has an all day seminar, so we won't be back until late. You seemed so tired this morning that we didn't want to wake you. Left breakfast outside your door. Hope you didn't trip over it

Keilann winced, her toe still throbbing.

Rest—her mom underlined this with several thick strokes of pen—*don't worry about anything else. Should be taking the 5:15 train home. Will call if plans change.*

So that was it. Keilann was really alone. She crumpled the paper into a wad and tossed it in the bin.

Keilann calculated as she made her way through the living room. *That means they won't be home until six at the earliest.* She paused at the French doors, her eyes trailing to where the grassy lawn was devoured by a dense wall of pines.

Plenty of time.

Though determined to set her plan in motion, Keilann found herself meandering around the house. She whiled away the better part of an hour picking through a bowl of cold, slightly stale, cereal. After the meal, she stripped down and allowed herself a long, hot shower. Keilann cranked the temperature dial as far as it could go, letting the scalding water splash against her skin, her mind reviewing the sparse details of her plan. By the time she was toweling off, Keilann was beginning to feel slightly foolish.

How are you going to find her? You don't know where she lives. You might not even know her real name. You're just expecting her to be there, waiting for you, a snide little voice criticized.

Keilann had no defense against this sound argument. She just had a feeling the girl would be there or would find her. She counted on the fact that whenever she had ventured to the stone circle, something usually happened. The only time the girl hadn't been involved was the day she had met Ben. Thinking of him brought a fresh flush to her face. Would it be so bad to find him in the circle? Keilann ran a comb through her hair, imagining what it would feel like if it were Ben's fingers instead. With a sharp jolt of pain, the comb's teeth were hopelessly tangled in a large snarl, and the daydream was cut short.

Besides, the voice continued after Keilann had regained control of her brush, *say you do find the girl there. Then what? How will talking to her solve anything?*

It had a point, there. In all actuality, she would end up embarrassing herself, if the girl showed up at all. Keilann hadn't figured exactly what she would say to the girl—to Gruoch—but she was tired of riddles and obscurity. If she could just talk to her, just know that Gruoch was a normal, ordinary girl instead of....

Instead of what? The voice broke in, sounding more than a little exasperated. *What else would she be? You shouldn't need proof that she's not some nightmare come to life. That's insane. You do know that, right?*

Keilann scowled at her reflection. Insane or not, she had to go. She needed answers, and this was the only way to get them. Who knows? They could end up getting on and becoming friends.

Yeah, good luck there, the voice snorted. *You can't even win an argument with yourself.*

By two o'clock, Keilann had run out of excuses. She had procrastinated as much as she could afford. If she was serious about meeting Gruoch, then it was time to go. Keilann wanted to give herself a buffer of time before her parents returned, just in case she had to wait for a few hours. Despite her resolute confidence, a gnawing doubt made her hesitate. What if the girl didn't show up after all? Or worse, what if she did and all of Keilann's questions were answered, but the nightmares kept going? How long could she stand them: a month, six months, a year more of horror and death every night? What if they never went away?

Keilann shivered.

That won't happen. They'll stop or....

Keilann took one last look at her reflection, her features marred by fleshy purple shadows and weary grey lines.

"Or I really am crazy," she whispered.

It was already beginning to rain by the time Keilann shrugged on a light jacket, the fat drops tinkling softly on the glass as she bolted the French doors behind her. She threw a wary glance at the sky and slogged through the spongy grass, her trainers kicking up mud and water.

She crossed under the trees and was swallowed by the forest, the mist stretching over the path at random intervals like a ghostly warning. She walked on, listening to the squelch of her shoes sucking in the mud, her mouth set at a thin, grim line. Once or twice, the path was lost in a dense patch of fog, droplets clinging to her face like sweat. If the way wasn't so familiar already, she might have been in danger of getting lost. But Keilann trudged on, despite a bitter disappointment sinking deeper with every boggy step.

Who would be out for a walk today? She had as much chance of meeting Macbeth himself as that red-haired girl, never mind Ben. More than once, she was close to turning back, taking her mother's advice and using her time to rest. Knowing that would've been the smart thing to do, Keilann pushed the tantalizing idea out of her way and picked up her pace.

The fog grew thicker and more opaque, as if trapped by the gnarled branches around her. There were very few sounds, the tension broken by unseen twigs snapping and the erratic shuffles of a foraging squirrel. Other than that, the forest was asleep. Each muffled noise made Keilann jump out of her skin with anxiety, her imagination full of invisible monstrosities. She forced herself to keep her eyes on the path, trying not to picture knobby, contorted hands reaching out for her, itching to drag her away into the fog.

What was that?

A finger trailed up her spine. Her skin prickled with a thousand red-hot needles. Keilann spun around. Her hands flailed out and smacked against an overhanging branch, it's thin, thorny arm adorned with a bright tuft of wool from where it had caught on her sweater. A burst of relieved laughter spilled out of Keilann, but was quickly cut short. The sound was far too loud, reverberating endlessly into the silent wood. She stood for a few more heartbeats, her feet unwilling to move forward but unable to go back. She peered into the fog, frantic for it to clear. It made her feel unwelcome and watched.

Finally, chilled with a fine glaze of cold sweat and rain, Keilann knew she had to move. Turning her back to the creeping mist, she splashed down the path at a brisk jog.

It can't be too much longer.

Doubt began to nibble away at her resolve. She should have been there by now. Maybe the fog was slowing her down more than she had realized. Though her lungs were already stinging, Keilann picked up the pace a bit more.

Just a bit farther.

Dark shadows of trees glowered at her, the mist distorting their trunks. Keilann frowned. There was something so familiar...hadn't she done this before? Without warning, the dream flashed before her eyes. Racing past silent, black forms. Stumbling through the darkness. Smoke in her lungs. A thick grey cloud closing in around her.

Keilann was at a full-on sprint now, her legs driven by the unbidden images. She tried to blot them from her mind, praying that the circle was close, not sure whether she even wanted to get there anymore, when a hulking stone materialized, looming directly in her path.

Keilann skidded to a halt about a foot from the rock, spattering its base with mud. She never saw it coming, the telltale minefield of jagged stone hidden beneath a deadly cloak of mist. Scanning the ground around her feet cautiously, she could make out about a half-dozen boulders slicing through the low-hanging fog like icebergs. Keilann winced. Her hand flinched instinctively to her shin where the thin white scars were just beginning to fade. Only sheer luck had steered her away from collecting more scars today. A wet, luke-warm breeze panted through the clearing, giving Keilann the disturbing impression that a giant, hairy beast was breathing down her neck. The vapor stirred and parted. Seven stones melted from the mist like shadows, their skin black and glistening. Crowned by straggles of wispy vapor, the stones looked like a group of hunched old crones huddled together against the cold, their gossiping voices a quiet murmur of rain dripping onto dead leaves.

Keilann stood awkwardly on the edge of the circle, biting her lip. She had the strange sensation that she had barged into a room full of people who, noticing her intrusion, had stopped their conversation. The last word still hung in the air, but she had just missed it. For no reason at all, Keilann had the distinct feeling that they had been talking about her. She stared warily at the edge of the circle. An odd quiver ran down her spine, whispering that the stones stared back.

Keilann's tongue flicked over her cracked lips, her throat like cotton.

"Hello," she said in a small voice.

Almost instantly, a dull red flush bloomed in her cheeks and crept to the roots of her hair. *I'm talking to rocks now?* Keilann scowled. *What's wrong with me?*

Shame burned away her childish apprehension. Keilann held her head high and marched into the ancient stone circle, keeping her eyes trained on the central ring of tufty grass. Despite the damp chill, a warm glow of pride filled the hollow pit of embarrassment from moments before. She made it.

Now what?

Unfortunately, this was the end of Keilann's brilliant plan: get to the stone circle. She sighed and looked around at the soggy trees, the comforting scent of decaying leaves and damp earth heavy in the air. Why did the circle always feel different every time she visited? The first time, it had been electrified with energy and completely terrifying. When she had met Ben, it had been comforting and warm. The third time...could she count that? The ache of fear and loss still throbbed in her head when she thought of the red-haired girl running from the death of her mother.

But no, Keilann shook her head. That had been a dream.

This time, she could taste the tension hanging like a steel web between the stones. This time the forest felt like it was holding its breath, waiting for something to break. Slowly, she unzipped her windbreaker and laid it on the grass.

Well, she thought, settling down onto the makeshift blanket, *I'll wait, too.*

She drew her knees to her chest and hugged them, listening to the sounds of the wood. Once or twice, Keilann thought she heard human footsteps. Her heart nearly drowned out the sound, blood pounding in her ears like a rushing wave. She stiffened, not sure if she were more terrified of meeting the red-haired girl or Ben, when the furry flicker in the brush revealed a squirrel bounding just out of sight. Keilann released her breath and slouched back into the ground. And waited.

Minutes passed and flowed together until she had lost count of them. Her head slumped against her palm. Overhead, a thunderhead rolled over in its sleep, releasing a fresh bout of raindrops. The rain wriggled down Keilann's hair and slithered under the collar of her sweater leaving icy footprints on her skin. She yawned and stretched her stiff limbs, her toes and fingers numbed with cold. Her gaze strayed from rock to tree branch, vacantly passing over her surroundings while her mind traveled back to yesterday.

How could so much happen in twenty-four hours, when most days it felt like nothing ever would? She thought about the interview with Jana, but when she got to the reveal of the burning man, Keilann shut her eyes against the memory. She blotted the image from her thoughts and forced her mind onto another topic, one that could hold her attention and keep her anxiety in check.

A warm, smiling face came into focus, one with a gap-toothed, lopsided grin. But he wasn't grinning now. He was leaning closer, so close...Keilann's eyes popped open, her face warm just from the hint of a kiss. Adrenaline shot through her veins. Keilann could no longer sit still. She paced the length of the circle three times, her hands clasped firmly behind her back, hoping to wear down some of her nervous energy. After a few minutes, she hazarded a glance at her wristwatch. It must have been at least an hour since she set out.

"What?"

Shaking with cold, Keilann stared at the cracked watch face.

It's broken, she realized. *It must be.*

She lifted her wrist to her ear. Dead. Keilann lowered her arm as she gazed at the watch mournfully.

I knew it. There's no way I've only been here for fifteen minutes.

Keilann slunk back to her coat and curled into a ball. Her watch had never stopped working before. It had been a gift from her grandfather, and she cherished it. Even when she had given the watch it's one scar—when she had left it on the kitchen counter of their old Chicago apartment and, in a moment of carelessness, sent it smashing onto the stone floor—even then it had still kept ticking. The watch wasn't pretty or expensive, but it reminded Keilann of her grandpa: plain, steady, and reliable. She knew that it probably just needed new batteries, but the absence of its reassuring pulse against her skin made her feel vulnerable and alone. To her horror, Keilann's eyes began to burn, her vision stinging with tears.

What do I do now? She sniffed miserably into her sleeve.

There was no way of knowing how much time she had already wasted. An hour? More? Keilann gritted her teeth at the thought of the scene waiting for her if her parents returned from Aberdeen and found her missing. Again. She tilted her head to the sky, but the darkening clouds held no answers for her. How could she have thought such a stupid plan would amount to anything? Half of her Saturday was gone, and what had she accomplished? A stiff neck and all the right ingredients for a nasty cold. If she had listened to her mom she would be snuggled in the warmth of her own bed, sipping hot chocolate and working on homework. Maybe Keilann would've even found an excuse to call Ben and ask him for some notes she had missed. And then, who knows what would've happened between the two of them in the empty house? They could've been alone for hours.

Keilann wanted to scream at her own stupidity. She wanted to throw something just to have the satisfaction of seeing it smash and then grind the broken bits into dust.

"Gruoch!" she screamed at the dreary trees. "Where are you?"

She listened to her voice echo through the wood, her hands clenched into white-knuckled fists. In the back of her mind, Keilann knew she was acting irrationally and found she didn't care. It felt good to yell.

"Come on out, Gruoch. I'm not afraid of you."

Blood pounded behind Keilann's eyes, her head splitting and voice growing hoarse from yelling at the top of her lungs. She was tired of feeling stupid. Tired of being pushed around by someone who might not even exist, tired of everything. Keilann was going to go home and never think about these ugly, old rocks or the stupid red-haired git again. Keilann sucked in a last, deep breath of air and bellowed.

"Gruoch!"

Almost instantly, the air around her fizzed and sparked to life. It crackled with wild abandon, making the ends of Keilann's hair stand and hover above her head. If she had noticed, Keilann probably would've run for it.

"You hear me? You're nothing but a—"

Before Keilann could finish, the air around her had coiled like a tightened spring and lashed out. Fueled by her unbridled emotions, the force of the release felt like an invisible fist had punched her in the stomach. She flew back, landing on her jacket with a painful thud. Stunned beyond words, she lay on her back, head whipping around. Shaken, Keilann tried to stand, but was instantly hit with a screaming wall of wind. It knocked her back on her butt, thrashing her hair about her face and threatening to send her flying once more.

Terrified of the sudden, inexplicable wind, Keilann scuttled back and hid in the hollow of one of the largest stones, its aged head bent over itself protectively. The wind roared like a freight train. Her jacket reared from the ground like a serpent and spiraled away. It was thrown into Keilann's face, the zipper catching on her cheek. She didn't feel the sting. She was too busy screaming. The sky, once a harmless, indecisive grey, had curdled to an inky black. Daylight was snuffed into darkness, and Keilann knew of only one thing that could cause such destruction. She had lived through several tornadoes back in the Midwest. But here?

She wound her arms around the stone, praying that she wouldn't be torn from it. The wind howled in her ears, carrying a deep growl of thunder. Keilann threw a panicked glance at the forest around her, expecting to see trees ripped up by the roots and thrown. What she saw instead made her arms slack and her muscles dissolve with fear.

The trees weren't moving.

Not a single branch or leaf stirred. It was as if the outside world was the same as she had left it and the cyclone was trapped in the circle.

Thunder boomed all around her. The earth quaked under Keilann's feet. She gripped the stone as her only lifeboat and squeezed her eyes shut.

Let it pass. Let it pass over me. Please, just let it leave, she begged.

The anger of the storm and thunder battered Keilann's ears, the wind so ferocious that it stole her breath. In her fear, she remembered the prayer her grandmother taught her when she was a small child. Focusing on the words, she could almost hear her Nokomis' voice rising like a sigh.

Gichi-manido wiidookawishin ji-mashkawiziyaan.

She repeated the prayer in her head over and over, the steady chant of her gram's gentle voice growing stronger, drowning out the storm. Keilann clung to the shred of hope, the words giving her strength. For the first time in years, she spoke them aloud, her tongue remembering the language she thought that she had lost long ago.

"*Gichi-manido wiidookawishin ji-mashkawiziyaan!*" she screamed into the wind.

As if on command, the storm died. Keilann's hair fell limp around her shoulders, and air returned to her starved lungs. For a few dizzying moments, the only sound she could hear was the banging of her heart as she lay almost pulverized against the stone.

Then, very slowly, Keilann opened her eyes.

*T*he smell of wood smoke was heavy in the air. Confused, Keilann tried to stand and shrieked in fear. The circle was gone.

Stillness. Silence, but different from before. Keilann unwound her arms from the rock and sat up. Her heart thumped in her ears and her head swam.

Where am I?

She squinted at the dimly lit space, but could make out only a few lumpy, disjointed shadows. Keilann twisted around. Blankets flowed around her feet and over the edge of the bed's dim outline. A soggy pillow was warped into odd bunches where her arms had hugged it tightly.

A pillow?

She was lying in a massive four-poster bed. Stone walls surrounded her, the room lit by the moon streaming through narrow windows along the wall. She could just make out a darkened fireplace, table and chairs, something that looked like a bear fur thrown on the floor, and an ornate dresser standing against the far end of the room.

Keilann's head spun. She tried to remember where she was supposed to be, what she had been doing. She stared in disbelief at the room around her. Something in her brain told her it wasn't right.

Where am I?

She froze. Slowly, Keilann raised her arm in the ghostly moonlight. It wasn't only pale, it was ivory. It was white.

It can't be. It *can't* be.

She grabbed a handful of her hair, which seemed to be pooled around her in impossibly long waves. She held it up in front of her face. Keilann screamed, throwing her own hair aside as if it could harm her.

Heavy footsteps clattered down the hall, and the huge wooden door next to the bed burst inward. Two men in what looked like renaissance costumes rushed to the bed, torches in one hand, glinting swords in the other.

"My lady!"

Keilann screamed again.

"Out of my way!" A stout woman in long robes with a messy brown braid thrown over her shoulder pushed her way past the guards. She sat right on the edge of the bed. "I'm here, my lady. Are you well? Shall I call for the physician?"

The woman's voice was kind and soothing, her round face flushed from running. She reached out a hand to stroke Keilann's hair. Keilann scooted as far back against the headboard as she could.

The woman frowned.

"My lady, did something happen to the baby?" She placed a hand on Keilann's stomach. Keilann gasped. Her stomach, which had never been flat, looked like a balloon. She put a shaking hand to her belly. It was hard, the skin stretched taut. She felt something move.

What's going on?

"A mirror," Keilann croaked. "Do you have a mirror? Please."

The woman nodded to the guard. He picked up a round piece of polished metal from one of the tables and knelt before the bed. Hands still shaking, she took the mirror from the man's gloved hands and held it up, afraid of what she might see. Staring back at her in the torchlight was the startled face of the red-haired girl.

Words failed her. She just stared, horrified and transfixed by the face in the mirror. The woman leaned in closer. Her clothes were scented with lavender or some other earthy flower, but it couldn't mask the smell of unwashed hair and body odor.

"My lady," she murmured just loud enough for Keilann to hear. "Was it the dream again?"

Keilann tore her eyes away from her reflection. She blinked at the pocked face of the woman, dazed.

"Dream?"

The woman threw a look over her shoulder at the guards. She leaned even closer, her face an inch from Keilann's.

"About the dark-haired girl in the stone circle?" Her voice was barely above a whisper. "Did you dream of the fey girl again?"

"Dark-haired girl?" Dark-haired girl! A face swam in her memory, skin the color of honey-eyed mead with hair as black as a raven's wing. She looked back down at the mirror now sitting on the bulge of her stomach, blinking at her milk-white complexion. Had it all been a dream? The stone circle from her childhood, the raging winds, the fear, it had seemed so real. She had been waiting for someone. Her brows furrowed. Another face surfaced, a boy's face, with blue eyes, auburn hair, and a lopsided smile. Who was he? She dropped her head in her hands and groaned. It felt like there were two people warring inside her. But who was she?

The woman seemed frightened. She grabbed Keilann by the shoulders.

"Gruoch?"

At the sound of her name, something shifted. The other warring half of her mind slipped away like a leaf in the current, and the world seemed to come back into focus. The light of realization transformed the shadows of the room. Her room. How could she have forgotten? Comforting outlines of familiar possessions surrounded her, but it was her best friend's face *that anchored the dizzy reeling in Gruoch's head. How could she have thought her a stranger?*

"I'm alright, Marjorie. It was just a nightmare."

Marjorie's face cleared. She put a hand over her heart, relieved.

"Leave us," *she said, turning to the guards. With another swift bow, the men were gone, closing the door behind them. As soon as they were gone, Marjorie grabbed Gruoch's cold hand in her sweaty one.* "What happened, my lady? I swear that when you woke you did not know me. You did not seem to know yourself."

Gruoch groaned and fell back onto the pillows, gathering the damp mess of sheets around her exposed shoulders. She closed her eyes, rubbing a hand across her swollen belly. The dreams had always gotten worse during a pregnancy, but this one....

"It was nothing," *she said with more cheer than she felt.* "Another nightmare. It passed. I'm fine," *she added. Marjorie was still looking at her as if she expected her friend to burst into flames.*

"If I were not a Christian woman, I would say the fey girl bewitched you. Who knows what she might have done to the baby?"

Gruoch tried to laugh it off, but it stuck in her throat.

Not the baby, she prayed. Please don't let me lose this one.

This one had survived so much longer than any of its siblings. She thought of the dream, of the fey girl, and a sudden chill of fear turned her spine to ice. It had felt so real, as if she had been drawn back to the home of her childhood. Back to the ring of seven stones where she had first met a dark, mysterious girl who had vanished when Gruoch tried to question her. She had lost her patience that day, and had dearly regretted it since. The fey were not quick to forgive.

Gruoch was so preoccupied within herself that she was deaf to the turmoil and upheaval without. At first, it was only a few distant shouts. The steady rumble of hurried steps and clip of hooves almost blended into the background of the night. Then there was shouting in the hall, and the heavy footfalls of the guards.

"What is it?" *Marjorie asked, wide-eyed.*

"Stay inside, my lady!" *one of the guards yelled through the door. Then their footsteps pounded down the hall and out of earshot.*

Gruoch's throat tightened.

"Trouble."

Despite Marjorie's protests, Gruoch threw off the coverlet and pushed herself out of bed. Waddling over to the nearest window with Marjorie fussing behind her, she braced herself against the stone and peered into the courtyard below.

She gasped.

Dozens of fiery pinpricks of light blazed in the darkness, casting a distorted shadow show of the scene on the stone walls. Men ran into each other, snatching gear, barking harsh orders over the scream of horses and sobbing women, the crush of people turning the courtyard below into madness. Gruoch's heart hammered in her chest. It leaped to her throat so quickly she was almost sick with the throbbing sense of foreboding in her stomach. Gruoch had no idea what was going on, but the fear and panic on the faces of the people was enough. The dream of an oncoming storm, the dark-skinned girl—had she been trying to warn her?

She dragged herself from the window.

"Marjorie, fetch my warmest cloak."

Marjorie gawked. "But, my lady! You cannot possibly go down there!"

Gruoch grabbed the cloak herself and threw it over her shoulders. Gawking and worrying wouldn't change what she had to do. And the first thing she had to do was get out of that room.

Grunting, she unbolted the heavy latch and threw the door open.

"What are you doing?" Marjorie screeched. "It isn't safe!"

Hand on her belly, Gruoch turned. Marjorie was the closest thing she had to a mother. She had been there when Gruoch's mother had died, when she was married off, and throughout her many miscarriages. She had always tried to protect her.

"I'm going to find my husband," Gruoch said calmly. "Wait here in case he comes looking for me."

Marjorie sputtered. "But—"

"Do as I say. I will return."

With that, Gruoch shut the door and heard the bolt slide into place. The hall was sparsely lit and gripped in a tense silence. No guards at their posts, no servants going about their nightly duties, no one. She hovered in the doorway, the unnatural quiet sending a chill warning prickling its way up her arms. Taking a deep breath, Gruoch gripped her cloak tighter around the bulge of her stomach and plunged into the stony darkness. Shadows tumbled around her, intensified by the dim rush lights, but Gruoch kept her eyes squinted down at the floor. She cautiously wound her way down flights of stairs, trying to ignore the squirming worm of fear that gnawed at her heart.

Rounding the last bend, Gruoch staggered into the main hall, dizzy and out of breath. It had been a while since she moved with such urgency. The oak doors had been flung open, distorted noise and light spilling over the chaos inside. Silhouettes rushed everywhere. No one screamed or shouted, but the dull tremor of panic was evident in every gesture.

Gruoch waddled past a huddle of men hoisting sacks of grain on their shoulders and finally stepped into the courtyard, her mind reeling. Here the noise and light were the worst— smoke from passing torches made her sensitive pregnant stomach somersault. People she barely knew grabbed her arm, twisting hard, their eyes wide in fear.

Why had they been woken in the middle of the night? What was happening? Gruoch coughed out smoke and shook her head, shrugging off their pleading hands. She did not know. Harsh orders of soldiers, cries of children and women mingled together.

Gruoch scanned the faces of the men. He was striding through the chaos as if immune to it, barking commands to his men while making his way to the stables. Her stomach unclenched. Now she would get some answers.

Seeing her, the man cursed.

"Woman, what the hell are you doing out here? Don't you know—?"

"I know nothing." Exhausted from her nightmares, the little patience Gruoch had was wearing dangerously thin.

"That," the man said slowly, his voice like ice, "is evident. Otherwise you would not be endangering our unborn child by exposing yourself to the foul night air."

"Husband," Gruoch said through gritted teeth. "I was woken by the chaos that you have not been able to control. Since no one can tell me what is going on, I thought to seek guidance from you. Is that not the duty of a wife?" She tried to keep the sarcasm from her voice.

"The duty of a wife is to obey, and so I command you: go inside." He turned, eager to be finished with her.

Gruoch switched tactics and reached for his arm. "Please," she said softly. "I am frightened. Will you not tell me what is happening or why you are leaving me?"

"He is coming," her husband said blankly.

He did not need to say the name. Gruoch's hand flew to her belly. Her stomach froze and dipped. One moment she was ice, the next blazing fire. Coming? Here?

A Dhia. Oh God. "How?"

Her husband barked out a short laugh. "The only way he could. With an army." The smile fell from his face, and he took Gruoch by the shoulders. "I am taking what men I have to protect our lands, but know this: he has trapped me well. I cannot muster more than fifty men in such little time."

His words sunk in. Her mouth opened and closed, but no words came out. He leaned closer to her. His voice dropped so only she could hear. "I have sent messengers to your father. If things go as expected, barricade inside until he can come for you."

Gruoch's throat was dry from the smoke, her tongue sticking to the roof of her mouth. She had to swallow hard before she could finally speak.

"What about—?"

"The child will be well cared for."

From behind her, a man called out. It was time to go. Her husband hesitated and kissed her cheek.

"Go inside."

Gruoch watched his back retreat, straight and proud as if he weren't heading for his death. The great doors were bolted, and an unnatural hush descended over the household. The hours ticked by as they huddled together in the damp safety of the keep. At times, Gruoch almost drifted off, but fear kept her alert. Fear of that horrible monster of a man, and fear of where her dreams would take her should she sleep. She held Marjorie's hand and prayed.

When her head lolled on her shoulders, Gruoch stood. She paced the room. Her feet soon ached. The stones pricked her heels like needles. Then she would sit again until her head dropped and started the whole wearisome process again.

So it went for hours.

The message came before dawn, the horizon rimmed with grey as if it too had kept watch through the night. Gruoch had fallen into a stupor, the face of the dark-skinned girl stained on the back of her eyelids. She was speaking, but Gruoch could not hear her voice. She leaned forward, trying to listen—and slipped off of her stool with a clatter. Bruised and embarrassed, she was just being hoisted to her feet when a bang echoed through the hall. The room froze, the men assisting her halted. All heads swiveled to the rattling doors.

Another bang, and then another.

One by one, the heads in the hall turned toward Gruoch. She stared back at them, realizing for the first time that she was in charge. Her face flushed and she straightened, shrugging the men off of her arms. The hall echoed with another knock, and the bones in her knees were suddenly changed to water.

Gruoch licked her lips and swallowed. Her throat felt like it was filled with dry, scratchy wool.

"Open it," she squeaked.

The heavy latch slid back with a thud, and the door creaked on its hinges. A narrow slip of a boy staggered through the entrance, doubled-over, wheezing and drenched in sweat, His small knuckles were red from knocking.

"They're...coming..." he panted, his hands on his knees.

The room went still.

"How many?" a woman asked from somewhere behind Gruoch.

The boy shook his head, gasping for air.

"And my husband?" Like her hands, her voice trembled.

He shook his head again, his tangled mop of white-blonde hair flopping on his forehead.

"What happened?" she asked.

"It was horrible!" he sobbed. "They were screaming. They wouldn't stop screaming! I ran as fast as I could. I thought he was going to kill me, too!"

Gruoch gripped the boy by his thin shoulders. "What happened? Was there a battle?"

The boy looked at her, tears and snot running white tracks down his grubby face. His eyes were wild with fear. "He took them and locked them in," the boy babbled. "He piled the *wood against the walls and burned them all. He burned everything. The smoke and the stink—" he shuddered. "They screamed. They still scream!"*

The boy collapsed in a heap. People rushed to help him, but Gruoch couldn't move. It was only when her palms felt wet that she realized how hard she'd clenched her hands. Her hands were red and slick with blood where her nails had bit into the skin. Her legs shook. The room swayed and tilted. Gruoch started walking. Marjorie called for her to stay, but she couldn't hear her. All she heard was the screaming in her head. Then, she ran.

She ran for her life. Men shouted from far away. Strange, rough voices. She heard a low rumble like a hundred snapping twigs. The boy's words came back in a rush.

"He burned them all. He burned everything."

Ash fell like snow outside. The delicate white embers littered the ground and caught in her hair. Coughing, Gruoch sucked in air, desperate to breathe. Her lungs were stabbed with ash and smoke. Her eyes burned. She tried to focus on the forest ahead to find a path, a way out. A large branch crashed to the ground behind her. Gruoch spun to see bright flames, the heat singing her face.

Run! Run! She heard her mother's voice in her head.

Gruoch lurched forward.

She stumbled forward, mud sucking at her legs, weeds piercing and tangling her feet. Too weak to struggle, she fell onto her knees—and into the river. She splashed into the current, scanning the riverbed for a stronghold—anything—and found a large boulder embedded in the hub of the current. Making her way to it was slow, for the current was swift at this time of year, and the weight of her belly and nightshift dragged. One wrong step and Gruoch would drown herself and the baby. She waded to the other side where the fire could not cross. Dragging herself through the mud, she flopped onto the opposite shore.

How long would it be until he found her? He was probably on his way. What would he do to a helpless widow and unborn child?

Gruoch could feel a cold steel sliding down her spine like quicksilver. She was not helpless. If he could murder her husband to avenge his father, then she could invoke the old covenant to save her child. Her husband had not been perfect, but he taught Gruoch how to survive. She was the widow of a defeated adversary, and his murderer had an honor-bound duty to protect her.

But would he honor it? How much honor could there be in a man who thinks nothing of burning his enemy alive along with fifty innocent men?

Help me, mother, Gruoch prayed.

She gripped the swell of her belly. She could do nothing to save those wretched men from their fate, but she would see that no more innocents were slaughtered that day. Gruoch would find a way to save her unborn child.

Or die trying.

Someone called her name from far away, but the syllables reached out like ripples in a pond, distorted and confused. She cocked her head to listen, but could barely hear over the bright crackle of flames trapped on the other side of the river. She strained her ears harder, but the noise only grew as if the whole forest was burning. A shiver ran up her spine, then another, her limbs jerking involuntarily with each chill.

Chill?

With a start, she realized that it wasn't the fire causing the unbearable noise. It was coming from inside of her own head. Her teeth were chattering. Her clothes, sodden and heavy, were clinging to her skin like a coating of ice.

I'm soaked from wading through the mud and water. I must look awful. She glanced down at herself to assess the damage. Her body was wreathed in fire and steam, rivulets of water evaporating from the heat of the flames. She opened her mouth to scream, but no sound would come.

Help! Help! She wanted to cry, but only a dry croak escaped her lips. *Where is everyone? Won't someone help me?*

Leaping onto her arms, angry red flames tangled themselves in her hair. Her head was burning, her cheeks and eyes flushed with fire, but still she couldn't stop herself from shivering. She beat at the hungry flames with her hands, her mind foggy from the smoke. Hadn't she been looking for someone, meeting someone? Or had she been running away?

Another chill shook down her spine, rattling through her ribcage so it became harder and harder to breathe. Was she burning or freezing to death? She felt like she was sinking into mud, her limbs growing heavier with the weight of the earth until she was certain she was being buried alive.

No! I'm still alive!

The flames ceased, and the world was black and quiet. Seconds or perhaps hours later, she was vaguely aware of moving. She was floating high above the forest. She could hear someone calling to her, but the trees hid him from view.

I'm here! She almost called out, but a warning flared in her mind. She had been running from someone. She hadn't wanted him to find her. She circled around the tree tops trying to catch a glimpse of him, spinning faster and faster until they melted together in a blurry mush of green. Her last thought was of a baby. Her baby.

I hope he's safe, she thought, but couldn't think why he wouldn't be. Before she could remember, her thoughts dissolved into sea foam and she let herself drift away on the tide.

Sound dribbled through a slit in the darkness.

Beep...beep...beep...

Keilann groaned and rolled over.

Why was her alarm going off? It couldn't be Monday already, could it? Dread tightened her chest as she swiftly recounted the days in her head. No, it was Saturday, only Saturday.

I must've forgotten to switch it off last night, she thought groggily.

Beep...beep...beep...

It didn't sound like her alarm clock.

Fiona, Keilann gritted her teeth.

She was always flitting in and out of the house. It wouldn't be the first time her alarm blared through the wall at blasphemously early hours. Keilann burrowed deeper into her blankets; a chill had settled into her bones overnight. Her plush, downy comforter seemed thinner and scratched against her face.

Why doesn't she shut that up? The beeping continued. Exasperated, she huffed and rolled over.

I'll have to do it myself.

In one clumsy motion, she threw the blankets from her and started to swing her legs over the edge of her bed and into something cool and unforgiving. Keilann gasped as shin collided with metal, her crushed nerves exploding with pain. Her leg jerked back. Instinctively, her hand shot forward to cradle the wound. Almost instantly, she drew it back, crying out at the sharp, stinging pinch on the inside of her wrist. Something was tugging at the back of her hand, like a weight.

Dazed, she looked around for the first time.

Her shin had struck against a thick metal rail, one on each side of the narrow white bed. The whole room was a gleaming white, sterile and silent except for the quiet beep of the machines that had woken her. They huddled around her, whirring, beeping and dripping clear liquids down long, snaking tubes. Dripping them into....

Keilann's eyes followed the tube as it curled under the bed rail, her stomach tightening. Slowly, she turned her hand over. The tube ended under a throbbing flap of skin, the cruel needle half-concealed by fat strips of white tape.

Keilann felt sick.

Wildly, she imagined ripping the thing out and throwing it to the floor. Then she had a thought that she couldn't explain, but filled her with an overwhelming terror. *What will it do to the baby?*

Impulsively, she put her hands to her stomach.

No! No, it can't be!

Fumbling with the awkward hospital gown, Keilann pulled up the fabric to expose her bare abdomen. Eyes wide in horror, she choked back a strangled moan.

She was empty. Her rounded flesh rolled over on itself, as if sagging from the loss that once swelled it with life.

It couldn't be....

Wait. It *couldn't* be.

She, Keilann, couldn't be pregnant. She never had been. So why...? She looked around the room again, her eyes truly seeing it for the first time. Keilann took in the machines, the cool white tiles, tubes, bed, the muffled squeak of shoes and monotone pages from the hall just outside the door.

A hospital, she felt as though she were coming out of a trance. *I'm in a hospital.*

And there, slumped in a chair next to her bed was an unmistakable and completely impossible figure that made her heart jig in her throat.

"Ben!" she croaked, her voice rusty from sleep.

The lanky limbs nearly jerked out of the cramped chair at the sound of his name. He lifted his head, groggily at first, and then snapped to attention. His hands gripped the worn armrests as he bolted upright.

"Keilann!" he gasped.

He leaned over into the light of a muted florescent lamp. The room was hushed in dark shadows, the window closed and curtained against the cold.

It must be night, she realized with a jolt.

The two of them sat in shocked silence, staring at each other.

Ben cleared his throat.

"Are we always goin' to meet like this?" he asked with a weak smile.

Keilann's brow furrowed. How *did* they meet? She had no memory of coming here. A bright orange blaze, a ravenous heat devouring her. Fire. She remembered fire all around her, *in* her, burning her eyes and arms.

Terrified of what she might see, Keilann held her hands up to the light. But there was nothing. No mark, no burn, not even the slightest red smudge. She was clean. Though she should have been relieved, the sight of her skin filled her with a deep, unshakable horror. Keilann knew that Ben watched her closely, but she couldn't stop staring at her hands.

"Honestly, if I knew ye were that desperate for my attention, I would've asked ye to come 'round," he tried again.

Keilann looked up at him. He had the same lopsided grin as always, but there was something else in his dark eyes that scared her. Ben was looking at her as if she were a wild animal who would explode or attack at the wrong move.

Her head spun. "What happened?"

Ben leaned forward, scooting his chair closer to the bed. "Yer in the hospital. Do ye remember?"

Keilann shook her head.

"Exhaustion is what the doctors say. I say stupidity. What the hell did ye mean, goin' out in the middle of a storm, an' when ye were already sick?" Ben cried, dropping his careful, cautious tones. His irritation, obvious concern, and blunt rudeness relieved her. That was familiar, at least.

Goin' out into a storm...bits and pieces floated back together.

"I was going to—I wanted to—" her brow knit in concentration.

"What, die? 'Cause ye damn near did. Ye were burnin' with fever when I got te ye."

"Fever?" She remembered burning, a hot white flame licking up and down her body. "What were you doing in the woods? My mom—" A bolt of fear shot down Keilann's spine. She was suddenly fully alert and upright, fear squeezing at her heart. "My parents!"

"Know everythin', calm down," he said, gently pushing her shoulder back toward the pillows. "I called them as soon as I got ye here. Yer da jess left to take Fiona home not ten minutes ago, and yer mum nipped down for a coffee. She's been sitting with ye all night."

Keilann stared at the darkened room, searching for a clock. All night. How long had she slept?

"How are you still here? Visiting hours must've ended ages ago."

Ben scratched his head, grinning sheepishly.

"Oh yeah, but, well, they only let family ride in the ambulance and I couldn't let ye go alone, so I sort of told them that I was yer brother."

Keilann gawked at him. The harsh light glared off of his pale skin and glinted red in his gingery hair.

"My brother?" she choked. "They bought that?"

Ben's grin widened.

"I was very persistent," he said wryly. "Once yer parents showed up, I let them in on it. They were so grateful I found ye that they insisted I stay."

"Don't they think it's a bit odd how you keep showing up?"

Ben shrugged. "As a matter of fact, so do I," he said with a slight frown.

"Ben, how did you find me? What were you doing out in the woods in such a horrible storm?" Keilann shuddered to remember it, the howling winds and driving rain. She had felt like Dorothy, chased by the merciless twister. Only Keilann hadn't landed in Oz.

The freezing water, the smoke and fire, the ashes and screams of the dead. Where had it taken her, and how did Ben bring her back?

Ben paused, his face creased in a puzzled frown.

"I dunno, but the storm was no' that bad. Jess a bit of rain and fog, really. I needed to get out of the house and went out for a stomp. I hadn' meant to go to the circle, but after so many years o' wanderin' around those woods, I guess it was jess my habit.

"I saw somethin' through the fog, somethin' lyin' in the center of the stones. I went slowly, thinkin' that it might be an animal. I didnae wan' to scare it off."

Keilann inhaled sharply. Had he seen the red-haired girl as well? But when he looked up at her, his face was lined with worry, not the astonishment or fear he should have been feeling.

"It was you, Keilann. I couldna believe it at firs'. I called yer name. I tried to wake ye, but when I touched yer face, ye were burnin' up with fever. I didnae wan' te pick ye up or drag ye. I was afraid I might hurt ye, but my damned phone never gets reception in the woods," he added bitterly. Keilann raised her eyebrows at the thought of stick thin Ben trying to carry her, but said nothing.

"Ye yelled at me when I touched ye."

Keilann gaped in horror. She had yelled at him?

Ben saw the look on her face.

"Well, not at me, exactly," he said. "Ye were delirious, ye didnae make sense. Ye kept yelling at people that weren' there."

Keilann buried her face in her hands, her eyes filling with embarrassed tears. "I'm so sorry."

Ben squeezed her shoulder. "Don' worry about it. Ye were sick. Don' think of it, I shouldna have told ye. I'm jess glad yer alrigh'."

"Why?" she moaned between her fingers. "Why do you even care? Why does this keep happening to me?"

Ben gave her shoulder another squeeze. He had no answer for her.

"I'm such a *freak*," she spat, hating every inch of skin, every roll of loose flesh.

"No," Ben said firmly. "Keilann, look at me. Ye are not a freak. Trust me, I've seen my fair share throughout my years at Mary Arden."

Despite herself, Keilann smiled.

"But why did ye go out there, Keilann? Why, when ye were already run down an' poorly?"

Bright images, the pungent smell of smoke, and spikes of inexplicable emotions tore rapid fire through her mind. She closed her eyes, trying to make sense of them.

"I was looking for...something," she finally murmured, opening her eyes.

"Was it worth it, then?"

Keilann shook her head, trying to hide the tears that she was too weary to fight. "I don't know."

Ben's eyes softened.

"Hey, the doctors say that ye have exhaustion. I'm guessing that means ye need rest."

Keilann slumped back into the bed. It somehow seemed more comfortable now. Rest. Sleep. Though she had just slept the day away, her eyes were hot and scratchy.

She heard Ben's chair scrape the floor as he stood, felt the bed compress under his weight as he bent over her. His lips were cool as they brushed her forehead.

Keilann's eyelids fluttered open in time to see his face close to hers, retreating back into the shadows. She grabbed Ben's hand, hugging his fingers to her chest. She was too tired to worry about being embarrassed or crossing lines. All Keilann knew is that she needed him close to her.

"Don't go," she pleaded, her words slurring drowsily.

Ben butted the chair against the railing as close as it would go, and slouched back into the position she had found him in.

"Wouldn't dream of it," he yawned.

The thin, soft skin of his knuckles rested under her fingers. She could feel the warmth of his hand radiating through the gown above her heart. The last sound she heard was the lullaby of his steady breathing, whispering through the air like a promise: *I'm here. I'm still here.*

It was the best sleep she'd had in months.

Keilann stared at her laptop, cursor poised at the top corner, the blank white page staring back. Her finger tapped out a light rhythm on the keys, keeping time with the blinking black bar.

Why haven't you written anything yet? it seemed to ask, the cursor's wink growing more accusatory with each passing second.

Keilann sighed. She scrolled the mouse up and down the page, stretched out her legs, grew stiff and crossed them again, got up and opened her bedroom window, re-arranged her pillows, closed the window, walked down to the kitchen to get a glass of water. When she finally looked at the monitor again, the page was still impossibly blank.

Pinching the bridge of her nose between thumb and forefinger, Keilann tried to rub away the dull throb behind her eyes. She shook out her hair and glanced over at the clock. She had been staring at her computer screen for over an hour.

This was getting ridiculous. She had to get something—anything—written. Hoping for a miraculous spurt of inspiration, Keilann snatched up the neon blue instructions from a towering pile of homework on her nightstand and scanned the list of requirements one last time:

1. Bring a *FRESH PERSPECTIVE* to the focus of your paper and *PERSUASIVELY ARGUE* why your topic is worth analyzing.
2. *EXPLORE* the deeper meaning behind the theme/character you have chosen.
3. *EXPLAIN* why the theme/character you have chosen is still relevant to today's society. What can society learn from it? Why should we still care about what your chosen topic says about human nature?

Keilann tossed the paper aside, slapping it back onto the disorderly stack of unfinished assignments beside her.

Twelve pages, the cursor blinked brightly on the untouched page, *twelve more pages.*

Bubbling with irritation and a slippery panic, Keilann folded her lap top with a firm click, shielding herself from the critical glare of the incomplete paper. No, it was worse than incomplete. At least the word incomplete implied that she had actually started it. She hadn't even typed her name yet.   Keilann leaned back, staring listlessly at the wintry grey soup outside her window. The sky looked just as she felt. The clouds looked more like limp mashed potatoes, stirred every once in a while by a half-hearted wind. When

Keilann had awoken in the hospital room Sunday morning, Ben had been gone. Gone home, her mother had said. His parents had come earlier to pick him up, insisting that Keilann needed to be with her family. In his place next to her bed, Keilann had found her mom reading a tattered paperback, just to keep herself awake. Her mother had pushed the chair back to its original place after Ben had left, erasing the closeness of the night before. When Keilann stirred, her mother's face lit up in a bright smile.

"Keilann!"

She threw aside her book, not bothering to mark her place. She kissed her daughter's forehead, the familiar gesture reminding her of another such kiss so powerfully that it made Keilann woozy as she sat up.

Her mom beamed for another moment before her face collapsed into a dark, livid frown. Trapped under her gaze, Keilann could feel the weight of her mother's anger, and worse, the hurt and fear that she had caused. What had it been like, Keilann wondered guiltily, to come home only to be told that your daughter had been rushed to the hospital? She picked at the thin cotton blanket, unable to meet her mother's eyes.

Why did she go outside? What was she thinking? Keilann had no answers, at least none that her mother would understand.

Or any sane person, really, she thought grimly. All Keilann could do was hang her head, apologize, and promise over and over that she would never do anything so stupid again in her entire life.

It would be an easy promise to keep. Or so she had thought.

After she had gone to the stone circle to confront Gruoch, something had changed inside of her. Keilann was different in a way she couldn't quite explain. She was no longer afraid of falling asleep. The very thought of taking sleeping pills now seemed ludicrous. The dreams used to terrify her but now they sparked only a deep curiosity, a need to understand where they came from and how these impossible people were connected with her.

There were many things Keilann couldn't explain. She had every right to be terrified of the red-haired girl, but she wasn't. She felt more connected to her than ever, and ached to know why. Every time she recalled a sudden flash of a dream or some small detail, Keilann would drag out an old notepad from her nightstand and scribble it all down before it slipped away again. So far, all she had was a jumble of strange notes that were nonsense at best.

Perhaps the dreams had lost part of their old fear because Keilann was not being forced to relive them night after night. After she'd come home from the hospital, the nightmares of the burning man and had ceased. Keilann had a feeling she wouldn't be dreaming of him again. Somehow she knew that she'd seen all she needed to see.

She still dreamed, but there was a benevolent quality to the dreams, softer and more pleading than alarming. It always began the same way: looming black shapes appearing like ghosts from the mist, stretching endlessly into darkness. It was impossible to tell where she was or how to find her way, but Keilann was never once afraid. In fact, she was inexplicably at ease, familiar with her surroundings as if she had been expecting to end up exactly where she was. Though the details were hazy and vague, Keilann knew she was heading somewhere important, somewhere she needed to be.

The trees were dark and ageless, charred by an ancient fire. Rough, blackened bark pulled away from trunks like curling hair. Here and there a burned out trunk stood like a used matchstick. But the scorch marks had begun to moss over, and beneath the peeling bark was the green of new growth. The hungry fire had blazed itself out years ago, and the forest was healing. She was in no danger walking among the trees.

Keilann never remembered hearing any sound, but a tugging at the back of her mind would always make her pause. She made herself be still, concentrating on the source of her summons.

Did a twig snap? Was someone calling her name from just behind that tree or miles away? Or was it in her head? She began weaving her way more purposefully through the maze of trunks and charcoal remains, following the sound that wasn't a sound at all. Then, peeking through the branches ahead, she would see a luminous silvery light beckoning her forward, pulsing like a heartbeat. She untangled herself from the last of the thinning trees, and there they were. The stones were waiting for her like old friends, the silver light surrounding them like halos. They hummed as she grew closer, a noise that reminded her of when she rubbed her finger along the rim of a wet glass. She could feel their song in the soles of her feet, vibrating up her bones. It was strong but somehow comforting, like a lullaby. The dream always ended when she finally found the stone circle, though Keilann would fight to stay asleep even as she felt herself waking. She knew that she was supposed to be at the stone circle for a reason, but never got to find out why.

Keilann snapped out of her reverie, shaking her head to dispel the humming from her ears. She had to focus. Gritting her teeth, she opened the laptop and refocused her eyes on the glaring computer screen, its page still staring expectantly. The notes from Jana sat unread beside her with the name *Gruoch* scattered across the paper like landmines. Keilann had an approved topic, she had the research, but she did not have the words. How could she write what she knew, or thought she knew, into an essay?

She settled instead on a harmless topic that would guarantee she stay well under the radar of Ms. Spark, muddling safely in the wash of mind-numbing, barely readable high school essays. She would write about the fictional character of Lady Macbeth and stay as far away from the truth as possible. Keilann picked up the notebook filled with Jana's notes, staring at the words for a few moments before closing the cover firmly and setting it aside. Her old copy of *Macbeth* sat waiting on the nightstand. Keilann would write an analysis of Shakespeare's Lady Macbeth, her ravenous ambition which ultimately led to her insanity and suicide, and figure out the dreams later.

Keilann frowned as she flipped through highlighted pages between Lady M's "unsex me" soliloquy and her guilty ravings as she slowly lost her mind. A grim caveat indeed for the women of Will's time: this is what happens when a woman tries to rule men. This is what happens when you forget your place.

Keilann snorted, propping the book open on her knees. *As if she actually had anything to do with it.*

From what Jana had revealed about her, the real woman behind Shakespeare's monster had very little choice in her own life decisions, much less those of a nation. Tossed about between two murdering husbands and a disappointed father, Gruoch probably stayed silent and out of the way as she was expected.

But what if she hadn't?

Keilann paused, her finger on the passage she had been searching for. What if she finally had stood up for herself, for what she believed in? A strange image flashed in Keilann's mind: a large-bellied, mud-stained figure clawing her way slowly, resolutely up a river bank with the flames of an old life blazing behind her. Keilann pressed her fingertips to her eyes and rubbed away the memory.

What was that about?

It seemed so familiar. Already the picture was fading. It was as if she had caught a glimpse of something bobbing on the surface of a lake, unable to get a real idea of what it was before it sunk back into the murky depths.

Three hours and five pages later, Keilann had an angry crick in her neck and the first half of a (mostly) passable term paper. This had been fairly easy writing. It had all been said before. She explained significant quotes from the play and copied what people who claimed to be PhDs on the Internet spouted about the corruption of human nature. Not exactly what Ms. Spark would consider a "fresh perspective," but at least it took up space.

Satisfied with her start and quickly losing motivation, Keilann hit "save," shoved the overheating computer from her lap, and stretched her cramped muscles. Her stomach squelched a raw, rumbling moan. She needed a break.

Snatching up her empty glass, Keilann arched her body in one last, luxurious stretch and plodded down the stairs. The slap of her bare feet on hardwood echoed in the empty house. It was Thursday, and Keilann would be alone for another few hours at least. She shuffled into the kitchen and began scavenging for snacks in the sparse cabinets. Pulling a face, she hastily shoved aside fiber bars and digestive biscuits in search of salty, satisfying junk food full of greasy carbohydrates. She opened a bag of cheese puffs and stood beside the sink stuffing handfuls in her mouth with an abandon that would appall her twig of a sister.

Brushing her hands on her jeans, Keilann crumpled the remains of the family size bag under her arm and tucked a package of fruit snacks with it to ensure a well-balanced lunch. Steeling what was left of her withering resolve, Keilann prepared for the hike back to her computer and unfinished essay.

She never made it as far as the first stair.

It was the light that distracted her, catching her eye as she rounded the bend in the hallway. A shower of gold flashes, dust motes dancing in and out of a sliver of pale winter sunlight: her parents' office door hung ajar. Keilann frowned, her body pausing half-turned toward the lonely flight of steps.

That was strange.

She was only going to close the door, but when Keilann caught sight of the neat rows of books just within, she was struck with a sudden inspiration. Her parents were both professors. Between the two of them, they had to own a Shakespearean text or two. Since Keilann was no longer using Jana's notes, her resources—which consisted mainly of lengthy *Macbeth* quotes and Wikipedia articles—could use a little padding.

The cheery, quiet warmth of the office drew her in. Keilann began wading through volumes of Chaucer, Woolf, Dickens, and Austen, methodically working her way through the history of English literature. At last she found an entire section on Shakespeare, picking out a heavily bound essay on his tragedies and another, slimmer book on Shakespearean heroines. Could Lady Macbeth be considered a heroine? Keilann nestled it alongside the cheese puffs.

Though she had found what she needed, Keilann hesitated to leave the warm office. What was the rush? She wouldn't be going back to school until next Monday, and that was still four days away. Keilann let her eyes linger over the shelves, drinking in the delicious smell of books, feeling glad for the first time that she was alone in the house with time to kill.

She almost missed it altogether, its nondescript spine faded and unimportant next to all the gilt lettering and leather jackets. But something in the title sparked Keilann's interest, and on a whim, she plucked it from the shelf and turned it over in her hands: *Aberdeen Architecture: A History in Stone*. She set her bags and books down on her dad's overflowing desk and began flipping idly through the dog-eared pages.

Keilann flicked back to the index and stopped dead. The very first category, labeled under prehistoric structural design: *Stone Circles, Early Architectural Wonders*. Without thinking, Keilann turned to the chapter.

She was greeted by a large, fold-out map, crisscrossed in squiggly blue and red highways that ran like arteries and veins through the white countryside. Fat purple dots were strewn everywhere, sometimes in thick clusters, sometimes scattered in lonely corners. Each was labeled with a number corresponding to a name and description on the back of the map. *Balkemback, Aikey Brae, Midmar Kirk, Strone Hill*, they marched on and on down the page, with strange names that almost sounded made-up.

Besides the map, the chapter was filled with tedious details of hypothetical construction diagrams and quality of stone. She could feel her eyes glazing over. Writing a paper couldn't be worse than this.

She was about to close the book, when a bold heading caught her attention: *Rituals and Burials.*

It is due mainly to the ritualistic nature of stone circles that many have become the center of myths and power struggles. The best example is in Lumphanan, where the famous battle between Macbethad and Malcom III took place in 1057. The stone monolith standing on the spot, known as Macbeth's Stone, is the site where he was believed to have been beheaded.

A hot rush of blood pounded in her ears, making Keilann lightheaded and slightly giddy. She flipped back to the map, but no, Lumphanan was miles away from where she lived. There was no way it was her stone circle. And even if it had been, why should that frighten her? She returned to the page, but the book had moved past Macbethad and onto a new topic.

Modern Mysticism

Stone circles have been long since believed to be portals of untapped, otherworldly energy. Visitors often report that stepping within the bounds of the circles causes immediate, at times violent, sickness, dizziness, and fainting spells. For those who consider the circles sacred spaces, these reported reactions are caused by intense energy currents channeled by the stones acting as conduits to the Otherworld. Modern pagans believe that the stone circles were purposely constructed where the veil between worlds is at its thinnest, allowing spiritual sustenance for those who seek it.

There are some circles, however, that even the most die-hard enthusiast will only reluctantly enter. These have often been the grisly sites of blood sacrifice. The dark history compels modern-day druids to avoid the "teeth of the Otherworld" as they are known, for fear of the ancient power that dwells within.

Normally, a paragraph like that would've elicited a snort and a roll of her eyes. Keilann's palms began to sweat.

Violent sickness, fainting, blood sacrifice—enough was enough. All at once, the room had lost its warmth and coziness. She snapped the binding closed and shoved the book back onto the shelf, knocking several of its neighbors loose. They thumped to the floor, their covers splayed like broken limbs, but she left them where they lay. Keilann grabbed the food she was no longer hungry for and pulled the door shut behind her.

She had just rounded on the staircase, her foot poised over the first step, when the front door suddenly clicked and muffled voices filled the hall. It was way too early for her parents to be home—what if they had come back early to check on her? Keilann's eyes widened. The books! She had left them sprawled on the floor!

Keilann swiveled on the spot, about to dash back, when a voice froze the blood in her muscles. A male voice, one she had hoped to never hear again. Barely able to move, she forced herself to peer around the corner and shrunk back into the shadows as if burned by the light.

It was him. He was here, in her house. Keilann's mind reeled in shock and fear. The dreams were nothing compared to the flesh and blood standing in her hallway. Panic welled in her throat, making it hard to breathe. How did he get in? What would he do to her now that she was alone? Keilann had seen too many horror movies to not think that he stood between her and the knives in the kitchen.

Helpless, she cowered, her body crawling with sweat. Childishly, she closed her eyes, but could hear his booming footsteps getting closer. He was going to find her. He was in the living room, turning toward the stairs. She couldn't stand it anymore, she had to see. Maybe she could surprise him, run up the stairs and lock herself in her room.

Keilann tensed, her muscles taut and ready to spring, when a slender, russet hand shot out from behind him, catching him by the shoulder.

"Not up there," a familiar voice said. "Let's just go on the couch."

Fiona's voice.

Keilann covered her mouth with her hand as her little sister turned the monster away from where she was hiding.

"Are we alone?"

His voice was a deep growl. Keilann willed her knees to stop shaking, to keep herself from buckling onto the floor.

Fiona nodded. She slid her arms around his broad neck, flashing him her most winning smile, the one she only used with boys: slow and coy, but devilish all at once. Then she moved in for the kill.

Keilann was rooted to the spot with no choice but to watch as her little sister wriggled closer and kissed Connor McBride.

21

Fiona broke the kiss off first, sliding her hand down Connor's chest with a wicked grin on her face. She took his hand and began leading him to the couch, her face alight. Keilann couldn't believe what she was seeing. Crouched in the shadows, her muscles stiff and burning, she watched her sister disappear behind the back edge of the new couch. She choked on the lump in her throat. Her eyes watered as she held back a cough.

Keilann was trapped. She couldn't run away, she couldn't speak up. The couch groaned under the weight of the two of them.

Keilann's knees shook. A wave of nausea swelled in her constricted throat. Couch cushions shifted. Someone was whispered. And then the unmistakable tear of a zipper.

Keilann gagged. She wanted to squeeze her eyes shut and slap both hands over her ears. How could this be happening right in front of her? Think! What could she do?

Cruuuunch.

Fiona's head shot up over the back of the couch, her perfect hair mussed, eyes wild.

A stabbing jolt of fear glued Keilann's feet to the floor. Barely daring to move her head, she looked down at the plastic bag in her arm. She had forgotten she was holding it. The bag crackled and squealed with every movement. Connor asked Fiona what was wrong and Keilann waited for his head to emerge beside her sister's.

Keilann inched back into the shadows. With an echoing bang, her heel collided with the lip of the staircase.

"What was that?" Fiona hissed. She jumped away from the couch. Her chest heaved as she hastily rearranged the wrenched collar of her shirt.

Connor was on his feet before she had finished tucking her shirt, and Keilann heard the zipper again. Another jolt like a hot electric current paralyzed her, but it was only the zip of his jacket.

"I thought you said your parents weren't home," he said, the familiar edge in his voice. Fiona didn't seem to notice his harsh tone. She cocked to the side, a frown on her face. "They're not." she said, shaking her head. "It's way too early to—"

Fiona's eyes widened, her whole body rigid.

"What is it?" Panic crept into Connor's voice this time, but Fiona wasn't listening. Her head jerked around to face the stairwell, glaring as if she could see Keilann through six inches of plaster. Keilann shrunk against the wall. What would Connor do if he found her there?

She gulped. What would Fiona do?

The last thing Keilann saw was the muscles in Fiona's jaw clenched and bulging. Then, her sister turned her back to the stairs, her movements taut and precise. Keilann felt her hairline prickle. Cold sweat leeched through her t-shirt and spread under her arms.

She knows.

Black spots popped and danced in front of her eyes before Keilann realized she was holding her breath.

"Maybe you should go." Fiona's voice was terse and cool, but Connor looked relieved.

He let Fiona lead him to the front door. They didn't linger in the front hall—*thank God*—Keilann let her breath out in a slow whoosh. The door clicked almost noiselessly behind them.

In the silence left behind, a rushing, pounding flooded Keilann's ears. She was still frozen to the spot like a thief caught in the act. Part of her wanted to sprint up the stairs two at a time and blare her music as high as it would go, pretending that she hadn't seen the hungry gleam in Connor's eye or heard the rustle of clothes as her little sister's hands fumbled with his jacket. The thought of what she almost witnessed—what she had, in all likelihood, merely postponed—literally made her skin crawl. Keilann wanted to blast scalding hot water on her body so she could shed it from her like a rotten orange peel. But she stayed.

The door creaked on its hinges, but only one set of footsteps echoed in the cold house. The hard heel of Fiona's wedges thumped down the hall in time with the pounding in Keilann's head and stopped just short of the couch. Neither of them spoke, though she could feel the cold anger radiating from the next room. The silence ballooned, punctuated only by Fiona's labored breathing and Keilann's thudding heartbeat, the plastic bag sweaty and slick in her hands.

"I know you're there. I know you saw."

Her voice was quiet, controlled, but it echoed as if she had screamed.

Keilann couldn't run away now, but she couldn't keep hiding. After a few seconds trickled by, a hot flush blossomed at the base of her neck. Keilann realized how foolish she must look and stumbled forward on numb legs.

Arms crossed, Fiona used every inch of her height advantage to glare down at Keilann as if she were an insect scuttling out from a rock.

"I can't believe you. You are so sick."

For one insane moment, Keilann felt like she had been in the wrong. She could've hung her head in shame. And then the numbness began to melt away from her tongue. Just picturing Connor McBride on top of her sister made her want to grab Fiona's shoulders and shake her until she saw what he really was.

Keilann drew herself up as tall as she could and glared back.

"How long has this been going on?"

Completely ignoring her sister's chilly tone, Fiona's face brightened as if a glowing light had been flicked on behind her eyes.

"Since after the first soccer match. Remember when I said I'd been out with friends afterwards? He tagged along and just stared at me all night. Couldn't take his eyes off me. I thought it was a little creepy at first, but he was so cute. As we were leaving he asked my friend about me. Can you imagine it? A senior interested in me?"

Keilann could imagine it. How Connor had charmed Fiona's innocent friend, easily getting the name he had hoped to hear: Fiona. Fiona Douglas.

"If anyone's sick around here, it sure the hell isn't me," Keilann muttered, angrier than she had thought. Angrier than she had been in a long time.

Fiona jerked back as if stung by the words, her arms uncrossing, mouth open in shock. "I'm not the one who was sneaking around, watching my sister and her boyfriend because I'm too pathetic to get some for myself!" she countered, her rising voice bitter.

Keilann ignored the jab. "Well, I'm not the one who was sneaking around when Mom and Dad were out of the house like a little—" She cut herself off. It wasn't Fiona's fault really, maybe she didn't know about Connor. He could've easily lied to her. If she could keep her voice even and her temper in check, maybe she could get through to her sister.

But Fiona's eyebrow had spiked at the unfinished sentence. Two spots of dark color rose in her cheeks, her eyes narrowed to slits.

"A what, Keilann?" she asked, her voice like ice. "Go ahead and say it. You're just jealous."

Keilann gaped. "Jealous? Are you crazy? Do you know what that moron has done to me all year?"

Fiona shrugged her thin shoulders. "I know that you liked him and he rejected you, so you started all of those fake rumors about him."

Keilann's head spun. She felt like Fiona had slammed her into the wall. Her mouth opened and closed, but she couldn't force the words to come out. "What did you—who told you that?" she croaked. But she already knew what the answer would be.

Fiona shot her a scornful glare. "Connor did. And he also told me the truth about those 'fight' rumors you and your friend Ben had going around. As if anyone would actually believe those."

Keilann lost it.

"That did happen! Ask anyone who was there. Connor McBride has been bullying me since I met him. That day, he came up from behind me and pushed me to the ground. Why would I make that up?"

Fiona sneered. "If that was true, why didn't you tell me when it happened? Why would you tell Mom and Dad that you hurt yourself playing rugby? Admit it. You've been lying about everything."

There was nothing Keilann could say. It was true. She had lied about everything, and now her sister was going to pay for it. It was all her fault. "There are things you need to know about him, Fiona." She fought to keep her voice from trembling. "He's lying to you."

Fiona snorted. "Oh, and that's so different from what you've been doing to me? You haven't told me the truth once all year."

"I'm doing it now. You've got to listen. He's just using you."

Instead of being horrified or angry, Fiona did something worse. She threw her head back and laughed. "Why would he be using me? He loves me!"

Keilann slapped her hand to her forehead and groaned.

"Are you listening to yourself, Fiona?" Keilann's voice was flirting with hysteria, the pitch rising with every word. "Connor McBride doesn't love you. He's just trying to get back at me! He. Is. Sick."

Fiona's face hardened into stone. She planted her hands on her hips, her body a cold fortress of sharp angles. "Yeah?" she said. The hatred in her voice sent a shiver down Keilann's spine. Fiona leaned forward intimately, as if she were about to share a secret. "Well, from where I'm standing, he's not the sick one. You are." She jabbed a sharp finger into Keilann's chest. "You're pathetic. You're just jealous that no boy is ever going to want to do with you what he wants to do with me."

Fiona leaned away from her sister's stunned face, smirking at the crumpled bag hanging limply from Keilann's hands. "Family size, huh?" Fiona glanced at the bulge hanging over Keilann's jeans, running her hands down her own flat stomach with a sigh. "Looks like you're nearly there." Without another word, Fiona tossed her hair behind her shoulder and sauntered from the room.

Keilann wasn't sure how long she stood there, blankly staring after her sister. Fiona's final words circled round and round in her head. Eventually, she moved her deadened muscles, forcing them to work again. She must have, because Keilann found herself in her room with the door bolted behind her. The cheese puffs were still in her hand, crushed to a fine powder in her fist. The fruit snacks were congealed and sticky from the heat of her body. Disgusted, she threw them in the trash. She wasn't hungry anymore. The computer's cheery screensaver blocked out the unfinished essay, bouncing back and forth over the monitor as if nothing had happened.

She saw it, but felt nothing. Her head was heavy, like each thought had turned into a grain of sand. Her heart pumped and contracted painfully in her chest.

How could I have been so stupid? How did I let this happen?

Keilann realized she was holding the books from her parents' office, her palms sweating into their spines. She set them down on the nightstand, the slender paperback on Shakespeare's heroines somersaulting to the floor. A torn sheet of paper slipped from between the covers and fluttered to rest beside it. Out of habit more than concern, Keilann bent down to retrieve the book and what she assumed would be a make-shift bookmark of blank computer paper. She was wrong.

Keilann was about to stick the slip of paper back inside the book at random, when the shadow of ink shone through the page. Not expecting to find anything, she hadn't noticed the writing on the other side. It was her mother's handwriting. The letters spiked and looped as if she had scrawled it in a great hurry, the ink bleeding as her hand flew by.

Gaa wiin daa-aangoshkigaazo ahaw enaabiyaan gaa-inaabid.

You cannot destroy one who has dreamed a dream like mine.

The paper blurred, but she could still see the words when she closed her eyes.

Gaa wiin daa-aangoshkigaazo ahaw enaabiyaan gaa-inaabid.

It wasn't until she buried her face in her hands that she realized she was crying.

22

"So what do ye want te do about it?"

Keilann sighed. That was one question she could not answer.

She had hoped that after telling Ben everything she had seen—and not seen—he would be filled with such righteous indignation and disgust he'd insist on doing everything in his power to save Fiona.

Instead of leaping into heroic action, however, he was sitting on her bed. Hands in his pockets, his long legs dangled carelessly over the side. Ben frowned at Keilann as if she had confessed a secret desire to shave off her eyebrows and dye her hair green.

Despite her initial delight in his surprise visit, Keilann had to admit that it was weird having Ben in her bedroom, sitting on her bed. After meeting in the woods so many times, the cluttered organized chaos of the room was claustrophobic and constraining. What was more disconcerting was that Ben didn't seem the least bothered by the news that Connor McBride was actively seducing Keilann's little sister.

She tried to hide her disappointment. "What would you have done?"

Ben chuckled. "I woulda lost my temper, charged into the room and gotten me arse handed to me. But at least he'd a known I disapproved."

Keilann gritted her teeth. How could he joke around about something so serious? "I tried getting through to Fiona," she muttered. *And to you.*

"And?"

"And..." The memory of her sister's cruel words made her throat sting like she had swallowed barbed wire. She shook her head.

Ben nodded. "Well, then."

"Well then what?"

Ben blinked at her. She hadn't meant to raise her voice, but why was he being so thick? "What?"

"You mean that's it? You're actually fine with this? We do nothing?" Keilann fumed.

Ben scratched his chin. "What do ye propose? Feel like challenging him to a duel or publicly shaming your sister?"

Keilann picked up a throw pillow and whipped it at Ben's head. "I'm serious!"

"Ow! So am I!" Ben cried, rubbing the side of his face. "What do ye expect, Keilann? You can't jess command two people not to see each other."

She gaped at him. "But all those things he's done—"

"Which you've told your sister," Ben pointed out.

"And all the things you've told me—"

"Which I told you so ye'd understand him better, not to judge him by. He's a frustrated and mixed-up person, Keilann, not a monster."

Keilann snorted. "Yeah, poor baby." She couldn't help rolling her eyes, even though she knew how childish it looked.

"And," Ben continued, "this may actually be good for him."

"Well, have him take his therapy sessions on someone else's couch with someone else's sister." Keilann stabbed at her homework so ferociously that the pencil tip tore it in half. "Damn it!"

Ben sighed and gently lowered her notebook so she would meet his eyes.

"C'mon, Keilann. When was the last time he went out of his way to bother you?"

Keilann couldn't believe her ears. "You're on his side!"

"I'm on no one's side," Ben insisted more firmly. "I'm jess sayin'—"

"And I'm sayin' that you're wrong. He's using Fiona to get back at me."

Ben's eyebrows shot up at her accusation. "Keilann—" he began, using his "be reasonable" voice.

"No, Ben! You weren't there! You didn't see what he was doing to my little sister."

"Well, neither did you—" Ben broke off when he saw the thunder in Keilann's face. "—but that's not the point," he added hastily. "The point is: did yer sister seem upset?"

Keilann thought of the coy look Fiona threw at Connor. The way her fingers slid down his chest and grabbed his hand.

"Well, no," she admitted reluctantly. "But that's only because she thinks that he's in love with her."

Ben pursed his lips. "So what if he is?"

"He's not," she spat out the words like venom.

"You really think he sought her out because he wanted revenge on you? Really?"

Keilann crossed her arms. "Why not? Aren't you the one who told me about the time he tried to frame another kid so he failed a drug test? He's not stupid, plus he's at least seventeen and Fiona's only barely fifteen. Your her dad's a cop. There's got to be a law against that!"

To Keilann's relief, Ben finally relented.

"Well, you do have a point there. Could you get Fiona to testify against him?"

Keilann bit her lip. "No, but I was an eye witness," she said, trying to remember everything she had seen on years of primetime cop dramas. "That has to count for something."

"But ye didn' really see anything," Ben reminded her gently. "It would be yer word against theirs, and if Fiona covers for him there's not much ye can do."

The throbbing crescendo of resentment building behind Keilann's eyes deflated. Ben was being calm and rational.

She hated it.

He was right, though. Not that she would admit that out loud, but she knew that Fiona was too infatuated to speak out against Connor. Keilann dropped her head in her hands, hot, frustrated tears burning in the corners of her eyes. She pressed her palms against her eyelids, willing herself not to dissolve into tears in front of Ben.

"There's got to be something I can do."

"There is," Ben said quietly.

Keilann raised her head.

"Tell yer parents."

It was so simple. She could. She could go to them right now and confess everything, all the damage she had woven with her lies unraveled and healed. Warn them about Connor, spill every last detail about Fiona's secret tryst, and—*and Fiona would never trust me again.* In time, she would speak to her. She may even see the wisdom of Keilann's intervention. But the bond of trust forged so tenuously between sisters would be shattered beyond repair. What if Keilann was wrong about Connor? Would it be worth it?

"I can't."

"Why not?" Ben asked, taken aback. "I don't know what he's capable of now. If you think he might try to force yer sister—"

Keilann set her jaw, her mouth a firm line. "Not until I'm sure there's no other way."

Ben nodded.

A brooding silence stretched between them, filled with the things they had left unsaid. Keilann absently traced a circle on her torn homework over and over until the scribbled line was dark and thick. She stopped and stared at what she had drawn, inspiration sparking at the sight of it. She looked at Ben and found him watching her. He didn't seem embarrassed that she had caught him and he didn't drop his gaze. Keilann flushed, wishing he would look away and not see the red coloring her cheeks.

She cleared her throat. "Ben, what do you know about stone circles?" She tried to keep her voice level and relaxed, her heart galloping in her throat.

Ben blinked at her, bewildered by the sudden shift in conversation.

Keilann forged ahead. If she didn't have the courage to do this now she never would. "You said you've been going to that one since you were little, but it's not in any of the travel books," she said casually.

"Is it not?"

Keilann shook her head. "I checked."

Ben leaned back against her wall, arching his back and stretching his legs. "Well, it's jess...here, innit? It always has been. There are circles like that all over Aberdeenshire. It isn't any different than the lot of 'em."

"Wanna bet?" Keilann muttered.

"Sorry?"

Keilann flushed. "Nothing." She paused and cleared her throat. "Have you ever heard what people say about stone circles having a kind of power?"

"New Age nutters?"

"Um, yeah, I guess," Keilann said carefully, flinching at the word 'nutter'. "Do you think that any of it could be true?"

"What, the 'spiritual energy?'" Ben drew sarcastic air quotes around the term, "or whatever they sae?"

Keilann nodded. She instantly regretted bringing up the topic.

Ben jerked his shoulder in an indifferent half-shrug. "Could be."

Encouraged that he didn't immediately dismiss the idea or laugh in her face, Keilann ignored her better judgment and ploughed on. "Have you ever..." Her voice trailed off. Ben looked at her, curious. She took a deep breath before totally losing her nerve. "Have you ever felt anything when you were there?"

Ben's steady gaze did not falter.

"In the circle?"

When Keilann nodded again, he pulled a face half-way between disgust and amusement. "Have I ever had a fit or started speaking tongues? No."

The hammering in her chest gave one final, excruciating thud and sunk into her stomach. She didn't want Ben to see how crestfallen she was, but he wasn't looking at Keilann. He was looking off to the far wall, his forehead puckered in thought.

"Mind ye, there are times..." Ben started quietly.

Keilann leaned forward, her anxiety a crushing weight. He suddenly broke out of his reverie, shaking his head as if dispelling the dangerous thoughts that loomed there.

"Forget it," he frowned. "It's mad."

"No!" Keilann cried, much louder than she had intended.

Ben jumped, surprised by the urgency in her voice. She could feel herself flush to the roots of her hair.

"You can tell me, really. Please."

Ben considered her for another moment or two, scratching the back of his head nervously. "Well, it's jess sometimes when I don't know if..." he broke off again, looking away. "Ye know the feeling you get, like you think someone is in the room but ye can't see 'em? Jess that. Jess that I'm not alone. But that's probably the woods doin' it to me," he added with forced cheerfulness. "Some squirrel or somethin'. It's nothin'."

Keilann took a deep breath and let it out in a rush. "Would you think that I was a nutter if I told you that something happened to me in there?"

Ben cocked his head. His lips quirked into a smile. "Depends on what ye think happened, I suppose," he said, folding his arms across his chest.

"I don't think that someone is in the room with me. I know she is. Things have happened out there that I can't explain, and the dreams I've been having for months—" despite her recent peace she'd made with her nightmares, Keilann shook uncontrollably. "Dreams about things I shouldn't—couldn't—know about. They scare me, Ben."

He blinked, nonplussed at her fear.

"Are you talking about the time ye were sick?" he asked slowly. "Keilann, ye had a concussion."

"I'm not so sure. These things keep happening to me Ben. Before and after I had a concussion. And who knows if it was actually a concussion?"

Ben's eyes narrowed. "What are ye sayin'?"

"I'm saying that some people have reported getting the same symptoms when they stay in a stone circle too long. What if the stones made me sick?"

Ben stared. "The stones."

Keilann nodded.

"Well, explain to me how I've never felt anything, then. I've been going to that spot since I could walk. If what ye say is true, then why has it never happened to me?"

The answer tumbled out of her mouth before she realized what she was saying. "Maybe you're not the one she was looking for."

Keilann wasn't sure where the words had come from, but as soon as they were spoken she knew they were true.

Ben gawked at her.

"She? Are you listening to yourself? Do ye really think that a ghost has come looking for you?"

Keilann frowned. "I don't think she's a ghost."

Ben grabbed her shoulders so quickly and firmly that Keilann gasped. "Please listen to me, Keilann." He looked directly into her eyes. "Yer scaring me with all this talk of stones and nightmares. Ye had dreams because of a concussion. Ye saw a girl because ye had exhaustion."

Keilann pushed his hands away. "I had exhaustion because of the nightmares I was having, the same dream every night for three months. Can you imagine? I was afraid to fall asleep. I would see terrible things every time I closed my eyes, Ben, and they all tie back to the same place."

Ben shook his head, utterly lost for words.

How could she make him understand? Keilann felt the familiar sting in the corners of her eyes—she had been so sure he would believe her. Now she was going to lose the only friend she had because he thought she was stark raving mad.

"Why don't you believe me?" she asked, her voice cracking.

Ben's shoulders sagged. He looked so tired, his eyes rimmed with grey that Keilann hadn't seen before.

"I don't think yer lyin'," he said carefully.

"But you don't believe me."

Ben sighed. "I don't believe that some moldy stones have mystical powers to transport people to some sort of spirit world. How could I? It's the stuff of fairy tales."

"How could everything people say about those places be made-up? They all report the same thing."

"All that proves is tha' they listen to the same nutters who get gubbed and have a sit in the woods. People will see what they want to see," he said.

"You think I want to see these things?" She seethed, hot anger boiling in her belly. An image of the burning man swam before her eyes. She blinked him away. "That I'm some desperate nut job? Is that what you think of me?"

Ben threw his hands up in frustration. "Of course not!"

"Then how do you explain it?"

"I don't know. It's all jess Folk stuff, fairy tales like I said. It gets into yer head." He raked a hand through his hair, exasperated. "Funny stories about people sayin' they met a stranger and talked for a few minutes in the morning, but when they walked out of the circle the sun was settin'. Legends of fairy folk taking men as lovers for a night only to have the poor souls wake the next mornin' as old men, or young still but a hundred years had passed by in that single night and all their family and friends were dead."

"The stories have had to come from somewhere," Keilann argued.

Ben pinched his nose between his thumb and forefinger as if fighting a migraine, shaking his head.

"I'm not saying that they're all real," she conceded. "But there's got to be some truth to some of them."

"Keilann," he said her name with a heavy sigh. "They're jess stories to keep kids from wandering off and gettin' into trouble. Only gullible, superstitious old women believe in that kind o' nonsense."

"My mother's people, they have the same kind of stories." Keilann's voice was steady now, but dangerously low. "I told you before how powerful a dream message can be. My grandmother believed that hers saved me from being miscarried like my older siblings. She believes that her dream did that. Do you think she's just a gullible, superstitious old woman?"

Ben lifted his palms up in supplication. "I don' know what ye wan' me te say."

"I want you to believe me!" Keilann slapped her hand down on the bed. "I'm not lying, and I'm not crazy."

"I can believe that." He put his hands on her shoulders again, but gently this time; comforting her, not restraining her. "But the rest, I jess don' know. I mean, ye ended up in a hospital, for God's sake. Jess promise me ye won' go chasin' after whatever it is ye've been chasin'. Rest this time, stay away from that daft circle, and see how ye feel about it in a few weeks, okay?"

Keilann bit her lip to keep herself from arguing again. Ben's face was lined with worry, his eyes pleading for her to stop. She felt like she was getting another doctor's mandate, but Ben's expression held her retort in check.

I've scared him, she realized with a pang. *I've scared myself.*

Ms. Spark raised her hand for quiet to make an important announcement, but Keilann couldn't focus on what she was saying. Despite the fact that it was the last day before holiday break, Keilann was more anxious than ever. There it was again. The prickle at the base of her neck, an instinctive warning bell incessantly tolling: *you are being watched.*

Keilann leaned her chin on her hand as if bored, her eyes darting left under her lashes, her thick curtain of hair blocking her face from view. This time she was sure she would catch him, but Connor McBride was still slouched over in his seat, his glazed, expressionless eyes staring off vaguely in the direction of the blackboard. She suppressed an exasperated sigh and doubled her efforts to pay attention to what Ms. Spark was saying about assignments over the holidays.

It had been like this for weeks, ever since the doctor had declared her recovered and sent her back to Mary Arden. At first, she thought it would be a relief to get out of the silent house—Fiona still wasn't talking to her—but the moment Keilann had stepped through the double doors, she had been swept into a whirlwind of pre-holiday chaos. Homework tripled. Exams loomed. And it was all she could do to keep from drowning beneath the ocean of new material with only patchy, mostly incomprehensible make-up work and borrowed notes for a leaky life preserver.

Had Fiona told Connor what had really happened, that Keilann knew about the two of them? Keilann had tried talking with her sister, only to get the same door slammed in her face with each attempt. A few times, she had reiterated her warnings and misgivings about Connor, but the only reactions this had produced were icy glares and a stubborn silence that had yet to be broken. Now whenever Keilann entered a room, Fiona made a point to leave as soon as possible.

After the last failed encounter, resentment had begun to fill in the cracks of Keilann's guilt and sisterly concern. Fiona was the one who had tried to smuggle a boy into the house behind their parents' backs. Fiona was the one who had slashed at her fragile sense of self-worth with words like razors. And yet she was the one acting like Keilann had wronged her, when all she was trying to do was protect her little sister.

Screw her.

If Fiona really wanted Connor's reeky breath on her neck, his vile, creeping hands on her body, then why should Keilann care? She was even beginning to think that they deserved one another.

Keilann shifted in her seat, blocking Connor's face with a tilt of her head. If Fiona had told him about her, he was doing a good job of hiding it. It was entirely possible that Fiona had been too humiliated, too mortified to tell him that Keilann had seen them together. It was possible that he knew nothing.

There were times though, like before, that she could've sworn he had been watching her. As if he had just turned away the moment before she noticed, ready to turn back when she looked away. This was paranoid, Keilann knew, and more than a little insane. But what about her life wasn't more than a little insane lately?

The old conversation with Ben was still bouncing around her head. *Jess promise me ye won' go chasin' after whatever it is ye've been chasin'. Rest this time, stay away from that daft circle, and see how ye feel about it in a few weeks, okay?* Maybe he was right. If she took a step back from the mess, she would probably see the situation more clearly. Given enough time, the dreams might even begin to make conventional sense. And if they didn't, she would deal with it her own way.

Whatever that might be.

"…have any questions, see me before you leave today and I'll be happy to explain further."

Keilann's head shot up from her hand. Ms. Sparks' words sent a rippling panic shooting to her fingertips.

Explain what? Explain what? Her bewildered mind spiraled into a desperate backtrack. *I missed it all!*

Cursing herself silently, Keilann honed her attention to pick up any hint of what her teacher was talking about. Ms. Spark was scribbling a date on the board. Imitating her classmates, Keilann jotted it in her notebook, clueless as to why. Before her teacher had time to turn and face the class again a single, cold tone blared through the halls, signaling the end of the period.

"Have a guid holiday!" Ms. Spark sang over the excited bustle of scraping chairs. It was the last day of term before the Christmas holidays began. Everyone was anxious to get out, especially the teaching staff. Everyone but Keilann. Connor grabbed his books and bolted with the rest of the class without giving her a second glance. Only Ben stayed behind, shifting eagerly in the doorway, a bemused expression on his face.

Keilann shook her head. "You go on. I'll just be a minute."

"I'll see ye after!" he called, and slipped into the noisy stream of students, letting the current carry him off to his next class.

Keilann's heart flip-flopped in her chest. Ben seemed as friendly as ever. But that was the problem. He was as friendly as ever, and neither of them had mentioned the kiss. He certainly hadn't kissed her again, not since the night in the hospital. Who could blame him? Had she been right to tell him about her dreams? In spite of everything, Keilann couldn't regret telling the truth to someone. It had felt too good to finally confide in Ben like a real friend, whatever the repercussions.

Even if he thought she was mad. If little things like insanity were going to scare him off, then she didn't want him kissing her. Or so she told herself. For some reason, Keilann no longer believed that the dreams were insane. Not completely, anyway.

Keilann approached Ms. Spark's overflowing desk. Her teacher shifted through papers, preparing for her next class. She glanced from arranging a pile of bright handouts, giving Keilann a knowing look as she brushed her hands together and straightened.

"Ah, Ms. Douglas. I had hoped ye'd come to see me."

A bolt of guilt pierced Keilann's chest, stealing the air from her lungs. Was it that obvious she hadn't been paying attention?

"Frankly, I've never been more disappointed in a student. I expected much more from you."

Keilann shifted uncomfortably. Though such harsh words stung coming from her favorite teacher, she couldn't help but feel that Ms. Spark was being a bit melodramatic. She couldn't have been the first student to ever daydream in class before.

"I'm sorry, Ms. Spark," Keilann mumbled politely to her shoes.

"I'm not the one who needs an apology, Ms. Douglas. Ye are the only one who is cheated when ye fail to live up to yer potential. And I have a feeling that this is not the first time it has happened."

What was this woman playing at? Did she really expect Keilann to get down on her knees and beg forgiveness for not paying attention in class?

"It was just the holiday break so close, I couldn't focus today."

Ms. Spark frowned at Keilann's apology, her eyebrow arching.

"I am speaking of yer paper, of course. What are ye talking about, Ms. Douglas?"

Keilann blinked.

"My paper? On Lady Macbeth?"

"Aye, I mentioned in class today that anyone who wished to inquire about their grade should see me directly after class. Isn't that why yer here?"

"Oh, uh, yeah," she lied.

Ms. Spark narrowed her eyes, but Keilann could've sworn she was fighting back a smile.

"Then as I said, I'm glad ye came te see me." Rifling briefly through a large stack of thick, white papers in various states of disarray, Ms. Spark produced what Keilann instantly recognized as her essay. A large, red "F" was scrawled across the top of the page. Just below the grade was a word written in all capital letters and circled twice:

INCOMPLETE.

Her jaw dropped.

"Surprised?" Spark said. "Imagine my surprise, Ms. Douglas, when I began reading your paper, not to find the brilliant and creative idea you proposed to me cleverly explored and defended, but this."

She dropped the paper onto the desk in disgust.

"What happened?" Spark demanded. "I saw ye do the research. I read yer notes. They were wonderfully insightful and original. Ye had the work done. It took ye more time to compile this load o' bollocks than if ye had jess used what ye already had. Why didn't ye?"

The red "F" swam before Keilann's eyes. She had failed. It wasn't as if she had never failed assignments before, but none as important or impactful as this term paper.

"I couldn't," she whispered.

"Ye wouldn't," Ms. Spark corrected. "There's a big difference, lass. Couldn't I can understand from some, but not from ye. Ye know what I think? I think ye weren't afraid of failing, but of succeeding. If ye proved to me that ye were more than capable of such work, than I'd start expectin' a higher level from ye every day. Or worse, ye'd start expectin' it from yerself. So ye thought it would be safer to sluff off and fly under the radar, did ye? Well, tough."

Keilann had never heard a teacher speak this way before, so brutally honest. It shamed and angered her all at the same time.

"I defended my thesis," she stammered, feebly. "I cited credible sources."

"It was a weak thesis that had been beaten to death by thousands of students before ye, unimaginative and uninteresting. And if I wanted to know what yer credible sources thought about Lady Macbeth, I would've bought their books."

"I'm sorry!" Keilann blurted in frustration. "What do you want me to say?"

Ms. Spark picked up the essay and placed it in Keilann's numb fingers. "I want ye te say that ye will do a better job this time."

Keilann blinked. "This time?" she echoed.

"Ms. Douglas, this term paper is unacceptable and its argument incomplete. Yer assignment is to revise and rewrite it according to previously approved proposal. If ye can do so over the holiday, I will consider changing yer grade."

The meaning of her words sunk in slowly.

"You're giving me another chance?" She couldn't believe it.

Ms. Spark nodded.

"Apparently I am. Just don't screw it up this time." She flashed Keilann a brief smile and waved her to the door. "Happy holidays, Ms. Douglas."

That night, Keilann tossed and turned in an uneasy sleep.

She was standing in front of her English class, reading aloud from her essay. She had to keep raising her voice, bellowing each line above Ms. Spark's boos and jeers from the back row. Keilann finally got so frustrated that she threw her paper to the ground and ran from the room.

Instead of the empty hallways of Mary Arden, she burst from the classroom into a vast, leafy forest, the trees overgrown and groaning with age. Her footfalls became muffled as tile gave way to a soft cover of pine needles and moss. Keilann slowed to a walk.

What a beautiful place, she thought, turning her face up to the warm, dappled sunshine. She meandered under the canopy, touching her hands to their scarred trunks, the ashy bark crumbling and falling away beneath her hands.

Maybe I'll sit here for a while. There was something she was supposed to be doing. But she'd worry about that later.

Yes, she thought lazily, sitting down here for a few minutes wouldn't hurt anyone. Keilann was just about to settle under a large, flourishing oak, but a tingle in her spine made her hesitate. It wasn't a sound, exactly. She felt it more than heard it: a humming buzz, like the sound of a hundred bumble bees right above her head vibrating in the soles of her feet. She turned her head in each direction, but there was nothing, no one else in sight. It was growing louder, more insistent, pulling her toward it like a magnet. A clear ringing, more sensation than sound, dragged her through the trees.

Then, peeking through the branches ahead, there it was: a luminous silvery light beckoning her forward, pulsing like a heartbeat. The stones were waiting for her like old friends, the silver light surrounding them like halos. She was about to step into the circle, to be a part of that light but something was wrong. There was a slight tremor to the edge of the chime, a disturbance she couldn't explain. She wanted to turn away, but her feet were rooted to the forest floor like the mighty oaks around her. A dark shadow fell across the flawless pool of light. Someone else was with her, standing just behind her. She turned her head—

Keilann bolted upright, her chest heaving, her sheets sticking to her skin with sweat. A solid, earthly sound had woken her from her dream, ringing through her ears.

Someone had been calling her name.

24

"What happened to you?" Keilann muttered, trailing her finger down the long paragraph.

Bent over yet another dusty volume on Scottish monarchs, she craned her neck to read the tiny passage at the bottom of the page:

*Gruoch ingen Boite **was the daughter of Boite mac Cináeda** son of Cináed (Kenneth) III. She is most famous for being the wife and queen of **Mac Bethad mac Findlaích** (Macbeth). The dates of her life are not certainly known. Sometime before 1032 Gruoch was married to **Gille Coemgáin**, with whom she had at least one son, **Lulach**, later **King of Scots**. The date of her death is not known.*

She sighed and slid the book from her lap: another disappointment.

Keilann had been working on her revised essay for hours, and in that time Scotland had gone through four different seasons. In the earliest hours, the sun had peeked through her window in bright shafts of golden light, only to be stolen midafternoon by great black clouds rolling over the valley. By the time she was on her fourth book, Keilann had to turn on her reading light because sheets of icy sleet lashed her window, suffusing the room with a wintry gloom. Now as she closed the last royal biography the public library had in stock, plump, fluffy snowflakes drifted in and out of sight like ash.

Where did you go? Keilann wanted to scream. But no one, it seemed, could answer her.

After Mac Bethad's death, everything that had been Gruoch stopped as well. There was no legend passed down through the ages, no mention of her whatsoever. It seemed that the only reason anyone knew who she had been at all was because William Shakespeare had wanted to impress King James I by writing a play about ancient Scottish monarchs.

Shakespeare wrote that Gruoch killed herself before Mac Bethad's final battle. Did he hear about that somewhere or did he just make it up for better drama? Some of Keilann's sources proposed her probable murder by her husband's enemies, her body dumped into a mass grave and forgotten. Still others guessed that she simply died in childbirth like so many others of her time. One or two more obscure texts suggested that she might have outlived her second husband, but none hazarded a guess as to how or where. Gruoch the woman slipped from history, leaving not even a whispered trail for Keilann to follow. She left the world as mysteriously as she came, and time was keeping her secrets.

Part of Keilann wanted to believe that she had survived, that she had found a way out at last. It would've been easy to disappear amidst all of the political upheaval following Mac Bethad's death. Was it naïve to hope that her enemies would just let her go, one of the only remaining competitors to the throne of Scotland?

Akiiwin. Come to me, Life.

The voice from last night rang in her ears. It had been a beautiful voice, soft and pleading. But had it been Gruoch? Keilann shook it out of her head. She promised Ben she wouldn't go chasing her dreams. There was enough work ahead of her as it was. Her hours of careful research had gained her no insights, no hints of anything conclusive. Keilann, like the rest of history, could only wonder and guess.

She was still inching through her essay when Ben showed up on her doorstep the day before Christmas. After hours of accomplishing very little, Keilann was frustrated and dangerously close to her boiling point. She never heard the doorbell ring, but her father's booming voice broke through the brooding silence of her room.

"Keilann! You have a visitor!"

Her spine straightened instantly and she leapt from the bed, scooping up her crushed, defeated spirits from the floor as she went. It had to be him. Who else would visit her? When the first days of break had slipped away with no word from Ben, Keilann had begun to steel herself to the reality that she probably wouldn't be seeing him until term began again in January.

He has other friends, she told herself sternly when her mind drifted from the paper. *You're not the most important person in his life. So what?*

It had gone on like this for days. She had almost given up hope, and here he was. As she hit the landing, Keilann realized she was sprinting and slowed herself to a casual walk. Suddenly she didn't want Ben to know about the thrill that tingled up her spine at the sound of his name; that he was the only person she had seen during the break. She rounded the corner, her face fixed in a relaxed, confident smile—and then she saw him.

"Keilann!" He waved like a schoolboy and gave her a grin that stripped her composure. She beamed.

Keilann's father took his cue. "Merry Christmas, Ben," he said, shaking the young man's hand. "Please thank your parents for us, and let them know that they're welcome here any time. We'd be delighted to meet them."

"Thank you, Professor Douglas. Happy Christmas."

Her father turned to leave and, to her horror, gave Keilann an exaggerated wink and a quick pat on the shoulder. Hot, blotchy patches covered her face. So much for relaxed and confident.

Ben grinned, his eyes glinting with laughter. "Nice guy, yer Da. I like 'im."

"So, what was that all about?" Keilann asked airily, trying to keep her voice light.

Ben straightened and gave her a little mock bow. "I have come here to formally invite yer family to the MacAlpin Hogmanay *cèilidh*."

Keilann stared at the unintelligible, lilting noises that must've been words.

"The MacAlpin what?"

"A *cèilidh*," he pronounced the Gaelic slowly, sounding to Keilann's ear like *kee-lee*. "It's a Scots celebration, a grand party with music, storytelling, dancing, and food. Plenty o' black pudding," he added with a wicked smile.

"But what's Hog-many?" she asked, too bewildered to pay any attention to his teasing.

Ben's jaw dropped.

"Ye've never heard of Hogmanay? How is it yer livin' in Scotland and ye've never even heard of Hogmanay?"

Keilann's eyes narrowed.

"After black pudding, I'm not sure I can stand anymore Scottish traditions."

"Hogmanay isn't food, Keilann," Ben laughed. "It's a holiday. The biggest holiday in the Scottish year: New Year's Eve."

Despite his obvious excitement, Keilann was skeptical. New Year's Eve had never been a particular favorite of hers. When she was little, the fancy food, fireworks, and permission to stay up until midnight had seemed like privileges beyond her wildest dreams. As she grew, however, the mystery and excitement surrounding the night slowly diminished until there was very little difference between New Year's and any other day. Just last night, she had stayed up well past three a.m. typing another revision of her paper. Midnight held no magical barriers for her anymore.

Ben translated the look on her face. "We're no' like the States. Hogmanay is bigger than Christmas here."

"Why?" Keilann couldn't see what all the fuss was about.

"Well, when Scotland became officially protestant way back in the day, they thought that Christmas was too Popish—too Catholic. So, they outlawed Christmas for about two hundred years or so."

"*What?*"

"Oh yeah," Ben said eagerly, nodding. "I mean, it's legal now, o' course, and we celebrate it, but back then with Christmas gone, people needed a different excuse to eat too much and get pissed. So, Hogmanay took over."

Keilann rolled her eyes.

"I bet that's exactly what the history books would say," she said dryly.

Ben shrugged. "Maybe no," he grinned. "But that's because it's the truth."

Keilann laughed. Standing here with her friend—even though it was freezing in the doorway—she felt better than she had in days. Being cramped into a room with an essay and a looming deadline for company doesn't exactly make for a very festive mood.

"All right," she acquiesced. She leaned against the door frame and crossed her arms. "What do you do on Hogmanay that's more exciting than essay writing?"

Ben's eyes lit up. "Well, like I said, ye have the *ceilidh*—and that can go on 'til the wee hours—but besides tha' ye have the fireballs."

"Are they like fireworks?" Keilann asked, trying to decipher what she guessed was more Scots slang.

Ben chuckled.

"No' exactly. Ever' year there's a grand parade from High Street to the West End and the whole procession swings giant fireballs o'er their heads the whole way. And there's fireworks, o' course, and—"

"What do you mean by 'swings giant fireballs over their heads'?"

"Well, they're giant balls on chains that get set on fire and swung around."

"Is that safe?" Keilann gawked.

"I s'pose it must be," Ben mused, scratching his head. "They've been doin' it fer about eight hundred years. Anyway, it's great fun. Will ye come with me?"

Even Keilann had to admit that giant fireballs sounded much more enticing than watching reruns and searching text books for a long lost woman. Maybe it was worth a try.

"My parents are already going to another party. One of their professor friends, I think. And Fiona is going to spend the night at a friend's house." Keilann really didn't need to speculate who that "friend" might be, or what kind of festivities he'd be planning to ring in the New Year with her little sister. She had seen enough of what they had attempted on the couch to guess.

"An' what about ye?"

Keilann scowled.

"I've got a date with an incomplete essay."

"Ye won' be done by then? Haven't ye been workin' on tha' fer days now? I did nae come to see ye before now so ye could finish with the damned thing."

Though it lightened Keilann's heart to hear that he hadn't simply forgotten her, Ben's words did little to lift her spirits. She shook her head glumly. At this rate, Keilann had no idea when—or if—her mangled paper would finally be complete.

Ben set his jaw.

"Then I'm havin' an intervention. I'm sorry, Keilann," he said, holding up a hand to stop her protests, "ye cannot spend yer first Hogmanay alone and workin', no less. It's no' right."

"I have to get this done."

Ben waved her words away with a flick of his hand.

"Ye will. Don' forget that the 2nd o' the year is a bank holiday so we Scots have enough time to recover from Hogmanay. Ye'll have plenty of time to finish if yer no' done by the thirty-first."

It was so tempting. A night out with Ben, even one filled with bizarre customs and the threat of dancing would be worth a few lost hours of homework.

"All right," she relented. "I'll come with you."

"Excellent!" Ben whooped, punching the air. "We'll drive ye to Stonehaven an' have ye back before it gets too late."

Keilann's elation did a small double-take, deflating slightly. "We?"

"Me family. Ye'll get to meet them all."

Suddenly, the solitary night of homework was beginning to look inviting and cozy.

"Don' worry," Ben laughed, seeing the frozen look on Keilann's face. "Ye won' have to impress anyone. They'll love ye. Oh, an' before I forget—"

Keilann gasped.

Horror, already swelling at the mention of having to meet Ben's family, amplified at the sight of a trim, square package tucked neatly under his arm. She hadn't noticed it until then: a gift wrapped in shimmering green paper that glinted gold as he handed it to her.

"But I didn't get you anything!" Keilann blurted, recoiling from the Christmas present as if it contained a live explosive.

Ben's gap-toothed grin changed into small, shy smile.

"Ye have."

A warm flush crept up Keilann's neck, making her whole face shine like a beacon. She couldn't look him in the eye, staring at the frosted cement beneath her feet as he pressed the gift toward her.

"Don' open it 'til Christmas," he said sternly. Ben gave her hand a quick squeeze and backed away from the house. It was only when Keilann heard the crunch of gravel under his long strides that she dared look up again, just in time to see him turn from the road and vanish between the wintry skeletons of the trees.

Christmas morning dawned damp and gloomy with heavy clouds hanging on the horizon almost as black and brooding as the atmosphere inside the Douglas house. The season, usually buzzing with festive parties, concerts, and shopping in the bright lights of downtown Chicago, had been quiet and subdued in the Scottish countryside. Though all of her family was at home during winter break, the absence of their relatives and friends sat between them at the dinner table and hovered over their conversations. The time that was supposed to be the most joyous of the year was turning out to be the most melancholy. It seemed to hit Keilann's mother the hardest.

As the days marched through December, her mom had grown increasingly distant and detached. In the past, she had greeted the holiday season with renewed energy and vigor, the promise of a long, revitalizing winter break just around the corner. This year, Keilann watched that energy drain away. Even their small fir tree looked limp and listless; its boughs weighed down with handmade ornaments that had survived the move, each one its own memory.

Still, it was nice to be together, like a sigh of relief after a long test. Despite their homesickness, they all made an extra effort to be cheerful and merry. Even Fiona noticed her mother's state and broke the silent ice between her and Keilann for the first time in weeks. She was civil and polite, thanking Keilann for her gifts and giving her sister one in return, but her generosity didn't last past dinner.

The best part of the night came when her dad stoked a bright, warm fire and turned on Christmas movies. Keilann settled down in a nest of blankets and pillows before the flames, a big tin of cookies Gram had shipped from Minnesota nestled between her and Fiona. This had always been Keilann's favorite Christmas tradition: drinking hot chocolate, eating cookies, and watching *It's a Wonderful Life*. Corny as it was, Keilann couldn't help but love it. Even though her family was in Scotland instead of Chicago, snuggling and munching together made it feel like home. As the final credits of the film faded into black, Fiona stretched out her long limbs and gave into a jaw-cracking yawn. She murmured a sleepy "Merry Christmas" and shuffled off to bed.

Keilann and her parents were left by the dying fire. Her mother's eyes were bright with tears, but that was nothing new. *It's a Wonderful Life* made them all tear up at the end, even though it embarrassed Keilann to admit it. Despite her red eyes, Keilann's mom looked more relaxed than she had in a long time. She got up slowly from the couch and kissed Keilann on the forehead.

"I'm so proud of you," her mother whispered. "You've done so well this year. Merry Christmas."

Keilann's throat tightened as she watched her mother gather up the mugs. If only she knew.

It was just Keilann and her father. She couldn't remember the last time they had been alone together. He was stretched out on the couch, arms behind his head, staring at the glowing embers.

"Merry Christmas, Kei."

"Merry Christmas."

Her father paused, looking at the dark doorway his wife had disappeared through. He frowned, his face haloed by firelight. "I know it's not the same. I know this move hasn't been easy," he said quietly. "I really appreciate everything you've given up. It's not completely awful for you, is it?"

He looked so small, so frail and helpless, that Keilann got up from the fire and hugged her father more fiercely than she had in a long time. He hesitated, shocked by her action, before wrapping his arms around her in a crushing bear hug. Her ribs felt like they were splintering, but Keilann didn't mind. His rough whiskers brushed the top of her head as he bent over to kiss her. She thought of Connor McBride and the burning man, the nightmares and taunts she'd endured. But then she thought of Ben and Chrisselle, of the stone circle she'd come to love and of the red-haired girl who was tied to her in a way she couldn't explain.

"No, Dad," she said, burying her face into his sweater to scratch away her tears. "Not by a long shot."

"I'm sorry I haven't been—" Her words failed. *Honest? Unselfish? Thoughtful?* All of those things were true. Keilann hadn't exactly made this move any easier on her family. But how could she say it?

Her dad released her from the embrace and put a warm hand on her head. "I know, Keilann. Me, too." He smiled, his face and lighting up his eyes. "You know I love you, right?"

Keilann nodded. He kissed her forehead once more, and followed after his wife to help with cleaning up.

She was alone.

Keilann crossed the room to kneel beside the tree, where one last gift was hidden under the small piles of sweaters, sweets, and flashy gadgets. Gingerly, she excavated the shimmering package, its iridescent paper glowing orange and copper in the firelight. She had saved her one real scrap of Christmas magic for the very end, hording Ben's present until she could open it in peace. Mindful not to tear the beautiful paper, Keilann slid a finger under the taped seam and pried the wrapping away.

It was a book. Its glossy cover shone proudly, the dying embers of the fire suffusing it in red. Keilann leaned forward. She tilted the book toward what was left of the fire, the soft glow splashing over the title, *Circles of Our Past: A Guide to Understanding Scotland's Greatest Treasures*.

She repeated the title to herself, stroking the smooth, waxy words with her fingertips. Curious, Keilann opened the front cover. There, as she had hoped, was a note written on the title page in a tidy, cramped hand. She expected it to say, "Merry Christmas!" but the message Ben left gave her far more comfort and joy than any generic holiday greeting.

It simply said: *I believe you.*

25

Everywhere else in Scotland homes blazed with light and song to welcome the New Year, but the eyes of Keilann's house were dead.

A tiny, metallic scratching and a dull *click* cracked the silence and the door pushed open without another noise. A dark silhouette was outlined in the dim moonlight, fighting to wrench a key from the lock. The door inched back, slowly nestling into the frame, cutting off the bluish-white light without its usual squeal. One last click and the deadbolt slid into place.

Keilann tossed her purse aside and sank against the wood paneling with a heavy sigh. Trails of snaking light were still waltzing through the dark like ghosts in front of her eyes, seared onto her corneas by the whirling parade of fireballs. Her feet were raw and blistered from dancing. She smelled like wood smoke and fresh air, and her legs were pillars of jelly.

It had been the best night of her life.

There had been no nightmares as Ben dragged her through the hopelessly complicated Scottish reels. No insults or stares as she shivered in the frosty air and watched the fireworks of Hogmanay. After a few glasses of the hot, spiced, very spiked punch, Keilann had even mustered enough courage to talk to a few of her blurry classmates. Ben had been right. Hogmanay hadn't been a bad way to begin a new year.

And it was a new year, a few hours from its very first dawn, but the stroke of midnight was still alive in Keilann's mind.

Ben had just finished bellowing the final slurred lyrics of "Auld Lang Syne," Keilann mumbling along as best as she could. He turned to her, throwing his arm around her shoulder, cheeks pink and eyes a bit too bright.

"*Uisge Beatha*," he slurred in Gaelic, handing Keilann a glass of amber-colored liquid and raising his own in a toast. "The water of life!"

The glasses clinked merrily and, following Ben's lead, Keilann threw her head back and downed the drink in one gulp. Her throat erupted in flames.

Keilann choked, slopping half of the liquid down the front of her dress.

"What is this stuff?" she gasped. "It's—" She coughed, tears streaming down her face—"horrible!"

Ben was doubled-over, laughing at her.

"It's whiskey!" he roared over the pounding music. "It'll give ye good health."

"It think it's killing me," Keilann wheezed. She felt like she had swallowed gasoline, her throat raw. Her cheeks flamed with the fire burning in her belly.

Without warning, Ben bent down and planted a heavy, smacking kiss on Keilann's cheek. "That's fer guid luck," he whispered in her ear.

Giddy with punch and something she couldn't quite name, Keilann wrapped her arms around his neck and pulled him into a close hug, the rough wool of his kilt scratching her bare legs. Before Ben could move away, Keilann leaned forward on her toes and kissed his warm, smooth cheek.

"For luck," she whispered back. Ben had given her a smile that made her toes tingle— or maybe that was the whiskey—and the dancing had begun again.

Coward.

Keilann opened her eyes, the flush warming her face only partly due to the alcohol. She chickened out, denying the punch-enhanced desire to do more than just peck him on the cheek. But in the end, she decided it was for the best. Ben was just being friendly. He had probably drunk too much whiskey—he might not even remember kissing her. But she remembered, and that would have to be enough.

Though almost certainly alone, Keilann didn't turn on the lights. Instead, she slid the glittering black heels from her throbbing feet and crept up to her room on tiptoes, stumbling around furniture and falling up the stairs. There were no lights peeking under her parents' door. Not wanting to take any chances, Keilann stifled a nervous giggle and forced herself to walk straight through the tilted hallway.

Is this what it feels like to be drunk?

She had no idea if she was swaying or the room was—or both. Keilann winced as the light of her own bedroom flickered on, blinking hard to focus her eyes. Staggering slightly, she forced herself to stand still.

I'm just buzzed, she decided confidently.

Not that Keilann had ever had any previous experience with alcohol. Her mother had never allowed any in the house and, though the girls had heard stories of their father's college days, her dad had given up drinking when he began dating her mom. Keilann's mother had a zero-tolerance alcohol policy. The thought of her reaction to Keilann's current state was more sobering than an ice bath. Her eyes darted nervously to the open door.

Relax. She won't be home for hours and by then I'll be perfectly fine.

It was probably a good idea to brush her teeth and rinse the tinge of whiskey from her mouth. Keilann veered into the bathroom and began untangling pins from her hair. Earlier in the night, it had been elegantly twisted and piled onto her head, but now it hung in damp, snarled strands knotted with hairpins. She shook out her limp curls, vigorously rubbing her tender scalp, and stumbled into her room. She staggered to her dresser and grabbed the first pair of sweatpants and the baggiest T-shirt she could find. Keilann yanked the clingy black dress over her head and watched the gauzy fabric float to the floor, glad to be rid of it.

The dress had been a birthday gift last year and was supposed to be a stylish, flattering cut, but she didn't like the feel of it on her skin. She felt naked, the dress exposed all of the ample, flabby areas of her body that Keilann usually tried to hide. She finally felt like herself with the cotton shirt on her skin, the merciful sweatpants concealing her legs from view. Keilann could've told herself that she had worn the dress for Hogmanay because it was the only formal clothing she owned, but she didn't feel like lying. She knew she had chosen it for Ben. Now that the warm glow of the whiskey was beginning to wear off, Keilann couldn't believe what she had done. She stared at the tiny pool of wrinkled fabric in horror. What had she been thinking?

Shaking her head in disgust, she kicked the dress into a far corner where she didn't have to look at it. She'd deal with that later. The bed stared at her, but she didn't feel like sleeping just yet. Her veins pumped with adrenaline and a hint of whiskey. She looked around her room, her lips pursed.

I guess I could do some research for my paper until I get tired.

Though knowing what she needed was in Jana's notes, Keilann ignored the notebook sitting patiently on her bedside table. She'd use it eventually. Besides, when would she get a better time to peruse her parents' office? There were still one or two potential sources she wanted to browse, and reading about Shakespeare would definitely put her to sleep. Throwing an old robe around her shoulders, Keilann snuck from her room and retraced her steps down the hall. At the bottom of the stair she turned right and pushed the door open, hoping to snatch up her books and leave without any notice.

A shadow rose from the desk. Someone was waiting for her in the dark.

Keilann yelped and jumped for the door.

"Keilann! What are you doing here?"

There was a click, and the figure behind the desk was bathed in the golden light of her father's lamp.

"Mom?" Keilann's hand flew to her chest to calm the panicked drumming of her heart. "You scared the hell out of me! I thought you were Con—uhh, someone else," she checked herself.

Keilann's mother sat back in the desk chair.

"I didn't mean to scare you. I thought I was alone."

Her voice was quiet and strained. In the lamp light, her face looked puffy, but

Keilann couldn't tell if her eyes were red or if that was the harsh glare.

"I just got back from Ben's." She glanced at her wristwatch, frowning. "When did you get back from your party? Is Dad home, too?"

Her mother hesitated.

"No, I don't think he'll be back for a while yet. I didn't feel like going." Her hands fidgeted nervously.

"You mean, you've been home all night by yourself?" Cold dread hit Keilann in the stomach. Something was wrong.

Her mom nodded wearily.

"But why?" Keilann pressed.

Keilann's mom fidgeted with her beaded shawl, not able to meet her daughter's eyes. She looked so lost, so helpless. For no reason, this filled Keilann with an inexplicable anger.

"I didn't feel well."

"So you're sitting in the dark all alone?" Keilann asked. "That'll make you feel better?"

She stepped toward her mother to force her to make eye contact, forgetting about the whiskey still flowing in her blood stream. Unfortunately, her feet hadn't forgotten. Her angry strides confused themselves into a staggering lunge and she stumbled into the back of the armchair.

Her mom shot up from the chair.

"Keilann! What's wrong?" She was at the chair, holding Keilann's face in her hands and searching her eyes. "Are you hurt? I—"

All at once, her whole body went rigid. The gentle hands cradling her daughter's face became talons. When she spoke, her voice was strong and calm.

"Have you been drinking?"

Keilann's mind whirled. *How did she know?*

Then it hit her. She forgot to brush her teeth. Her breath still reeked of whiskey and whatever had been swimming in the spiced punch.

How could she lie? Her mom could smell the proof on her breath, had seen her stumble. But how could she admit to the truth? Keilann's uncle had been killed by a drunk driver. Her grandfather survived the crash but was left paralyzed for life. Keilann had been warned through these stories, by seeing her grandfather in his wheelchair, and now she had betrayed her mother anyway. Hot tears of shame pricked the edges of her eyes. Her mother still held her face, waiting for a denial.

But Keilann said nothing.

Instead, she braced herself for the volcano of her mom's anger to erupt through the ice. Would she give Keilann "the speech" reliving her brother's four day struggle in the ICU before his battered body finally gave up? Or would she storm from the room and refuse to talk to Keilann for days as she did to Keilann's father on the occasions he had come home from a party tipsy?

Her mother's face quivered as if on the brink of shouting and crumpled. She bowed her head, crushed her daughter to her chest in a fierce hug, and wept. Sobs rippled her shoulders as tears began to soak through Keilann's nightshirt.

"I don't want to lose you, too!"

Keilann was frozen. Shock and fear numbed her senses.

What was she supposed to do when a parent acted like a child? Afraid to move, she let her mother hug her, arms hanging uselessly at her sides. In all the years since his death, her mom had never openly cried over the loss of her brother like it was breaking her heart all over again. Keilann felt like a monster. Like the lowest, slimiest scum, but still she stood and did nothing.

Finally, her mother released her, leaving a pool of tears on Keilann's shirt. She crumbled into the chair and rocked back and forth, hugging herself as if to hold herself together. "What have I done?" She moaned like a wounded animal. "What have I done?"

"Mom, it's not your fault," she cried over her mother's sobs.

Keilann tried to place a hand on her mother's back, but she recoiled from her touch. Her wails doubled.

Please let Dad come home soon. Please let him hear. Knowing she had to do something, she knelt beside her mother, careful not to touch her. "Mom, I'm so sorry," Keilann said calmly and clearly, trying to hide her panic. "I'll never do it again."

Her mother shook her head in wordless anguish. Tears rolled off of her cheeks and dappled the armchair with dark shadows. Suddenly, Keilann realized what must have happened.

"Oh, no. It's the university, isn't it?"

Mom blinked up at her. "What?"

"The program cuts. Did you lose your job?"

Mom passed a weary hand over her eyes. "No. It's not that." She closed her eyes and rubbed her forehead.

Now it was Keilann's turn to be confused. "Then, what? What could be so bad?"

Mom took a great, shuddering gasp and words flooded out of her faster than Keilann could understand them. Tumbling between sobs, Keilann strained her ears and strung the broken words together.

The miscarriages?

Her mother had never spoken of the children that almost were. They were only ever mentioned in reference to Gram's dream. From an early age, Keilann had quelled her curiosity and learned without being told that her dead siblings would always be a mystery. So why was her mom suddenly talking about them now after years of guarded silence?

And what could Keilann say? What did people usually do in a situation like this?

She gave her mother's shoulder an awkward pat.

"It's okay, Mom," she crooned over her mom's rasping sobs. "You've still got me and Fiona."

Keilann's mother rocked back and forth, shaking her head.

"You don't know," she choked out. "My fault...all my fault..."

"What are you talking about?" Keilann asked, bewildered. "You didn't do anything wrong."

Her mom stopped rocking and lifted her head. Her face was blotched and puffy from crying. Her mascara ran in black rivulets down her face like ceremonial paint.

Keep talking, a voice inside of her urged.

Keilann licked her lips nervously. "It wasn't your fault Mom," she said in what she hoped was a soothing voice, forcing herself to look into her mom's tearstained face. "Those miscarriages weren't your fault."

Her mom frowned. "Miscarriages?" she repeated blankly. "What did you say about miscarriages?"

Keilann had not planned on this. If her mother was not talking about the miscarriages, what was she talking about? "Isn't that what this is all about?"

"Oh, Keilann..."

Her mother covered her face with her hands. She no longer rocked and wailed, but somehow this new stillness was worse.

"Please, tell me what's going on." Keilann spoke softly, gently, remembering the way she had heard her grandmother soothe a skiddish horse.

Keilann's mother shook her head, refusing to look her daughter in the eye.

"I know something's been bothering you. Ever since the move you've just been acting so, so—"

Her mom's head jerked up, her eyes widened into terrified spheres as if Keilann had accused her of doing something shameful. Keilann chose her words with care.

"—different," she said slowly, dragging the word through multiple syllables. Her mother's expression was impassive, but the fingers that gripped the chair arms were white at the knuckles.

"I thought it was just the move at first, but now—"

Keilann wavered on the edge of resolve. If she stopped now, she could still get her books, go back to her room, and keep pretending nothing was wrong. Cross this bridge, and there might not be any going back. What if she found the answers she'd been hunting down, only to discover that she had been happier not knowing? It would be easier to run away from the truth, but would it be better? For the first time in her life, Keilann didn't think so. She thought of the red-haired girl, of Gruoch, and the same feeling settled over her: she had to know. Taking a deep breath, she looked directly into her mother's eyes.

"Mom, I want to know."

Her mother paused. Her dark eyes bored into Keilann's. "I had an abortion."

The words ripped through the air and punched Keilann in the chest. She couldn't breathe. She stared at the woman before her. So many thoughts fought to escape that she opened and closed her mouth several times, like a fish gasping for water, before she could finally speak.

"All this time? Why? Why did you lie to Dad? To everyone?"

Keilann's mother shook her head, her eyes far away.

"You don't understand, *Akiiwin*." Her mom sighed. When she looked at Keilann again, her eyes brimmed with fresh tears, but her voice was steady. "I didn't lie about the miscarriages twenty years ago."

Keilann opened her mouth to protest, but her mother held up her hand.

She closed her eyes. "The abortion was six months ago."

Keilann gasped. She couldn't help herself. *Impossible!* Six months ago? Her brain fought through the shock and linked cause with effect. That would mean....

"I found out just before we left Chicago."

Pregnant. Her mother had been pregnant, and she never knew. Never even considered it. Things like that didn't happen to middle-aged, comfortable mothers. They just didn't.

"Why didn't you tell anyone? Why didn't you say anything?"

Keilann's mother pressed her hands to her face, splaying her fingers over her eyes to hide the tears washing her cheeks.

"I was so scared. You have no idea." Her words were thick. She took a shuddering breath and exhaled the tears from her voice. "We were leaving for a new country, a new life. The other pregnancies...."

Her mom lowered her hands and wrapped them around Keilann's so quickly that she didn't have time to even think about pulling away. She couldn't work her numb fingers to squeeze back.

"I was so happy when you were born, *Akiiwin*. So grateful that you were alive and whole." Her mom cleared her throat. "And then when I almost lost Fiona, when the doctors didn't think she'd make it to term. They told me to expect the worst. I had to stay on bed rest for five months, and even then she was born three weeks early. Did you know that?"

Keilann shook her head.

"And that was when I was young and healthy enough to bear children, but a pregnancy at forty-five? Even under the best conditions, there wouldn't be much of a chance.

During a stressful and exhausting relocation, where there was no option of bed rest? I was terrified. I couldn't live through another miscarriage, I just couldn't. The doctors told me my body wouldn't even be able to survive another high-risk pregnancy. I waited until your father had left and I...I...."

The last of her resolve crumbled. Keilann's mother curled into herself, cradling her head in her arms. This was a grief far beyond tears.

Keilann wanted to say something comforting, her conscience prodding her with a hot brand of guilt. All this time. She should've said a thousand different things, but found that she only wanted to ask one question.

"Does Dad know?"

"I tried." Her mother closed her eyes again. "I couldn't," she shook her head. "I promised myself that I would tell him everything after we had settled into our new life. But then the time came and it felt too soon, and then too late. Every time I spoke or laughed, it felt like a lie. It ate away like a cancer, but I was afraid that living with the truth would be worse."

A heavy silence stole any words Keilann had thought to say. The logical part of Keilann's brain kicked and squirmed. From somewhere outside of her body, she heard herself speak. "Mom, you have to tell him. You were scared and did what you had to do. You could've died."

Her mother raised her head, her face was burning with such a ferocious hatred that Keilann shrank back.

"But I could've lived, don't you understand? The baby could've lived. She's dead because of me, because I was afraid that it would be too hard. How will I ever be able to protect you or Fiona?"

Her mom's shoulders slumped under the weight of her grief. Six months of regret sapped her reserves of strength like an ulcer. Six months, and all that time Keilann had thought she was homesick. She had never bothered to think. Never bothered to ask.

I'm the one who should be ashamed.

Her hands trembled uncontrollably, but she forced her fingers to bend around her mothers and squeezed.

"I'm sorry," Keilann choked out. "I'm so sorry."

Keilann's mother raised her eyes, looking at her daughter as if seeing her for the first time.

"You don't hate me?"

Keilann started.

"Hate you? How could I hate you? You had to make a horrible choice that had death on both sides." She paused. "I just wish you hadn't faced it all alone."

Keilann's mother squeezed her hand. Overcome and exhausted, she closed her eyes and slumped back in her chair.

"You have to tell Dad," Keilann added gently.

Her mom remained still for another beat as if gathering strength. She took a deep breath, opened her eyes, and dabbed at the corners of her eyes with her shawl.

"I know," she sniffed.

Keilann gave her hand one last squeeze and helped her mother to her feet.

"C'mon, I'll make tea."

She started heading for the door, but her mother stayed where she was. She stood motionless, staring out the window at the trees. Their boughs shimmered with moonlight.

"I see her everywhere. I dream of her, my little girl," she murmured, just loud enough for Keilann to hear.

Keilann frowned.

"Her?" she echoed, taking a step back toward her mother. Mom was dangerously close to spiraling back into depression. If Keilann could only get her out of the office.

Her mom nodded, her gaze far away again.

"Sometimes, she's a baby. Sometimes I see what she would've been like as a woman."

Keilann inched closer, her arm reaching around to steer her mother from the window.

"Tall and strong, with red hair like your father."

Every cell in Keilann's body froze. Her arm hovered above her mom's shoulder, joints stiff with fear. She knew her mother was still talking, but she couldn't hear a word.

"A red-haired girl?" Her voice was high-pitched and much too loud. "You've been dreaming about a red-haired girl?"

Startled, her mother turned from the window.

"What is it? What's wrong?"

The room lurched, as if someone had hooked Keilann around the navel and tugged. The floor tilted up. Her mom rushed forward and caught Keilann by the shoulders.

"Keilann!"

"I'm alright! I'm alright!" she shrugged off her mother's hands and sunk into the arm chair.

"Keilann, you're scaring me. Why in the world does dreaming about my daughter matter so much?"

Keilann clenched her hands into fists to keep them from trembling. She took deep breaths until the black spots disappeared from the edge of her vision.

She looked up at her mother. It was finally Keilann's turn to confess.

"Mom," she sighed. "That girl is not your daughter."

26

Keilann had first heard the story of her grandmother's life giving dream as a lullaby, a bedtime story whispered to pacify her in the crib. There had never been a time that she didn't remember knowing it by heart. The story had grown with her, a fixed point in her identity that never faltered. It never occurred to Keilann to ask questions until she was almost ten-years-old.

"The spirits speak through dreams, *Akiiwin,*" Keilann's grandmother explained one summer holiday. Dusk closed in on the small cabin, the lake beyond as smooth and dark as blue velvet. They had been sitting on the back porch overlooking the water. Her grandmother leaned back on the legs of her favorite faded lawn chair, eyes half-closed as if listening to a concert of mosquito buzzing and loon calls.

"If you want to ask for guidance, you must be prepared to listen."

Keilann sat cross-legged on the floor beside her, picking at a swollen mosquito bite on her knee.

"Did you ask for your dream about me, *Nokomis?*"

Her grandmother said nothing. Keilann thought that maybe she hadn't heard, or worse. What if she had angered *Nokomis* by questioning her great secret? After a few minutes pause, her grandmother slowly lowered the front legs of the chair and turned to face Keilann.

"Tell me, do your mother and father teach you only what you ask them to?"

Keilann stopped fidgeting with her mosquito bite and frowned up at her grandmother. "What d'you mean?"

"Do your parents only teach you about life when you ask a specific question, or do they tell you things you need to know without you asking?"

Keilann crinkled her nose. "They tell me what they think I need to know. Especially rules," she added with a petulant scowl.

"Why?"

"Because I wouldn't even think of what to ask about most of the time," Keilann admitted. "They know things that I haven't even heard of yet."

Nokomis took Keilann's sticky, chubby fingers into her own soft, wrinkled ones and patted her hand. "Of course they do, *Akiiwin.* That is why the best lessons are the ones you don't have to ask for."

Keilann's frown deepened. "So, your dream was a lesson?"

Her grandmother gave a single, slow nod. "In a way." She held up her hand before Keilann could begin a new string of questions. "But I will not tell you how. Not yet."

Keilann clamped her mouth shut, biting back her words. She slouched into herself and scratched her mosquito bite with new vigor. But she hadn't given up. She had one last card to play. "Well then how am I supposed to know if I get the same kind of dream? How will I know if it's a lesson or not?" She looked up at *Nokomis* hopefully.

But her grandmother's eyes were already closed again, her head nodding in tempo with the night music of the lake. "You must learn to listen, *Akiiwin*."

It had seemed so simple so many years ago. But now, trembling in the worn office armchair with her mother kneeling beside her, Keilann knew that she had failed. She hadn't learned to listen. Worse, it seemed that she had gone deaf. If she was lucky, the damage wouldn't be permanent, but there was only one remedy that could help at such a late stage.

She told her mother everything.

For the first time in years, Keilann held nothing back. She couldn't if she had wanted to. The words gushed from her lips like spouts of water from a broken dam. She expected to be exhausted after telling the whole story, but as the words flowed out of her they loosed a massive weight from her chest and bore it out of her on the current. Nothing else could've done it. Keilann needed the full, cleansing force of each word to break its iron grip.

Once released, an untapped reserve of strength sprung from the spot, as if her guilt and fear had been corked and suppressed for months. She sat-up straighter, finding that she could meet her mother's eyes. Finally, after what seemed like hours, the flow ebbed into a trickle, her throat raw and scratchy. The burning man, red-haired girl, and stone circle all lay at her mother's feet, waiting for her to kick them aside or embrace them.

Keilann's mother sat back on her heels, rubbing her chin with the nail of her thumb. "And you're sure that it's her. That it's always the same red-haired girl?"

Keilann nodded. "Always."

Her mom braced her hands on her thighs and stood. Her knees creaked and popped. She shrugged off her shawl and shook her hair out of its clip. Keilann watched her, thinking that she looked younger than she had in months. Her mother leaned her weight against the desk and crossed her arms.

"So that's who she is," her mother breathed. Her body relaxed, relieved that she wasn't being haunted by the ghost of her unborn daughter. Relieved, Keilann thought, but wistful. She had lost her last connection to a child she would never know.

"You believe me?" she gawked. "Just like that?"

Her mother shrugged, brushing away doubt with an absent flick of her wrist.

"I've been living through the same dreams for the past five months, Keilann. How could I not believe you?"

At that moment, Keilann felt like she was seeing her mother as a small child would: impossibly strong, incalculably wise. Not once did her mom ask why she and her daughter had been plagued by an onslaught of nightmares. Unlike Keilann, she did not try and talk herself out of believing or rationalize its impracticality.

Guilt ate away the acid in her stomach. Why hadn't she been honest with her mother before tonight? How much pain could Keilann have saved both of them?

"Those awful nightmares," Mom added with a shudder. "I just can't believe that you've been living with those horrible images and haven't said a word. How did you do it?"

Keilann blinked. "What d'you mean 'how did I do it?' You've been doing the same thing this whole time."

Her mom shook her head again. "I never dreamed of fire. I don't think I could bear what you've told me. Seeing that night after night," she shuddered. "I dreamt of a red-haired girl. Mostly, she was a little girl—an infant or a toddler—but sometimes she appeared older. Once in a while there was another woman with her, but she was always a half-blurred form in the shadows. I'd see the woman out of the corner of my eye, but I could never get a good look at her. She disappeared after a while," she added quietly.

Keilann found herself nodding along with her mother's story.

"Her mother," she said simply. "I've seen her, too. She—" Keilann bit her lip. For a few seconds, she couldn't speak. Talking about the girl's mother made her throat constrict and her eyes sting, though she couldn't explain why.

Keilann swallowed hard. "She died."

Her mom's hand flew to her chest. "You saw this?"

Still fighting against the swelling balloon of sorrow in her throat, Keilann could only nod.

"Oh, Keilann..." Her mother rushed to her, crushing Keilann to her heart. Warm arms encircled her. Keilann closed her eyes, hot tears leaking into her lashes and down her cheeks. Her mother didn't think she was crazy.

She had her mother. Broken and wounded as they both were, she could still hold her and stroke her hair. A steady stream of tears dripped down her chin, but Keilann was not sobbing, she was mourning. The overwhelming weight of her secret was finally lifted, and she could recognize and weep over the tragedies she had witnessed. They had really happened. Those people had really died. Sharing these visions with her mother, Keilann finally saw the red-haired girl and the burning man for who they were—human beings. They were not monsters lurking under her bed. They were people, suffering, straining, and seeking as she did. The ghosts of the old house were nothing but empty shadows.

She was free.

Keilann's mother held her long after her tears had dried. Then gently, as if handling a fledgling bird, she released her. "But you've seen her?" She leaned forward, searching her face. "You've actually seen her?"

Keilann nodded. "At least, I think I did."

Her mother sucked in a breath. "I can't imagine."

"She scared me at first, but maybe she was afraid as well." Keilann shrugged. "I don't think either of us expected one another."

Her mom pursed her lips. "You don't believe she's a spirit?"

"No, no, definitely not," Keilann said firmly. The red-haired girl was too earthly, too human, too alive. But how could that be? Gruoch had lived almost a thousand years ago. How could she be living?

"At least, not when she's in the stone circle, anyway," she decided, pushing the rest of her jumbled thoughts aside. Keilann couldn't be expected to solve all of the mysteries of the universe in one night. "She is definitely alive when I see her, like we are walking through our own lives and they somehow intersect. I don't think any of this was her choice either."

"Little very rarely is," Mom said with a sad smile. "So what do you believe has caused it, this strange intersection?"

"It's the stone circle," Keilann insisted. "It's got to be. There's something there. When I'm in the circle, I feel different. I see and hear her. The dreams are more intense and hit me without warning. I usually don't even remember falling asleep. I just kind of slide into them, like I open a door and walk into her life."

The corners of her mother's mouth quirked. "Like the time you were playing rugby?"

Keilann flushed, squirming uncomfortably in her seat. She had come clean about what had really happened that night in the circle, but didn't feel like it was the right time to tell the truth about Connor McBride. She recounted the dream and the spinning sickness, and just let her mother assume that she had gotten the bruises from passing out and hitting a stone. At any rate, Keilann didn't try to correct these assumptions. Her mother had been through so much. What would she do if she knew that the boy bullying Keilann and the one Fiona was secretly dating were the same person?

No, she decided, *I'll tell her soon, but not tonight*. Divulging her first earth-shattering secret was more than enough for one night.

Keilann cleared her throat.

"The circle is the only link I've been able to come up with," she continued a little louder, determined to appear unfazed even though her face was still hot. "It's the only common denominator between us."

"Then you have to go back."

"What?"

Hadn't she just finished explaining to her mother what it was like in there?

"Don't you want to know why all this has been happening to us?"

"Of course I do!" Keilann snapped. "But I can do that without going back there. I can do research, put the pieces together."

Her mother shook her head.

"I don't think you can, Keilann. This isn't a situation that logic and examination can solve."

"I've done pretty well so far, haven't I?" Keilann asked. A huffy edge sharpened her words. "I figured out who she was."

"You've done very well, especially considering the nature of your nightmares. I know you're afraid to go back, but you won't help anyone by hiding."

Keilann closed her eyes. The latest dream replayed behind her eyelids: a song like a lullaby, drawing her to the stone circle, luminous and humming. It called to her through the mist.

"Will you come with me?"

Keilann's mother placed a hand on her shoulder. "I don't think it would do any good. You've been given a gift. You've been shown much more than I have. I don't think she would reveal anything if I came along."

"You think what I've been going through is a gift?"

Her mom nodded, her face grave. "A very sacred one, and one that I cannot and will not interfere with."

Keilann shrugged her mother's hand from her shoulder. "How can you say that?"

"I know it has been difficult for you, but an apowawin is not supposed to be easy."

"A vision quest?" Keilann gaped. "You think these dreams have been a vision quest?"

"An *apowawin*, the most powerful kind: the dream quest. It can awaken you to a new sense of self, if you have the courage to follow it."

"But Gram told me about vision quests! They're spiritual and peaceful. They aren't supposed to be like this!"

To Keilann's surprise, her mom laughed.

"Spiritual and peaceful! Does that sound like you, *Akiiwin*?" Her mother chuckled. "A vision quest is different for each person. It is a way to find your purpose, your true self. How would you be able to do that if it didn't give you what you needed?"

"You think I needed to have nightmares about people burning alive?"

Her mother paused, considering her words carefully.

"I think you needed to see beyond yourself, to share a journey with someone that needed help as much as you did. You have almost reached the end of that journey. Will you abandon her now?"

Keilann said nothing. She had always thought of the red-haired girl as an obstacle, a burden to figure out and remove as quickly as possible. Did she really need Keilann as much as her mother claimed?

"'The duty of animals is to live; the duty of humans is to dream,'" her mom continued, reciting her father's favorite quote. "You remember the old tales, the ones *Nokomis* and *Mishomis* told you. *Gichi-Manido* created life by dreaming of its endless possibilities and then creating them. When he created human beings, he gave us a part of himself: the power to dream and create as he does. But he is clever, *Akiiwin*, he doesn't always play by the rules we have dreamt up for him. You thought you had been fervently seeking the answers to a mystery, but what you have really been doing is seeking yourself."

"I'm scared." Keilann hung her head in her hands. "I don't know what to do."

Her mother put her arm around Keilann's shoulders and helped her stand.

"Yours is the hardest task of all," she said, taking Keilann's face in her hands. "You have to listen."

Keilann was abruptly very aware of how late it was. The roller coaster of emotion she had been riding the past hour had drained her body of its last reserves. She let her mother lead her up the stairs, her mind a maelstrom of erratic thoughts.

A vision quest? Could such a thing really exist? And her mother's confession, the abortion—it was too much to take in. She didn't want to think anymore.

Keilann fell asleep to the sound of someone singing. She couldn't make out the words, exactly, but it was bittersweet and sad, a lullaby to ease her mind into sleep.

Come to me, it seemed to say, *come to me*.

The voice was so familiar. Before she could place it, the song ended and Keilann drifted off into a dreamless sleep.

The song ended.

Keilann opened her eyes and winced at the daylight overflowing her window. Someone had been singing to her—*ugh*, had the sun always been so *bright*?

Massaging her temples with her fingertips, Keilann tried to grind away the painful drumming the whiskey had left behind. She couldn't remember a face or a dream, just the lullaby. Keilann pressed her fingers harder against her throbbing skull, willing her head to clear. Without knowing why, she had the impression that something had startled the singer, almost as if someone else had snuck up behind her. There hadn't been a scream or cry for help, but something definitely wasn't right.

"Owwwww!"

Keilann tried to sit up. Her movement triggered the dull throb into an explosion of ripping pain, as if her corneas were being wrenched through the back of her skull. She was going to be sick. The agony in her head shot nauseating ripples to her stomach. She concentrated on taking slow, deep breaths. The uprising in her belly quieted and she was able to—slowly—roll out of bed.

Never again, she swore vehemently. *I will never touch that awful stuff ever again. I'll go to Mom right now and promise.*

Her heart contracted with such force it squeezed the air from her lungs.

Mom.

The events of last night tumbled together: the whiskey—*oh God*, the whiskey—her own confession, and her mother's revelations.

The abortion.

The thought she had been avoiding threw a bucket of cold, sobering water over her head. Its icy syllables chilled her spine. The dream, the singing, it didn't matter. Her mother needed her. Gruoch could wait. Brushing the hairspray-matted tangles from her hair and pulling on fresh clothes, Keilann rubbed the sleep from her eyes and glanced at the clock. At first, she couldn't figure out why the numbers weren't making sense. Then she did a double-take.

2:30? Two-thirty in the afternoon?

How late had she and her mother stayed in that office? Her whiskey infused brain struggled to churn out the calculations. She had come home from the party well past midnight. Talking with her mother, time hadn't seemed to pass at all, but the clock said otherwise. Had her father still been out at the party when she finally dragged herself to bed or had he been home the whole time, sleeping through the turmoil below?

Sweeping her half-brushed hair into a messy ponytail, Keilann risked a quick confrontation with the mirror. She had no idea when Mom was planning to finally confide in Dad, but until she was ready Keilann had to appear as normal as possible. Not as bad as she expected: a few smudges of last night's mascara and blotches of eye shadow were scrubbed away with a tissue. There wasn't much she could do about her hair without a shower, but it would have to do for now. She was giving herself one last look-over when a dark flutter in the mirror behind her made her freeze. There was something in the room with her.

Keilann spun around. The slight breeze from her movements stirred another quivering flutter in her wake, the dark feathers rising and falling like a sigh. It had appeared as if Asibikaashi, the Spider Woman, had woven it while Keilann slept. The bloodroot yarn looped in an intricate spider web, black-striped feathers trailing from the tightly-bound ring of willow. The dreamcatcher was slung over the far bedpost. She recognized it at once, though she still couldn't believe it was there. Keilann stepped toward it, feeling like she had been caught in a dream between the threads. She reached out through the years of time. When she curled her fingers around the soft yarn, she was six years old again, her mother's strong hands helping her shape her first dreamcatcher.

Keilann stroked the soft feathers. The story of the dreamcatcher rushed back to her. How her mother told of how *Ashibikaashi* had saved the world by catching the sun in her web, bringing life to their people. She smiled, remembering how clumsily she had twisted and knotted the bright yarn until her mom had taken pity and untangled it. But brittle childhood dreamcatchers were supposed to wear and snap, a lesson that all things pass. Over time, Keilann had forgotten about its existence. How had her mother kept it safe and whole all these years?

Keilann unhooked the dreamcatcher and laid it out on her bed, smoothing the glossy feathers so they splayed like a fan. Catching the dark and letting in the light. Maybe they all needed more of that.

Leaving the dreamcatcher to rest from its long night of guarding her, Keilann crept from the room and poked her head into the cool hall, feeling like a snake tasting the air for danger. The house was quiet and still. As she neared the end of the hallway, a murmur of muffled voices floated up from the rooms below. Keilann cocked her head. From the office came the sound of two voices, and that low, rumbling growl was definitely her father. Keilann leaned forward, straining to hear her mother's reply, but it was too soft to hear. She took the stairs one at a time, pausing between each step to listen. The last thing

Keilann wanted to do was blunder into what could possibly be the most important and devastating conversation of their marriage. Though she couldn't hear any sobs or tremors catching in either voice, she had witnessed her mother cry last night and had no desire to see it again. On the contrary, as Keilann's feet touched the landing, her mother's voice sounded stronger and clearer than it had in a long time. Perhaps she had poured all of her tears into her confession last night. Perhaps she had no more to cry.

Keilann followed the voices down the hallway, tracing her footsteps from last night back to the office. The door was flung open, bright sunlight thrown against the scrubbed wall in a patch of dazzling white. Her mom's voice drifted out of the door, but Keilann could only snatch at random words. Hovering on the edge of the light, Keilann hesitated. The voices had stopped altogether. Had they heard her? She craned her neck around the doorframe.

Neither of her parents looked at her. In fact, they didn't seem aware of her presence. Her father sat at his desk, the wooden swivel chair facing the window, a cold mug of coffee forgotten behind him. Keilann's mom stood beside him, a comforting arm on his shoulder, but he didn't look at her. Keilann couldn't see his face, but the limp slouch of his shoulders told her that he knew.

"I'm so sorry," her dad said to the windows.

Keilann's hand flew to her mouth, stifling a gasp. Her father's voice, usually so cheerful, sounded like the rattling husk of an old man.

Her mom stiffened. After all the pain and isolation of the past six months, what would she possibly say?

"It's no one's fault."

Her father shook his head. "But if I had—you never once—if you'd only felt like you could talk to me."

Keilann's mother knelt beside him, as Keilann had knelt beside her just a few hours ago. "I'm talking to you now, so listen." She cupped her hand around his chin and turned his face to meet hers. "It's not your fault. It's no one's fault."

He shook his head, but didn't argue again. He reached up and took her hand, holding it to his left shoulder as if afraid that she would disappear when he let go.

Keilann decided that she had played spy long enough. Now was clearly not the time for interruptions, however well-meaning. Wanting nothing more than to leave unnoticed, she shifted her weight to her back foot and leaned out of the doorway to tiptoe back upstairs. Before Keilann could duck out of sight, her mother's head twisted at the sound of creaking floorboards and spotted her. Burning with shame, Keilann expected her mother's face to darken with indignant anger. Instead, it broke into a relieved smile. She motioned to her to wait. Murmuring in her dad's ear, her mom gave his shoulder a final squeeze and crossed the room in a few quick strides. As Keilann watched her mother walk toward her, she couldn't help but think how different she seemed. Grief had changed her. This morning she stood like steel tempered by fire. She was a little scorched in places, but hardened enough to bear her husband's sorrow without breaking.

Her mother was at the door before Keilann realized she had no idea what to say to her. She couldn't pretend last night hadn't happened or what was said hadn't changed everything. Where did they go from here?

Her mom put her finger to her lips and shooed Keilann into the hall, easing the door shut behind them.

She turned to her daughter.

Keilann opened her mouth. "Hi."

A small, amused smile brushed Mom's dry lips. "Good morning—or afternoon, I should say," she said after a cursory glance at her watch.

"Are you...is Dad..." Keilann groped for the right question. "Did you tell him?"

The smile flickered and faded. Her mother nodded. "He knows."

"Is he okay? Are you okay, Mom?"

"Not okay...better. It'll be a while before any of us are okay," she said after a pause. For once, Keilann believed her. "Did you sleep alright? No nightmares?"

"Yeah. Thanks, Mom."

Her mother shrugged. "It was yours anyway. I just kept it safe until you needed it."

Keilann opened her mouth to ask how she had kept it for so long, but her mother cut in before she could speak. "Keilann, will you do me a favor?" she asked with a slight frown. "Could you go talk to your sister?"

"Fiona? Yeah, sure," she said, taken aback but reluctant to deny her mother anything.

"I think she needs someone." Her mother glanced over her shoulder. "We'll be talking for a while."

"I'll talk to her," Keilann said. Though whether Fiona would talk back was an entirely different question.

"She's upstairs. If you need me—" she gestured to the office. "*Miigwetch, Akiiwin.* Thank you for everything you've done."

Keilann winced. Everything she'd done—or hadn't done—seemed to be the root of most of their problems. But there would be time enough for self-pity later.

Though her mother was just a flight of stairs below facing her demons, Keilann could not bring herself to face her little sister. The two hadn't spoken for weeks. The most words passed between them over break had been "Merry Christmas" or "Remote. Now."

Not that Keilann's mother knew what she was asking her oldest daughter to do. Keilann hadn't told her anything about Connor or the almost hook-up she had barged into and the girls had been very careful to act normally around their parents. Between the two of them, Fiona had made it clear to her sister that she wanted nothing to do with her. But last night had changed things. Not just for their mother, but for the whole family. Suddenly, a few spiteful insults and arguments over a boy seemed petty. She stared at Fiona's door, willing her hand to knock, but there it hung, limp at her side.

Just get it over with. Keilann clenched her jaw and rapped her knuckles, business-like, on the door.

"Fiona? I'm coming in." She wasn't about to give her little sister the option of sending her away this time.

Surprised to find the door unlocked, Keilann turned the handle and swept through the door, closing it behind her before Fiona could argue. She expected an onslaught of indignant protests, but was met with a wet sniffle. The room was dark and the blinds shuttered. Keilann had to blink a few times before her eyes adjusted to the gloom.

"Fiona?"

Another sniffle. Keilann groped her way to the bed and made out the form of her little sister, curled in on herself like a stray cat hiding in the corner.

Oh boy.

"Are you okay?"

Fiona gave a great sniff and leaned forward. The reading lamp next to her bed clicked on, splashing a circle of pale light over her face. Her eyes were red and puffy.

"I guess Mom told you," she said, dragging the sleeve of her loose grey night shirt across her nose.

It was a few moments before Keilann could speak. Fiona, not primped and dressed at this hour? If she thought her own hair was hopeless, Fiona's was worse. It was a mass of knots slicked to her head by old hairspray and sticking out at odd angles. Keilann couldn't remember the last time she had seen her sister wear sweatpants, but the ratty, washed out shirt was vaguely familiar. Keilann thought she looked more like her old self than she had in years. The news must've hit her hard.

"Yeah," Keilann said gently. She sat on the opposite corner of the bed. "Can you believe it?"

Fiona buried her head in her hands.

"I never thought...."

Her words were lost in tear-filled wails. Keilann surprised herself, reaching across the distance and silence with a fierce hug. Here she was, comforting two crying people in the past twelve hours. She was getting good at this.

"There's nothing you could've done about it," Keilann cooed, rubbing Fiona's back.

"How—did—this—happen?" Fiona sobbed.

"It's okay, it's going to be okay," she soothed, quickly expending her pool of reassuring phrases.

"I just can't believe he would do something like that!" she cried, wiping more snot on her damp sleeve.

Was she serious? Keilann let go of Fiona, staring at her from arm's length.

"Fiona, how can you blame him? It's no one's fault," she defended her father, echoing Mom's own words.

Fiona smacked Keilann's hands from her shoulders. "How can you say that!" she screeched. "You of all people. I thought you'd be on my side."

"It's not Dad's fault. He didn't even know about the baby!"

Fiona stopped. She stared at Keilann as if she'd never seen her before. "Oh my god, Keilann, what are you talking about?"

Keilann stood and stepped away from her sister. "What are you talking about?" Fiona scooted to the edge of the bed, ogling her sister. "Keilann, are you pregnant?"

"What? No! I thought—didn't you? I'm not pregnant!" she insisted, a bit too loudly. "Didn't Mom tell you?"

Then it hit Keilann: *she didn't know.*

Fiona's eyes narrowed. "Tell me what?"

"Well, last night we were talking about the babies she's...lost. I thought she might've told you about them, too, and maybe that's why you were so upset today," Keilann said carefully.

Fiona blinked. "You mean the miscarriages she had, like, twenty years ago? That's a bit morbid," she added, crinkling her nose. "Why the heck were you talking about that? Besides, how could they've been Dad's fault? He had nothing to do with them."

"Nope, nope, he sure didn't," Keilann agreed with an anxious giggle. Why hadn't Mom told Fiona? Did she not think her younger daughter could handle such news?

She could've at least warned me, Keilann grit her teeth. "Anyway," she added, trying to smooth the situation awkwardly. "We're talking about you, aren't we? Something's definitely up. I can tell."

Fiona was suddenly sullen, picking at the frayed edge of her cuff. "Mom didn't tell you about what happened?"

Keilann shook her head. "I'm not so sure that she did, actually."

For a moment, Fiona seemed on the brink of shrugging it off and reestablishing the icy silence between them. But her bottom lip began to quiver and she broke, the story bursting out of her in a gush. "It was awful!" she moaned. "I went to a party with him last night."

Keilann's stomach dropped out of her body, her palms slick with sweat. What had Connor McBride done to her little sister?

"We were having fun, you know? And then he disappeared. He said he was looking for a friend. I didn't want to be clingy, so I stayed with our group and watched a movie."

Thank you, thank you for not being alone with him. Keilann let go of a breath she hadn't been aware of holding. She could see where this story was going.

She cleared her throat. "And did Connor find his *friend?*"

Fiona closed her eyes, as if she could see him cheating on her in her own bed. "I found him in one of the back rooms with her." The waver in her voice hardened into bitterness. "He was mad at me. Can you believe it? Me! Said I was just a little girl and it was none of my business, but if I still wanted to...still wanted to sleep with a senior I could come back later."

Fiona ducked her burning face out of sight. Her eyes refilled with tears.

Keilann gaped. A vicious hatred simmered in her belly. Part of her wanted to fling a triumphant "I told you so" at Fiona, turn on her heel, and stomp from the room. Looking at her little sister, her makeup smeared and her confidence shattered, part of her also wanted to hug her.

"Fiona—"

She threw her hands up. "Don't say it, Keilann. Please don't say it."

Keilann paused. "Is it over?"

Fiona dropped her hands and glared at her sister with some of her old pride. "You think I'd do that? You really think I'd go back to that—" She took a deep breath. "He was a senior and he actually *looked* at me, Keilann. But I thought he wanted me—just me. I thought...." Fiona shook her head.

"You told Mom about this? About everything?"

"Well, not everything," Fiona admitted, a bit sheepishly. "She was still up when I came home last night bawling my eyes out. I told her that Connor was just a boy I liked. I didn't tell her about...you know."

Her head snapped up as if a terrible thought had struck her. She grabbed Keilann's arm. "You won't tell her?"

Keilann bit her lip. Should she? Look at where all of the lies had gotten them so far. It might be better to just come clean. But that was not something she could decide. Keilann had finally been released from her secret. Only Fiona could choose when and if to do the same.

She looked her sister steadily in the eye. "I won't tell them anything."

Fiona sighed and fell back against her pillows. "You were so right about him," she said in a small voice. "Thanks for not rubbing it in my face."

Keilann shrugged and headed for the door. "We all do stupid stuff. You sure you're okay?"

Fiona nodded. "Keilann?"

Keilann turned around in the doorway.

"I'm sorry about what I said. I was really mean. I didn't mean it."

Though Fiona's insults rang through her head every time she looked in the mirror, Keilann shrugged as if she had forgotten them.

"Where are you going?" Fiona asked.

"Me?" Keilann sighed. "I'm off to write my paper."

Fiona frowned. "That essay? I thought you were almost done."

Keilann gave her a half-hearted smile. "So did I."

Kicking her door shut behind her, Keilann flicked on her light and powered-up the old laptop. It whined to life, unenthusiastically shaking the dust from its programs. Gently, she slid the dreamcatcher from her bed and draped it over the bedpost. She was going to need all the help she could get. As her computer whizzed and hummed, Keilann traipsed straight past her distinct, thoughtfully selected piles of books and grabbed the ragged notebook from her nightstand. It was stuffed with Jana's details of Gruoch and her tumultuous life. Exactly what she had needed all along.

The laptop chimed groggily, and Keilann pulled up the file she had been cobbling together since the first day of break. Eleven pages filled with quotes and statistics, professional opinions and historical documentation. All it lacked was a conclusion and a bibliography, and the nightmare essay would be behind her. Instead of typing, Keilann dragged the mouse over to the menu and hovered over a command. Without a moment's hesitation, she hit "Delete."

A little warning box popped up before her.

"Are you sure?" it asked, trying to make her see reason.

Keilann had never been surer of anything in her life. Another swift click of the mouse, and the essay was gone.

With a heavy sigh, Keilann cracked her knuckles and shook out her fingers.

It was time to start over.

28

The schoolyard was packed with stragglers catcalling, yelping, and whooping. Students fell over each other, slipping in the wet, heavy snow that had finally rolled in with the New Year. A rogue snowball whizzed past Keilann's nose, but she kept walking, her eyes fixed on the glowering double doors. Everyone else tried to squeeze out a last few seconds of break, but she was on a mission.

"Just keep walking," she muttered out of the corner of her mouth, her breath escaping in tiny white clouds.

Pale-faced and tight-lipped, Fiona nodded stiffly.

She hadn't mentioned it, but Keilann knew the queasy knot of dread and loathing coiled in Fiona's stomach. Meeting Connor before they had even started the second term was the last thing either sister wanted, and it was Keilann's mission to see Fiona safely to her first class without incident. How, exactly, she was going to prevent Connor McBride from harassing her little sister when she hadn't been able to stand-up to him herself was something she'd have to work out later.

They stepped into the warmth of the entrance hall and shook the frozen droplets from their dripping hair. It was even noisier inside with students lounging on the stairs, reuniting at lockers, and furiously scribbling a last-ditch effort on a forgotten assignment. Fiona hesitated, her dark eyes darting from face to face. Keilann pretended not to notice, brushing snow from her coat that wasn't there to begin with. After a few moments, Fiona's shoulders relaxed, and she turned to Keilann with a fleeting, breathless smile. Connor was nowhere to be seen.

Pushing their way through throngs of students, they made it to Fiona's locker with only seconds to spare. Looking perfectly normal, Fiona began stuffing books into her locker. Keilann searched her little sister's cool expression for cracks.

"You gonna be okay?"

Fiona cast a glance around the hallway. A blonde head bobbed into view. Keilann watched her sister's whole body go rigid. But when the boy turned his face toward them, it was only a blonde stranger neither of them recognized. Swallowing, Fiona gave her sister a grim nod.

"Don't worry about him," Keilann said, trying to sound dismissive. "If you see him, just ignore whatever he says because it won't be true. You don't owe him anything."

She wasn't sure if Fiona had heard her. She was staring at the muddy puddles spreading from her shoes. Her lower lip trembled, but then she nodded again.

Keilann pressed her hand.

"You'll be fine. No matter what happens, remember that you're pretty and clever and he's an ugly old arsehole," Keilann joked, miming a thick Scottish accent.

Fiona rewarded her with a nervous grin.

"I'll see you in a few hours. At least you won't have to see him in class."

Unlike me.

The signal rang through the halls, and the listless students stampeded into action. Fiona set her jaw and marched off toward her first class without another word.

The first day's the hardest, Keilann reassured herself as she followed the flow of bodies up the stairs. As if she knew what it was like to have been cheated on. As if she knew what it was like to have been in a relationship.

She'll get better.

Distracted, Keilann turned the corner to Ms. Spark's room and slammed into a solid wall wearing a school jumper.

"Whoa, steady on! Still not tipsy from tha' wee dram, are ye? Or did I give ye a thirst fer whiskey?"

Keilann scowled up at Ben, bending to gather the fallen books at her feet.

"Ugh, I can't believe you made me drink that crap," she said, pulling a face.

Ben laughed, scooping up Keilann's precious essay from where it had been knocked to the floor, saving it from being trampled by an onslaught of classmates. "As I recall, I don' believe I made you drink anythin'." He looked down at the paper in his hands and read the first few sentences. "Is this it then? The reason ye holed yerself up for most of yer holiday and why I haven't talked to ye since Hogmanay?"

Keilann flushed. "Oh, sorry. And yeah, I had to rewrite it."

Ben was aghast. "All of it? Everythin' ye worked on?"

"Yup," Keilann nodded grimly. "It just wasn't right."

Ben's eyebrows shot up skeptically. "Was it worth it?" he asked, placing the stapled pages into her outstretched hands.

Keilann gently cradled the essay, frantic not to smudge a single word or crinkle any pages. In the past two days, she had written, edited, and rewritten her essay until, bruised and bloodied, it resembled something like the truth. She could only hope it would be enough.

Squaring her shoulders, she dropped her bag onto her desk and flashed Ben a quick smile.

"We'll see," she said brightly.

"Hey—Keilann wait." Ben laid a hand on her arm. The urgent tone in his voice caught her by surprise—he was suddenly eager and hesitant at the same time. She gave him a puzzled look, waiting for him to speak.

"Umm...are ye free after school?"

She nodded. "You wanna get chips or something?" she asked, trying her best to seem normal.

Ben's worried expression broke into his normal gap-toothed grin. "Since when do ye say chips?"

Keilann tossed a braid over her shoulder, pretending to be offended. "Hey, I've been through Hogmanay and I've even eaten black pudding without dying. I'm Scottish now. I'm allowed to say chips."

Ben threw up his hands in surrender. "How can I argue with such sound logic? Scottish ye are then, and chips it'll be."

Keilann smiled back and turned away from him, her head in a warm daze. *Is this what flirting feels like?*

Keilann stopped in front of the podium where Ms. Spark was leafing through papers, settling herself in after the long holiday. She waited for her teacher to notice her, forcing herself to be calm.

"Ah, Ms. Douglas!" Ms. Spark looked up from her work. "I trust ye had a pleasant holiday and, I hope, a productive one?"

Keilann flourished her finished paper proudly.

Ms. Spark graced her student with a benevolent smile as she paused to receive the essay. She set the paper on top of the ones scattered across her podium and leaned back to scan the first page.

"Mmmmm," she said, her sharp eyes flicking over Keilann's painstakingly constructed argument. Ms. Spark only spent a few seconds over each page, but as she flipped to the end, she gave Keilann a satisfied nod.

"Good to have ye back, Ms. Douglas."

Keilann dashed back to her seat just as the final bell tolled, flashing Ben a thumbs-up. Too late, she noticed Connor had been watching her. Grinning like a cat that had finally caught his mouse, Connor returned the thumbs-up and faced forward, refusing to make eye contact with Keilann for the rest of the period. But Keilann couldn't help staring at him, snakes crawling in her stomach.

The rest of the day rushed by in a giddy whiplash of emotions; one moment dreading the meaning behind Connor's smirk, the next euphoric when she thought about having chips with Ben. She tried to catch him up at lunch, but felt like Ben was only half-listening. He told Keilann he was relieved that Fiona wasn't involved with Connor anymore and seemed to think that was the end of it. Maybe Connor would just want to ignore them and be ignored in return. Keilann wanted to believe that, but the look on

Connor's face that morning had told her it wasn't over yet.

By the time her last class ended, she nearly jumped out of her skin with anticipation. She stuffed books and handfuls of homework into her bag as quickly as she could and hustled to Fiona's locker. Out of breath for the second time that day, Keilann leaned against the cool metal of the locker and watched as a river of students ebbed into a stream, and then into a trickle. She checked her watch.

Where is she?

They had agreed to meet at Fiona's locker directly after school. Tapping her foot impatiently, she watched the minute hands on her watch slowly crawl past a quarter of an hour. Something was wrong. Maybe Fiona was outside with her group of friends. Keilann waited until she was alone in the empty hallway. Why didn't their parents ever let them get cell phones?

Pushing off of the lockers, Keilann made her way back through the hall, dragging her feet in case Fiona breezed in at the last second, yelling at her for not being outside. Her foot was on the first stair before she heard a sound that made her freeze. A familiar sound, one that made the hairs on her neck stand at attention: Connor McBride.

She turned at once, head cocked, her ears strained. Keilann sped down the side corridor—an art wing from the looks of it—and stopped. It was empty like the main hall, but somehow darker. There were no windows here. She tried to listen over the sound of her thudding heart.

Say something, she pleaded. *Talk again, you bastard.*

Instead, she heard another voice; small and shaken, but very familiar.

"No."

Fiona.

Her voice was louder than his, and it pulled Keilann down the hallway toward what looked like a photography dark room. Connor's voice boomed behind it, but she couldn't make out any words. What would that matter anyway? With a last deep breath, she forced her shaking arms to grasp the latch on the door and pull as hard as she could.

It was locked.

No! No!

She yanked and yanked again, thudding her palms against the metal barrier between her and her sister. The voices inside stopped, but Keilann kept pounding. The latch suddenly clicked and the door slid open, light spilling into the room.

Connor McBride's face was twisted in fury.

"What—" he snarled. Then he saw who it was, and his whole body relaxed, reminding Keilann of a cat again. A cat toying with its prey.

He narrowed his eyes and gave Keilann a lazy grin. He leaned against the door between her and Fiona. Fiona was a frozen shadow bathed in red light, back pressed to the sink behind her.

Keilann was too horrified to speak. Her brain tried to find the words to throw at the monster, but she found none.

"Pocahontas! I was jess catching up with yer sister."

Shaking from head to foot, she met Connor's glare with one of her own.

"Leave Fiona alone, Connor," she said. Her jaw was stiff but the words came out strong and clear. "I swear to God, I'll call the police if you don't let her out of there."

Connor's smile widened, dripping with cruelty. He pulled Fiona forward and draped a long, lazy arm over her shoulders. She winced at his touch, her face white with fear, her eyes wide and pleading. Keilann darted forward and grabbed Fiona by the shoulders, jerking her from Connor's surprised grasp. He didn't have time to react and his hands slacked as Fiona's thin frame slipped through the door. Keilann pulled her sister behind her. She could feel Fiona's body tremble. She gripped Keilann like a life vest.

"Don't you touch her, don't you ever touch her again, you monster!"

Connor stepped into the hall. He towered over both girls. Keilann wanted to run and scream, but held her ground. Mostly because her legs had been replaced with jelly.

Now what?

Connor took another step toward them.

"What?" He asked innocently, his arms outspread. "Don' like to think o' yer darlin' slut of a sister with me?"

The insult coursed through Keilann like quicksilver. She clenched her fists.

"If you ever call her that again, if you ever touch her—"

Connor advanced to a hair's breath away from Keilann's face and crossed his arms. "Ye'll what?" he jeered.

Connor's face was like thunder. Before he could yell or charge, Keilann shocked herself by speaking up.

"I'm tired of this!" she snapped in his face.

Connor's eyes widened in shock.

"You don't like me? Fine. Let's agree to ignore one another and leave my sister out of this. You don't even like her. Just let this stupid grudge go and after this year we'll never have to see each other again."

Her words ran out and she was left stunned by their calm clarity. Where had that come from? Was it something like courage? All she knew at that moment was that she had faced far worse than Connor McBride, walked through fire and made it to the other side unscathed. Connor's childish tantrum no longer frightened her.

This is what growing up feels like. Keilann wondered if Connor would ever feel anything like it.

. Connor said nothing. He just glared.

Keilann wrapped an arm around Fiona's shaking shoulders. "C'mon. Let's go."

She turned to lead Fiona down the hall, but Connor's rage finally found his tongue.

"You bastards! You're not gettin' the best of me!" he screamed. "I'm gonna make sure everyone at this school knows fer years that yer sister is nothin' but a dirty little wh—"

It happened so fast. Bone connected with bone, and with a stomach-churning crunch, Connor fell to the ground. He bellowed in pain and clamped a hand to his shattered nose, blood spurting from between his fingers and spattering the ground with red. He scrambled away from Keilann on his hands and knees. He cowered with his back against the wall. Shocked beyond words, Fiona gaped open mouthed as Connor staggered to his feet and ran out of sight without looking back.

"What the hell did I miss this time?"

It was like a dream. Keilann turned, and Ben was already at Fiona's side. He stared as Connor ran away from Keilann with a bloodied face.

Keilann glanced at her hand and turned to face them, breaking the silence.

"You're right, Ben," she said cradling her throbbing, swelling knuckles. "That really does hurt."

Keilann stumbled into her room, her head spinning. She could hear the phone click into its cradle in the kitchen below and the murmur of her parents voices floated up to her once again.

Only this time, Fiona's voice was with them.

After the last phone call, they had finally released Keilann, telling her to get some rest. They needed time to spend with their youngest daughter alone. Careful to protect her bandaged hand, Keilann flopped down on her bed, her bones settling against the soft cushion of her mattress. Thanks to Ben's dad, her parents were on their way to officially filing charges against Connor McBride. Ben and his father had only just left an hour ago, Ben filling in his side of the story of the previous accounts of harassment Keilann had faced. Would Fiona finally tell her parents the whole truth about Connor?

Keilann found that she didn't really care as long as he wouldn't be able to hurt her again. She expected to feel a thrill of victory, of triumph over her tormentor. Instead, she felt tired. Keilann found that she pitied a life so sad and twisted as Connor's. What would his father do to him when he found out about the charges? Keilann closed her eyes, thinking of the kind of parents he would never know. The kind she had.

Yes, she pitied him. But not enough to regret breaking his nose.

I did that.

Keilann sat up. A year ago she wouldn't have had the guts. She wouldn't have believed she could do such a thing.

So who am I now?

With her good hand, she gently removed the dreamcatcher from its perch and stroked the soft, timeworn yarn.

Who am I?

Keilann stood, dreamcatcher in hand, and walked to the window. She squinted at the dazzling colors of the sunset, peering into the dark depths of the trees to where she knew the stone circle waited for her.

"Okay," she said at last. "I'm ready to listen now."

Keilann stood outside the stone circle, the toes of her grubby trainers poised on an invisible line. She was so close. She swore she could hear the stones hum again, just like in her dreams. It was almost like singing, a vibration that ran up her legs and down her arms, tickling the balls of her feet through her shoes. Though she heard no distinguishable voice, Keilann was reminded of the lullabies her mother used to sing to her: soft and sweet, but powerful and reassuring.

She lingered on the edge, drinking in the forest around her. It was so beautiful. Why hadn't she ever noticed before? Keilann fixed her eyes onto the craggy faces of the seven stones, as if committing their individual details to memory. Some were crumbled. Most had abrupt, almost violent gashes wrenched into their sides. Several stones leaned away from the circle as if one good breeze would knock them over for good. One or two still stood stall, their proud forms unbent by time. She looked on in silence, letting the sounds of the living forest mingle with the hum of the stones and wash over her until she lost track of the moments.

She looked but did not dare touch or join them—not yet. The gritty stone faces had been sculpted a hundred thousand times during their lonely lives. They were as familiar as old friends now, inseparable from Keilann's new identity, but still cold and distant as strangers. She felt the hairs rise on the back of her neck as if the stones knew she was there. As if they waited for her.

Her fingers tightened around the precious bundle clasped to her chest. Another step and her world would change forever. Entering the circle now, no matter what happened afterward, would mean throwing away her old absolute definition of the universe and accepting something new and yet unspeakably old; something much more formless and frightening. That something had the power to ignore time, death, and logic, in order to knit two lives together. Or was it bigger than that? As Keilann looked back on the threads of her life, she could see how they looped and interlocked, branching out and weaving together since the day she had been born. And before that, her grandmother's dream, her naming ceremony—was all of it connected? She could feel the threads nearing the center, drawing her to the stone circle before she had drawn her first breath.

Her head reeled. The idea made her so dizzy she had to lock her knees to keep from swaying. She fought against the urge to close her eyes. It was too big, too confusing. The mere idea of it split her head.

She trained her eyes at a point between gaps in the stones. Keilann focused on the murky horizon to settle her nerves. Mist clung to the damp hollows of trees, sinking through her wool jacket and coating her bones. Stiff with cold, she stretched her limbs and blinked the sleep from her eyes. Keilann wasn't used to getting up before dawn, but she had wanted to be in the stone circle at sunrise, not a moment before or after. Most of her fingers were numb, but she only held her bundle tighter.

Keilann felt like *Asibikaashi*, the Spider Woman, perfectly balanced on her sinewy web, ready to capture the sun and bring life back to the People. Here she was in her web of stone, waiting for the first light of day. But would it bring life or death with its purifying fire?

The world ignited. The sun's fiery head crested over the trees and splashed the feathery evergreens crimson and gold. Above the canopy, the black velvet of the still sleeping sky was dyed with an almost colorless blue. Thousands of nameless stars dissolved behind a blanket of pale rose and burnt orange as the sun climbed higher.

Keilann squinted at the blinding flare of light and squeezed the dreamcatcher to her thudding chest. She took a deep breath and let the air out slowly.

Gichi-manido wiidookawishin ji-mashkawiziyaan.

"Great Spirit, help me to be strong."

Keilann closed her eyes and stepped into the circle.

30

Nothing happened.

Keilann touched a hand to one of the humming stones. It pulsed gently beneath her fingertips, but Gruoch did not appear. She stepped to the center of the circle, her brow furrowed. All week she had dreamed of the lullaby calling her to return. All week she had waited, wanting to deal with the aftermath of Connor McBride before she returned to such a sacred place. Keilann felt it was necessary to wait, to purge herself of the last darkness before she stepped into the light. Now, it seemed, she had waited too long.

Keilann laid the dreamcatcher down in the center of the ring where snow still clung to the dead grass in clumps. Navigating the circle of yarn like a compass, she shifted the hoop back and forth until each of the seven points of the web lined up with one of the seven standing stones. A chill breeze shivered through the stone circle and she drew her mother's shawl tightly around her shoulders. It was simple: heavy, dark wool embellished with one ribbonwork blossom—red, yellow, white, and black—in each corner. Drab compared to the fancy shawls beribboned with sunbursts of gaudy color like the ones she'd seen at childhood pow wows, it was one of her grandmother's making. Keilann could feel the warmth and love of *Nokomis'* patient hands in every stitch. The shawl was not flashy, but neither was she.

Keilann threw her arms out, the cloth clutched in her hands and draped across her back like wings. She closed her eyes, swaying with a gentle side-step to the pulse of the singing stones. Tilting her arms, she twirled around and around, kicking up her legs as the air charged and crackled, dancing to the lullaby in her head. Keilann was wearing muddy trainers, not beaded moccasins and ripped blue jeans instead of a jewel-bright jingle dress, but that's who she was: a girl of two worlds. They conflicted and clashed and made her who she was. No ceremonial drums spurred her on, just the distant echo of a faded melody, sighing as if carried on the wind. Caught up in the steps of the dance, Keilann didn't notice at first that the song was no longer just in her head. It was all around her. Dipping and swirling, the stone circle was a grey blur, her feet barely touched the ground as she picked up her pace.

It was working.

The song ended abruptly, cut off mid-tune. Keilann's foot stomped down on the final note, and she could feel that it had worked before she even saw Gruoch. She lowered her arms, opened her eyes, and there she was. As if she had been waiting for Keilann to appear, Gruoch was standing tall, proud, and impossible in the center of the circle, clutching a well wrapped bundle to her chest.

Keilann had feared, prepared, and yearned for this moment since she had first seen the red-haired girl, but now that they were both here, she had no idea what to do. She couldn't exactly call her the red-haired girl anymore. She was definitely no longer a girl. Her face had not lost its wild beauty, but it was weathered and hardened now, as if carved and sharpened by time. Keilann could've almost believed it was a different person except for her eyes. There was no mistaking the dark intelligence of her eyes, smoldering beneath her brows like blue-grey smoke.

They stood only yards apart, sizing each other up as they had the very first time Keilann had stumbled into the stone circle. Only this time was different. This time, she wasn't going to run away. But what was she *supposed* to do? Keilann felt like there had to be some ritual to perform or maybe a task to complete. How else did a vision quest end? Should she speak? Whatever power resided in the seven stones had joined the crooked paths of their lives, changing them both for a reason. What on earth could she say to possibly sum that up?

"Hey."

Gruoch wasted no time. Steeling her spine, she took a halting step toward Keilann—just one, as if not to frighten her. Keilann's muscles tensed at the movement, but she fought the urge to bolt. She didn't come all this way to run away now. She came here to find herself. Whatever that meant.

Clenching her jaw to keep it from shaking, she forced herself to mimic Gruoch and stand straight and firm. Gruoch never increased her speed, never took her eyes off of Keilann's. She took one step, and then another, inching toward her as cautiously as a deer with its tail half-raised, uncertain if the next step would be forward or in flight. Keilann stood her ground, and Gruoch kept moving closer. Yards shrunk into feet, and soon the two were only inches apart. She could feel the same hum that surrounded the stones emanating from Gruoch's skin as if she were enveloped in a barrier of static electricity.

Do I feel the same way to her? Keilann wondered, gazing into her companion's dark, fearless eyes. But there was something else in her eyes, something softer and far more human: hope. From this distance, Keilann could see the age-weary lines on a face that was not yet old. She remembered the night of fire that Gruoch had lived through—that she had somehow shared with her—and the bitter unknown that she had yet to face alone.

Or was she alone? Gruoch was still carrying the bundle, pressed to her heart as if a treasure beyond imagining. Why bring it all the way out here to the stone circle?

Her gaze followed Keilann's, and slowly, as if every inch was breaking her heart, she lifted the bundle from her chest and held it out. Keilann licked her lips, the salt of her sweat stinging her tongue, her throat parched from dancing. With shaking hands, she met Gruoch's in the middle. A sharp tingle shuddered down her elbows at the touch. The bundle was heavier than she expected, and warm from Gruoch's body. Nestling the bundle in the cradle of her arm, Keilann lifted a corner of the cloak and peered inside.

A pair of dark, intelligent eyes peered back at her. With a cry, Keilann flung the rest of the outer cloak back and lifted up a blinking child.

It was a baby girl.

Keilann stared at the child in awe. A baby girl. The child smiled at Keilann. So the history books were wrong. Gently, Keilann cradled the baby to her chest and kissed her forehead. *Good luck, little girl. You're going to need it.*

Keilann rewrapped her in the warmth of the cloak and handed her to Gruoch with a shy smile. The red-haired girl snatched her baby to her chest and nuzzled her face into the smooth baby-down of her head. For the first time since she had appeared in the stone circle all those months ago, the girl looked up at Keilann and smiled. It was a beautiful smile, startlingly white, that lit up her eyes and made the girl look years younger. Keilann couldn't help but smile back, and when she did she felt something pass between the two of them. Worlds apart and as impossible as this meeting was, something like friendship had formed. How had Keilann ever been afraid?

Gruoch placed her hand on the baby's head and spoke in a strange language. Keilann couldn't make out the words, but somehow she understood what Gruoch was doing. She was giving her daughter a blessing in the sacred ring of stones to protect her, to bring her life and safety. The red-haired girl stopped talking and looked at Keilann. Keilann reached out a hand and gently placed it on the child's head, joining Gruoch in her blessing.

"*Beatha,*" Gruoch said.

Keilann blinked. Did that mean they were done? She took her hand off the baby's head, her fingers tingling.

Gruoch frowned. Without warning, she grabbed Keilann's hand. Keilann flinched, but there was no electricity, no blinding pain this time. Gruoch laid Keilann's hand back on the baby's head.

"*Beatha,*" she said again, and Keilann finally understood.

"*Beatha,*" Keilann repeated. "That's a beautiful name."

31

Keilann woke slowly, unwilling to let the dream fade. She could feel herself sinking back into her body. Her spirit grew heavy with bone and muscle. But it hadn't been a dream this time. She had been there, had held the baby girl in her arms and felt the weight of the tiny life in her arms.

Beatha.

The name sounded so familiar. She let the Gaelic syllables play in her mind. *Beatha.*

Ben's voice echoed in her head. "*Uisge Beatha!* The water of life!"

Life, *Beatha* meant "life." Gruoch had named her daughter after life, just as Keilann's own mother had. Just like her grandmother's dream.

A moment ago, she and Gruoch had been as one, the lines of their lives meeting in a perfect "V." But now, as she was jostled back onto the rough gravel of her own path, she could feel Gruoch leave her, the threads holding them together pulling away from each other for the final time. Trying to hang onto her was like trying to capture smoke. Her thread slipped from Keilann's fingers and disappeared into the infinite pattern of life like a drop in the ocean.

Wait! I'm not ready yet. Her head began to ache, a dull, throbbing pain splintering behind her eyes.

What did it all mean?

She became aware of her body jerking from side-to-side, of someone trying to shake her awake.

Not now, I'm trying to think.

The shaking grew more persistent. She tried to ignore it, but already she was losing her grip, beginning the swift descent into consciousness. Whoever was waking her up was shouting her name. Why did they have to be so loud? Awareness spread throughout her limbs and with it, pain. Her feet were tingled with icy needles. She couldn't feel her fingers or ears at all. The hard, frosty ground was pressed against her side. The cold gnawed its way through her mother's shawl.

"Please, please wake up!"

Keilann opened her eyes.

"Oh! Yer alive, thank God." The boy's lanky form sank back onto the ground, exhausted. "Don' ye ever do tha' to me again!"

It was Ben.

Sweat beaded on his brow. He sat before her, panting as if he had run through the currents of time to pull her back. Keilann blinked and looked down at herself. Her body was curled stiffly around the dreamcatcher clutched in both hands, her mother's shawl still wrapped around her shoulders. And she was cold.

Lifting her head, she tried to sit up, but her muscles were too weak and stiff to respond. Keilann fell back onto the ground, her whole body shaking with cold fire.

Cursing under his breath, Ben leapt to his feet and helped her up.

"An' I suppose yer not gonna tell me why yer here? Again?"

Keilann's jaw chattered. She couldn't control the violent shivers convulsing through her limbs. She couldn't remember a time she had been this cold.

"I...had...to," she gasped.

Ben snorted and whipped his heavy winter coat from his arms and threw it around Keilann, rubbing her arms to awaken the frozen blood. Keilann watched him, entranced by his movements. There was something so familiar about how he moved.

"Ye had to what? Get hypothermia and die? Yer lips are blue, fer Christ's sake!"

He shook his head and continued to rub her arms. After several minutes, she began to feel her body warming to his touch.

"You always come," Keilann croaked. "How do you always come for me?"

Ben shook his head again. "Dumb luck. If I hadn't been out fer a walk—"

Keilann frowned. Something didn't feel right. "Yeah, but every time?"

Ben shrugged. "I guess I can jess hear ye bein' stupid from me house, is all."

"Ben, stop!"

Her cry echoed off of the trees. Birds startled and flew away in a rustle of fluttering wings. Ben jumped back, his eyes thrown wide in concern and surprise. She grabbed his shoulders with numbed hands and peered into his face. Keilann looked into his eyes, and her heart stopped. She had always loved his eyes, dark grey flecked with blue like a winter sunrise. So dark they were almost liquid. Like blue-grey smoke.

"Oh my god...." she breathed.

She stared so long that Ben's discomfort began to gel into real fear.

"What? What is it Keilann? Yer scarin' me!" he cried.

Keilann released him and sat back on the hard ground. Her head was spinning. It couldn't be.

"Beatha," she whispered. "*Beathan.*"

"What?" He ventured, his eyes darting nervously. "Fer God's sake, tell me what's goin' on!"

"Your name," she said, bluntly. "It's your name."

Now Ben looked truly frightened. He leaned forward and took Keilann by the hand. "Aye, that's me name. Can ye remember yers?"

Keilann dropped his hand and slapped him on the shoulder. "I know my own name, you idiot! I was asking about yours! What does it mean?"

Ben's brow furrowed. "What the devil does that matter now? My name isn't important," he said. "What's important is getting ye inside with a hot drink in yer gullet."

He reached for her, but Keilann stubbornly remained on the ground.

"Ben, your name is more important than anything else right now!" she cried, throwing off his arm and crossing her own tightly against her chest. "I'm not going anywhere until you tell me."

Ben gave her a hard look and sighed, throwing up his hands.

"Alrigh'! Fine! Don' let me get in the way of ye freezin' te death!" he growled. "If it really means so much te ye, I'll tell ye. It means, 'life,' alrigh'? Same as yers."

Keilann closed her eyes, the pain in her head mounting. "Why—?" she began, but her voice failed her. It was too much.

Ben guessed her question. "Why didn't I tell ye before? I didnae think ye'd believe me. When ye told me what yer name meant, I almost didnae believe ye myself. It was jess too weird. But there ye go, funny old life, innit?" he added a bit too cheerfully, clearly trying to get Keilann to forget about it and move.

But she shook her head. "No, why were you named Beathan? Did your mom have miscarriages like mine?" *Like Gruoch? Like Mac Bethad's mother?*

"No, no, I told ye before it's jess an old family name, been passed down fer generations to the eldest child. There's an old story about the name protectin' children from harm, but it's all jess nonsense. It doesn't matter."

It mattered. It was Ben.

Keilann might have stumbled into the stone circle, but Ben had always been drawn to it. Every time it had called, he had answered. It wasn't just luck or coincidence that he found her when she had tapped into its ancient power. Gruoch had asked the stones to bring Life to her children, and that's exactly what they did. The prayers of Gruoch had knitted the two of them together, beginning with her grandmother's vision. The dreams led her to where she would find the stone circle. The stones had brought *Akiwiin*, Life, to Gruoch's child.

But it meant more than that, Keilann realized. If Ben was a Son of Life, that meant that Gruoch and her daughter had escaped Macbeth's fate. They had survived. Tears welled in her eyes and crystallized in the winter air. For once, Keilann didn't try to stop them.

"Keilann, what is goin' on?"

She looked up at Ben and laughed at the puzzled frown on his face.

"You should probably sit down," she said, wiping a hand across her eyes. "I have a feeling that this is gonna to take a while to explain."

32

The seams of the old duffle bag groaned. The threadbare grey nylon bulged dangerously under the strain of Keilann's last minute packing. She pressed her body weight down on the bulk of the clothing, muscling the teeth of the zipper closer until, wriggling just enough give from the bag, it finally whizzed shut.

Sweaty and exhausted from hours of packing, she flopped onto the bed, grateful for one moment's rest amid the hectic blur of the past few weeks. Between final exams and graduation, Keilann had little time to think of anything else until today, and the airplane was leaving tomorrow. It was now or never.

The plane! The ticket!

She bolted from the bed, nearly tripping over two other suitcases and stubbing her toe on a third. Keilann spun around in a frenzied panic, patting down her shorts even though the ticket couldn't possibly be in her pocket. She flipped over the comforter on her bed and shook out her sheets. Did Mom have it? Or worst of all: could she have packed it? Keilann stared at the disgruntled bags, shuddering at the thought of tearing their contents apart only to repack them, again.

She put her hand to her mouth, making an internal checklist of possible locations. *Think, Keilann, think. You put them somewhere safe. There!*

A gleam of thick, glossy paper flashed and waved in the summer breeze wafting through her open window. Keilann scrambled for the nightstand. She tossed aside her graduation cap and diploma to reveal—her heart skipped a beat. A sturdy, block-lettered airplane ticket was tucked safely inside her passport, as if to patiently wait for her to remember where she had left it. Pounding the air with her fist, she kissed the passport booklet and stowed it in her purse. Keilann had been having nightmares for weeks that she'd get to the Aberdeen airport, only to realize that she'd lost her ticket. In one dream, airport security had accused her of attempting to stowaway to America and hauled her into prison. Unlike the last time she'd flown, however, she hadn't had a single dream about crashing.

Keilann smiled to herself as she lugged the last duffle bag over to the door. Even if the fear of a plane crash haunted her dreams tonight, she had a feeling she could deal with it. She'd had worse nightmares.

With a relieved sigh, Keilann wiped her hand across her brow and surveyed her room one last time. A limp, distorted web of knotted yarn and broken twigs caught her eye, drawing her back to the bed. It was her dreamcatcher, or what was left of it. The solid ring of willow which had held for so impossibly long was finally cracking. The twigs poked through the yarn like bone shards. Soon the dreamcatcher would be unrecognizable, a wreck of tangled feathers and yarn. A sharp pang of loss jabbed at Keilann's ribs. Though she knew it had survived long after most childhood dreamcatchers, it was that much harder to see its ruin. Made of willow specifically because the supple branches would someday dry out and break, a child's first dreamcatcher was meant to teach her about the fleeting nature of life, its death helping her to cherish life while it was hers.

Keilann stroked the sleek black feathers like the face of a beloved friend. It was time. Her dreamcatcher had guarded and watched over her until she could stand on her own, and she had to let it go. There would be plenty of time to begin a new one this summer—an adult dreamcatcher. It would have no feathers adorning it and would be made from a solid hoop instead of willow. Strong enough to see Keilann through the next stage of her life.

Wherever that might be.

The balmy summer air tickled her neck and whispered in her ear. Keilann turned to the open window, the warm sunlight shining on her chestnut skin. In the dark hours of the morning, before another day had dawned, she'd be leaving this place.

But there was one last thing she had to do.

Keilann meandered through the green light of the trees, checking her watch every few minutes. She didn't want to be late, but she couldn't help dragging her feet just a bit. Who knew when she'd be able to walk in this wood again?

Tears stung her eyes, but Keilann rapidly blinked them away, tightening her hold on the warm bundle in her arms. She didn't want him to see her cry. Up ahead, the sunlight broke through the trees, greedily lunging into the open patch of canopy and filling the stone circle with light. She looked around and back at her watch. Still early.

The stones basked in the warmth of the sun, their faces glowing in the warm light. It had been such a gloomy, rain drenched spring. A dry Scottish summer day was a rare gift. The perfect way to say goodbye.

Why couldn't it have been raining like it does three-hundred-and-sixty-four days out of the year? Keilann grumbled inwardly as she spread the cool blanket over the tufts of ankle-length grass. *Why'd it have to go showing off today?*

She sat down to wait, tearing off a piece of grass and shredding it between her fingers. After a few minutes, she stood up and paced around the circle, running her hands along each of the stones, busying herself with saying her goodbyes so she didn't have to think about him. About what she'd been planning to say, and how on earth she was going to leave him after seeing the look on his face.

Keilann rested her head against the sun-warmed stone, shutting her eyes against her tears.

"What am I going to do now?" she groaned.

"Funny," came a quiet voice from behind her. "Tha's jess what I was thinkin'."

There he was, just like the first time she had met him, leaning against one of the stones and staring at her with such sadness it made Keilann's heart ache.

She turned to him, her lips quirked in a weak smile. "Hey, don't you know you're not supposed to sneak up on people like that?"

Ben shrugged and walked toward her. "I guess I never learn."

In that moment, Keilann forgot all of her practiced words and determined dignity. She threw her arms around his waist and hugged him to her fiercely, holding and breathing him in as if it could keep him with her after she'd gone. As if she could leave a bit of herself behind.

"Oh hell," Ben growled. His arms enveloped Keilann, crushing her into his chest. "Here I thought I was gonna get to be all manly fer once," he said with his head on hers, his words muffled by her hair. "An' I'm blubberin' like a wee bairn."

Keilann let go of him and wiped her eyes with the back of her hand. "We're being stupid. It's not like I'm leaving forever."

Ben returned a half-smile, but his eyes were still red.

"I don' think it's stupid te cry when yer girlfriend is abandoning ye for six months."

Keilann threw back her head and laughed.

"Abandoning? Ben, I'm visiting my grandparents in Minnesota. And I have a tablet now. We can Skype all the time."

He nodded in relief. "Aye, at least ye have that." He bit his lip. "I know ye have te go, it's jess...." His eyes slid away from hers.

Keilann cocked her head. "What?"

"Well, what if ye meet someone?" Ben ground the toe of his shoe into the dirt, unwilling to meet her eyes. "What if ye don' want te come back?"

Keilann shook her head. There would be precious little time to find the answers she craved, and she certainly wasn't going to waste a second of it ogling over boys.

"I'm going to be with my mother and grandparents, not exactly leading a wild college life in the big city of Edinburgh."

Ben blinked. "Wait, how is it that yer the one leaving, but I'm still the one in trouble?"

"I'm just saying that you might be too busy to miss me. There will be plenty of homework and girls at the university," she said, only half-teasing. Her heart leapt to her throat. She'd be gone a long time.

"Aye, well, if ye wanted te keep me on a shorter leash, ye shouldna leave. Who knows what I'll get up te, all alone and me such a gullible country lad? I need a city girl te help me."

Despite herself, Keilann felt a poisonous sting of jealousy bite her insides. "Well, I'm sure you'll have no problem finding one."

Ben let out a bark of laughter and hugged her again. "Ah, ye daft eegit. I meant ye. Can ye no' stay?"

Keilann pushed away from him gently. "I can't. I'm leaving tomorrow."

"Aye, fer the whole summer," Ben said grimly. "But do ye really have te take a semester off as well?"

Keilann nodded.

There were questions that had been put off too long. The only place she could find the answers was the Rez. She had planned this trip with her mother for months. Keeping her mom's mind on beating out the details seemed to help keep her focused. Though better, Keilann's mother still didn't seem quite whole. Keilann was hoping that a few months on the Rez with her family could heal what damage the year had wrought on her spirit.

But it wasn't just for her mother's healing, it was for her own as well. Keilann wanted to learn more about her heritage, hear the stories of her grandfather, and finally learn the secrets of her grandmother's dream. Her own dreams were over, but her vision quest had only just begun. Keilann still had much searching to do before she fully understood what had happened. Somehow, she felt that heading back to her family was a step in the right direction. One thing she did know was this: in bringing Life to her children, Gruoch had given Keilann a new life as well.

"I brought you something." she said, breaching the loaded silence between them.

Keilann knelt beside the blanket and scooped up the warm bundle in her arms. She stood and held it out to Ben. He took it from her. Holding it in one hand, he peeled the aluminum foil from the top. The tempting aroma of warm bread and melted butter wafted through the opening.

"Wha' is it?" Ben asked, sniffing the air tentatively.

"Fry Bread," Keilann said proudly. "My grandmother taught me how to make it, and I'm going back to learn everything else that I can from her."

Ben ripped off a chunk of crispy bread and popped it in his mouth. His eyes widened. "If all of her food tastes like this, I wouldna be surprised if ye never came back."

Keilann laughed. "Better than Black Pudding, huh?"

Ben snorted, choking on another piece of bread. "I never said that."

They sat on the blanket, the warm breeze ruffling their hair, talking like normal, sharing the Fry Bread until nothing was left but an oily shell of aluminum foil. After they had talked about Mary Arden, the Rez, and what they were going to do when she came home for Christmas, the conversation fell into a comfortable lull. Keilann leaned back on her hands and closed her eyes. She listened to the rustle of leaves and calling birds, inhaling the spicy scent of earth and heather. She had wandered into the stone circle feeling like an alien, lost and alone in a strange world. It was only when Keilann was leaving it behind that she realized how much she belonged to this place.

Ben wiped the oil from his hands and lay back on the blanket, his arms flung wide. Keilann laid next to him, her head on his shoulder.

"Jess promise me ye'll come back," he murmured, drowsily.

"I'll come back," she promised.

She thought of Gruoch, of how no matter where her bitter, turbulent life took her, she always found her way back to the stone circle. One way or another.

"I'll find my way back here," Keilann whispered to the stones, laying her palm on the warm soil. "I'll always come home."

Julia Lee graduated from University of Wisconsin-Whitewater with a degree in Secondary English Education and has taught Shakespeare and advanced composition classes. While attending college, she had several short stories published in the literary arts magazine, *The Muse* and won first-place prize for prose in the university's annual writing competition in 2008.

Her passion for books, writing, and chocolate are unequalled. She currently lives in rural Minnesota with her wonderful husband, and is always working on her next novel.

The following authors and sites have been very helpful during my research into the subjects of Ojibwe language and culture, Scottish language and history, and, of course, stone circles:

Banai-Benton, E. (2010). *The Mishomis Book*. Minneapolis: University of Minnesota Press.

Blundell, N. (1998). *Scotland*. New York: Barnes and Noble, Inc.

Grant, I., & Cheape, H. (1997). *Periods in Highland History*. New York: Barnes and Noble, Inc.

Kerrigan, M. (2006). *The Secrets of Scotland*. New York: Barnes and Noble, Inc.

Nicholas, J.D., & Nyholm, E. (1995). *A Concise Dictionary of Minnesota Ojibwe*. Minneapolis: University of Minnesota Press.

Oram, R. (2006). *The Kings and Queens of Scotland*. Stroud: Tempus Publishing Limited.

Spadaro, K.M., & Graham, K. (2001). *Colloquial Scottish Gaelic: The Complete Course for Beginners*. New York: Routledge.

Treuer, A. (2012). *Everything You Wanted to Know About Indians But Were Afraid to Ask*. St. Paul: Borealis Books.

http://www.educationscotland.gov.uk

http://www.native-languages.org (Native Languages of the Americas)

http://www.stone-circles.org.uk